WHERE WE
Bloom

New York Times and *USA Today* Bestselling Author
KRISTEN PROBY

&
AMPERSAND
PUBLISHING, INC.

Where We Bloom

THE BLACKWELLS OF MONTANA

KRISTEN PROBY

&
AMPERSAND
PUBLISHING, INC.

Where We Bloom
A Blackwells of Montana Novel
By
Kristen Proby

To every woman who's ever been afraid to speak up for herself.
Billie's backbone is something to behold.

Spicy Girls Book Club

TBR

Reading List:
Slave to Sensation by Nalini Singh
The Pucking Wrong Number by CR Jane
Crossroads by Devney Perry
Steal My Heart by Laura Pavlov
The Playboy by Marni Mann
King of Wrath by Ana Huang
Rise of the King by Bella Matthews
The Proposal Play by Lauren Blakely
If You Love Me by Helena Hunting
Broken by Sadie Kincaid

Last Autumn

I like him, this handsome *stranger* who approached me at my bookstore right before closing. He asked if he could take me to dinner, and honestly, I wasn't sure. I mean, he's hot as hell at well over six feet tall, with dark hair and the greenest eyes I've ever seen, and it looks like he has muscles for days beneath his white button-down shirt and black slacks.

He's sexy.

And did I mention his glasses? Yeah, he has the nerve to wear black-rimmed glasses that might have made my vagina salivate.

But he's ... broody.

I'm not a broody person. And yes, I read enough romance novels to know that the grumpy-sunshine combination can be hot, but that's fiction. In real life? I've never been attracted to the grump. And this guy has *intense* written all over him.

Despite that, I said yes, and two hours later, here we are, finishing dinner at Ciao, my favorite restaurant in Bitterroot Valley, with the handsome stranger sitting across from me. We shared the appetizer of Italian nachos, a *huge* entrée of pasta, and tiramisu for dessert. I'm not afraid to eat in front of a man. Yes, I'm a curvy girl, and I know how to dress my body, and I'm not ashamed of it.

I like to eat.

But the portions here are so large that I suggested we share, and I think it was the right call.

The best part of this dinner, though, has been the conversation. This guy—I didn't get his name—is intelligent, and he *listens.*

Which, in my limited dating experience, seems rare.

"I might be in a food coma," I admit as I sit back and sip the last of my after-dinner coffee, watching him. "That was delicious."

"Everything about this evening has been delicious," he replies, holding my gaze through those sexy-as-fuck glasses. I feel the warmth from his words spread through me.

He may be broody, but he's charming. And he's hardly taken his eyes off me all through dinner.

"May I be blunt?" he asks, his light accent coming through. I don't know where he's from in Europe, but I know he's not American.

"Of course, please do."

"I'd like you to come back to my suite with me. Stay the night with me."

The hand lifting my water glass to my lips pauses halfway as I stare at him, and then I slowly lower it to the table.

"Is that so?"

"Yes."

"Why do I feel like you're a man who usually gets what he wants?"

His green gaze holds mine as he waits quietly, his finger tapping the side of his wineglass, watching me as I decide what to do. He's sexy, there's no doubt about it. He held my hand on the way here from my shop, and it made my whole arm tingle.

I'm not an impulsive person. I certainly don't have sex with someone on a first date.

But I like him. And a chance to have sex with a man like this one may never present itself again.

And did I mention that he's sexy?

"Where are you staying?" I watch his lips twitch, and his face relaxes as if he were worried I'd say no.

"At the ski resort."

I nod slowly, take one last sip of my water, and ignore the butterflies currently doing the Macarena in my stomach.

"All right."

His eyebrow wings up. "Just like that?"

"It seems so."

He pays the check, offers me his hand, and guides me

through the restaurant. I like walking beside him. He's such a big man, but I feel perfectly safe when I'm next to him, which is an odd thought, considering I don't typically feel *un*safe.

When we're standing on the sidewalk, I turn to him.

"I can meet you up there. My car's parked behind my shop."

This tall, hot-as-hell stranger steps closer to me, and with his finger under my chin, he lifts my face so he can look into my eyes. Did all the air rush out of Montana just now? Because it's suddenly harder to breathe.

"I don't want to let you out of my sight in case you disappear on me. I'm only here for one night, and I plan to take full advantage of that. I'll make sure you get back to your car safely in the morning."

Wow. After swallowing hard, I simply nod, and he kisses my forehead before leading me to a massive black SUV parked across the street.

My stranger opens the passenger door for me, makes sure I secure my seat belt, closes the door, and then circles the hood to the driver's side.

"You know," I say as he backs out of the parking space and heads toward the road that leads to the resort, "we talked all through dinner, but I never asked you where you're visiting from."

I'm watching his profile as he drives, so I see it when his lips tip up at the side, and I wish he'd give me a full smile.

I saw his eyes light up when I said something funny,

and those lips tipped up too, but he has yet to grace me with a full grin.

I bet it's devastating.

"Perhaps we shouldn't divulge too many personal things tonight." He shoots me a glance before he reaches over and sets his hand on my thigh, then gives it a little squeeze.

Just that simple touch makes my nipples pucker. I bite my lip.

We had animated conversation at dinner, but we never talked about anything too personal. Obviously, I discussed my bookstore a bit, but never my family or friends. He asked me questions about the store and the town.

But really, we've kept things quite surface, and I don't really mind. He's only here for this one night, and if he wants to keep things mellow, I'm down for that.

I stare at his hand, then cover it with my own and glide my fingers over his, enjoying the way his skin feels against mine.

"As long as you don't have a wife somewhere who assumes you're being faithful to her and your six children, that's fine with me."

To my absolute shock, he laughs. *Laughs.* And it lights me up inside. It's the kind of laugh you give when you're tickled with someone.

And his smile is as devastating as I expected. It makes my heart speed up into hyperdrive.

"That's not exactly a denial."

He shakes his head and glances at me again. "No. I'm

not married, and I don't have any children. Certainly not six."

"Great. I don't either."

He leaves his SUV with the valet and takes my hand again to escort me into the lodge. After riding the elevator to the top floor, he leads me to the suite at the end of the hall, opens the door, and gestures for me to walk in ahead of him.

This room is *fancy*. Or set of rooms, I should say. A wall of windows in both the living area and the bedroom gives a spectacular view of the ski mountain and the beautiful trees beyond.

"Great room." I immediately kick off my shoes, because that's just habit, and the next thing I know, I'm spun around, back against the window, and he's framed my face in his hands and is kissing me.

Not a tentative first kiss. No, this man *consumes* me, as if he's wanted to do this to me since the moment he first saw me, and I'm not sure I've ever felt so wanted.

So damn sexy.

His mouth is *amazing*. Not too hard, not too wet. He growls against me, those hands drift down to my ass, and then he *lifts me*.

I let out a yelp and wrap my arms around his shoulders. I'm not a little woman.

"I've got you," he says against my lips as he carries me to the bedroom. "And as much as I'd love to fuck you against that glass, I'd have to kill anyone who got a look at you, so we'll take it to the bedroom."

I smirk. I can't help it.

He's not going to kill anyone over a one-night stand.

But it's an amusing thought.

And then all thinking goes out those windows as he sets me on my feet. My hands dive for the buttons on his shirt, and he unfastens the belt I have around the green dress I'm wearing.

"You're fucking gorgeous," he says as the belt hits the floor.

With a grin, I push his shirt over his shoulders, and when it joins my belt near our feet, I let my eyes roam over smooth skin and muscles that aren't for days. They're for *years*. His abs are so defined, I want to lick them.

I want to nibble them.

And my hands are all over him.

"Lift your arms, beautiful girl." I comply, letting him pull my dress over my head. He discards it, and I'm standing before this Greek god in just my pretty purple bra and panties, my many flaws on display for him. "Christ Jesus, you're gorgeous."

We're not touching now, just staring at each other, taking each other in. His chest heaves. His hands fist at his sides.

"Your pants," I whisper, meeting his eyes. "Please."

His jaw clenches.

"I like it when you ask nicely." He steps out of the slacks, along with his boxers, and *oh. My. God.* "My eyes are up here, angel."

Angel. I'm going to die tonight. I feel it coming.

I swallow hard.

7

"And you have nice eyes, but holy shit, have you seen *that*?"

I'm scooped up again and am lying on my back in the middle of a soft island of a bed, and he's hovering over me, kissing up my chest toward my chin.

His hands explore me everywhere. Over my sides and hips. My thighs. And then his palms skim up to my breasts. His thumbs brush my nipples over the bra, and I arch into him.

"Every fucking inch of you is perfect," he growls against my ear. "If there is anything that I do that you don't like, you just say so, and it stops. Got it?"

I nod, biting my lip as I watch his lips move.

"I need your words, angel."

"I understand. Same goes."

He gives me that smile again before twisting me onto my stomach. He unfastens my bra before he pulls my hips back so my ass is in the air and my face is against the bed. Then his mouth is *right there.*

I hear him inhale. His hands ghost over the globes of my ass, and then he swipes his tongue through my slit, from my clit all the way to the back door, and I moan.

"Look at you," he murmurs before doing it again. "Already so damn wet."

It starts out gentle, and then it's anything *but*. He licks and then sucks on my clit, pushes a finger inside me, and I push back against him, needing so much more. I feel like if I don't get him inside me *now*, I'll spontaneously combust.

"You like that?"

I nod, and then there's a smack on my ass.

"Words, angel."

This is going to be the best way to die.

"Yes, I like it."

"Good."

He pushes in another finger, stretching me, and I moan again, still pushing back against him, wanting so much more than his fingers.

Just as I'm about to come apart with the most intense orgasm of my life, he stops.

And I frown back at him, but then I realize he's rolling on a condom. He flips me back over, braces himself on his hands beside my shoulders, and pushes the crown inside me. I grip his sides, my nails digging into his skin.

"Take a breath, angel." He brushes his nose over mine so gently, I take that breath.

Why do I love it when he calls me angel so much?

With my eyes on his, I inhale, and then he slides all the way in. My legs are hitched on his hips, my hands slide to his back, and to my surprise, he lowers his forehead to mine.

"Christ, you're snug," he whispers. "Your pussy fits my cock perfectly."

I feel like I've just been given a gold medal.

He covers my mouth with his, then he starts to move, and I can't help the whimper that pushes through my throat.

"Are you okay?" he asks as he tucks his hand under my ass, tilting my pelvis up.

"Never better. Don't you dare stop."

He cups my cheek and jawline, and picks up the tempo, making my spine tingle and every muscle clench around him.

"Oh fuck."

"That's right. Come for me. God, you're so bloody gorgeous."

His accent is thicker when he's aroused, and before I know it, I'm shattering into a million pieces, holding on to him for dear life as I'm thrown off the sexiest cliff *ever*.

With a roar, he follows me over, cants his hips into mine, and shivers with his own climax.

He lowers to his elbows, bracing himself. Pushing his hands into my hair, he brushes his nose down my jawline, making me shiver.

"Are you okay, angel?"

"If I die because of the best orgasm of my life, please tell my family it was worth it."

With a proud grin, he kisses me, softly this time. Leisurely. As if we have all the time in the world to lie here, in this opulent bed, and soak each other in.

This man, this stranger, is a grade A kisser.

Finally, he rolls to the side, disentangles himself from me, then takes my hand and pulls me from the bed.

"Where are we going?" I ask with a laugh.

"Shower," he replies. "I'm going to clean you up, then get you messy again."

Well, yes, please and thank you, hot stranger. Sign me up for that.

Connor

I jolt up from a dead sleep and pull air into my lungs, taking in my surroundings.

Waking up in a strange place is nothing new to me. It's part of my job.

I'm in Montana. I was supposed to leave yesterday, but my plane had a problem, and we had to postpone until today.

And then I met the most beautiful woman I've ever seen in my bleedin' life.

I glance down and frown when I see that the bed is empty, and a brush of my hand over the sheets tells me she's been gone for a while.

Pushing the blanket aside, I walk to the living room, where I find my dark-haired angel curled up in one of the leather armchairs by the windows, a blanket tossed over her lap, watching the snow outside. She's wearing my shirt from earlier, and it's sexy as hell on her.

I don't know when the snow started, but the trees are already covered in white, and the flakes falling from the sky look like the size of my fist.

"It's the first snowfall of the year," she says without turning to look at me. Her voice is raspy, her beautiful long hair tangled, and I need to get my hands on her again more than I need air.

"Have you slept at all?" I ask and scowl when she shakes her head.

"I don't sleep much. But I won't say anything else because we're not sharing personal things." She grins over at me, and her whiskey-colored eyes go round when she sees that I'm naked.

I want to ask her a million questions. *Why* doesn't she sleep well? How does she like her coffee in the morning? When can I see her again?

What's her bleeding name?

If I was a man who did relationships, I'd claim this woman as mine.

But I'm not.

However, I plan to enjoy the hell out of her while I have her, so I kneel in front of her, pull the blanket off her lap, and spread her legs, hooking one of them over the arm of the chair.

"Uh, you don't have to—"

Before she can finish that thought, I lean in and wrap my lips around her clit, flick the little bundle of nerves with the tip of my tongue, and grin when her hands twine in my hair and *pull.*

I love that she's not gentle.

That she's not fragile.

And with a growl, I push my tongue inside her and lap at her juices.

"Ah, shit," she moans. "God, you're so damn good at that."

With a growl, I pull her out of that chair, sit, and straddle her over me. She immediately takes my cock inside her, sinking down until I'm buried inside her. She circles her gorgeous hips before she starts to ride.

I unbutton the shirt, lean in and suck on her nipples, tease them with my teeth, and with my hands planted on the globes of her bloody phenomenal arse, she rides me until I feel the orgasm gather, lifting my balls. I press my thumb to her clit, making sure she comes with me.

Her movements falter as she cries out, coming apart on my lap, and once she's finished, I lift her and pump my cock until I come in thick ropes all over her stomach and tits.

"No condom," she whispers, grinning at me. "Good call."

Still catching my breath, I stand with her in my arms and take us back to bed.

"Come on, we're going to work on that sleep."

"You know, I'm not a small person," she says as she wraps her arm around my neck, still catching her own breath as she presses her sweet face to my neck. "I'm not used to being carried around."

"You're small compared to me," I reply. I don't want her to think she's anything but perfect, just the way she is.

I fucking *love* curvy women.

"I won't sleep," she informs me, dragging a finger down my neck. "And I don't want to keep you up. I'm fine in the chair."

"You're fine in the bed, and you won't keep me up."

She starts to protest, but I silence her with a kiss.

"I want you with me, angel."

I lay her down, and once I've fetched a warm cloth from the bathroom and cleaned her up, I curl up behind her, tucking her back against my front. We lie like this for a while, watching the snow through the windows. But then, to my surprise, she wiggles around, presses her face to my chest, wraps her arm around my waist, and sighs as she loops one leg through mine. She snuggles into me so tightly, as if she's worried I might get away from her.

I kiss her head and hug her close, breathing her in.

I've never felt such an instant connection to someone. I don't remember the last time I was this attracted to a woman. I'm not in the habit of keeping someone in my bed overnight, and I'm not a cuddler.

That's too personal.

But this lass had me trapped in her spell from the moment I saw her.

I glance at the clock. I'm leaving in five hours.

And I spend every minute of those holding her. She was wrong. She fell into a deep sleep and relaxed against me. I washed her face in the shower earlier, so she's free of makeup and even more stunning.

The snow stops at around six, and it's time for me to get ready to leave. My angel is sleeping so well, I don't want to wake her.

Okay, the truth is, if she wakes up, I won't want to leave her.

And I have to go.

So I cross to the walk-in closet and dress, grab my already packed bag, and carry it through to the front door of the suite. Then I return to her and watch her for a few moments. She's still in my shirt. *She can keep it.*

I wonder, briefly, if she'll hang on to it or discard it.

"Take care, angel," I whisper before leaving the suite and quietly shutting the door behind me. I stop at the front desk and ask them to send up coffee and everything on the breakfast menu in two hours, then have a driver take her to her car whenever she's ready. Then I leave for the airport.

Although I know I'll be back in Bitterroot Valley often to see my sister, I also know that I won't repeat this night with that glorious, stunning, and witty woman.

Because I'd lose myself to her, and there's no room for that in my world.

Chapter One

BILLIE

This is my very favorite day of the month.

One Monday a month, I leave my bookstore in the capable hands of my two employees and drive the four hours to Big Sky, Montana, to shop. The only time this doesn't happen is when it's too snowy and the roads are treacherous.

But it's summertime, which means that for the next few months, I'll be able to come to this resort town and buy clothes on my usual schedule.

I'm a self-professed fashionista. I love clothes, especially expensive, high-end labels, but I don't have the budget for that when it comes to buying brand-new.

That's where Big Sky comes in.

This ski town isn't so unlike Bitterroot Valley, except it's where the rich come to vacation and own vacation homes. Mega celebrities, billionaires, you name it, and these wealthy women send their hand-me-downs to the local thrift store.

A little secret I discovered by mistake a couple of years ago, and I'm so glad I did. I find a place to park, then walk down the block to the darling boutique-style thrift shop and push inside.

"How are you, Martha?" I ask the owner, who's hanging what looks like a red wool coat on a hanger.

This store is the cutest. It doesn't look or smell like a thrift shop. It's styled like an adorable fashion boutique, and I always feel fancy when I come in to browse through the racks and hunt for amazing finds.

"Oh, no complaints here. How's the bookstore life treating you, Billie?"

"It's the best. I brought that series you requested and a few bags of donations as well."

Not only do I buy from this thrift store but I also donate back anything that I've grown tired of or just didn't work for me.

Because although I'm a clothes horse, my little house can't hold all the pieces I'd keep if I had the space.

"Oh, that's great, thank you," she says with a smile. "I held a few things back for you because I knew they'd sell fast, and I wanted you to get first dibs."

Those magical words make my tummy flip, and I've already pulled two dresses and a pair of slacks from a rack to try on when Martha returns, pulling a rolling rack of clothes behind her.

"That's not a *few things*." I quickly twist my long hair up into a knot. It needs to be out of my way so I can try on clothes.

Martha laughs and takes my finds from me so she can

start me a room, and I immediately hurry over to the rack to comb through it.

"This is a Gucci blouse," I call out to her as my adrenaline spikes. "And it's in my size! That never happens."

Unfortunately, not all fashion houses offer their ready-to-wear clothes in larger sizes, but every once in a while, I find something.

In fact, this whole rack is full of designer pieces in my size.

"Who donated this stuff?" I ask as Martha joins me.

"A governor's wife," she says with a shrug. "I swear, she must have brought me half of her closet. These are last year's pieces."

"Who cares?" I laugh and step back. "I'll try it all on."

"I figured you'd say that. Let's get started."

Every piece fits me like a glove. A Dior shift dress, a Louis Vuitton blouse. Chanel, Hermes, and Valentino. Some of the items still have tags on them.

"I'm going to give you everything for three hundred," Martha says.

"There's easily twenty grand in clothes here, and that's on the conservative side," I reply, shaking my head. "I should pay you at least one thousand."

"*Used* clothes, and besides, you'll bring them back to me when you're finished with them."

"This might be the best day of the whole year. I feel like I should buy a lottery ticket," I inform her as I pull on the long maxi dress I wore here and follow her to the

19

counter where we dig in, folding everything and gently placing it all in the two totes I brought.

"Billie?" Her voice sounds tentative.

I raise an eyebrow at Martha. "Yes?"

"I'm thinking about selling the shop."

I feel my eyes go wide, and my heart stutters.

"Oh, why? It's such a great place."

"My parents are in Arizona, and my dad's health isn't great. I feel like I should be there with them, you know? I have a serious case of daughter guilt."

I bite my lip. "I get it. Mine moved to Florida a few years ago, and if my dad wasn't well, I'd want to be closer to him, too. It's a tough decision. Is the shop struggling?"

"No. Actually, I do well, and I love it so much," she replies. "You're not my only client who comes from far away to pick through rich people's castoffs. I stay really busy. Why, do you want to buy it?"

She giggles at that, but I'm not laughing with her.

I can't really *afford* to buy this shop, and it's four hours from where I live, so I really shouldn't entertain the idea.

But I get 90 percent of my wardrobe here. And the day trip over each month is so good for my mental health. It's really the only day that I *don't* work. I don't stop by the shop to restock, or shoot an email, or change the display window. I listen to music or audiobooks in my car and empty my mind. Not to mention, my favorite restaurant is here in town, and I always treat myself whenever I'm here.

"No, of course not." I shake my head. "But do me a

favor? Please give me a heads-up before you sell. I love it in here."

"I'll keep you posted. I'm not convinced that selling is the right move, but I've considered it. I know it would be a stretch for you to own two businesses in two vastly different places."

"One is hard enough, as you know."

Martha helps me load the totes into my car, then I hug her goodbye. I'm hungry and have a long drive ahead of me, so I walk down the block to the cutest boutique hotel I've ever seen. Because we're in the mountains, you'd think it would have a rustic lodge feel, but it doesn't. It's classy, with beautiful sage green and burnt orange colors. The lighting is moody, and it makes a person feel ... *luxurious.*

Not that I've seen many boutique hotels. It's not like I travel the world often or anything, but this place is adorable. I wish I could afford to spend a long weekend here.

But, given that this is the playground for the ridiculously wealthy, I'm quite sure I can't afford the nightly rate.

I can, however, afford to eat in the restaurant.

I'm shown to a table by the windows, and once I take a seat, I pull out my phone to check my messages. I have a group text thread with my Spicy Girls Book Club girls that always has some activity.

Starting that book club is one of the best things I ever did. Not only did it bring me closer to my best friend and now sister-in-law, Dani, but it also brought my other bestie, Skyla, into my life. Add in the other ladies, and I have a kick-ass group of women around me.

I never take it for granted.

Millie: *Did you make it to Big Sky, Bee?*

Oops, I didn't see that earlier. Millie owns the coffee shop right next door to my bookstore, and I've known her all of my life. She's the best.

Me: *I did! Sorry, I didn't see this message earlier. I'm having lunch before I get back on the road.*

Skyla: *Did you find some fun things this time? I want to see everything!*

I grin and look up to thank my server, who just brought me some warm bread and water.

"Hello, miss. I'm Travis, and I'll be helping you today."

"Thanks, Travis."

"Have you had an opportunity to look over the menu?"

I don't need to. I know exactly what I want.

"I have," I reply with a smile. "I'll have the whipped feta dip because it's absolutely addicting."

Travis grins as he writes on his pad. "It really is. What else can I bring you?"

"I'll have the grilled chicken Caesar salad, no anchovies."

"I can do that. Anything to drink?"

"Just an iced tea, please. And also, for dessert, I'll have the huckleberry crème brûlée."

"You're living your best life, my friend," Travis says with a wide smile before he walks away to put my order in. Travis is cute. He's tall with almost white blond hair and one hell of a smile, complete with dimples.

Adorable.

Not nearly as sexy as Connor Gallagher. My stranger. The man who not only fucked my brains out one night late last year but has found ways to corner me and kiss the hell out of me at every opportunity since then. He's Skyla's brother, a detail that I didn't know until I saw him at my niece's dance recital several months after that night, where he dragged me out back and kissed the fuck out of me.

And ever since then, it's been the same. Family dinner? Stolen kisses. Trip to Europe to watch Skyla dance? All the fucking kisses. He even stormed in on a book club meeting several weeks ago and dragged me into a supply closet, where he proceeded to give me an orgasm in three-point-seven seconds.

He's *everywhere*. And because he's my best friend's brother, it's not exactly possible to *never* see him, but I can be an adult when he's around.

I can be civil.

I can keep my hands and my lips to myself.

Because as much as Connor makes it clear that he's attracted to me sexually, he's *never* indicated that there's anything else there. I don't even have the jerk's phone number, for God's sake. And I'm through with meaning-less sex. When I'm with Connor, I lose myself to him, but in a good way. I feel safe. I feel ... *content*. God, I slept the best I have in years when he took me to bed with him that night, and I haven't slept that well since. But the last time, when he kissed the hell out of me in that closet, I told him he didn't get to do that to me anymore because I feel used. Even if I *love* the way he towers over me, making me feel petite, something I've never felt before. And even if I *love* how he treats Skyla, knowing that's the extraordinary way he'd treat his partner.

I don't *just* want sex with him. There, I admitted it. He intrigues me, and I know he's a good man.

I want more. Just like Dani and Skyla have recently found with my brothers. I want that for myself. I deserve more.

And he won't give me more.

If he wanted more, he'd have asked for my goddamn phone number. I'm done feeling used by that ridiculously sexy Irishman.

Chapter Two

I swear to Christ, I'm seeing things because it's impossible that the bane of my existence, the one woman in this world who can make me hard just by breathing in her scent, is sitting in my restaurant.

I'm so fucking gone over her, I'm conjuring her everywhere I go now.

Except I'd bet the deed of this hotel that it's her. No one's that beautiful except for my angel. No one sets me on fire like she does.

"Mr. Gallagher, we'd like to show you the projections ..." The manager of my Big Sky property drones on about business, but I can't take my eyes off the woman sitting by the window. Her dark hair is pulled up into a messy knot on her head, showing the long lines of her neck and shoulders.

Her long dress is flowy around her perfect curves, and to my surprise, she's in sandals.

I don't think I've ever seen her in anything other than

heels, and I've seen Billie Blackwell often over the past nine months or so. This is as casual as it gets for her, and I want to leave these arseholes and join her.

What is she doing here?

The server approaches her, and as she smiles up at him, I want to growl. Once she places her order, she checks her phone, sips her tea, and watches the people outside.

I don't hear a thing that happens in this meeting.

But I know every move that my angel makes.

"How do you feel about that, Mr. Gallagher?"

I turn back to whatever this idiot is pointing at on a piece of paper and nod. "Fine."

"Excellent, now—"

He continues, but I turn back to watch my girl. It's fucking intoxicating to watch her eat. She's not shy at all about her love of food, and I wish I was sitting with her so I could share her meal the way we did that first night at the Italian place. I want to hear the way she hums with approval. I want to see her face when she closes her eyes and savors the flavors on her tongue.

I sit back and watch her make her way through each course of her meal. With each plate set in front of her, she does a little dance in her seat.

I've never met anyone who exuded so much joy over something as simple as a meal.

I'm not surprised when the server delivers dessert to the table, and Billie claps with happiness, her whole face lighting up. It's a punch to the gut.

Christ, she's beautiful.

I flag the server down.

"Yes, sir?"

"I'd like her check added to mine," I reply, gesturing toward Billie.

"You got it." He nods and walks away, and I notice that the rest of the table has gone quiet, but I don't care.

I'm not even sure I need to be a part of this meeting.

"Sir, we can wrap this up if you'd like," the manager says, and I nod.

"Thank you. I'll be heading back to Bitterroot Valley today."

"But we thought—"

"It wasn't a question," I reply and shake both of their hands, dismissing them, and then I sit alone and watch Billie as she finishes her dessert and checks her phone again, smiling at something she sees. Is it a message from another man?

The mere thought makes my hand fist and my jaw clench, which is completely unreasonable.

It's none of my business if she's seeing someone. She made it clear a couple of weeks ago, when I dragged her into the supply closet at her shop, that she wants nothing to do with me.

"I won't do this with you," she says, her voice shaking. "No more. No more kisses at dance recitals and family dinners and at the fucking coronation of a king. No more messing with my head, Connor. I'm sure it makes you happy to know that I enjoyed fucking you. I can't help myself from responding to you when you touch me, but I

am done letting you use me. You don't get to do that anymore."

I've tried. I've kept my distance over the past few weeks and made sure that if she was going to be somewhere, I *wasn't*. Yet the thought of staying away from her forever is pure fucking torture. Each day is getting harder and harder. All I want is this woman.

The server approaches her table, and she asks for the check, but he shakes his head and must tell her it's been taken care of because she frowns.

I stand and start her way.

When she sees me coming, her gorgeous eyes widen, and all of the blood drains from her face as if she's seen a ghost. Or her worst nightmare.

I fucking hate that.

"Thank you, Travis," I say. The young man nods, and then he's gone, and I take the seat across from Billie.

"What are you doing here?" she asks with a scowl.

"I own this place."

She blinks at me, then seems to wilt. "*You* own this? The hotel, too?"

I nod, fiddling with the silverware on the table.

"Well, shit. I love this place."

"You do?" I lift an eyebrow in surprise and feel oddly ... proud.

"It's a beautiful hotel. I've never stayed here, but I always eat here whenever I come to town."

"And how often is that?"

She nibbles her lip. "Once a month."

"You make a four-hour drive once a month?"

"It's closer to eight hours because I go back the same day. I'm actually about to head out now. I just wanted to eat first."

"I'll walk you to your car, then."

She doesn't argue as I stand and button my suit jacket, and with my hand pressed to the small of her back, I lead her out the front door to the footpath.

"I'm that way." She points to the left, and without thinking about it, I link my hand with hers, walking beside her, making sure she's on the inside of the footpath.

Her fingers curl around mine, settling something in me, the way she always does when I touch her.

"So what brings you all this way once a month?" I ask.

"We don't share personal things, remember?"

I scowl down at her, but she doesn't look up at me, and I don't push her. When we reach her car, I pull my phone out and send a text to Miller.

> We're leaving for BV now. Pick me up outside Thrifty Threads.

> Miller: On my way.

"Well, I guess I'll see you around," Billie says and circles her SUV, unlocks it, and lowers inside. But when she pushes the ignition, nothing happens. I see her narrow her eyes, and she tries again, and after the third time, she simply rests her forehead against the steering wheel.

29

It's a good thing I'm here.

I circle the bonnet and open her door. "You can ride back with me."

"I have this, Connor. I'll make some calls."

"No, you'll let me handle it, and you'll ride back with me. I was heading back now anyway. My last meeting just wrapped up."

Okay, that's a lie. I was supposed to be here for two more days, but plans have changed.

"Seriously, thanks for the offer, but I can call Brooks. He'll call someone, and they'll tow me back. I can catch a ride with them."

"If you think for one moment that I'll let you ride for four hours from here with a strange tow-truck driver, you've lost your bloody mind, angel."

Miller pulls up right behind her.

"Now, get in my fucking car."

Billie narrows her eyes at me, then sighs. "Fine, I'll ride back with you. But I'm not leaving my clothes behind."

She stomps to the back of her SUV, opens the hatch, and points at two plastic totes full of clothing.

"I have to take these, too."

"They'll fit in the back, miss," Miller says. "Please, allow me."

"Oh, hi, Miller," Billie says as she steps back to let Miller get the totes. He takes them in one trip, stacking them on top of each other, and I close the door behind him.

"Lock it up," I say to Billie, gesturing to her car.

"Obviously, it's not currently worth stealing," she grumbles, but she presses a button on her fob, locking the vehicle, and I escort her to the back of my SUV.

She climbs into the back seat, and I walk around to join her on the other side.

"I'll have our things sent to us," I inform Miller as I pass him, and he nods in return. Once we're all seated, Miller starts the car, and we're headed toward Bitterroot Valley.

Billie seems intent on staring out the passenger window.

"So tell me about those clothes."

She's silent for so long, I don't think she'll respond. When she sighs and turns my way, I want to drag my knuckles down her cheek.

I want to pull her into my lap and feast on her delicious, plump lips.

I want to feel her against me so badly.

But I don't touch her because she wouldn't welcome that.

"I bought them at the thrift store," she says. There's no shame in her tone, no hesitation.

But I'm seeing red.

"Why are you wearing secondhand clothes?"

"Okay, you can press pause on the judging." She points her finger at me. "I'll have you know that filthy rich people live in or stay in Big Sky."

"That's not news to me."

"Of course, it isn't." She huffs a breath and rolls her pretty eyes, and I feel my lips twitch. I fucking love her

31

sassy side. "They also discard their hardly worn clothes and donate them to that shop, and *I love it.* Here, look."

Before I can stop her, she unfastens her seat belt and flips around on the seat, diving backward to the totes behind us. Her arse is in the air, and my heart stumbles as fear spears right through it.

"Get back in that seat belt, Billie." I wrap my arm around her waist and glare at Miller in the mirror, making it clear that he had better not wreck this car and hurt her.

The fucker grins at me.

"Billie, I'm not kidding. Sit your arse down."

"I know it's here somewh—aha! Here it is." She flips back around with several garments in her hands and refastens her belt. "Look. This is a *Dior* skirt, in my size, with the tag still on it. It was more than two thousand dollars brand-new. Look at the tag. *Look.*"

I glance down but don't reply. *This* is how she affords to look the way she does. Always put together, always classy, like she just stepped off a Paris runway.

She sets the skirt on her lap and reaches for the other piece of clothing.

"This is a Louis Vuitton blouse with the tag still on. Fifteen hundred dollars! It's insane. This stuff is brand-new or nearly new, all of it is luxury, and I only paid three hundred dollars for *all of it* because Martha, the owner, knows I'll donate it back when I'm finished with it. It's an insane deal. I love clothes so much, but there's no way I could afford to dress like this normally. Oh! Let me show you—"

She reaches down to unbuckle again, but I cover her hand in mine over the clip and growl.

"You'll stay where you are, or I'll spank your arse."

"You're a bully." There's not much heat in her voice as she narrows her eyes at me. "I wanted to show you the Hermès coat I found. It's gorgeous and so soft."

"It's July," I remind her.

"It won't always be July," she counters and gestures at the clothes still in her hands. "I just need to put these away."

I take the garments from her and toss them over my shoulder into the back.

"If those get stained, I'll kick you in the shin."

I raise an eyebrow. "If they get stained, I'll buy you new ones."

I fucking *hate* that she's wearing someone's castoffs. I'll buy her whatever she wants. Hell, I'll take her to Paris, New York, wherever she wants to go to shop until she has everything she could want.

"I don't want new ones," she replies as if she's talking to a child who doesn't understand the words coming out of her pretty little mouth. "I want *those.* Besides, there's so much waste in the fashion industry. Fast fashion drives me bonkers. Sure, you can get a cute top for sixteen dollars off some site, but by the time it's been washed twice, it's no longer worth wearing because it's misshapen and shrunk three sizes. So it gets tossed, and then something else is bought, and all of that goes into the landfill. Yes, luxury costs a lot of money, but the materials are so beautiful and well made. Sure, my dry-cleaning bill is more than some mortgages, but I don't care. It's worth it."

She shrugs and crosses her arms over her chest.

"Glad you asked, aren't you?"

"I know it's surprising to you, but I'm interested in hearing about these things. I like knowing more about you."

"Right." She sighs and looks out the window. She doesn't believe me.

"I have a question. What happened to that funny, intelligent, kind woman I had dinner with and shared the best night of my life with last year?"

I watch her roll her lips together and narrow her eyes. Her cheeks flush, and her breathing increases.

"You want to know where she went?" she asks softly.

I catch her chin in my fingers and make her look at me. There's a vulnerability there, and it makes me want to pull her into my arms.

"I do, aye."

"That girl is no longer available to you." She turns in her seat to face me but glances at Miller.

"He's not here," I say, and she nods.

"I had no issues with a one-night stand with a sexy man I met by chance and had a good time with. There's no shame in that. It was fun. It made me feel good. No harm, no foul. Sure, the whole leaving without saying goodbye thing bruised my feelings a bit, but I got over it. It was a nice memory to tuck away and pull out once in a while to admire."

She clears her throat, and I want to fuck her right here, in the back of this car.

"But it turned out that you weren't a stranger, Connor. You're my *best friend's* brother. The same best friend who will probably marry *my* brother. So it's not like I can avoid you. You're *everywhere*. London? There you are. My store, Birdie's dance recitals, even the house I grew up in, you're there. And I could be a grown-up about that. I could shake it off and laugh about it. What a coincidence! Crazy small world. But when you're near, you want to put your stupid magical hands all over me and kiss me until I can't think straight."

She's ranting now. The words are pouring out of her, and I have no intention of stopping her because I need to know everything she's saying.

I should have asked a long time ago.

"You want to put your hands on me and make me lose my mind, but that's it. Then you walk away like I'm a stranger, and you're so fucking *cold*. I don't even have your phone number. I don't even know where you live. I don't really know anything about you at all, except you run an empire, and you're the brother of one of the sweetest people in the world. That's it. So it's not like it was a random hookup that was fun, and then I can just get on with my life. And I'm worth more than the five minutes of good you're willing to give me whenever we happen to be in the same room together. Orgasms don't cut it, Connor."

She shakes her head and looks outside again.

"I'm an adult," she mutters. "I can be civil."

"What was that?"

"Nothing."

"Billie, I'm sorry. You're right, I've been a daft idiot, and I shouldn't have treated you like that. I'm so fucking attracted to you, I—"

"You know, I don't want to hear it." She shakes her head again, sounding weary. "I just deserve more respect than what you've been handing out. That's what I'm trying to say."

I push my hand through my hair and blow out a breath.

She's absolutely right.

"I'm going to nap." She leans against the door and closes her eyes, and I take that time to watch her.

Billie Blackwell *is* the most beautiful woman I've ever seen. I didn't realize she was Skyla's friend that night when I asked her to dinner and then to my room. When I discovered she was one of the friends Skyla had been talking about, I was stunned.

I didn't think I'd ever see her again, and there she was, standing right in front of me. And I couldn't help myself.

I can never seem to help myself where she's concerned.

If she's nearby, I want to have my hands on her. I want to consume her.

I want to claim her.

But I'm pure shite when it comes to relationships, and this woman is close to fifteen years younger than me.

It wouldn't work.

Yet I can't stay away from her.

Her breathing has evened out, and I notice Miller looking at me in the mirror.

"She's good for you, boss," he says.

I glance her way again. Her head is angled badly, and she'll get a crick in the neck like that, so I unbuckle her belt and slide her across the seat until she's next to me.

She opens her eyes, but she's still out of it.

"What are you doing?"

"Hold on," I say softly and secure her with the other belt, then pull her against me. "I've got you, angel. Just sleep."

She's so sleepy that she doesn't fight me. She wraps an arm around my middle, nuzzles her face into my chest, and goes right back to sleep.

I've spent the past four hours holding her, breathing her in. She slept the entire rest of the drive as if she was bloody exhausted. I remember her telling me before that she doesn't sleep well. She was going to drive for four hours, but she was clearly too tired for that, making me irrationally angry.

I wish I knew why she doesn't sleep at night. Does she have nightmares? And if so, what are they about? Or is it that her mind is simply too busy to quiet down?

I want to know everything.

But I don't have any right to.

Because although I held her and let myself drag my fingers over her soft skin, I also decided that after this, I won't touch Billie again. She's right in that our families are connected now, so I'll have to see her from time to time, but I won't seek her out. I won't pull her away to steal a moment with her.

I won't be that guy.

I have so much respect for this hardworking, incredible woman. She deserves everything she desires, including a man who knows how to open up to a woman outside of the bloody bedroom.

Miller pulls up in front of her small house in Bitterroot Valley, and I press a kiss to her head.

"Wake up, angel. You're home."

She stirs, yawns, and then sits up and stretches. The material of her dress pulls tight against her breasts.

Fuck me.

"Wow, did I sleep that whole time?"

"You did, aye." I unbuckle her belt, then mine, and step out of the vehicle to keep me from wrapping her in my arms and pulling her close. How can I have just spent all afternoon hugging her, and I still want more?

She climbs out of the car and walks up to her door to unlock it.

Just a key. No keypad. No alarm. No cameras.

She should be in a safer house.

"I'll get those," she says as Miller lifts the totes out of the back of the SUV.

"No, miss, I have them. I'll set them just inside."

She nods. I've never seen the inside of her house, and I'm jealous of my own bodyguard as he walks in to set down the totes.

"Thanks for the ride," she says to Miller, offering him a smile when he walks out the door.

"My pleasure," he replies with a nod and walks past me to the vehicle, where he'll wait.

"I already sent messages to have your car towed," I inform her. "It should be at Brooks's garage first thing in the morning."

"Oh, just let me know what I owe you for the tow." She bites her lip, and I shake my head.

"You don't owe me anything."

"I can pay for the tow truck, Connor."

"I said no." I sigh and push my glasses up my nose. Christ, I love her sassy mouth, but I also miss that sweet side of her from that first night. I wish she'd smile at me. When she smiled, laughed, gasped, moaned, she lit up my whole world.

But she doesn't smile. She's scowling.

"You want to put your hands on me and make me lose my mind, but that's it. Then you walk away like I'm a stranger, and you're so fucking cold. I just deserve more respect than what you've been handing out."

She's not wrong. And I don't deserve those smiles anymore.

"Fine. Thanks."

"You're welcome." I nod and turn to walk back to the SUV, but she calls out my name.

I fucking love it when she says my name.

"Connor?"

I turn and raise an eyebrow.

"Thank you." Her voice is softer, and those delicious lips lift in a small smile. "I appreciate your help."

"You're welcome," I repeat, gentler this time. I shove my hands in my pockets and make myself walk to the car before I beg her to forgive me and let me have her in my life.

I can't do that to her.

It wouldn't be fair.

Chapter Three

BILLIE

I'll never sleep tonight. Not after sleeping on the drive home. I can't believe I did that. When I told Connor I was going to nap, I'd planned to just close my eyes and pretend to sleep so I didn't have to talk to him and humiliate myself more.

I can't believe that I sat in that car and told a *billionaire* all about my used-clothes habit. Sure, they're luxury brands, but I explained it to him as if he doesn't know what Dior is.

I'm pretty sure his white button-down cost more than all the clothes I bought combined.

Not to mention, his sister, Skyla, wore a couture Dior gown to a benefit earlier this year. He didn't need me to give him a lecture on ready-to-wear clothes from fashion houses, and the sad state of fast fashion in our society.

Although, I really do love everything I bought today, and I enjoyed talking about it.

"I'll just unpack it all and hang it up and forget about my stupid fashion lecture to the billionaire," I grumble as I drag one of the totes into the primary bedroom. This house used to have four bedrooms, but I converted the smallest one, which happens to be next to the primary bedroom, into a beautiful closet and dressing room. I did it all myself with a closet kit that I ordered online.

Okay, I didn't do it *all* myself. My brothers helped.

I painted the walls in a soft blue, the floor is hardwood, and the lighting is specifically designed to perfectly showcase my racks, shelves, and the area in front of the mirror so I can see myself well while dressing.

My clothes are hanging, organized by color. On the left are work and dressy clothes. On the right are casual ensembles. And in the middle is an island dresser where I house all of my pretty unmentionables and pajamas. I saved one drawer for jewelry.

One by one, I pull out each garment from the tote, shake it out, and hang it up, replaying the conversation in the car earlier.

Not only did I go on about the clothes, but *then* I humiliated myself more by basically whining about the fact that he didn't want me. For the love of all that's holy, I should have just launched myself out of the vehicle. Road rash would be more comfortable than this horrible embarrassment I feel. I should have just told him this *is* the real me and left it at that, but no. I had to rant and rave about my *feelings*, and that's so mortifying.

But when I fell asleep, he pulled me against him,

which was an unexpected surprise. He was warm and hard, and I'm fairly certain there were times when I woke up enough to feel him kissing my hair or brushing his fingers up and down my arm.

There are moments when he looks at me, or during those moments when I slept against him, that I feel like he wants to be tender. He wants to talk or just be near me, and it's not simply sexual. But he holds himself back, and it makes me want to scream.

I hang a Chanel scarf and sigh.

I said my piece. The rest is up to him.

"I need to move on," I whisper as I open the second tote and continue hanging my finds. "If he eventually comes around and decides to ask for my number or start an actual conversation, fine. But he probably won't. So I need to move the fuck on."

When the last item of clothing is hung, I carefully select my outfit for work tomorrow and hang it near the mirror, then I take a hot shower and climb into my pajama pants and the shirt I wear to bed every night.

Connor's shirt.

It doesn't smell like him anymore because I've washed it about a hundred times, which makes me sad. But it's so soft and big on me, and for reasons I haven't examined too closely, it comforts me.

"Stupid," I mutter as I pad into the kitchen and pour a glass of water. I stand at the sink, looking out the window to my postage-stamp-sized backyard as I sip the water, and then turn off all the lights, make sure the doors are locked, and head to my bedroom, where I'll lie awake and stare at the ceiling all night.

What a bizarre day. Exceptionally fun shopping with Martha, as always, and a delicious, peaceful lunch ... *that Connor paid for*, and then a strange car ride home with the mercurial Mr. Gallagher. My mental health day was hijacked. Here's hoping next month's trip is less eventful.

"We're going out," Dani informs me the following Saturday afternoon. She found me in the dark romance section of my store, and she's got her hands on her hips, smiling at me.

"Hello to you, too," I reply with a laugh as I shelve a copy of *Haunting Adeline*. "I can't go out tonight. I have a book and a bottle of wine waiting for me."

I'm so fucking tired. I didn't sleep all week because I kept overthinking the whole car ride from Big Sky with Connor, and all I want to do is relax. My shop is closed on Sunday, so I get to sleep in tomorrow.

"You're coming," Dani says, scowling at me. "We haven't had a girls' night out in *months*."

"We had book club last week."

"That's not the same, and you know it," Skyla adds, surprising me as she walks around the bookcase.

"You're ganging up on me now?"

"Yep." Dani smiles and tucks her dark hair behind

her ear. "We need it, Bee. Bridger's off this weekend, so he's staying home with Birdie. Alex is coming, too."

Dani's twin sister missed book club last week, and I haven't seen her in a while.

"I do miss Alex," I say with a resigned sigh. "Fine. I'll come. Where are we going?"

"Just to the Wolf Den." Skyla claps her hands. "Huckleberry margaritas are calling our names, and we can play some pool, or dance, or just talk. Who knows, maybe you'll find some cute tourists to flirt with."

I shake my head, putting all thoughts of that to a stop right away. "No. No more tourists for me."

Not that Connor was really a tourist. Hell, I don't know what Connor was.

Sexy. Connor was sexy.

"What time?" I ask.

"We're thinking around seven? That way, we can have dinner, too."

"Cool, I can be at home with my book by nine."

Skyla rolls her pretty green eyes. "We're going to have fun. Wear something scandalous."

"I will if you two will."

"I don't own anything scandalous." Dani laughs. "But I'll dress up a bit, and I'll text Alex. She has lots of sexy clothes to wear."

"I'm so bloody excited," Skyla says with a little shimmy. "I'd better get home and get ready. Oh, and Beckett said he's happy to be the driver tonight and give everyone a ride home, so we can all drink if we want to."

"My brothers are so chivalrous." Sarcasm drips from

45

my words, and the other two laugh. "Like I want my brother to pick me up while I'm drunk and wearing something scandalous. I'd never live it down. Luckily for me, this is a tiny town, and I can walk home if need be."

"You'll get a ride, and that's the end of it," Skyla counters, pointing her finger into my chest.

"You're as bossy as your brother."

Skyla just smiles. "I know."

The girls leave, and it's already time to close the store for the day. By the time I get home, I have just over an hour to get ready and meet my friends downtown.

Maybe this won't be so bad. It'll be good to see them, have a couple of drinks, and then come home and read for the rest of the night. I can be social.

I can be fun.

And it might take my mind off a certain sexy Irishman.

"Seriously, you are *smokin' hot*," Alex says as we clink our glasses together. "That dress should come with a warning label that says, *I will blow your fucking mind*."

I giggle and look down at the red slip dress. It's gathered just below my boobs and flows down in a way that hides my tummy and ends just above my knees. It's held up with spaghetti straps, and it's the first time I've dared to wear it. But it's perfect for summer, and with my hair up in a twist, it makes me feel sexy.

"So many heads turned when we walked in here," Skyla agrees as she reaches for some nachos. "You're getting laid tonight, friend."

A laugh bubbles through me, and I shake my head. "No. I'm not. But thank you all for the huge boost to my ego. You're the best friends ever."

"Of course, we are, but every word is absolutely true," Dani replies smugly. Our table is full of the appetizer menu, we all have our margaritas, and I have to admit, this really is exactly what I needed. A chance to talk and laugh and hang out with my girls.

"Why is that guy over there chewing on a match?" Alex wants to know. "He's got it clenched in his teeth like you would a toothpick. What the hell? Does he think it's cool? Is he prepared in case he has to quickly light something on fire?"

"Stop staring at him." I smack her arm. "He'll think you're interested in him."

"I want to ask him what his thought process is here because seriously, what the hell?"

"Maybe he's a pyro." I shrug.

"Don't say that," Dani replies, shaking her head, and I immediately feel bad. Dani's husband, Bridger, the fire chief and my big brother, had to deal with an arsonist last year, and it was horrible.

"Sorry. Too soon." I shake my head. "What are you guys reading right now?"

"I'm in my mafia romance era," Alex says with a sly smile. "I'm consuming all things Neva Altaj."

"Oh, I've heard good things. I need to get more of her stuff in the store." I nod and turn to Dani. "How about you?"

We spend the next half hour discussing books, and there's a lull in the music coming from the jukebox, so I stand.

"I'm going to stretch my legs and put some music on," I inform my friends, who all nod.

"Play some Sidney Sterling," Dani calls out, and I nod.

The Wolf Den is always busy, especially on a Saturday night, and we're in the heart of tourist season. Usually, a live band would be playing, but for some reason, there isn't tonight. That's okay. The jukebox is just as good in a pinch.

I skirt around a group of guys playing pool and grin when one of them catcalls me. I know, it's not terribly feminist of me, but it boosts my ego a bit more, and I send them a little wave as I approach the jukebox and plug some cash in.

Once I've chosen five songs, I start back to the table, but suddenly, a body stands in front of me.

"Well, hello, gorgeous."

I'm in heels, which puts me at eye level with this guy. He's a little drunk, and his eyes are on my tits.

"Excuse me."

"I'm talking to you." He reaches out to put his hand on my hip, but I move away, evading him.

"Don't fucking touch me."

His eyes jerk up to mine, and he sneers. "What, do you think you're better than me or something?"

"Or something. You have a good night."

I go to walk around him, but he grabs my arm, pulling me to a stop, and I round on him, my patience long gone.

"Oh, hell no," I yell in his face. "I said *don't fucking touch me*, you asshole. Who the hell do you think you are? Keep your hands to yourself, or I'll remove them from your ugly body."

"You're a fat cunt," he says, holding his hands up. "Jesus, try to be nice to a bitch."

"No. You weren't being nice. You were being a slimy, creepy, predatory asshole. No one, not *one* woman in this bar, wants that from you or anyone else. Learn some fucking manners, you piece of shit."

I walk away, and the guys at the pool table applaud.

"We were about to come help, but you didn't need it," one of them says with a proud smile. "He won't bother you again."

"No. He won't."

With my chin high, I return to my table, and my friends are all watching me with wide eyes.

"What?"

"You're so fucking badass, Bee." Alex shakes her head. "Like, *I* would do you right now."

I laugh and take a sip of my drink. "I don't get assholes like that. Get some liquid courage in them, and they think they're the boss of everything. I'd have punched him if I had to."

"Have you taken self-defense classes?" Skyla asks me.

"I have four older brothers," I remind her with a smirk. "They taught me to punch before I started kindergarten. That asshole doesn't scare me. I outweigh him by a solid fifty pounds."

There's a heartbeat of silence, and then more laughter around me, and the jerk is forgotten.

We all get up to dance, and when we return to the table, we order fresh drinks—because you just never know—and eat some more of our food.

I admit, the room is a little fuzzy from the alcohol and the endorphins of a good night spent with my girls.

"I'm so getting laid tonight," Skyla says with a sloppy smile. "I know it's your brother, Bee, and I apologize, but holy shite, the man knows what he's doing. He can do this thing with his fingers that I can't get enough of."

"Ew."

"Bridger, too," Dani agrees. I feel a little sick to my stomach at the thought of my brothers having sex. "The orgasms are insane with that man. And his mouth! He says the sexiest things."

"Yes!" Skyla high-fives Dani, making me blink. "The orgasms! I didn't know it was possible to have that many in one night."

"If you keep talking about my brothers"—my words slur slightly—"I'll talk about yours, my Irish friend."

Skyla laughs, waving me off. "I don't honestly care. Connor's almost forty. The man obviously has sex."

"And he's too good at it." I don't know why that makes me grumpy. Probably because it's been so long since he did it with *me*, so he's probably moved on to having it with someone else.

That lucky bitch.

I want to kill her, whoever she is.

"Anything new happening there?" Alex asks, and I shake my head.

"Nothing's going to happen, either."

"You never know," Dani replies, but I sigh and eat a mozzarella stick.

"I'm pretty sure I know. Okay, maybe I should get Connor off my brain and have sex with one of these lucky men tonight."

I turn in my chair, and we scan the room. The guy at the pool table, the one who told me he'd make sure the asshole didn't bother me again, is handsome. He's muscular with blond hair and blue eyes, and his forearms are sexy when he leans over the table to shoot at a ball.

"I think the one you're looking at is gay," Alex says, leaning toward me.

"Why?"

"Because he's been holding hands with the other hot guy all night."

As soon as she says that, hot pool guy walks over and kisses the other hot pool guy, and I grin.

I know that guy.

"Well, damn." With a fresh idea in my mind, I grin at my friends. "Wait. Maybe they're bi, and they'd like a third."

I smile at the girls, who all whoop and clap and encourage me to go ask.

This is gonna be hilarious.

"I *dare* you to go ask them that," Dani says. "You're safe. We're right here. Do it. Right now."

"What do I get if I do it?"

"Free yoga classes for the rest of your life," Skyla offers.

"You already give me that." I laugh at her as she frowns into her glass.

"Oh yeah."

"I'll pay for your dry-cleaning for a *month*," Dani says with a knowing smile and winks as she sips her drink. "And I'm not kidding."

"That's a lot, friend."

"I know."

"I'll split it with you," Alex offers, getting in on the action.

"I'm in too," Skyla says. "We'll pay for your dry-cleaning for a month if you go ask those sexy boys over there if they'd like you to join them with their ... *sticks*."

"You guys think I won't? Just watch."

"Go proposition those men, friend. If they accept, be careful. Make sure they wrap it up." Alex pats me on the arm.

"Oh my God, what if they say yes? I never considered that!"

My friends laugh some more, and I'm on the verge of laughing.

"You don't *have* to do anything," Dani reminds me,

patting my shoulder. "This is all in fun. Go do it. Think of all that free dry-cleaning."

"Fine." I down the last of my margarita in two gulps, then stand and straighten my dress. As I walk to the two men playing pool, I'm determined not to be embarrassed or panic. I can do this. I look good tonight.

"Well, hi there," Number One says with a charming smile. "Do you need us to save you from that jerk?"

"I think you know the answer to that," I reply with a wink. "I don't usually need saving from much."

"Good girl," Number Two says, and I can't help but remember the way Connor said that in my ear.

Good fucking girl.

A shiver runs through me, and I take a deep breath. I *so* need to get that sexy Irishman out of my head.

Then Number Two's eyes widen in surprise. "Billie?"

"Hey, cousin."

Gabe leans in to kiss my cheek and grins at me. "You look like you're up to no good, baby doll."

Gabe is a *flirt.*

"What can we do for you?" Number One asks.

"I honestly came over here so my friends would pay for my dry-cleaning."

Number One's eyebrows climb. "Now we need to know everything. Have a seat, beautiful."

I climb onto a stool, and both men hover close by. I wish I could say that I feel tingles of excitement, but I don't.

Not one fucking tingle in sight.

I mean, obviously I wouldn't for my cousin, but not even Number One is giving me a spark.

Goddamn you, Connor.

"So we're all women over there, right?"

"A gorgeous group of women," Gabe agrees, eyeing them over my shoulder.

"And most of those girls are going home to men tonight. My brothers, in fact, but that's a long story. Anywho, I'm a little tipsy, and I mentioned that *you're* a handsome fella." I point at Number One, who preens while Gabe chuckles. "But then it was pointed out to me that you're with him"—I point at Gabe, who smiles back—"and I said, what if they want a third?"

I swallow hard. *I cannot believe I just said that out loud.*

Gabe starts to cough.

"I mean, you're my cousin, and that's not happening in this or any other lifetime, but the girls don't know that because Alex and Dani haven't recognized you yet, and I *really* wanted them to pay for my dry-cleaning. So I was dared to come over here and ask."

"How much is your dry-cleaning?" Gabe asks.

"It averages over a thousand dollars a month."

"Holy shit," Gabe says. "Yeah, I'd do it, too."

"Do you want an answer to your intriguing question?" Number One asks.

"Wait." I hold up a hand. "What is your name?"

"I'm Adam," Number One says.

"Adam and Gabe. Got it. I'm Billie, Gabe's cousin on my dad's side. Nice to meet you, Adam. Okay, you can give me an answer so I can take it back to the table, and we can talk about it." I push a stray strand of hair behind my ear.

"If you weren't his cousin, fuck yes, we'd take you home with us," Adam says as his eyes move from my face, down my body, and back up again. "We love to share, sweetheart."

"Shut up." I roll my eyes, but Adam leans in and plants his lips at my ear.

And there might be half a tingle.

"You're fucking gorgeous, baby girl." His fingertips ghost down my arm. Gabe's gaze catches mine, and he winks at me.

"You know, that's the nicest thing anyone has said to me all day," I reply and then give them a sassy smile. "I'll go relay the message."

Adam chuckles and kisses my cheek. "I'm glad we could help with that dry-cleaning bill."

"So that's Alex Lexington?" Gabe asks, gesturing to the table with his chin. "I haven't seen her in over a decade."

"She's single." I waggle my eyebrows. "Shall I send her over?"

They share a look, and Gabe nods. "If she's interested, by all means."

"Oh, this is fun." I grin and turn around to return to the table, and when I sit down, all I can do is grin at Alex.

"Well?" Dani demands, waving her hand in front of my face. "Did they make you short-circuit?"

"What happened, then?" Skyla asks. "You can't just sit there and smile."

"Oh, they'd be down for a threesome," I reply, taking a sip of Alex's drink. "But not with me."

"Huh." Alex eyes them and sips her drink. "With who, then? You're hot as fuck tonight."

"That's Gabe Blackwell, friend. And he's eyeing you up, so you should go over there. They're hot, they're nice, and holy shit, they'd rock your world."

"Hmm." Alex sips her drink and eyes the two men, who are staring right back, smiling. "Gabe has changed a *lot*. Jesus, it's been a long time since I've seen him."

"He's so different," Dani agrees.

"Looks like they're hoping you'll go over there." I gesture to Alex in a Vanna White way, and they both nod. "Do it, Alex. For all of womankind, I'm begging you to go have sex with those two men."

She bites her lip and looks at each of us. "Yeah?"

"Yes," Dani and Skyla say at the same time.

"But be careful," Dani adds.

"See you bitches later."

"Tomorrow, with a full report," I call out after her as she grabs her purse and saunters over to the men, who smile at her and hold her hands, and then they send me a wink and a smile.

I wave back as if to say, *it's all good. Go have fun,* and then sigh in happiness.

"You know I feel good about the fact that I just helped one of my closest friends have some great sex tonight."

"We don't know if it's great sex yet," Dani reminds me.

"Look at them," I reply. "Also, trust me. She's going to have a lot of fun."

"Now I'm sad because you're the only one not getting some this evening, and you look incredible," Skyla says. We all watch Adam and Gabe surround Alex, and I'm excited for my friend.

Good for her.

"I'll live. Trust me."

Just then, Bridger and Beckett stroll inside, looking for their girls.

"We're taking you home," Bridger says to his wife, planting a kiss on her lips as his hands dive into her hair at the back of her neck.

I notice Alex leaving, walking between the two men, a huge smile on her face.

"Who has Birdie?" I ask Bridger.

"She ended up going to Holden and Millie's for a few hours to watch a movie, and it's not over yet, so I'm here to claim my wife before we pick her up."

"Come on, Irish," Beckett says to Skyla, taking her hand and pulling her to her feet. "I have plans for you tonight."

"I'm so grossed out right now," I grumble into my drink.

"I'll take you home," Bridger offers, but I shake my head.

"I think I'll have one more, then I can walk home or call a rideshare." I shrug a shoulder.

"I don't like leaving you here after you've had this much to drink," Dani says with a scowl. "I'll stay for a while longer with you, and we can grab a rideshare together. Bridger can meet me at home when Birdie's done with her movie."

"No." I shake my head, but my brothers don't look convinced. "Honest, I'm fine. You know I can take care of myself. Those brothers of mine taught me how to fight. I can kick some serious ass if I have to."

"I wouldn't cross her," Beckett agrees with a laugh. "But if you need a ride, just call us, Bee. Seriously, it's not a problem to come back and get you."

"Yeah, yeah." I blow them all a kiss as they stand to go, then I take my drink to the bar. I don't want to sit at that table by myself.

"One more," I say to Brenda, the bartender. She winks at me as she takes my glass, then grabs a clean one to make me a fresh drink.

She passes it to me, and I lay down some cash, then take a sip, leaning against the bar.

"Hi."

I turn my head to the right and see a guy smiling shyly. Not at all my type, and I'm absolutely going home alone, but I'm not a rude person.

"Hello."

"I'm Bill."

"You're kidding." I give a little laugh and sip my drink.

"About my name? No, I'm not kidding."

"I'm Billie."

His smile grows, and he turns on his stool to face me. "Well, isn't that interesting? Does this mean we have to get married?"

I wrinkle my nose. "Bill and Billie? I don't know, what's your last name?"

"Williamson."

I snort, sending myself into a coughing fit. I have to turn away so I don't cough in the poor man's face.

When I turn back around, he's still grinning at me, and I pick up my drink and take some sips and try to clear my throat.

"You know, Bill, as nice as that offer is, I'm going to have to pass."

"Just sex, then."

Ugh, now he's turning into a creep. What is it with creepy men tonight?

"I don't really like the idea of crying out my own name in the middle of sex, Bill. It just doesn't sound like a good time to me."

"Don't knock it until you've tried it."

The room starts to spin even more, and my vision is cloudy. I push my drink away. I guess I went over my limit.

I don't like this feeling. This out-of-control, dizzy, like I'm going to fall down feeling. Why didn't I leave with the others?

"Are you okay?" Bill asks, sounding truly concerned.

"Fine. I'm going to call a ride."

I pull my phone out of my purse, but he puts his

hand over mine, and it falls from my fingers to the bar, as if I can't control my fingers to hold on to it.

"Shit."

"I'll give you a ride, baby."

"No thanks. Don't call me baby." My words are slurred. Jesus, I only had a few sips of that drink. I shouldn't be this out of it.

"Come on, *baby*, let's get you outside in the fresh air."

"Don't want to."

"Sure, you do. The air will feel good." He wraps his arm around my waist to keep me up because my knees want to buckle. He pulls me against him and plants his lips on my temple. Gross.

No, I don't want to go with you. Why am I going outside with Bill? Why do I feel so dizzy?

Fight him off, Bee. You know how to—and it hits me.

"You ... you drugged me."

"Don't say it like that." He pushes us through the crowd of people and out the door. *Why isn't anyone stopping him?* "You already wanted it. I just gave you a nudge."

"Said no." God, I hate how faint my voice is. How loose and out of my control my body feels. I should be able to kick this fucker's ass, but I can't even make my feet work right.

"Look at this dress, Billie. You're practically begging for my cock. Don't worry, I'm going to give it to you. I'm going to give it to you so good, you'll want more. I'm going to fuck your throat, your pussy, and your ass before the night is through. You'll be soaking in my cum, and begging for more, like the good little slut you are."

I shake my head. So dizzy. *No. No.* This can't be happening. I'm pushed against the side of a truck. He has his hand up my dress, and his mouth on me, and I want to throw up.

Stop. Please fucking stop.

Suddenly, I'm falling to the ground, and he's gone, and I sink down to the concrete.

Oh God.

Chapter Four

CONNOR

I didn't want to be at home alone tonight, so I came into town to the Wolf Den. Thought I'd have a drink at the bar, watch the game, and sit among humanity for a few hours.

What I found when I got here put me in a bloody foul mood.

Billie was with my sister and their friends for a while. They seemed to be having a good time, and I hung back, just to make sure they were safe. I thought about calling Miller in to look after them as well, but then decided that they were fine, and there was no harm in the fun they were having.

Then my angel, my bumble bee, walked over to flirt with two men, and I almost went out of my fucking mind when it looked like she might leave with them.

Are you kidding me?

It's one thing to know that she's not mine, but it's another entirely to watch her be propositioned by not one but *two* wankers at the same time. They looked at her like she's gorgeous, which she is, and they wanted to get their dicks wet.

Fuck that.

But, to my surprise, she walked away with a laugh, then filled the girls in and shook her head.

Interesting.

Even more so when the woman I know as Alex leaves with said two men. What I don't understand is why Billie didn't leave with them. Why did Bridger and Beckett collect my sister and Dani, then leave my girl here alone?

Why the fuck didn't they give her a ride home?

I'll be giving the Blackwell boys a piece of my mind the next time I see them.

Billie walks up to the bar, just about four stools down from me. She hasn't noticed me here, and I'd like to keep it that way.

I'll make sure she gets home safely, then I'll call it a night.

"One more," she says to the bartender, then pays for her drink and takes a sip.

Of course, the arsehole on her right starts to talk to her. A new song comes on the jukebox, drowning out most of their conversation, but I see her wrinkle her nose at him in disgust, and it makes me grin.

I love that my girl doesn't have a poker face.

She starts to cough, and then they talk for a few more minutes—which I tolerate … *just*—and then that prick has his arm around her, and he's escorting her out of the bar.

What in the actual fuck?

I notice her phone is on the bar, so I grab it and slip it into my pocket as I hurry after them. When I get outside, he has her cornered against a truck, his hands and mouth on her, and Billie looks ... limp.

He.

Fucking.

Drugged.

My.

Angel.

The fuck?

Seeing red, I yank the piece of shite back by the collar and punch him in the nose, breaking it and sending blood spraying all over the place. He moans and covers his face with his hands.

When I glance back, I see Billie sliding down the truck and sitting on the concrete, and I want to kill this arsehole.

"Hey!" he cries out, waving one hand out in front of him. "What the fuck, man!"

"Did you fucking drug her?"

"What we're doing is none of you—"

I pull him up by the shirt and punch him in the jaw three times, satisfied when I feel it give under my knuckles. It's either broken or dislocated.

He moans again, his eyes rolling back in his head.

"Answer me, you worthless piece of shite."

"She wanted me," he mutters as blood runs down from his nose and into his teeth. "Fucking slut wanted it."

Grabbing his wrist, I twist it and feel the bones give, ignoring the keening wail this idiot lets out in response.

"I should kill you." My voice is calmer than I feel as I let go and watch him drop onto the concrete, twisting in pain. "But my girl wouldn't like that."

With him writhing on the ground, I turn and pick up Billie and carry her to my SUV, get her settled in the passenger seat, and buckle her in. I kiss her forehead and brush the hair back from her face with shaky hands. She moans, and pure rage and helplessness consume me as her eyebrows pull together and she whimpers.

"Sick," she says.

"Are you going to be sick, angel?"

She nods, and I unbuckle her in time to pull her over the side of the car. She throws up, barely missing my shoes.

Not that I give a fuck. She could retch all over the car, all over me, and I couldn't care less. It's the fact that she's hurting at all that has me out of my bloody mind.

"Good." I use my shirt to wipe off her mouth. "Good girl, you need to get that poison out of you. Did you drink the whole thing, baby?"

She whimpers again. Her eyes are closed, and I need to know how much she drank.

"Billie. Can you look at me?"

She forces her eyes open and scowls. "Connor?"

"It's me. You're safe, angel. Did you drink the whole drink?"

"No. Few sips."

Thank Christ.

"I'm taking you home, bumble. I've got you."

I get her buckled back in, then spare a look at the idiot on the ground. He's sitting up, cradling his wrist against his chest. I rush around to the driver's side and pull out of the car park, watching Billie closely as I navigate through town.

"I live ten minutes away," I assure her as I reach over and press the back of my hand to her forehead. She doesn't feel warm, but her breathing is shallow, and she keeps whimpering. "Billie, can you hear me? I need you to talk to me, angel."

"Thirsty." She licks her lips, and her head moves back and forth against the seat as if she's agitated. I wish I could pull her into my arms and comfort her.

"Okay, it's okay, gorgeous, we'll get you some water. It's not far now."

I should have killed that motherfucker. I'm going to ruin his life.

The gate at my property recognizes my vehicle and automatically opens, and I drive down the long driveway to my house. I bought this ten-acre property earlier this year when I decided to buy the ski resort that had burned down last Thanksgiving and rebuild it as a Gallagher Hotels property. I knew I'd be here for the entire build and didn't want to live in a hotel.

For once in my adult life, I wanted a home base.

And this house suits my needs well. It's more of a mansion, with mountain views and a lodge aesthetic, but the best part is, it's private, with a guesthouse for Miller and other men I might have with me at any given time.

The lights are on inside, and I scoop Billie into my arms and carry her in and through to the family room off the kitchen, where I spend a lot of time. It's comfortable, with a deep sectional sofa, and I can grab anything she might need from the kitchen.

"Here, *a stór*," I say as I settle her into the corner of the sofa. "I'm getting you water. Do you feel sick again?"

"Tired," she mutters, nuzzling against the back of the couch. "Sleep."

"Let me get some water in you."

I rush to the kitchen and grab a water bottle from the fridge. I help her take a few sips before she lies back and seems to fall into a restless sleep.

"Fuck me," I mutter, rubbing my hand over my neck.

I call her brother Blake. Ironically, I have all of her brothers' contact info, but I don't have hers.

Having hers would have been too tempting.

But the Blackwells have brought my sister into their family, and I needed to know how to reach any one of them in case of an emergency.

Blake's phone rings three times before he answers.

He wasn't sleeping. He's breathing too hard for that.

"What?" he barks into the phone.

"I need help," I reply. "Your sister was roofied at the bar tonight, and I want to make sure I'm doing everything right."

"Fuck," he growls. Then I hear him say, "Sorry, baby, I'll be right back."

"Sorry to interrupt." My voice is as dry as the desert, and Blake doesn't acknowledge it.

"Tell me everything," he says, his voice hard.

"I didn't see him slip it in her drink. I happened to be at the bar, keeping an eye on her."

"Not creepy at all."

"Fuck you. This guy started hitting on her, she had a coughing fit, and then sipped her drink, and things got weird. Pretty sure that's when he slipped it in the glass. He took her outside, and by the time I got there, he already had her pinned against the side of a truck."

"Jesus Christ. I'm on my way."

"No need. I beat the shite out of him and brought her home with me, Blake. She threw up before we left the car park."

"This is my sister, Gallagher. I need to examine her and make sure she's okay."

"I hear you, and if she hadn't thrown up, I would have taken her straight to the hospital."

He's silent for a few beats, and I can imagine he's extremely torn right now. The Blackwell brothers love their baby sister and are very protective of her.

I'll take her to the hospital if she needs it, but right now, I wonder if she's better here where it's quiet with soft lighting. *But I don't fucking know if that's the right thing.*

Blake sighs. "Do you know how much she drank?"

"She said a few sips. She's been agitated, and she was confused. She's sleeping now."

"How's her breathing?"

It was fast in the car, but as I stare down at her now, she's breathing in long, slow breaths, like in normal sleep.

"Actually, fuck this." Blake's suddenly ringing through with a FaceTime call, and I accept. His hair is a mess, and he's not wearing a shirt. His jaw is tight. "Show me."

I turn the camera to my angel and get closer to her.

"Her breathing looks normal to me. She asked for water."

He's quiet for a moment, obviously listening to her, and I watch her as well. Christ, she's beautiful. *I fucking hate that this is happening to her.*

"Okay, it doesn't sound like she got much in her. Here's what you'll do. You're going to watch her like a fucking hawk. If she wakes up, get her to drink water. Water is her friend. If she needs to throw up, that's fine too. If she starts having trouble breathing, you call an ambulance right away. Don't fuck around with that. I'm assuming she had drinks before that, and that's where it gets tricky with these fucking drugs. Both alcohol and any roofie are depressants, and that's when people die. If she didn't get too much in her, her breathing is good, and she's already thrown up, I'm comfortable with you keeping her there and watching her. If literally *anything* changes, you get her to the fucking hospital."

"Got it. Thank you." I turn the camera back to me and pace the room.

"No, thank you. Sounds like you saved my baby sister from being raped and fuck knows what tonight."

I have to sit down because my legs feel like they're going to give out on me. *Both alcohol and any roofie are depressants, and that's when people die.* Fucking hell, thank God I was there.

"I have to call the police. This piece of shite doesn't get to go free."

"Call Chase Wild. Do you have his number?"

"Yeah, after the mess with Skyla earlier this year, I have his number."

"He'll take care of it."

"Thanks. Go back to your ... date."

"I plan to."

He hangs up, and I immediately dial Chase Wild, who *does* sound sleepy. After giving him the same rundown, he asks, "Do you have a name?"

"No."

"Then how am I supposed to find the son of a bitch?"

"Check the hospital," I suggest. "I broke his nose and his wrist. Maybe his jaw. He'll be needing medical attention."

He's quiet for a moment. "Good. Fucker. There'll be video surveillance of that parking lot. I'll take care of it. He might press charges against you for assault."

"I'm fucking terrified." My voice couldn't get any drier.

"I'll need to talk to Billie."

"When she's conscious, I'll make it happen."

"Thanks, Connor."

I hang up and drag my hand down my face, then watch Billie, still sleeping on the couch. I grab her water

70

and head to my bedroom, where I change my clothes, tossing away the shirt with the vomit and blood on it, and set out one of my T-shirts for her. I grab her phone out of my pocket and set it by the bed, then I return to her downstairs and see that she hasn't moved.

But her breathing is still good, and she looks peaceful.

I nudge my arms under her and lift her, returning to my bedroom.

She stirs and nuzzles herself against me. I love that she snarls at me like a champ when she's awake but seeks me out when she's asleep.

I shouldn't love it.

But I do.

Every instinct tells me that Billie is mine. Watching her flirt and talk with other men tonight was a torture I wouldn't wish on anyone. It felt like my heart was being ripped from my body.

I want her smiles and her laughter. Only me. If she's going to flirt, I want her to flirt with *me*. And no one, not one other bloody arsehole, gets to put his hands on her.

I set her on the bed and work quickly to get the dress that looked so damn delicious but is now a dirty, wrinkled mess off her, and then slip the T-shirt over her head. I help her lie down, and when I grab her phone, I discover it's not locked. She doesn't have decent security at her house, and she doesn't lock her phone. My angel and I are going to have a conversation about her personal protection. I put my number in her contacts and send myself a text so I have her number as well. After tonight, I need to be able to reach her.

I climb into the bed and curl myself around her. I don't want to just watch her breathe. I need to feel it. I want my hand on her soft stomach so I can feel it move up and down with each inhale and exhale. I need to feel her warmth and reassure myself that she's safe and whole.

"I'm so sorry, bumble," I whisper against her hair as fear sets in. Jesus, I could have lost her tonight. "I was right there, and I didn't stop it. I didn't want to piss you off by intruding on your night, but from now on, fuck that. This won't ever happen to you again."

Blake's words echo through my mind.

You saved my baby sister from being raped and fuck knows what tonight.

The mere thought of it has me pulling her close.

No, this will never happen again.

I stay awake all night, keeping my eyes and ears open, watching and listening for any signs of distress from my girl, but she sleeps through the night. She has moments of whimpering, of shifting, as if she's having bad dreams, but then she quickly drifts off again.

At around seven in the morning, she starts to stir.

She whimpers and rolls toward me, loops her arm around my waist, and buries her nose in my chest.

"What can I do?" I ask her softly. "What do you need?"

"Bathroom," she mumbles, but she doesn't move. "Gotta pee."

"Good." The more she gets flushed through her, the better. "Come on, let's get you to the bathroom, angel."

She's still *very* impaired, but she's able to walk with my help to the bathroom. Her eyes are glassy and half open, but when we get inside my bathroom, she pushes on my chest.

"No. Out."

"It's fine. I can help you."

"No." She shakes her head and whimpers again. "Out."

I sigh and set my jaw but press a kiss to her forehead. "I'll be right outside."

She's leaning on the vanity when I walk out and shut the door, and I listen intently as she shuffles around. I can hear the tinkle of her doing her business, the flush of the toilet, and she even washes her hands, which makes me grin.

Even wasted, she's a sanitary girl.

Finally, I can't stand it anymore, and I push the door open and find her leaning on her hands, her head bent forward as if she's sleeping standing up.

Christ.

"I've got you." Carefully, I lift and carry her back to the bed and get her settled under the blankets once more. She takes a couple of sips of water, but then she's too sluggish to keep drinking.

"Your house?" she asks with a whisper.

"Aye, baby, I brought you home with me. You're safe. He didn't do anything to you."

She blinks her eyes open and looks up at me for just a second. "Scared."

"You don't need to be scared." I kiss her forehead and her cheek. "Just sleep this off."

I want to crawl in with her, but my phone lights up, so I walk to the other side of the room and accept Chase Wild's call.

"Gallagher."

"Well, we found him," he says grimly. "Jesus, you fucked him up, Connor."

"Told you. He deserved worse."

"Yeah, well, his story is different from yours, of course. Claims you came out of nowhere and attacked him for no reason."

"Right. Would you like a photo of Billie lying in my bed, *still* out of it?"

"I don't need it," Chase says. "Side note, how is she? Christ, I've known Billie all of her life. Is she okay?"

"She will be. She's still presenting as very drunk. And she didn't even get much of that shit in her. I can't even imagine if she'd drunk the whole thing, Chase."

"It's fucking scary," he replies. "Anyway, I don't need a photo because I have security footage from the bar that shows exactly what happened. She's clearly shaking her head, and he attacks her anyway. I can't prove in that video that she'd been drugged, but she's clearly inebriated. I wanted to check in on her and let you know that we have him. Once he can be released from the hospital, he'll be arrested for sexual assault."

"Good."

When my call with Chase is done, I turn to look at Billie, who's sleeping peacefully. And just when I start to join her, my phone rings.

Again.

"Bloody hell," I grumble as I accept the call. "Gallagher."

"How is she?" Blake asks.

"She's sleeping." I fill him in on how she was a few minutes ago.

"That's normal," he says. "She'll probably sleep most of today. She'll have the hangover of her life when she's finally lucid again. I'll come over later when she's more with it and get an IV of fluids in her. It's good that she used the bathroom and sipped some water. Just keep doing what you're doing. If she's not awake and more with it by midafternoon, call me."

"Aye, I will."

With a sigh, I walk over to the side of the bed and stare down at her. A lock of her dark hair has fallen across her face, so I reach down and smooth it away, then let my fingers glide down her cheek.

The fact that anyone would want to hurt her makes me feral.

I should work. I have calls to make, emails to send, and work to look over. I should be in my office today, following up with contractors and the architect. I'm sure my assistant is frantic, wondering where I am despite it being a Sunday.

But nothing is more important than the woman in my bed.

So without overthinking it, I climb under the covers and pull her to me. Immediately, Billie curls around me, nuzzles her nose in my chest, and sighs, almost as if in relief.

"Just sleep, bumble bee."

Chapter Five

BILLIE

Someone shoved a huge wad of cotton in my mouth. My head feels like it's split open and my brains are spilling out. Every joint in my body aches.

I'm pretty sure I'm in Connor's bed. I remember waking up at some point and seeing him. I felt him. I *smelled* him. Did I ask? I think so. Honestly, I don't remember much, and trying to think about it only makes my head hurt more.

I moan and roll onto my back, but I don't open my eyes because that's going to *hurt*.

"Are you awake?" It's whispered above me, but it still sounds like he's screaming.

"Shh," I reply. "Too loud."

He chuckles softly. I wish he was lying down so I could curl around him, but he's not. I can tell he's sitting up, his back against the headboard. I do have vague memories of his arms around me. Cuddling me against him.

It felt too fucking good, and it just puts me in a bad mood.

Or helps the bad mood that I already have.

"I need you to drink this."

I sit up enough to sip some cool water, then fall back to the pillow. Why is his bed more comfortable than my *own* bed?

Wait. I'm in Connor's bed.

A whole slew of questions bombard my bruised brain.

What does his house look like?
Did we have sex, and I forgot?
Did he pick me up at the bar?

"Did we—" It's a whispered question. He brushes a piece of hair off my face.

"No." That's not whispered, and it echoes through my skull, making me cringe. "What do you remember, bumble?"

"Quiet," I reply and try to blink my eyes open. There's light from outside, but it's muted by pretty curtains. Beige, I think. The bed is the size of Rhode Island, the linens are soft and luxurious, and I want to burrow down in them.

So I don't. I fling the covers off, and let the cool air drift over me, waking me up more.

"I don't remember much." My voice sounds like sandpaper. "The girls. Drinks. Alex going home with my cousin and his boyfriend."

Connor's fingers drift through my hair, and I close my eyes. That actually feels good.

So I should tell him to stop.

But I don't want to. Why do I love it so much when he touches me?

"How did I get *here*?"

"I went to the bar to have a drink," he says. God, he can just play with my hair like that for the rest of my life, and it won't be long enough. "Saw you there. Some arse-hole spiked your drink."

I frown, but I don't open my eyes again. When he removes his hand from my hair, I want to pull him back, already feeling the loss of his touch.

"I don't remember an asshole. Wait, the asshole after the jukebox? The one I almost punched out?"

"No, this was after the girls left, and you sat at the bar."

I slowly move my head side to side. "I don't recall that part."

"That's not surprising. He pulled you out of the bar and had you up against a truck by the time I got out to you."

I open one eye and squint up at him. "And you saved me?"

"I stopped something bad from happening to you, aye."

I blow out a shaky breath as the magnitude of that situation hits me. Fuck, I was almost *raped*?

The back of my nose starts to tingle as tears fill my

eyes, and then Connor is lying next to me, pulling me against him, and God, it feels so *good*.

"Shh, nothing happened, Billie. I promise."

"I'm so hungover," I mutter against his chest. I want to melt into him. I want to *enjoy* this feeling of safety.

But I can't because it's not real.

"And I'm so fucking pissed off."

"You should be angry." His voice is grim. "Chase Wild will want to talk to you when you feel up to it. And Blake's been calling throughout the day to check on you."

"Blake knows?"

"I had to call a doctor," Connor says. "And he's your brother."

I groan, and roll out of his arms, and cover my face with my hands. "That means my whole family knows."

With a cringe, I sit up and the room spins a bit. I don't feel drunk anymore, but I'm super woozy, and everything hurts.

And I'm so fucking grumpy.

"Can I get you food? You should drink more water."

"I want to go home, Connor."

He's quiet for a heartbeat. His hand is on my back, and I have to take a deep breath so I don't launch myself back in his arms and beg him to simply hold me.

This feels too good.

And I don't trust it.

"I don't love the idea of you being alone, angel."

"I'll be fine." I move to the side of the bed and let my feet dangle, but I don't stand yet.

I'm not convinced I won't fall on my face, and that would be humiliating.

"We can move downstairs," he suggests softly, as if he's hoping I'll stay with him. "Watch a movie and eat something while you get your strength back."

"Connor." I clear my throat, and he doesn't say anything, just listens. "I appreciate your help more than you know. I hate to think—well, I won't even say it out loud. Thank you for everything. I mean that. And I really, *really*"—my voice hitches—"don't want to be a bitch to you because you've been so nice to me, but I'm in a super pissy mood right now, and I don't feel good. I need to go home. Please, take me home. Or have Miller drive me."

He's quiet for a minute, then he lets out a gusty breath. I feel him stand from the bed and hear him pad around to me, where he squats and cups my cheek, making me look him in the face.

"Promise me you'll call one of your brothers or Dani, or Skyla, to come be with you."

I want to tell him to piss off but remind myself that he saved my ass last night.

Maybe my life.

So I take a deep breath.

"I will. Blake will probably want to come check me out."

He searches my eyes for a minute and nods. "Okay. You wear that shirt home. I'll get you some shorts. Don't move."

He kisses my forehead as he stands, then he's gone. When he returns, he's put on jeans and a T-shirt.

Connor's usually in dressier clothes, and every time I see him dressed casually, it makes my loins stand up and applaud.

Even when I feel like I'm half dead.

"Here." He holds the black workout shorts out for me to step into. With my hands braced on his shoulders, I stand, and he works them up over my hips.

I'm standing here in his T-shirt, his shorts, and my thong from last night.

"Where's my dress?"

"I have it," he replies. "I'd like you to drink the rest of this bottle of water before we go."

"I'll take it with me."

He starts to argue as he stands, and I take his hand in mine, holding on tight, silently begging him to understand.

"I *need* to go home." It's a whispered plea. "Please, Connor."

His jaw tightens. "Then I'll take you home, angel."

He honestly needs to stop being nice because I really just want to cry. And that's not helping.

Connor doesn't release my hand as we walk slowly through the house. I get glimpses of wood beams and gleaming floors. Beautiful furniture. A stunning kitchen.

When we get to the front door, he helps me into my shoes from last night and leads me out to his SUV.

"These heels go with the shorts so well," I mutter and glance over to see Connor's half smile.

"My shoes are too big for you," he says. "But I'll get you some if you want them."

"No. I'm just going home anyway."

I lean my head back and close my eyes as he takes off down the driveway. I can tell he's going slow, taking the turns carefully. I want to look in the side mirror to see what his house looks like, but I just don't have the energy.

It doesn't matter.

I'll never be back here again anyway.

I feel him ease onto what I assume is the highway because he picks up speed, and I look around to see where we are. It's not too far from my family's ranch, actually.

I don't know why that surprises me.

But I don't say anything.

"Are you all right, then, beautiful girl?" he asks.

Connor's Irish accent has always done things to me. It makes my stomach clench and my core tingle.

It's sexy as hell.

But add in the compliments, the sweet touches, the light brushes of his lips? I can hardly resist him.

Damn him.

"I will be," I mutter and cover my eyes, blocking out the sunlight. "Once I find all of the pieces of my skull and put them back together again."

Before long, he pulls into my driveway.

"Wait for me." He turns off the engine, then pushes out of the vehicle and hurries around to my side, where he opens the door and helps me to my feet.

"I'm walking you in. You can argue, but it's still happening."

I'm wobbly enough in these stupid heels that I don't protest.

I let him lead me to the door, and I unlock it, and we step inside. It's already late afternoon on Sunday, and I feel my shoulders fall in disappointment.

"What's wrong?" he asks with a concerned scowl.

"I lost my whole day off," I reply as I kick out of the heels and rub my hands over my face. I don't even want to think about what last night's makeup must look like right now. "I have to get ready for work tomorrow already, and I missed family time at the ranch."

"I'm sure the family understands," he says. "What can I do to help?"

Damn him for being so nice to me right now.

"You've helped plenty," I remind him. "And I'm about to turn into a pumpkin. Don't worry, I'll call Blake. You can go."

He shoves his hands in his jeans pockets and frowns at me. Dammit, he looks too good standing in my house. Like he could just help me in the kitchen or sit with me in my library even though said library is tiny, and I don't need to imagine this man hanging out with me at home.

"Connor." It's a whisper, and finally, he nods.

"Let me know if you need anything," he says as he turns away. "I'll come to you anytime, or I'll send whatever you need over. I mean it."

I don't know why, but that makes me scoff. "I don't have your number."

"Yes, you do," he says over his shoulder. "It's in your phone. Get some rest, bumble."

And with that, he leaves me standing here, and I'm a fucking mess.

But this is what I asked him for. I asked him to bring me home and leave me alone, but now I want him here with me.

I'm pissing myself off. Get it together, Billie.

First, I call Blake.

"Tell me how you're feeling," he says in greeting.

"Like hammered shit."

"I'm coming over with a banana bag," he informs me. "Are you home, or are you still at Connor's?"

"I'm at home. And I hate bananas."

"It's an IV, and you're getting it."

"I hate needles more, and you know that."

"Too bad. Three minutes."

He hangs up on me and I toss the phone onto the couch before walking into my closet to change out of Connor's shorts—but I leave the shirt on—and exchange them for light, loose athletic pants. With a detour to quickly wash my face, I have just enough time before there are two knocks on my door, and Blake strides right inside, carrying his old-fashioned doctor bag with him.

"You left me with Connor all night," I inform my brother.

"Reluctantly. He followed my instructions to care for you," he replies with a scowl. "He did take care of you, right? Do I have to kill him?"

"No, he took care of me." I sit on the sofa, too tired

to get into it with him. "But I don't want Connor to be my caregiver."

"Why not?"

"For girl reasons."

My brother, the doctor, pulls out a large IV bag and clips it to the lamp beside the sofa, and starts fiddling with tubes and then pulling out tape and gauze and the dreaded needles.

"Have you had sex with Connor Gallagher?" he asks me. There's no judgment in his tone, and there shouldn't be because Blake has a *lot* of sex of his own.

"A long time ago," I confirm, then watch as my big brother's eyes narrow. "But not last night."

"Jesus, Bee, he's got to be close to fifteen years older than you."

"I didn't know that at the time, not that it matters. I'm not telling you the whole sordid story. I don't ask about all of your many conquests. I don't want to know."

"Give me your arm." I hold it out, palm up, and he presses the pad of his finger against the skin of my inner elbow until he seems happy with the vein he's found, then wraps an elastic band around my bicep.

"Look away," he murmurs, his head bent over my arm in concentration. "You hate this part."

Doing as I'm told, I look to the left and think about adding some bookshelves to the far side of my living room. I feel the prick in my elbow, but then it's gone. Blake pulls the needle out, leaving the tiny catheter in my vein. He secures it with tape and gets the fluids flowing.

"I'm getting you some water. Have you eaten anything?"

"No, I woke up less than an hour ago." I watch him saunter into the kitchen. He fills the large tumbler I use for water and brings it to me. "I have some soup in the fridge."

"I'll heat it. Do you have enough for two?"

"I have enough for six," I reply and sip my water. Using my toes, I scoot my ottoman over to put my feet up and close my eyes, listening to my brother bustle in the kitchen.

"Have you talked to Chase?" Blake asks.

"Not yet. Did they find the guy?"

"He was in the hospital," Blake replies as he pulls the bowls of soup out of the microwave, wraps each one in a towel so they're not too hot to hold, the way our mom used to do, and brings them into the living room. He passes me one before he sits in the chair opposite me. "He'll be there for a few more days yet."

"Wait. Why is he in the hospital?"

Blake scoops a noodle into his mouth. "Connor didn't tell you?"

"Tell me what?"

"He beat the hell out of that guy. Broke his nose, his jaw, his wrist."

My own jaw drops, and I stare at my brother in shock as my chest warms. *Why is that so hot?* I wish I'd seen that. "Seriously?"

"He'll have to have surgery on the jaw. The wrist will

set fine. And as long as you follow through on pressing charges, he'll be charged with sexual assault."

"I'll definitely press charges against that piece of shit."

"Good."

"So Connor beat the hell out of that guy for me?"

Blake grins. "Yep. He told me about it when he called me last night, but I went in to see for myself this morning. That dude is fucked up. Serves him right for drugging and laying his hands on my baby sister."

Connor did that for *me*.

I admit, that doesn't sound like the actions of someone who just wants sex and nothing more. However, he could have been acting out of kindness or obligation. He is an alpha male personality, so perhaps it was his big-brother vibes. Like he'd want someone to do the same for Skyla.

Like if he saw anyone being treated that way, he still would have stepped in.

It doesn't mean that it was explicitly for *me*.

"You're thinking way too hard for someone who feels as shitty as you do."

"How do you know I feel shitty?"

"You look shitty," he replies, grinning when I narrow my eyes at him. "You should start feeling better soon, though."

I already am. Between the food, this IV, and the water I've drunk, I'm starting to feel human again. My head isn't pounding, and the cotton is mostly gone from my mouth.

"I'm sorry you're spending your day off playing doctor to me."

"I don't *play* at being a doctor," he replies. "And you're my best girl. Of course, I came to check on you. I have tomorrow off, too."

"Two days in a row?"

"I know, there was a schedule mix-up. I'm not complaining. It doesn't happen often."

"Any plans?"

"Errands, house stuff. The usual. Check on you."

"I'll be at work."

He frowns over at me. "Jesus, Billie, take a day off. Recuperate."

"I'll be fine." I wave him off and set my empty bowl aside, but he shakes his head.

"As your doctor—"

"You're not my doctor. That's not ethical."

"I want you to stay home. Rest. Lots of fluids and good foods."

"No." He starts to argue, but I hold up a hand. "I'll drink lots of fluids and eat good food, but I'm not staying home."

I won't be able to sleep anyway.

Without replying, he takes our empty bowls to the kitchen and loads them into the dishwasher, then returns to me and sits by me on the couch after checking the bag that's now half empty.

"What are you doing?"

"We're going to cuddle," he says as he wraps his arm

89

around my shoulders and tugs me against him. "It's good for you."

"Cuddling is good for you?"

"Yep."

"What if I don't want to?" *He knows I want to. My big brother knows that touch is my love language.*

"I want to." He kisses the top of my head. "I want you to know that Connor went above and beyond last night, Bee. Aside from kicking that asshole's ass, he helped you when you threw up—"

"Oh God."

"—and watched you all night. He didn't sleep, so he could monitor your breathing and make sure you weren't in distress. It wasn't just a matter of getting you somewhere safe and letting you sleep it off while he did the same."

Now I feel like a jerk for kicking him out of here earlier.

"He could have just dropped me off at the ER."

"He could have," Blake agrees. "But he didn't. And I can tell you that when he first called me, he was scared as fuck."

I turn so I can look up at my brother. "He was?"

"Yeah. And Connor doesn't exactly strike me as the kind of dude who lets much faze him."

No. He doesn't me, either.

"I thought you should know. I don't have a clue what's going on with you two. From what I've seen, you dance around each other. You look at each other like you want to devour each other, but I watch you fight it. Both of you."

"Are you trying to set me up with him?"

"Just telling you what I know and see. I love you."

I sigh and settle against him. "I love you, too. Stop interfering."

"I'm not."

"Not yet."

"Do you like him?"

I sigh again and feel stupid tears threaten, so I swallow hard. "Yeah, but he doesn't—"

"Maybe stop assuming what Connor does or doesn't think and pay attention to what he *does*. Because like you said, he could have just dumped you off at the ER and washed his hands of the whole situation. Instead, he nursed you through the worst of it, and I'm not lying when I tell you he was afraid."

"If he was that scared, why didn't he demand you come over? It's not like any of you to hold back if you think I'm in trouble."

In fact, I need to check my cell. There are probably a gazillion messages. I'm honestly surprised they haven't all landed on my doorstep, including Dani and Skyla.

"I tried. He was ... scared *for you*, but confident he could care for you. He listened to everything I said, and when I checked on you early this morning, it was clear he was doing a good job."

"Huh. I don't want him to be scared because of me."

He kisses my hair again. "Just something to think

about. Now, hand me the remote. We're going to watch TV."

"The bag's almost empty. You can go home."

"Nah. I'm hanging out with my best girl."

"You're annoying as fuck, Blake."

"I know. I love you, too. Oh, and by the way, the rest of the family will be here in about thirty minutes. I can't hold them back anymore."

"Shocker."

Chapter Six

CONNOR

"**W**hy am I in bloody fecking Dublin?" My board of directors shifts uncomfortably in their seats, looking at each other and out the window. Basically everywhere except at me.

Because they know they've fecked up.

Fiona, our real estate lawyer, clears her throat. "We called you in because the new property in Stockholm is exceeding budget forecasts. Environmentalists are upset about water rights, and building the structure close to the lake is causing an issue with ground stabilization."

"It would be best if you could make a trip over there," Ronan, my chief of marketing, bravely adds. "You have the magic touch with people, Connor."

I stare at them both and feel the others in the room shift in their seats again.

"I explained to you all that I'm in Montana for the next two years." I stand and walk to the windows, looking out over the city of Dublin, then turn back to the room. Nine faces stare back at me. These are the people who I work side by side with to keep Gallagher Hotels running. They represent everything from legal, marketing, and hospitality to regional market knowledge and construction. I'm the head of financials, but I have more people for that, too.

We run an empire, and since my father retired three years ago, I'm the head of that empire.

And right now, I'd like to fire all of them for calling me here the day after I dropped my bumble bee off at her house after being drugged by that piece of shite.

"I'm not the only one on this board capable of doing site visits," I add.

"No, but you're the one who *has* done the majority of the site visits for the past decade," Fiona reminds me. "More than that, actually. The people in our hotels know and respect you."

"They'll learn to know and respect the others on this team," I counter. "Because I'm not going to bend on this. The Bitterroot Valley and Big Sky properties are my focus for the next couple of years, with quarterly trips back to Dublin for meetings with all of you. I'm not flying to the Maldives, or London, or bloody Stockholm to smooth over ruffled feathers."

"You're expected at a site visit in Maui next month," Sean, my head of contracting says. "We just bought the property, and you need to approve the plans so we can start construction."

I just stare at the man I've worked with for ten years.

"He's gonna blow," Ronan mutters, looking at Fiona, and she stands to address the rest of the room.

"Please give us a few moments with Mr. Gallagher," she says. "We'll reconvene in thirty minutes."

The rest of the table stands and exits the room, leaving me with Fiona and Ronan.

"What in the bloody hell has gotten into you?" Fiona asks, scowling at me. "You're a grumpy bastard, but you don't usually speak to your board that way."

I pace next to the long table, then walk back to the windows and stare outside.

This isn't the view I want to be looking at.

"What's up with the site visits?" Ronan asks.

He's been my best mate since we were at university together. We played rugby together, and because he's the best in the fucking world at what he does, it was a non-issue to bring him into Gallagher Hotels.

When I came to the head of the board, I brought Ronan with me.

He even married my ex-wife. The woman sitting directly across from him.

"Now he's not speaking to us." Fiona sighs.

"I'm fecking pissed," I reply and turn back to them. "I didn't need to be brought in here for this. It could have been handled with a Zoom call, and you know it."

"Stockholm is an issue," Fiona presses. "They're threatening lawsuits, Connor."

The words *I don't bloody give a shite* almost leave my mouth.

And I've never said something like that when it comes to business. *Never.*

Instead, I take a breath. "It's time to start delegating this out. I won't pull back completely, but I've been traveling the world nonstop for fifteen years, as you said, Fi. I'm fecking tired."

Her pretty blue eyes widen, and she tilts her head, looking at me closely.

"You've met someone, Connor Gallagher."

I shake my head, but Ronan chuckles. "I never thought I'd see the day. Who is she, then? Obviously, she lives in Montana if you want to stay there."

But I study Fiona. We were married for less than five years, and I admit that the relationship ended because of me.

Because I wouldn't sit still.

Because the business was more important.

But she doesn't look hurt.

"Stop it." She reaches out to pat my shoulder. "You'll not hurt my feelings for this. You and I weren't meant to be married, and that's the truth of it. I could have traveled with you, and I chose not to. Besides, I married the love of my life—"

"That's me, mate," Ronan says with a wink.

"—ten years ago, have two gorgeous children, and am perfectly, blissfully happy. So get over yourself and just be bloody honest about what's going on here."

"I *am* being bloody honest," I counter. "For the first time in my life, I don't want to travel so much."

"And you met *her*," Ronan adds, but he's not ribbing me now.

"And I should be there, right now, rather than here for a meeting that could have been an email. I have meetings with the city *and* the county this week. I'm meeting with the architectural firm. I *am* working in Montana, you know, building a brand-new resort from the ground up, spending nearly half a billion dollars. And I want to be hands-on with this one."

I know that the resort in Bitterroot Valley will be special, and I want my hands on every piece of it.

And that has nothing to do with wanting my hands on every inch of a certain bumble bee.

"We've seen the schematics," Fiona reminds me. "It's going to be bloody gorgeous, and I can't wait to see it in person. But I'm personally asking you to go to Stockholm on your way back to Montana to spend *one day* taking meetings and talking to the people there. One day."

"It won't be one fecking day, Fi. It'll turn into a week or more, and we both know it."

She's already shaking her head. "One day. I promise. I'll tell them you have a family emergency or something, and we'll get you out of there. Twelve hours of meetings."

"Twelve hours." My eyebrows lift.

"I said it would be one day. I didn't say it wouldn't be a long one."

"I'll work on finding someone else to do the majority of the site visits," Ronan adds. "Or we split them up among the board. The properties should know all of us, not just you. You've just never had a problem with the travel before."

No, I didn't have a problem with it. I thrived on it. I still enjoy travel and am proud of our properties, but I no longer want it to be my lifestyle.

Of course, the woman I want in Montana won't give me the time of bleeding day, but I'm working on that.

"Tell us about her," Fiona says as if she can read my mind. "We're your best friends, Connor."

"There's not much to tell right now. She doesn't want to have anything to do with me."

They both stare at me for a moment and then, because they're a couple of arseholes, they start to laugh.

Not just a chuckle.

No, face down on the table, laughing until tears drip down their faces.

"I hate you both."

That makes them start again, and I fist my hands and pull out my phone. It's still the middle of the night in Montana, but I miss my angel.

And I left Miller behind to keep an eye on her. If I can't be there to make sure she's safe, the one man I trust most in the world will do it for me.

In fact, a message from Miller waits for me.

Miller: She's safe, sleeping in her bed. She smiled when the flowers were delivered. Didn't work a full day. Looked tired when she went home around two. Hasn't left since. I'll check in on her tomorrow.

I was pissed that she went in to work at all. If she were mine, I would have insisted she stay home to heal.

Her work ethic rivals mine, which is one of the things I'm attracted to in her.

"Are you two quite done?" I lift an eyebrow as they wipe their faces. Fiona pulls a compact out of her handbag to dab at her makeup.

"This is the best day of my life, no offense, my love," Ronan says to his wife.

"None taken, as it might be mine as well," she says with a wide grin aimed at me. "A woman, with a heartbeat and breathing the air around her, has told you no? The irresistible Connor Gallagher?"

"Shut up."

"Obviously, she's brilliant," Ronan adds. "A bloody goddess who knows her mind if she isn't willing to put up with your shite."

"I don't know why I call you my friends."

"Because we love you, and you know it." Fiona walks to the wet bar in the conference room to make herself some tea. "You can be quite charming when you want to be. But if you want it to work for the long term, you're going to have to open up to her."

I scowl at my ex-wife, but she just smiles.

"And that's not something you do," she finishes.

No, it's not something I did with *her*.

Or anyone else.

And the thought of opening up to Billie scares the fecking shite out of me, but I know that she's right because the woman basically said the same thing herself.

"I'm not saying that to bring up old hurts," she adds. "It's simply the truth of it."

"Listen, I didn't come here for advice. I came because someone"—I eye Ronan, who simply smiles at me— "made it sound like the bloody world would end if I didn't get my Irish arse to Dublin straight away. Now I find out you just missed me."

"That's not true." Ronan shakes his head. "Stockholm—"

"Jesus bloody hell," I grumble, rubbing my hand over my face. "Fine, I'll go to Stockholm for *one* day. One, Fiona, or I'll fire your arse."

"You can't." She bats her eyelashes at me. "I promise, I'll do my best to have you out of there in less than twenty-four hours."

"You promised me it *would* be that not half an hour ago." I glare at her, but she doesn't even pretend to look intimidated.

Because she's not.

"I'll do my best."

Three fucking days. Fiona is on my list because what was supposed to be *one* day turned into three, but I think I've managed to avoid a lawsuit, and it seems that feathers have been smoothed out.

I also made it clear that other board members can answer questions and make decisions, and I'm not the only person to call.

Time will tell if that actually happens.

It's Friday, and I'm finally back in Bitterroot Valley. We flew all night so I could be here before the bookshop closed.

Miller's waiting on the tarmac with the SUV.

"To the bookshop," I say as I walk toward the vehicle.

"I assumed that was our destination." He nods, and then we're both in the car, driving away from the airport. "Sir, if you'd like, I can begin the process of hiring a man for her."

I scowl at Miller in the rearview mirror. "What do you mean?"

"If you want a detail protecting Miss Blackwell, I can hire someone to do so, so I'm available for you. *You* are my job."

I narrow my eyes. "Your job is what I tell you it is."

"I'm dropping the formality for a minute because

I've worked for you for eight years." He shakes his head. "And I hate to disagree with you, but *you* are my priority, Connor. Always. The fact that you left me here, where I couldn't protect you, so I could babysit a woman who doesn't need me? That's a waste of resources."

"She'd been fucking *drugged*, Miller."

"Yes, by a stranger. Not a stalker or an ex-boyfriend. Not by someone she knows. It was a random thing that happened in a bar, and while upsetting and absolutely *not fucking okay*, it was a one-off. I've kept tabs on the idiot who did it. He's not even from here. He's from Vegas, for Christ's sake. He's no threat to her. But there is always a threat to *you*."

"I don't want anyone else protecting her," I mutter and rub my hand over my face. "If I'm in town, it's fine."

"You sound ridiculous." I'm *this close* to firing his arse. "One, there's no threat. Two, you don't live with her. It's not like you're with her all the time to save her from the *non* threat."

"I'm getting really bloody tired of this speaking freely shite, Miller."

"I won't stay here again to babysit and stalk your girl-friend or whatever the fuck she is while you travel *without protection* all over the goddamn world. That's not what I was hired to do. So if you want me to hire someone for her, I will. Otherwise, I'm done."

"Are you threatening me?"

"I'm telling you how it is. Your safety is paramount. You put yourself at risk this week, and I don't work that way. Sir."

I grind my molars together. Was I being irresponsible and rash? Maybe, but dammit, she'd just been violated, and I didn't want to leave her. Miller, begrudgingly, is not wrong. Had I known I'd be gone as long as I was, I would have taken him with me and hired someone to watch my girl. However, Miller is the best there is, so I know I need to acknowledge his point here.

Seems I'm smoothing out all kinds of feathers this week.

"We'll hire someone to be on standby. If we have to leave town, I want someone watching her. Not fucking *stalking* her but making sure she's safe."

When Miller pulls up in front of the shop, I climb out of the car and stride inside.

I'm still wearing the suit I wore yesterday, but I took the coat and tie off when I boarded the plane. I'm fucking tired as hell, but I need to get my eyes on my angel and make sure she's okay.

And there she is.

She doesn't see me, so I hold back and take her in. It feels like I'm breathing for the first time in five days.

Her dark hair is down, hanging in loose curls. She's wearing high-waisted camel-colored slacks with a sleeveless green blouse tucked into them. Her makeup is flawless and understated.

She's barefoot. She kicked off her black heels, cast them aside a few feet away from her, and she's stocking shelves.

Billie Blackwell is more beautiful than anything I've ever seen. Just being this close to her makes every nerve in my body sit up and take notice, and my dick has joined the party. I want to cup that gorgeous face and kiss the breath out of her.

She glances up and sees me, pauses, and swallows hard before returning to setting books on the shelf.

"You look amazing," I say as I approach her.

"Better than the last time you saw me," she replies, trying to make a joke.

"It's not funny." Without thinking, I reach out and brush my fingers through her soft hair. "It's pleased I am to see you looking well, bumble."

"I hate that name," she mutters, but I don't reply. She closes her eyes and seems to lean into my touch, but only for a heartbeat before she pulls away again. "What brings you in?"

"You. I just landed a few minutes ago. I've been in Dublin and then Sweden this week."

Her eyebrows climb in surprise. "You're probably exhausted. You should go home and rest."

"Are you worried about me, angel?"

She bites that plump lower lip and shakes her head, fighting a smile. "Just using common sense. Thanks for the flowers earlier this week."

"You're welcome. How do you feel?"

"I'm all recovered. Monday was rough, but I'm fine now. Thanks again for all your help."

"You don't need to thank me. I wanted to stop in to say hello and check on you for a wee minute. And I brought you something."

Her eyebrows pull together in a frown as I pull my hand out of my pocket, but she pulls back as if it might bite her.

"It's just a necklace."

Her wide amber eyes find mine, and she shakes her head. "That's not *just* anything. That's a Van Cleef & Arpels necklace."

"It's a shamrock," I argue, looking down at it. "In malachite. Just a token from Dublin, angel."

Her mouth bobs open, then closes again. Her gaze falls back to the bit of gold and gemstone in my palm.

"Can I put it on you, then?"

"I should *not* accept that." She bites her lip, her cheeks darken, and I've never wanted to simply *hug* someone so badly, while at the same time, I want to boost her up against this bookshelf and fuck her into next week. "But it would be rude to say no to a gift."

"And you don't want to be rude." A smile tugs at my lips as I unclasp the chain, and she lifts her hair, turning so I can fasten it around her neck.

Her fingers brush over it as she turns back to me.

"Just as I suspected," I murmur.

"What?"

"It's gorgeous on you. I'm relieved that you're feeling better, bumble."

"Connor." She frowns but still holds the pendant in her fingers. "Um, thanks. This is really ... unnecessary."

"It's just a trinket, *a stór.*" I turn to walk away, happy with the way this interaction went. I can tell by the look in her eyes that she's starting to soften. "I'll see you on Sunday."

"Sunday? What's happening on Sunday?"

"Family dinner." I wink at her over my shoulder and walk out of the store. I need some bloody sleep.

Chapter Seven

BILLIE

I've never been nervous about spending the day at my family's property before. At the place where I grew up. My home. My safe place, where no matter what, I'm welcome and loved.

Until today.

Even before, on days when I knew Connor would be here, I wasn't exactly nervous. Annoyed and maybe slightly uncomfortable but never nervous because this is my turf.

But today, my nerves are all over the place after everything that happened last weekend, then he showed up at my shop on Friday with this ridiculously expensive *trinket*. I thought he was still messing with me. All week, I couldn't figure him out. He looked so torn when he left me at my house on Sunday, and he sent flowers on Monday. And then *nothing* for the rest of the week.

Until Friday, when he turned up in person and gifted me with a little *trinket* from Ireland. Because apparently, he'd been thinking of me while he traveled. And I'd be lying if I said that didn't make me feel good.

But a text would have sufficed. I don't need expensive gifts.

I just want to talk to him.

I shake my head and pull my sunglasses off as I park in front of the family farmhouse. I'm here fairly early in the afternoon, but to my surprise, Bridger, Dani, and Birdie are already here.

This makes me happy because I'd like to talk to my girls before Connor arrives.

And I don't have to go far to find them.

On the deep porch that wraps around the entire house, Dani and Skyla are curled up in what looks like new furniture, with a pitcher of something on ice and several glasses on a table next to them.

"You're here," Dani says with a bright smile. "And just in time. We made strawberry lemonade."

"With no liquor, right?" Just the thought of drinking alcohol makes me sick to my stomach.

"No liquor," Skyla confirms, and her eyes sober. "I'm so sorry, Bee."

"Stop." I wave her off and admire the furniture. It looks ... *cozy.* Like you'd want to curl up and take a nap out here. "You guys already came and checked on me every day last week. You have nothing to be sorry for. I'm an adult, and we didn't know a creep was at the bar that night. Now, tell me about this fabulous new furniture."

I sit and draw my legs up under me, getting comfy as Dani pours me a cold drink.

Summer has its claws into Montana, and it's *hot*. But here, in the shade of the porch, with a light breeze blowing through, is lovely.

"I want to nap out here," Skyla says, passing me a glass. "The second I first saw this porch, I knew it would be perfect for naps in the summertime, and this couch will be ideal for that."

"I might join you," I reply with a wink. "We can both fit."

"You're welcome anytime." She grins.

Skyla's been with my brother for several months and lives here on the farm with him. She has the prettiest red hair I've ever seen, with green eyes just like her brother's, and she looks amazing today in a simple blue sundress.

Dani's in black capri pants and a white T-shirt that shows off her curves, her dark hair up in a bun, and she's watching me with those shrewd blue eyes.

Dani and I have sat on this porch together most of our lives. When we were kids, it was usually because she was running away from her abusive father, and we'd sit here, eating ice cream together.

I love that she's married to Bridger. There was always magic between them and knowing they finally made their way to each other makes me so happy.

And the fact that my two best friends are with my brothers means I get to see them all the time, which is the best bonus ever.

"You're quiet." Dani interrupts my thoughts.

"I need advice," I admit with a sigh, just as Skyla's gaze falls to the necklace I'm wearing.

"Well, that's lovely," she says with a knowing smile. "Where did you get that new necklace, Bee?"

I bite my lip as Dani looks back and forth between us. "What am I missing?" she asks.

"That's a *very* nice Van Cleef & Arpels piece," Skyla explains.

"I still don't know what that means." Dani shrugs.

"It's a luxury jewelry brand." I swallow hard. "It was a gift."

Skyla's already grinning.

"From who?" Dani wants to know, tipping up her eyebrow.

"Connor." I frown down into my glass. "He came to the bookstore on Friday and said he got me this *trinket* in Ireland."

"Wow," Dani breathes.

"It's so beautiful," Skyla says at the same time.

"This isn't a *trinket*." I set my glass down in frustration. "It's a several thousand-dollar piece of jewelry, you guys. It's not a keychain, or a postcard, or whatever you buy at cheap tourist shops."

"My brother is *never* going to buy something from a cheap tourist shop." Skyla shakes her head. "And to him, that is an inexpensive gift."

My mouth opens, and I scowl and lay my head back against the new outdoor sofa.

"That's insane."

"No." Dani reaches over to take my hand and give it a squeeze. "He's rich, Bee. It's not insane because the money is insignificant."

"Exactly," Skyla agrees. "I know it's not easy to get used to."

"No, you don't." I laugh with the comment, and the others laugh as well because it's true. Skyla would have no idea what that's like. She was born into massive wealth.

"That's fair," she says. "I don't know. But I can empathize and understand that it would be overwhelming."

"I don't want gifts from him," I admit, chewing on my bottom lip.

"Are you sleeping with him again?" Dani asks, and I shake my head.

"No, there's been no sex and no kissing. Like I told you guys on Monday, he was amazing after the *incident* but never crossed a line. He was ... great, actually."

We're quiet for a moment as another breeze blows through, and we enjoy the quiet around us. I can hear cows mooing in the distance. Riley, Skyla's big dog, is curled up on a bed of his own nearby, snoring away. Suddenly, it occurs to me that the men and Birdie are nowhere to be seen.

"Where are the others? Bridger, Birdie, and Beckett?"

"Out at the horse barn," Dani replies. "Riding for a few hours. Blake's out there with them, too. Brooks should be here soon."

I nod, tucking a stray piece of hair that fell out of my topknot behind my ear.

"I can sleep when I'm with him," I finally admit, looking their way.

Dani's eyebrow climbs.

Skyla frowns.

"I thought you said you're *not* having sex," Skyla says.

"We're not, but when I'm with him, I can *sleep*. And I've been an insomniac since I was a teenager. I don't sleep well. But with Connor, it's like my body just lets go, and I sleep like the dead, and it's *so good*. I don't need expensive necklaces. I just want a nap date."

Dani snorts. "A nap date?"

"Yes. I want him to invite me over and let me curl up around him and sleep. You have no idea how good that sounds, you guys."

"With no ... *sex*?" Skyla asks.

"Okay, fine. Yes, I'm so fucking attracted to him that I can hardly breathe when he's nearby. All he has to do is touch me. No, strike that. All he has to do is look at me with those amazing green eyes, and my body is on fire for him. I want the sexy time, but I don't *just* want that."

"And you've told him that?" Dani asks.

"Yeah. I told him that I want more than to be used for sex. And then I didn't hear from him for a while, so that's my answer."

"Wait." Skyla holds up a hand and pulls her eyebrows together. "It's not that simple, Bee. You need to understand that Connor doesn't open up to people. He's quite guarded, and that's the truth of it. I'm not going to betray any of his confidences even though I want to because I love you and think you're good for each other. Just know that what you've asked of him isn't easy."

I tilt my head, watching her, but before I can reply, I

hear voices coming from the direction of the barn, so we table this discussion for now.

Have I even considered that? That it could be difficult for Connor to open up to me? My brothers are not all exactly talkative, but I don't think they've had trouble talking about life. Was I only thinking of my own feelings and needs? *That would be a big, fat yes, Bee.* I didn't consider him at all.

And when I think back to how he cared for me last weekend, how worried he looked, and then what Blake said later that night, I can see that Connor cares.

I finger the green shamrock at my throat and sigh just as Birdie hurries up the porch steps and launches herself into my lap.

My six-year-old niece is the apple of my eye, and I love her more than just about anything.

"Hello, baby bird," I say as I kiss her head.

"I'm happy to see you," she replies and lays her cheek against mine. She's done that since she was a tiny baby, and it squeezes my heart.

"I'm happy to see you, too. Did you go for a ride on one of the horses?"

A car door slams, then the rumble of a motorcycle engine comes to a stop, but I don't look up. I'm enjoying these cuddles from my sweet girl and soaking her in.

"Yeah, we took a ride. Next time, you should come, too."

I hate just about everything about farm life, except for the horses. I love being near and on the big animals.

"Next time," I agree softly and hug her closer. I

didn't realize until just this minute how much I needed to be snuggled.

It doesn't happen very often.

"Are you okay?" Birdie whispers in my ear, making me smile.

"I'm so much better now that you're cuddling me," I reply with a whisper of my own. My girl sighs happily and settles in against me, so I kiss her some more.

"How are you feeling?"

I open my eyes and look up to find all four of my brothers—that was Brooks's motorcycle that pulled in—watching me with concerned eyes.

"I'm great," I reply, offering them all a smile. "Really. All is well."

"Yeah, that's why you're clinging to my daughter like she's a lifeline," Bridger says, and I notice movement out of the corner of my eye when Connor sits next to Skyla.

That must have been the car door I heard.

"I just needed some snuggles, okay? I don't get them often, and no one snuggles like this girl." I kiss her cheek, and she smiles at me.

"Did you get hurt?" She presses her hand against my cheek as her face falls into a worried scowl.

"No, baby. Your daddy and uncles are just super nosy." I brush my nose over hers, making her giggle. "You don't need to worry about a thing. Ever. Now, what are you making us for dinner?"

"It's taco night," she exclaims. "And I'm grating the cheese."

"Yum."

"Come on," Dani says, standing and holding her hand out for Birdie's. "Let's go get dinner started."

Birdie gives me one more squeeze, then she climbs off my lap and follows Dani, Bridger and Blake inside. Beckett winks at me before taking Skyla's hand and following the others.

"I haven't seen you yet," Brooks says. He pulls me up and into his arms, squeezing me *hard*.

I feel Connor's gaze on me, but I don't look his way because this hug is making me emotional.

Brooks is the oldest of us, and I'm the baby. And although all of my brothers have always been my protectors, Brooks takes that role the most seriously.

"I'm sorry." His voice is gruff. He smells a bit like motor oil, thanks to his auto repair shop, and fresh air, thanks to riding on his bike.

"Stop." I shake my head and pat him on the chest. "Seriously, I feel fine. Maybe a little hungry, but there are tacos inside, and I'm always hungry whenever anyone mentions Mexican food. As evidenced by my hips."

I think I hear Connor growl behind me, and Brooks pulls back.

"Don't you *ever* put yourself in that kind of a position again, little girl." He's glaring at me, but I know it's a front.

He was scared. Brooks is rarely scared, but when he turned up last Sunday, I saw true fear in his eyes. It took Blake and me about thirty minutes to reassure him that I was okay.

"Right." I roll my eyes. "Because it was *my* fault. But

don't worry, I'm never drinking alcohol again. Just the thought of it makes me want to toss cookies."

Brooks shifts his gaze to Connor. "Thanks again."

"Nothing to thank me for," the man replies, speaking for the first time since he arrived.

"We both know that's not true," Brooks replies before turning and walking inside, leaving me alone on the porch with a certain sexy Irishman.

"Well, that went better than I thought it would. They all hover. It's the side effect of being the youngest out of a bunch of boys." I lower my butt to the chair across from Connor and rub my hands up and down my thighs. His gaze moves down my body, over my pink tank top, my simple denim wide-leg capris, to my sandal-covered feet. And when those green orbs return to my face, there's heat in them.

Christ, he's beautiful. He's in jeans himself and a plain black T-shirt that shows off the defined muscles of his biceps, which always sends my lady bits into overdrive. Every time he's dressed casually, it's a punch to the gut.

His dark hair is tousled, his chiseled jaw covered in a light stubble, and I wonder if he slept well last night.

I know I didn't.

"How are you?" I ask him, and by the way he presses his lips together, the question seems to take him by surprise. I want to reach out and take his hand, so I fist my own and keep it in my lap. His eyes fall to watch the movement, and his jaw firms. "Doesn't anyone ever ask how you are?"

"Not often." He pushes his fingers through his hair and nudges his glasses up his nose. "I'm well, thank you for asking."

So he gets formal when he's taken off guard.

I feel like so many things are falling into place, and I'm seeing him through a different lens.

"I guess my whole family must have reached out to thank you for what you did."

He narrows his eyes. "Aye."

"Even my parents?"

He doesn't look away from me. "Aye."

With a nod, I reach up to finger the pendant at my throat and bite my lip. "Are you hungry?"

He stands and offers me his hand. Without hesitation, I take it, soaking in the warmth from his touch, and let him pull me to my feet.

And when we're just inches apart, he tips my chin up so he can look me in the eyes.

"Tomorrow," he murmurs. "I'd like to spend the day with you."

I almost agree, and then I blink. "I can't." I see his face close off and hurry to explain. "I would like that, but I really can't. I only have two employees, and I want two people in the store at all times. Tiffany is having a medical procedure done and can't work tomorrow, so I have to go in."

He seems to visibly relax with that explanation.

"What day would work for you, angel?" he asks.

"I can take Friday." It feels so far away, but I want

Tiffany to have enough time to recover. "She'll be back at work on Friday."

Connor nods and leans in to press a kiss to my forehead. "Friday it is, then. Let's go inside."

"Connor—"

He cuts me off and kisses my forehead once more. "Friday."

It's Tuesday night, and I'm so fucking tired.

God, I wish I could just sleep through the night like a normal person. But I can't. I've done all the meditations, the affirmations, the mental exercises. I've tried medications, but they make me too drowsy the next day.

Melatonin gives me nightmares.

Magnesium helps, but then I took too much of it and couldn't get out of the bathroom.

Nothing works.

I'm finally home from work, and it's late in the evening. Later than usual for me, but my second employee, Emily, had a family emergency, leaving me alone at the shop for the afternoon. I had too much to do after I locked up to simply walk away and come home.

Hopefully, Emily will be able to work tomorrow.

I've just kicked off my shoes, like I do every night as soon as I walk through the door, when my phone pings with an incoming text.

Expecting it to be Skyla or Dani, I wait to check it until after I've changed into comfortable clothes and washed my face.

But when I look at the screen, I'm surprised to see that it's Connor.

> Connor: How was work today?

I frown, then look over my shoulder as if someone's there to laugh. As if this might be a joke.

Connor Gallagher is *texting me*, asking about my day?

This is new.

Chewing on my lip, I type out a response.

> Busy, which is good, but I was left alone for the afternoon, so I just got home. Long day. No complaints, though, because I killed it in sales. How was your day?

I pad into the kitchen and stare at my empty fridge. I didn't make time for the grocery store, let alone any kind of meal prep this week. I'm considering calling Old Town Pizza when my phone pings with a response.

> Connor: Meetings all day. About to go into another one but wanted to check on you. What's for dinner?

With a chuckle, I send him a photo of my empty fridge, then type my response.

> Pizza, I think. I should really get to the store sometime this week. What are you having? Something fancy in your fancy meeting?

The bubbles dance on the screen as I pour fresh water into my tumbler.

> Connor: I'm having a steak. If you were here, I'd share it with you.

Holy shit, who is this man, and what has he done with broody Connor? He's flirting with me.

> Maybe I'd make you buy me my own steak. I'm pretty hungry.

His response is immediate.

> Connor: You can have whatever you want, bumble.

I still hate that nickname, but my lips twitch.

> Have a good meeting.

> Connor: Good night.

I place my pizza order and take a shower while waiting for it. The timing is perfect because the doorbell rings just after I've combed out my wet hair and slathered on my moisturizer.

But when I open the door, it's not the pizza delivery kid.

It's Miller.

"Miss," he says with a nod. "I have some things for you. Do I have your permission to bring the bags into the kitchen?"

"Uh, sure." With a scowl, I step back from the door, then watch, stunned, as Miller proceeds to bring in three trips of groceries, *many* bags in each of his hands with each trip.

"Would you like me to put these away?"

I blink at him. "Why did you bring me groceries?"

"Boss's orders." He offers me a half smile. "Would you like me to put them away, or would you rather do it yourself?"

"I'll do it. Um, thanks. Do I tip you?"

"No." Miller actually laughs now and walks to the door. "Have a good night, miss."

Before he can shut the door behind him, the pizza delivery kid arrives, smiling at me.

"Hey, Billie, here's your order."

"Thanks, Curt." I smile and pass him his tip money. "Take care."

"You, too," Curt says before pocketing the cash and whistling his way down to his car.

I notice Miller watches, not leaving until after Curt pulls away, and I send him a wave before I close the door, pizza box in hand, and stare at the bags on my kitchen counter.

Between bites of pepperoni with extra cheese, I systematically go through all the bags, setting everything on the countertops so I can take it all in.

"I won't eat this much in a month," I mutter as I

survey all of the vegetables, fruits, and meats. Pretty much everything and anything I could possibly need to make anything my heart desires, including my favorite coffee creamer.

How did he manage that?

I finish the crust on my pizza and send Connor a message.

> The grocery fairy just visited my house disguised as Miller! I wonder how that happened?

Within seconds, his response comes in.

> Connor: I have no idea.

My lips spread into a wide smile as I type my response.

> Thank you. You didn't have to do that. I just ate half a pizza.

I start sorting and putting all of the groceries away. It's a good thing my fridge was pretty much empty, to begin with. Otherwise, this wouldn't all fit. Just as I put away the last of it, my phone pings.

> Connor: I don't know what you're talking about.

I roll my eyes, but I'm still smiling.

> Have a good meeting.

Chapter Eight

CONNOR

I've been waiting all week for this. I cleared my schedule, much to the dismay of the people I was supposed to meet with today, but I don't give a bleedin' fuck.

This is the day my angel can give me, so it's hers.

Everyone else can kiss my arse.

"You're sure you won't let me drive you?" Miller asks as I set the cooler in the back of the Jeep Wrangler I bought for this occasion.

"No." I shake my head at him. "You're a bloody mother hen, mate."

"I'm your fucking *bodyguard*," he replies, then clears his throat. "Sir."

"I'm taking her for a drive, not into downtown London," I remind him. "There's a tracker on this Jeep that *you* added yesterday. You'll know where we are all day."

He still doesn't look happy.

"I'm getting her to myself, and I'll not fuck that up. I don't want anyone listening in today, even you."

Miller steps back and nods before he walks toward the guesthouse.

Everything about today has me outside of my comfort zone. Everything except my angel.

I get her all to myself.

Here's to hoping I don't fuck it up in the first hour.

Blowing out a breath, I start the Jeep. We took off the doors, but I wanted to keep the soft roof on so Billie doesn't get too sunburned.

I texted her this morning and told her to wear something comfortable.

I can't wait to get to her.

It's another beautiful, sunny morning as I drive into town. I understand why they call Montana Big Sky country because on a clear day like today, the sky is so blue, so damn *big*, it takes the breath away.

And I'm going to enjoy it with my angel today.

I park in front of her house and have just gotten out to walk up to the door when it opens and my tongue sticks to the roof of my mouth.

Jesus fucking Christ.

Her hair is up in a high ponytail. She's in the same loose dress she wore in Big Sky several weeks ago, with her strappy sandals and sunglasses. She has a small handbag slung across her body, and when she looks up at me, she smiles, making my heart stutter.

She's also wearing the necklace I gave her, making me want to puff my chest out.

"Hi," she says and glances at the Jeep. "Is that new?"

"Aye." I swallow and walk toward her as she pushes her sunglasses up onto her head. "I thought it would be fun for today."

"You still haven't told me where we're going."

"No." I can't resist leaning in to press my lips to the top of her head, breathing in her lavender scent. "I haven't."

Her eyes drag down my torso, down my legs, and I smirk when they find mine again.

"I like it when you're dressed like this," she admits.

"Like what, bumble?"

"Casual."

"Why is that?"

She bites that lip, and I don't think she's going to answer, but finally, she says, "Because your arms are fucking *delicious* in a T-shirt. There. I said it."

I laugh as I pull her against me for a hug, wrapping the arms she seems to like around her and squeezing her close as I plant my lips on the top of her head, enjoying how she fits against me.

"Come on, then," I say as I lead her to the Jeep. "Let's go."

I get her buckled in, the cage door closed, and then I circle the car and hop in behind the wheel.

"It's a long drive," I inform her. "Are you comfortable?"

She frowns over at me. "How long?"

"All day."

Now her eyebrows climb. "Where are we going? Canada?"

I grin and don't stop myself from reaching out to drag the back of my fingers down her cheek.

I'm letting go today.

I'm indulging in my need for her.

And based on the way she leans into my touch, she's here for it.

"No, not Canada. Just a long drive. I want to be with you today. Just you. No noise, no other people, just you on this pretty day."

She tips her head, examining me, then nods. "That sounds really nice. And I promise not to fall asleep."

With a laugh, I start the engine and pull out of her driveway.

"You won't offend me if you fall asleep."

"I'll offend *me*. I don't want to miss this. Besides, it's a nice day, and there will be lots to see."

"My thoughts exactly."

Once I'm on the highway leading us out of town, I rest my elbow on the center console and open my hand, waiting.

Without hesitating, Billie leans in, threads her fingers through mine, and holds on.

And we stay like this as we drive a couple of hours out of town. She points out a herd of elk. The wind whips around us, and it's too loud to have a conversation, but that's okay.

The quiet between us is comfortable, and she's smiling each time I glance her way.

Thank Christ, this was a good idea.

It's close to noon when I turn off the highway near Flathead Lake and drive us close to the shoreline, with a view of the mountains beyond. I park facing the water and cut the engine. We sit in silence for a moment, taking in the breathtaking view of the lake and the mountains.

"I haven't been here since I was a kid," she says softly and takes a deep breath. The roof on the Jeep gives us valuable shade, but there's a nice breeze blowing through to keep us cool. "My parents brought us here a couple of times to go camping, which I thought was so silly."

"Why silly?"

She reaches for my hand, and I feel everything in me go still.

I'm always the one to reach for her. She never initiates physical contact with me, so seeing her hand reach out for mine has my heart hammering.

"For a couple of reasons," she continues as if she didn't just turn my life upside down. "First of all, we literally live in the woods. We could walk twenty feet and go camping."

"Do you enjoy camping?"

She wrinkles her nose. "And that's number two. I *hate* camping. Spend the day outside, doing whatever? Fine. I can do that. But I do not ever want to sleep outside."

"I don't either."

She looks my way, her eyebrows lifted. "Really?"

"Aye, I have a perfectly good bed to sleep in at night."

"Exactly." She nods once. "Also, I know this makes me sound, I don't know, weak maybe—"

"You're not weak."

"But I don't like getting dirty. I didn't enjoy living on a farm. It's sweaty, dirty work, and I don't like it. My brother can have it."

"That's not weak," I reply, rubbing my thumb in a circle against her soft skin. "I don't particularly enjoy dirty work, either. I work my arse off, but I don't get filthy while doing it."

"Same." She sighs and leans her head back on the seat. "Oh, I forgot my water bottle at home."

"Here." I let go of her hand and open one of the coolers in the back, pulling out a bottle of water for her, and she wrinkles that nose again. "What is it?"

"Nothing, thank you."

"No." I pull the bottle out of her reach. "You made your disgusted face."

"I don't have a disgusted face."

"Aye, you do, bumble. And you made it. Tell me why."

"I just don't love that particular brand of water, that's all. But I'll drink it because I'm thirsty."

"It's just water."

Her eyes go wide as I crack the top for her and pass it over.

"No. That's where you're wrong. All of the different brands of water taste different. Haven't you noticed that?"

"I can't say that I have, no."

"Well, I have."

"And this one isn't to your liking?"

"Not particularly." She drinks down several gulps and secures the lid once more. "But that's better. My throat was dry. Want some?"

She offers me the bottle, and with my eyes on hers, I take it, unscrew the lid, and place my lips where hers just were, tipping it back to drink.

It tastes fine to me.

"Shall we stretch our legs? There's a path over there."

"Sure." She pushes her sunglasses back on and waits for me to round the hood to help her down.

My heart is hammering. It always is when she's close, but I'm about to do something I haven't done in ... well, ever.

"I'm surprised there aren't a ton of tourists here," Billie says as she slips her hand in mine—as if it's the most natural thing to do, and she does it every damn day —and walks beside me on the trail.

I don't bother to tell her that I called the state park bureau and had this area cleared for us today.

Finally, we settle into a comfortable silence, enjoying the cool air when we walk into the shade of tall evergreens, and with a magnificent view of the lake, I gesture to a fallen log.

"Let's sit," I suggest. She nods, then brushes off the bark as if she can get rid of every speck of dirt, and then sits.

I can't help my smile as I sit next to her.

I'm not touching her now, simply sitting a couple of inches away.

And I start to fucking talk. Because this is what she needs from me, and I need *her*. More than anything else, I need this woman in my life, so I'll give her anything she needs to make that happen. Even if I have to open my mouth and be honest with her.

So here I am, taking my chance. I've never felt the need to shift gears in my life. Work and family have been my priority for as long as I can remember. But I see Fiona and Ronan together, and I know they're so damn happy because they're partners. Equals in everything. Fiona is the air Ronan breathes, and he is to her, and *I want that*. I want that connection. I don't want the endless ... aloneness that comes with, well, being alone.

More than anything else, I need this woman in my life.

"Growing up a Gallagher was a privilege and a curse," I begin, watching as a bald eagle swoops and plucks a fish out of the lake before flying off with his lunch. "Although I never wanted for anything, I also learned at quite a young age that I couldn't truly trust anyone. Well, that's not entirely true. I trust my family and Ronan, my best friend. I met him at university."

"Are you still in touch?" Billie asks me quietly, hardly moving, as if she's afraid I'll stop telling her my tale.

"Aye. He's on the board of directors of Gallagher Hotels, and he's married to my ex-wife."

I look over in time to see her gaze whip to mine, her eyes wide.

But she swallows and looks back out at the lake without asking me any questions.

"We're all friends, the three of us. And I trust them. But as a whole, I learned young that when someone figured out my name, and if they connected the dots to my father, they wanted something from me."

Billie pushes her hand through my arm and laces her fingers with mine, leaning her head on my shoulder, and it's the connection to her that I need to keep talking.

"I don't open up to people easily. I'm not good at talking about my feelings, or asking for help, or conversation at all, really, unless it has to do with work. I can talk to a room of investors all day long. That's only one of the reasons that my marriage to Fiona didn't work. She wanted more, and I wouldn't give it to her."

I lean over and kiss my angel's hair, breathing her in, enjoying the way her soft hair feels against my lips.

"Notice I said *wouldn't*. Not *couldn't*."

"I heard you," she murmurs before kissing my bicep and then turning her gaze out once more.

"When I do find someone to trust, it's forever, and I'm fucking loyal, Billie."

She nods. "We have that in common. So is that why no names that first night?"

"Aye. It made things less complicated, and I was so bloody attracted to you, I had to have you. I didn't know—"

"I know." She doesn't let go of my hand, but she sits up and turns on the log so she's facing me now rather than the lake. I turn to look her in the eyes. "Why are you telling me all of this now?"

"Because I still want you," I reply instantly, not even having to think about it. "And I was fucking that up without realizing it. Falling into old habits. It's not simply about sex with you, although, I can't lie to you, angel. I want you more than I want my next breath."

Especially when you give me that stunning smile like you are right now.

"But you need more from me, and it surprised me to realize that I want to *give* you more. I simply don't know how to go about it."

"Sure you do." She tips her head to the side. "You're doing it right now. You've been doing it all week."

When I frown, she continues.

"Spoiler alert, Connor, but we're having a conversation right now, and I'm learning more about you. You texted me every day this week. You've been flirty and funny. You stocked my fridge, which I admit threw me for a loop, but in a fun way. And I love this necklace." She rubs her fingers over the malachite. "I love that you thought of me while you were traveling, but I don't need expensive gifts."

"It wasn't expensive."

"Yes, to normal people, it was expensive. I love it, but I don't *need* it. Honestly, this is what I like the best."

"What's that?"

"This date. A simple drive, a nice conversation, flirty touches. You're dressed all sexy, and I can't wait to get you naked again."

And just like that, my dick is engaged, and I pull her onto my lap, making her chuckle as she presses her hands to my chest.

"That can be arranged at literally any given moment, bumble."

She laughs and kisses my cheek, then she gets serious again as she cups my face in her sweet hands.

"Thank you for telling me this. I want to know so much more, but it's a good start."

"I have to be honest with you because this isn't a game for me. I'm not now, nor was I ever trying to *use* you. Never, angel. I simply can't stay away from you and want to touch you all the time. I'm not good at the rest of it, but I'm willing to try. If it means I get you in my life, I'll do my best."

"Thank you," she whispers and tips her forehead against my own.

"There is one more elephant in the room to discuss."

"The fact that I don't want other women to see your arms?" she asks, making me smile.

Fuck me, I smile so easily when I'm with her.

"No, my age."

She frowns at me. "Why?"

"You're twenty-seven."

"Almost twenty-eight. A few weeks away from that, actually."

"I'm nearly forty, Billie."

She nods, watching me as if she's waiting for me to spell it out for her. Finally, she rolls her pretty eyes at me, and I narrow mine.

"Roll your eyes at me again, and I'll take you over my knee."

"You're not old enough to be my father, although you sound like one right now."

"Technically—"

She frames my face in her hands. "I don't care, Connor."

"Others might care."

"Do I look like a woman who gives two fucks about what others think? Look at me. I'm plus-sized, and I eat whatever I want, wherever I want."

My hand grips her arse, and I scowl at her. "Your body is fucking perfect, angel, and I don't ever want to hear you say otherwise."

"I know. But *other people* don't think so, and I don't care. I live my life on my terms, and as long as I'm not hurting anyone else, it's my own business. No one else's."

"I'm not trying to talk you out of seeing more of me," I remind us both. "I'm simply making sure you're okay."

"I'm way better than I was," she admits.

I grip her chin in my fingers. "If that ever changes, you tell me."

"You'll be the first to know."

Unable to hold back any longer, I cover her lips with mine, and she opens up to me so sweetly, wraps those arms around my neck, and holds on as I devour her.

God, I've missed her. Her pillowy lips on mine, the way her voice rasps when she moans, and the way her body lights up under my touch.

I've missed everything.

"Why did we have to drive so far away to have this conversation?" she asks against my lips. "We need a bed, Connor."

I chuckle and tighten my hold on her, bury my hand in the back of her hair and keep her mouth on mine, still not getting enough of her.

And when we finally pull apart to catch our breath, I drag my thumb over that bottom lip, still wet from my kiss.

"We're not having sex today," I inform her. Her gasp, followed by the narrowing of her eyes, makes me chuckle. I've received thousands of accolades in just as many boardrooms, and yet, her two responses do something for my soul that nothing else has ever done.

She gives me hope that I might be able to do this. Try for more.

Billie wiggles her arse over my hard cock, making me swallow and curse under my breath.

"I beg to differ," she whispers.

"I drove this far on purpose. We're doing all the things you said you love. Talk, flirt, touch. I brought lunch for us to share. And then I'm taking you home."

"And no sex," she repeats, her lips pouty.

So I bite them because I can't fucking resist her.

"No sex," I confirm. "Come on, let's have lunch."

I guide her to her feet and lead her to the Jeep, where I pull out the folding chairs I brought along, and unfold them, gesturing for her to sit.

"Is this the cheapest date you've ever been on?" she

asks as she leans back in the chair, stretching her legs out before her.

"I don't think so." I pull out the sandwiches from the cooler and unwrap them, set them on a tray, then open the charcuterie my cook made for us, setting it out as well.

Billie hums in approval, and I feel it in my cock. Christ, I'd love for her to make that sound while she's choking on my dick.

"Really?" She frowns and snags a square of cheese. "You've been on cheaper dates than this one?"

"I mean, I bought the Jeep."

She holds up a hand, choking on the cheese. "Wait. You bought the Jeep *for this date*?"

"Of course."

She's shaking her head, looking at me like I just grew a watermelon out of my chest.

"What? It seemed appropriate for today."

"You bought a whole car *for one date.*"

"We'll use it again." I unwrap my sandwich and take a bite. "Eat your lunch, bumble."

Chapter Nine

BILLIE

I have *so many* questions. First of all, Connor was married. *Freaking married.* I want to know all about that. How long were they married? When? How long have they been divorced? He says they're still friends, so was the divorce amicable? She's on the board of directors, so does that mean that he sees her often? None of it is my business, but I really want to know.

We're headed toward Bitterroot Valley, and I turn to watch his profile as he drives. His jaw is tight. His left hand grips the wheel, but his right holds my hand, not too tight. It's as if he's holding stress all over his body, but he's making a conscious effort to be gentle with me.

His gaze drifts over to me, and those amazing eyes, so fucking green it almost makes me ache, smile at me. His lips inch up on the side, and he raises an eyebrow, as if to ask, *are you okay?*

And I smile and nod at him. He gives my hand a squeeze and turns his attention back to the highway.

About twenty minutes later, he pulls into a gas station and stops next to the pump, turns off the engine.

"You pump your own gas?" I ask him, surprised.

"Not often," he admits with a laugh. "But I do know how. Do you need anything from inside?"

"I'm going to quickly use the restroom," I reply, unbuckling my belt. I hurry inside and find the public restroom, cringe at the state of it, then hover over the toilet, relieving myself.

When I get back outside, Connor has pulled the Jeep into a parking spot, making room for someone else to pump gas, and before I can climb in, he walks straight for me, frames my face, and kisses the hell out of me, right here in the parking lot.

Gripping his wrists, I lean in, pressing my breasts against him, soaking this man in. I feel like a selfish idiot. I wasted so much time. I should have just had a conversation with him months ago, but I didn't know.

I can't read minds, for fuck's sake.

And, I can admit, neither can he.

Finally, he pulls away and rests his forehead against my own.

"I've been thinking about that since we got back on the road," he confesses. "It should hold me over until we get into town."

I smirk and tap my hand against his chest. "There are places to pull over in case you change your mind."

With a wink, I climb into the Jeep and secure my seat belt as Connor walks into the gas station. Holy hell, the man's ass in those jeans could end wars. When does he have time to do all of this working out? Between his arms and his abs and that ass, he has to spend time in the gym, but I know he's as much of a workaholic as I am, and I don't have time to go to the gym.

Okay, I could *make* time. I'm awake all night, but no one wants to work out when they can't sleep. Besides, I haul boxes of books all day, so I do lift weights.

A few minutes later, he walks out of the gas station, and I feel my jaw drop because cradled in his arms have to be at least ten brands of bottled water.

"What did you do?" I ask with a laugh as he swaggers over to me, a half smile on his delicious lips.

"I bought every brand they have," he says, standing next to me. "So you can choose the one you like the best."

I blink at the bottles, then up at him, and feel my heart soften even more. "This one is my favorite." I point at the one by his elbow and pluck it from his arm. He sets the rest of the bottles in the cooler in the back seat.

I open the water and take a drink, and as I'm sliding it into the cup holder, Connor sits next to me. Just like every other time he's sat next to me, I feel calm. Happy. *He's so thoughtful. Intentional.*

Then Blake's words come to my mind.

"He didn't sleep so he could monitor your breathing and make sure that you weren't in distress. Maybe stop assuming what Connor does or doesn't think and pay attention to what he does."

"Thank you, Connor."

"For what? Water?"

"No, and yes. For being so thoughtful and looking for water I would drink."

He shrugs. "No problem, angel."

Angel.

He's called me that from the beginning. *Doesn't that show you what he feels about you, Bee?*

In less than forty-five minutes, we're back in Bitterroot Valley. Connor pulls into my driveway and cuts the engine. I turn in the seat to face him.

"I'm grilling steak for dinner," I inform him, not letting go of his hand. "You should join me. You did promise me the whole day, after all."

He nods, watching me carefully. "I'd like that."

"Great." I push out of the Jeep and lead him to the front door, where I unlock it and step inside. After I kick out of my sandals, I turn to him. "Make yourself comfortable. Do you want something to drink?"

I don't know why I'm suddenly nervous, but my stomach flutters in overdrive as I pad to the kitchen and open the fridge.

"I have water, iced tea, some beer that I'll never drink now—"

I feel the heat of him as he moves behind me and wraps his arms around my shoulders. He hugs my back to his front, immediately settling my stomach.

"This is nice," I whisper, leaning against him.

"I don't want you to be nervous, not now."

I turn and wrap my arms around his middle as I stare

up at him. "I'm not exactly good at being nervous. It doesn't happen often."

"Then why now?" He drags his knuckles down my cheek, then his hand is in my hair. Pushing his fingers through the strands, he's putting me into a blissed-out coma. "We've been together all day."

"The last time you were in my house," I say, "I couldn't bring myself to care because I felt like shit. I was *so* grumpy and couldn't get you out of here fast enough."

He purses his lips, waiting.

"I'm sorry if that hurt your feelings."

"My feelings are fine," he replies, and his eyes narrow. "Do you want me to go?"

"No." I shake my head and grip his shirt. "Absolutely not. It's just, *now* I have my wits about me and am a tiny bit self-conscious about my house. It's a good house, but it's small, and—"

He shuts me up, thank all the gods, by covering my mouth with his. That hand in my hair fists, holding me where he wants me as his tongue brushes over mine.

I can't help the moan that slips out of my throat. Jesus, I want to climb this man like a tree, and he told me *no sex* for today.

That seems highly unfair.

"Never, *ever* feel self-conscious with me, angel," he murmurs against my lips. "I'm perfectly comfortable here. As long as I'm with you, I've never been better."

"Okay." I lick my lips, still tasting him on me. "How do you like your steak?"

"Medium," he replies.

"Good because that's the only way I know how to grill them." I laugh as I step away from him to pull out the ingredients for steak with salad and rice pilaf.

"What can I do?"

"Nothing."

He takes my hand, pulling me to a stop, and drags one finger down the side of my neck, making me shiver.

"Keep flirting with me like that, and your *no-sex* rule for today goes out the window," I inform him, making his lips spread in that full smile that I love so fucking much.

"What can I do to help, bumble?"

"Do you know how to start a grill?"

"I'm a man. Of *course* I know how to start a bloody barbecue."

I snort, making his eyes narrow. "Hey, you're stupidly rich. I don't know if you're up to speed on what us commoners do every day."

Connor smirks and leans in to whisper in my ear, setting my skin on fire.

"You're so fucking gorgeous, I can hardly breathe."

I was *not* expecting that.

He pulls away and winks at me, and I shift back and forth on my bare feet.

"Uh, thanks."

I watch him walk out the back door onto my tiny patio to light the grill and let out a long breath.

Holy shit.

He's kept me off balance all day. I've known this man

for the better part of a year, and I've never seen him drop his guard the way he has today. I've never seen him be so physically affectionate and even a little silly. He's laughed and smiled more at me in one day than in the whole time I've known him.

And, God, how I love his laugh. I want to make him do it all the time.

Just as I start chopping vegetables for the salad, Connor walks back inside and takes over washing the ones I haven't gotten to yet.

"You're handy."

"Despite being rich?" he asks, raising an eyebrow.

"Yep." I whip the kitchen towel at him, swatting him on the butt. He lunges for me, making me shriek as I move away, but before he can catch me, his phone rings.

"I have to get this."

"Go ahead." I'm still laughing when I grab the knife and continue slicing the cucumber. To my surprise, he doesn't leave the room. He simply answers.

"Gallagher."

I glance over and see him scowl as he stares out at the living room, listening to whatever the person on the other end says.

"When?" His voice is sharp. Direct.

It sends a shiver down my spine, and my panties flood.

Why do I love that so much? That hard, unrelenting, demanding tone.

I know how it sounds in the bedroom when he's

143

driving me wild with his fingers, with his mouth, with his cock.

And fuck me if I don't miss it.

"Send Sean first thing in the morning and let it be known that if they can't back the fuck off, we'll dump the entire bloody project. No, I'm not bloody kidding, Fiona."

Fiona. His ex-wife.

"I'm not playing this game with them. Bleedin' hell, there are plenty of other sites to build a resort on in Sweden."

He hangs up and blows out a breath. His jaw muscles tick, his shoulders are tight, and I don't know why, but I want to touch him.

Setting the knife down, I walk up behind him, wrap my arms around his middle, and rest my cheek against his back, hugging him.

And slowly, the tension seems to seep out of him.

"It'll be okay," I murmur as his hands cover my arms. "Sometimes people just suck, Connor."

And now it's *my* phone ringing, making me scowl as I pull away from him and look at the screen.

It's Emily at the shop.

"Hey, Em."

"Hi, I'm so sorry to call you on your day off."

"No worries, what's up?"

I move back to continue cutting the cucumber, pinching the phone between my ear and shoulder, and Connor resumes cleaning vegetables next to me.

"I caught a shoplifter."

I narrow my eyes.

"Did you call the police?"

Connor's head whips over to look down at me.

"Of course. They just left. The kid was arrested, and we filed a report, and everything is fine, but I didn't want to wait to tell you until you got here tomorrow."

"I appreciate that. Who was it?"

"A teenage girl. I actually felt really sorry for her because I could tell that she just *really* wanted to read the book she tried to steal and likely can't afford it."

"But we have a no toleration policy," I finish for her.

"Yeah. She was upset. She'll probably be released to her parents."

I turn and lean against the counter, and Connor reaches over and tucks a piece of my hair behind my ear. I offer him a small smile.

"You did the right thing, Em. Thanks for letting me know. How's Tiffany feeling?"

"Oh, she's fine. She's ringing up customers now."

"Has it been busy today?"

"Steady all day. Have you considered hiring more help? I don't see us getting slower in the offseason."

"I have some interviews on Monday," I reply. "We definitely need more help. I'm gonna go now, but let me know if you need anything."

"Will do, boss. See you."

I hang up and look up into worried, insightful eyes. "It's all fine."

"Sometimes people suck," he says, echoing my words and making me laugh.

"That's true. What wise words."

"A brilliant and beautiful woman recently told me that." He winks, and we resume our tasks. "You're going to hire more help?"

"Yes, definitely. Two, maybe three more. The store is busy, and more often than not, I'm being called away from the floor for other things. I'm in contact with indie authors about collaborations, which is *so* exciting and not something I ever thought I'd do. I'm constantly buying new stock and starting to schedule book signings. It's a lot of admin work on my end, and I'd rather have employees on the floor with customers while I handle the back end."

"You're growing," he says, dragging his hand down my spine. "Good for you, bumble."

"I might eventually buy the space next to me. Not the coffee shop side, obviously, but the other side, if it ever comes available. I could use more space, and it hasn't even been a year. Anyway, I won't bore you with that."

"Do I look bored?" He raises an eyebrow and leans his hip against the counter. Folding his arms over his chest, he faces me as I finish the vegetables.

"No, you look ..." I lift a shoulder. "You know what? Never mind. I've boosted your ego enough today."

He laughs and cages me in, bracing his hands on the counter on either side of my hips, his face just inches from mine.

"You look amazing," he murmurs. "You've been tempting me in this dress all bloody day, showing me just a hint of the curves that make me so damn hard, I can hardly stand it."

He leans in closer and drags his lips up my throat, sending heat spearing through me. My nipples pucker, and my core tightens with need.

"Listening to you take control of your business has my own control hanging on by a thread, angel."

"You like it when I'm bossy?"

"I like it when you're the boss," he says. "Your work ethic turns me on. The whole time you were on that call, I wanted to strip you bare and bury my face in your gorgeous wet cunt and feast on you."

Holy. Fucking. Shit.

He's nibbling my shoulder, and his hand moves up my side and cups my breast. His thumb brushes over the tight nipple through my clothes, and it makes me arch my back against him.

"Connor."

"Say it again." He bites my chin, then covers my lips but doesn't kiss me. "Say it, angel."

"Connor." It's hardly a whisper now, and he groans against me.

"My name tastes so bloody delicious on your lips."

Then he's kissing me, pressing the hard length of his dick against my stomach, nibbling and devouring my mouth, and I don't want him to stop.

With a whimper, I cling to him, needing so much more from him.

But he breaks the kiss and rests his forehead against mine, and I growl.

Growl.

"Connor."

"No." There's that firm voice again, but his hands are gentle as they frame my face. "You asked for *more*, and I'm giving it to you today."

"I lied." I swallow hard and lean in to rest my forehead on his chest. "Just use me for sex. It's fine."

He laughs and kisses the top of my head as he takes my shoulders and pulls away from me.

"I'm hungry." He lifts an eyebrow. "Would you like me to put the steaks on the barbecue? It should be warm enough by now."

"Yeah, you should probably leave the room so I can call you names and flip you off behind your back."

He laughs again and swats my butt as he takes the plate of steaks off the counter and walks toward the door.

"Go ahead, then. Curse me out."

With a wink, he walks outside, and I blow out a breath.

"I only have myself to blame," I mutter as I get to work, checking on the rice. "I'm the needy one who wanted *more.* Stupid bitch."

"Call yourself a bitch again"—I jump because I didn't even know he'd walked back inside, and Connor presses his mouth to my ear—"and we'll have a problem."

He kisses my cheek and pulls out his ringing phone, but he doesn't answer it. He checks the screen, then slips it back into his pocket.

"You can answer that. It doesn't bother me."

"It's not important," he replies, shaking his head. He sips his water, watching me. "What made you decide to open a bookshop?"

"I mean, who *wouldn't* love to own a bookstore?" With a smirk, I pull salad dressings out of the fridge for the salad and set them on my small table in the breakfast nook beside the kitchen. I converted my dining room into a library, so this is as fancy as I get. "I've always been a bookworm. I went to college for business administration and knew that I'd own my own business. I *hate* working for someone else."

I glance over and see him lift a brow, humor in his intense gaze. "Is that so?"

"Yep. I want to be the boss. I don't take direction well." I bite my lip, suddenly flustered because I took direction pretty damn well during our one night together.

By his quick intake of breath, I can tell he's thinking the same thing.

"When it comes to *work*," I clarify, and he smirks. "Anyway, I've known for a long time that I wanted to open a store. I joined a local women-in-business group, and that's been hugely helpful. Once a month, we listen to guest speakers. People like London Ambrose-Montgomery and Sophie Harrison. Women who are *killing it* in business. It's inspiring. Anyway, I started networking with those girls long before I opened the shop."

"Hold that thought." He kisses my forehead before walking back out to flip the steaks on the grill, so I simply follow him. We'll keep an eye on them together.

"This is easier." I shrug. "I waited a while to open my place because I knew I wanted that specific location, and the former owners didn't want to sell."

He tilts his head, listening, but I can see he's growling on the inside. *Protective man.*

"I knew, I *know*, that being next door to the coffee shop was the way to go. Who can resist buying a coffee, then wandering through a bookstore? I didn't want to be across the street or down the block. I needed to be *there.*"

"How did you get them to sell to you?"

"I slept with the former owner for a year. Blow jobs twice a week, and even let him do anal once a month." I tuck my hair behind my ear as his hands fist, and his eyes narrow menacingly. "Worked like a charm."

He grinds his molars together, and I hold his gaze with my own for about ten seconds, then I can't stand it anymore.

I double over in laughter.

"I can't do it. Oh God, that was funny. Your face!" I wipe a tear from the corner of my eye as Connor reaches out, clasps his hand over the back of my neck, and closes the gap between us. He makes me look him in the face.

"You're going to pay for that, *mo rúnsearc.*"

"Oh, I hope so." I pat his chest and grin, practically glowing. "The owner was an old friend of my dad's and decided to retire. I offered him fair market value, and he took it. No sexual favors required. But he was stubborn about it for a while. I don't know how I'm going to get the owners on the side of me to sell when I'm ready to do it. They don't live here and use it as an investment property."

"There's always a way," he says before turning and taking the finished steak off the grill. He passes me the plate, then turns off the propane, and we make our way inside, fill our plates, and sit at my small table.

As we eat, I keep watching him, looking for any signs that he's uncomfortable in my simple house, but he looks at ease, which makes it easy to chat about everyday things.

When we've finished eating, Connor helps me put the leftovers away and load the dishes in the dishwasher, and then I show him to the door.

I want to ask him to stay.

I want to talk him into breaking the no-sex rule for today, make me go crazy with lust and need, and then hold me while I sleep like a baby, the way I do when I'm with him.

But I don't have the guts.

He made it clear that nothing more is happening today, and I refuse to be that needy girl who begs him to hold her while she sleeps.

"You're quiet," he says when we reach the door.

"I was just thinking that I had a nice time today." I smile up at him and let my hand rest at his waist as he cups my face and bends to press his lips to mine. This one is a sweet kiss, loaded with promises of more for later.

"Me, too. Thank you for dinner."

"Thanks for everything else."

He pulls me to him for a hug, and then the door is open and he walks through it to the waiting Jeep.

"Lock your doors, bumble."

"Yes, sir."

His jaw ticks at that, and I send him a sassy grin. Once he's backed out of my driveway and driven away, I close the door, lock it, and let out a long breath.

Holy shit, Connor Gallagher just swept me off my feet.

Chapter Ten

CONNOR

I had one whole day with her, and now I fucking miss her.

It took everything in me, every ounce of self-control, to walk away from her after dinner yesterday. Being with her is as easy as breathing. I wanted to stay, to ask her more questions, to simply hold her.

Sleep beside her.

And that's not something I usually think about. No other woman, not even my ex-wife, made me contemplate the idea of curling up in bed to simply *be* with her. To fuck? Of course. But to hold and show affection?

I've never given it any thought.

Until my bumble bee.

"Sir, did you hear me?"

I drag my hand down my face and turn to Lyle, my site manager, then push my glasses up my nose.

"So the main lodge is here." I point at the plans

before me and look up and point at the land. We're on-site today, and I'm approving phase two of the build.

Phase one is already under construction. The condos were the first to break ground because private investors own those. Some owned them previously and chose to stay. Others took the insurance money and ran, selling to others.

I'll own the penthouse that I had added to the plans.

"As you know," Lyle continues, "other buildings will be over there. Shops, restaurants, and equipment rentals. You've added downhill bike rentals in the summer."

Among other things.

I nod, scanning the area and picturing it perfectly in my head. Of course, the renderings we've had done make it hard *not* to see it clearly. This resort will be stunning.

And it will make me a lot of money.

It's hot today, and I'm in a suit, so I shed my coat, roll my sleeves, and take off my tie. For the next several hours, we tour the mountain, making sure everything is in place to begin the next phase of construction.

My phone pings with a text, and I pull it out of my pocket, pleased that it's my angel.

> Angel: Did you seriously send this?

> Angel: *Photo of a case of water*

> You need to stay hydrated. It's your favorite.

Yes, I sent a case of her favorite water to the bookshop just to make her smile. Because her smile is my favorite thing.

> How are you today? Is your shop busy?

I want to go in and see her, but I have to be here for this. Then I have work to catch up on from yesterday.

"I have to take this call," Lyle says, stepping away from me and giving me a few minutes to enjoy my girl.

> Angel: It's Saturday, so we're busy. I hope the interviews on Monday go well because I'd like to start being open on Sunday as well. Holy shit, now flowers are being delivered?

I can't help but laugh at that. I love that she doesn't have a filter and says what she's thinking. She's not shy in the least, has no poker face, and it's a breath of fresh air. It makes me wonder how I've survived so many years of *yes-men* who've bent over backward to appease me but have never shown interest in me as a person.

She's one of a kind.

Christ, I want to see her.

A few seconds later, my phone rings.

"Hello, bumble."

"You bought out the whole florist," she says, her raspy voice a little shaky. "Summer just said that you bought *all of the flowers*, Connor."

And I'd buy her more if they'd had them.

"I hope you like them."

155

"Like them?" She huffs a breath, then chuckles. "The *whole* store? You couldn't save some for someone else? What if someone has an anniversary or something?"

"Not my problem. Tell me you like the flowers, *mo rúnsearc*. And the water."

She's quiet for a moment, and then her voice is soft, and I ache to touch her. "I like the flowers and the water."

"Good. I'd like to take you to dinner tonight, if you're free."

"I'll be finished here around six thirty."

I smile. Something that's been happening more often. "I'll be there, bumble. Have a good afternoon."

"You too. And Connor?"

"Yes?"

"Thank you."

"My pleasure."

I pocket my phone and nod when Lyle raises a brow, wondering if I'm ready to move on.

"Let's wrap this up," I tell him.

I have to get ready for a date.

Her back is to me when I walk into the bookshop. Bouquets cover every available surface, filling the space with fragrance and color. Was it over the top to buy every bloom available at Paula's Poseys?

Yes.

I don't care. She deserves them.

She's wearing the blue Dior dress she bought that day in Big Sky, her dark hair is in the usual curls down her back that never fail to make my fingers itch with the need to touch, and she's wearing black heels that make me think of her naked and writhing with her legs on my shoulders.

I want this woman more than I've wanted anything else in my life. Her body, with all its curves and soft skin, is my fantasy brought to life. I know she was kidding yesterday when she said she'd fucked the owner of this place to get him to sell, but at that moment, I saw red.

I wanted to kill a faceless man at the mere thought of him having his hands, or his cock, anywhere near my angel's perfect arse. Hell no.

And I'll make it crystal clear to her that she's mine.

Later.

She laughs at something her employee says, then turns around and stops short when she sees me, but the smile doesn't leave her gorgeous face. I walk straight to her, tip her chin up, and cover her lips. I want to deepen the kiss, to brand her here, but I respect that these are her employees, so I keep the kiss light.

"I missed this face," I whisper against her lips.

"You saw it just yesterday."

"Still missed it," I repeat before pulling back. Now that I get a good look at her, I can see the fatigue in her eyes. She reaches up to press on the tension on her neck as she turns to her employee.

"This is Emily," she says, turning to me. "And this is Connor."

"Hello," Emily says with a polite smile. "I know you sent the flowers to the boss lady here, but I'm taking some home, so thanks for the flowers."

I nod and shove my hands in my pockets. "Enjoy."

"Oh, we are," Emily says, walking off to return some books to a shelf.

"They won't all fit in my house," Billie says. "So I handed some out. But I'll have you know, I kept my favorites for myself."

"As you should. Are you all right then, *mo rúnsearc?*" I brush the pad of my thumb under her eye, and she leans her cheek into my palm, closing her eyes as if she's exhausted. "We don't have to do dinner. We can simply relax."

"You're going to deprive me of carbs?" She narrows her eyes, clearly teasing me. To my surprise, she takes my hand in hers and kisses my palm, sending a jolt of awareness up my arm and down to my cock. "Absolutely not. I'm hungry, Mr. Gallagher, and you promised me pasta."

"Then I best feed you."

Christ, I'll give her the moon if it'll make her happy.

She smiles softly and turns to Emily and another woman I didn't see before. That must be Tiffany.

"Ladies, I'm heading out. Have a good day off tomorrow."

"You too, boss," Emily says with a smile and a wave.

With my hand on the small of Billie's back, we walk

to the front door and step outside. Miller stands in front of my SUV and nods at us as we step onto the footpath.

"We're going to walk to the restaurant, Miller," I tell him.

"Hi, Miller," Billie adds with a smile. "Are you having a good day?"

My right-hand man cracks a smile and nods at Billie. "Yes, thank you, miss. I'll be parked in front of the restaurant when you're finished."

But he doesn't climb inside the SUV. He walks behind us down the block until we're safely inside the restaurant.

"I'm Casey, your server tonight," we're told as we sit. She writes her name in crayon on the white paper and passes the menus. "Can I get you started with something to drink?"

"I'll start with water," Billie says.

"Same for me," I reply and nod as she walks away.

"I have questions," Billie begins, setting her menu aside and leaning on the table, giving me her undivided attention.

And I *want* her undivided attention. All the damn time.

"That makes two of us," I reply. "Go ahead. Ask away."

"First of all, do you want to get what we got last time and share?"

"And do you remember that, angel?"

She purses her lips. "I have an excellent memory."

"As do I. That works for me."

159

"Good."

The server returns with waters and a basket of bread with garlic piled on top of it. Billie grabs a slice and keeps talking.

"Sometimes Miller's with you, and sometimes he isn't. Why is that?"

I take her free hand in mine and rub my thumb over her knuckles. She's not wearing any rings, but she has on the necklace I gave her.

"Miller's with me most of the time," I admit. "Some days, I go out on my own, but that honestly pisses him off."

She lifts an eyebrow, but we're interrupted by the server. I place our order, and when we're alone again, she takes my hand once more and sips her water.

"Why do you have him with you?"

"For protection."

She blinks at that, her eyebrows pulling together in a frown, and my angel suddenly looks concerned. I don't ever want her to worry about anything. "What do you need to be protected from?"

I shake my head, ready to brush it off, but her hand tightens in mine.

"Don't fucking sugarcoat it," she says, her voice low enough that no one else can hear her. "Just tell me."

"I don't always deal with good people. I can be ruthless in business. I don't care if I'm liked as long as I get what I want."

"People want to *hurt* you?" Her jaw firms, and she

squares her shoulders. "You don't need Miller. I'll kill them myself."

"I have no doubt you could do that." I can't help the smile that spreads over my face because she looks so fierce. It feels good to know that she'd try to defend me in any way she could. Not that I'd ever let her put herself between me and anyone else. "But you don't have to worry about anything. It's mostly a precaution, and that's the truth of it. Also, when he drives, I can work."

Her gaze searches mine as if she's making sure I'm telling the truth. She must believe me because she nods. The Italian nachos are set in front of us, and I discover I'm hungrier than I thought I was.

"What are your questions for me?" Billie asks.

"What are you wearing under that dress?"

She doesn't even pause in her reply. "Something that will make you sweat when I get you home."

I reach over and brush her hair behind her ear. "All you have to do is exist for that to happen."

She smirks, but I don't miss the satisfaction that moves through her eyes.

"How long have you been divorced?"

Ah, here we go. After our talk yesterday, I wondered when she'd dig into this topic. Not that I have a problem discussing it with her because if the roles were reversed, I'd want to know, too.

"More than ten years. Maybe closer to twelve now, actually."

She reaches for another nacho and chews. "Was it amicable?"

"As much as divorce can be." She's watching me with serious eyes, and I lean back in the chair. "I was twenty-three when I married her and almost twenty-eight when it was over. I'd known her a long time. Her family and mine are friends, and when it was suggested that we'd make a fine match, I didn't balk at it."

"It was an *arranged* marriage?" Her eyes widen at that, and I smile.

"Not like that, no, and she'd be mighty chuffed if she thought I said so. It was … *easy*, I guess is the word for it. Fiona's a lovely woman. She's pretty"—Billie narrows her eyes, and I squeeze her hand, enjoying her wee show of jealousy—"and we got along well. We still do, but just as friends."

"So you married her because you liked her well enough and she fit into your world?"

"Those were my reasons." Our entrée is set in front of us, and when we confirm that we don't need anything else, the server leaves. Billie and I both grab a fork and eat from one plate. "She would likely tell you that she thought she was in love with me at the time."

Billie nods thoughtfully, but there's no judgment there. "Interesting."

"She hated how much I traveled for work. I wasn't home much."

"Where was home base?" she asks.

"Dublin. That's where our headquarters is, although my family is originally from Galway. Have you ever been?"

Billie's smile is easy and soft. "No. I'd never used my passport before we all went to London last month."

I'm going to take this woman *everywhere*. And I can't fucking wait. I want to show her the world. Every corner of it.

"So she lived in Dublin while you flew all over the place."

"Aye." I nod and push my glasses up my nose. "She could have come with me, but she preferred to stay in Ireland. And I was determined to earn my seat as CEO of Gallagher Hotels."

"So really, it sounds like you wanted different things."

"We did."

"And no kids?"

I quirk an eyebrow at her. "I didn't lie to you when I told you that I haven't any children, angel."

"Just checking. Besides, Skyla would have mentioned it." She chews thoughtfully. "And now Fiona is married to your best friend?"

I feel the smile come when I think of the two of them together. "That's how it should have been all along. Ronan and Fiona are amazing together. And they have two gorgeous boys."

"A happy ending for them." She smiles, setting her fork aside.

"You can't be finished eating, angel. There's still a lot of food here."

"Pasta is filling. I ate a ton of nachos, and I'm about

to have dessert. Trust me, I've had plenty." She wipes her mouth with her napkin.

"Let's talk about you now." I set my own cutlery aside. "No long-term relationship for you?"

"Not currently," she says, grinning when I lift an eyebrow. "Well, let's see. I dated a little here and there through high school and college. Nothing super serious."

"Were all the boys you knew just idiots?"

She smirks at that. "I'm picky, Connor. There's really no other way to put it. And I don't have much of a filter, and you already pointed out that I have a *disgusted* face."

"You do, aye."

"Yeah, well, can you imagine how well it goes over when a guy I'm not in any way attracted to approaches me, and I'm trying to be kind and let them down easily, but I have that look on my face because I don't even know that it's there?"

God, she's amazing.

"You simply walk around Montana hurting feelings, then, is that it?"

Now, she drops her face in her hands. "No. It's not like I'm approached all that often. Anyway, I dated one guy in college for about six months, and he took me home to meet his family."

She looks up at me with that disgusted face firmly in place.

"I have to know what happened."

"In all fairness, he had told me, no, *warned me*, that he was close to his mother."

"Oh no.

"And my stupid ass thought, *Oh, isn't that nice? He has a good relationship with his mom.* But that's not what it was, not even close. The *second* I stepped into that house, that woman had it out for me. She asked him, right in front of me, why he would date a fat girl."

My hand fists on the table, and she keeps going.

"He did tell her to stop being mean. But she didn't stop. At one point, he went to the bathroom, and she leaned over and informed me that she'd never let me marry him. That she'd do everything in her power to make sure he knew what a piece-of-shit whore I am, and he'd dump me before the night was over."

"What's this woman's name?" I ask before taking a sip of my water.

My angel, my perfect girl, laughs.

"I don't find this to be funny at all, bumble."

"Oh, it's funny, all right." The smile on her face is one of utter, smug pleasure. "He came back into the room and sat next to me but didn't touch me. Now, that boy had been fucking me six ways to Sunday for three months."

"I thought you said you'd been seeing him for six months?"

"Hey, despite what his bitch of a mother said, I held out for three whole months." She snorts at that. "We're sitting there in her living room, and he won't touch me, so at this point, I knew it was over. There was *no damn way* I was going to keep seeing this guy. Despite what she said, I'd had no illusions that I'd marry him anyway."

I hate her saying those words about anyone.

"I was twenty-one. I wasn't getting married anytime soon, and if she'd asked me, I would have told her that we were just ... seeing each other, I guess. I wasn't trying to trap that boy into anything. I say boy because he was twenty-two and called his mother *Mommy.*" She sips her water, and I'm enthralled. Listening to her tell a story is fascinating. "So she asked me what I was majoring in, making general conversation, but then she asked why I'd had an STD when I was seventeen."

My blood runs cold, but I don't move a muscle. That woman is about to lose everything she loves for doing that to my angel.

"Connor." She reaches over and takes my hand, and her face has lost all its humor. "I was a virgin when I was seventeen. I've never had an STD in my life."

I frown, clinging to her hand. "Then what was she talking about?"

"I denied it. Told her she didn't know what she was talking about. Her son proceeded to scoot away from me, scowling as if I was suddenly a rabid dog and he might catch something if he touched me. I was *so* mad."

She shakes her head and takes a deep breath.

"Now, what I'm about to tell you is likely the worst thing I've ever done in my life."

"You can tell me anything, baby."

She nods, then looks down at the uneaten dessert neither of us realized was delivered. Biting her lip, she shrugs and scoops up a mouthful of dessert.

"I demanded to know why she thought that about me. And she finally admitted that she'd searched my name in the database at her hospital. She was a nurse, and she totally broke every HIPAA law in this country when she did that. The hospital she works at is *big* and is tied to most of the clinics in that town, along with a lot of clinics and medical centers in western Montana. So when she found someone in the system by the name of Willa Blackwell, she thought that was me. Because Billie is sometimes a nickname for Willa."

She swallows and keeps talking. Christ, I want to scoop her up and set her in my lap.

"My given name is Billie. Everyone knows that my parents have a thing for B names. Not that his mom knew that. Anyway, she invaded that girl's privacy trying to dig up dirt on *me* and broke the law and the terms of her work contract."

"And what did you do about that, bumble?"

"I called her boss, told him what she'd done, and she was fired. Then I called the police, and she got into *huge* trouble for HIPAA violations. Finally, I told her son that he had better cut that umbilical cord because no girl would ever put up with that bullshit, least of all me. When I left their house, I called Brooks to come get me since I was one hundred miles from home without a vehicle."

"This is the worst thing you've ever done?" I grin at her. I can't help it.

"I got her fired. I ruined her entire career, but it wasn't just because she called me fat or made me feel less than. It was because there's some girl out there whose rights were violated by that woman, who's supposed to care about and take care of people. What if that girl had been raped or had a boyfriend who was cheating on her, and she didn't know? It's *no one's* business why that happened to her, and the fact that she went hunting for it disgusted me. And I was having none of it."

"Good girl. And what happened to her?"

"She'll never work as a nurse again," she replies. "Beyond that, I'm not sure. I didn't keep track. I was just so *pissed*. The weird thing? He was actually a nice guy and not a jerk at all. I mean, he was never going to be *my* guy, but he was decent. Never pressured me, had a sense of humor, nothing really super wrong with him. But wow, his mother was a piece of work. Okay, enough about that. I had one boyfriend after that for about a year, and *he* was *not* a nice guy. He hit me exactly once, and that was all it took for me to tell him to fuck right off."

"And what was *his* name?" I ask, hating that I asked the question about her dating history in the first place.

"Are you going to make him disappear for me, Mr. Billionaire?"

"Yes."

Her smile falls, and she swallows hard, watching me. She wanted morally gray? She found it.

"Not worth it."

Leaning in, I motion for her to meet me halfway over the table. When my mouth is next to her ear, I whisper, "No one touches you in anger and lives to tell about it, angel. You'll give me a fucking name."

She turns her face and kisses my cheek, brushing her

nose against me. "Thank you, but in this case, it really is unnecessary. He's already dead. Hiking incident two years ago."

Billie sits back and cringes. "Sorry you asked?"

"Yes, but not for the reason you think. I hate that you went through any of that."

"And I hate that you were once married to literally *anyone*, even if she *is* a nice, pretty girl from an appropriate family who ended up happily married to your best friend. So I guess we're even."

We stare at each other across the table, and I marvel *again* at how incredibly strong this woman is. One would think a younger sister of four brothers would be weak or entitled. Spoiled, even. But Billie is intelligent and thoughtful, so I'm not surprised that I feel that same connection with her from the first night we met.

The only thing that's different is her eyes. *She's so ... fatigued.* And it's only just past eight o'clock.

"Why do you look so tired, angel?"

She blinks at the sudden change in subject. "I didn't sleep well last night."

"I'm taking you home with me."

It's not a question.

"Ready when you are."

Chapter Eleven

BILLIE

Miller turns onto the driveway leading to Connor's house. When we go around the bend and the sprawling mansion comes into view, my jaw drops.

I didn't even know this house existed out here. It's what I would call rustic but still fancy. If you took a cute little rustic cabin, the kind you might find in a Hallmark Christmas movie, and fed it steroids for about ten years, this is what you'd get.

I bet it's *stunning* all dressed up for the holidays.

"Wow," I mutter, taking it all in as Miller stops in front of the house in the circular driveway.

"You've been here before," Connor reminds me.

"But I didn't see it," I reply and turn to him. "I was too busy trying not to die to check out your cozy mountain getaway."

He smirks, but his eyes are hard as he reaches out to drag his finger down my cheek.

"Let's make happier memories here, bumble."

Connor pushes out of the SUV, and rather than walk around to open my door, he simply reaches in, pulls me across the seat, and helps me to my feet.

"Thanks, Miller," he says as he takes my hand and leads me toward the door.

I glance back over my shoulder and give Miller a grin and a wave, and then we're inside, and I can't help but say, "Wow," again.

"These windows," I murmur, walking through the great room to stand at a wall of windows with a killer view of the mountains. The ceiling in here has to be thirty feet tall, and the furniture is soft brown leather with area rugs in burnt orange and brown. "I hope you put a ridiculously huge Christmas tree right here."

I plant my feet in the center of the windows and look up, raising my arms over my head as if *I'm* the tree.

"And tons of garland along that railing." I point up to the second floor, where a catwalk must connect the house's two wings. God, those wrought-iron railings are gorgeous.

When I look over at Connor, he's watching me with his hands in his pockets, leaning against the wall. He's in navy slacks and a light blue button-down. His sleeves are rolled almost to his elbows, and his top two buttons are undone. His dark hair is tousled, likely from pushing his hands through it throughout the day.

He's so fucking handsome. So tall and broad and muscular. He could give Henry Cavill a run for his money, and that's saying a lot.

"Sorry, I didn't mean to be bossy about holiday decor. It's just really the perfect spot for a tree."

"I'll take it under advisement." His lips pull up at the sides, the way they do when I amuse him. I've learned that full smiles from this man are rare, earned, and spectacular. He pulls one hand out of his pocket and holds it out for me. Without hesitation, I cross to him and slide my palm against his, loving the way his warm hand engulfs my own. "Do you want a tour then, angel?"

"Sure, I'll take a tour."

He kisses my forehead—forehead kisses are *not* overrated. If anything, they're underrated and should be doled out more often—and then leads me through the house. The kitchen is any chef's dream. I'm *not* a chef, but if I were, I'd want to cook in there all day. Again, I can picture myself in there with my mom and Birdie and my girls baking holiday cookies, but I press my lips together, keeping that thought to myself.

"This is my home office," he says, pointing at an open doorway as we walk down the hall, and I peek in to see a massive desk with both a laptop and a desktop computer, two possibly thirty-four-inch monitors, a wall of books, and more windows with a view of the mountains. "There are three guest bedrooms and bathrooms on this floor."

With that, he leads me to the stairs and shows me more guest rooms, a fully equipped home gym—I *knew* he worked out—and another office that looks like it's never used, given the empty desktop. On the opposite side of the catwalk is the primary suite, and it takes up the entire second level of this side of the house.

"I remember glimpses of this room," I murmur as I walk through and drag my hand over the cream comforter. The windows are framed with pretty beige drapes. A closet the size of my entire house makes me salivate. How did I miss that last time? Even drugged, I should have noticed my dream closet.

Attached is another lounging space with a deep-cushioned sofa, a television, and more bookshelves.

"You're a bookworm," I say, turning to Connor in surprise.

"I like to read," he replies, pushing his glasses up his nose, and it makes me grin.

"We have something in common."

"We have plenty in common, bumble."

My eyes skim over the titles. It seems my Irishman enjoys thrillers and fantasy, which shouldn't surprise me, but if I'm being honest, it really does.

"You read Nalini Singh?"

"I do. Have you?"

"Have I? Oh my God, she's fucking brilliant."

"Come on, let's complete this tour, and we can talk books later."

I press my lips together—holy shit, reader Connor just totally upped the sexy factor here—and follow him to the bathroom, which is more beautiful than I remember. The shower is big enough for a party of six, with glass walls and a beautiful mosaic that mirrors the mountains outside. The double vanity is marble, and there's a soaking tub that's … full.

"Did you leave the water in the tub when you left today?" I ask him. "With bubbles?"

"I've never used this tub," he says with a half smile, pulling me against him, my back to his front. He brushes my hair to the side and kisses my neck, making my nipples pucker and my core tighten.

"Then how?"

"I have staff here," he murmurs. "And I messaged ahead. I want you to get in this tub and soak for a bit. Do you want wine?"

"No, thank you. No alcohol ever again. At least, not for a good while."

He sighs against me and peppers two more kisses on my skin. "I'll get you something else, then. Get comfortable, angel."

After pulling away, he walks out of the room, closing the door behind him, and I stare at the tub. He had someone fill it, just for me? How many people work here? Why does *one person* need *staff*?

"Billionaires," I mutter as I carefully take off my Dior dress and hang it on the hook behind the door. I remove my matching pink bra and panties, then find a hair tie in my handbag, which I'm glad I hadn't set down anywhere else in the house. After securing my hair up, I slip into the steaming water and sigh as it envelops me.

Oh holy hell. This is luxurious.

Maybe I need to invest in a hot tub. Maybe a good soak each night would help me sleep better.

I'm contemplating that when the door opens, and Connor returns carrying a cup of tea, which he sets on a skinny table next to the tub.

"Was it still hot enough?" he asks.

"They must have filled this thing with boiling water because it's still really hot. Are you getting in with me?"

He bends over and kisses me, so tenderly, so softly, it makes my toes curl. With my head back, his finger glides between my collarbone and up my throat to my lips.

I can't wait to get my hands on this man.

"No. I'm going to let you relax for a while longer, then I'll dry you off and put you to bed."

I lift an eyebrow. "I don't have a watch on me, but I don't think it's even nine yet."

"Those are the plans. Drink your tea."

"Bossy, aren't you?"

"You have no idea."

He saunters out of the bathroom, and I decide to enjoy this hot water, and the hot tea he brought me.

When the tea is gone, the bubbles have popped to nothing, and the water is tepid, Connor returns with an enormous, fluffy green towel and offers me his hand to help me stand.

When I'm out of the water, he wraps me in that towel and pulls me against him. Hugging me close, he rubs his hands up and down my back and kisses my head.

Never, not once in all of my life, have I felt as sexy, as secure, as *safe* as I do when Connor holds me.

"You changed," I mutter against his gray T-shirt. He's in matching sweatpants, and it looks like he took a shower because his hair is still damp. "Did you shower?"

"Aye. I used a guest room. I didn't want to bother you."

"Yeah, because lounging in that fancy tub and watching you shower ten feet away from me would have been too great a burden to bear."

"I like it when you're sassy," he says before leading me out of the bathroom to the bedroom. The bed's been turned down, the lights are dim, and I'm ... sleepy.

I have the sexiest man alive *right here*, and all I want to do is curl up around him and sleep.

Am I broken? Because the sex is top-notch, and I want that, too. I want lots of it.

But fuck, I'm so tired.

"Come on, bumble." He drops my towel, then reaches for another of his shirts and slips it over my head. He doesn't touch my skin. He doesn't even let his eyes drop below my chin.

"Question."

He raises an eyebrow, and I don't climb into bed quite yet because I want to ask this while I'm standing.

"It used to be that you couldn't keep your hands off me, and now that we're spending time together, it's the opposite. Are we not—"

He frames my face in his hands, and he crushes his mouth to mine, gripping me like he never wants to let me go as he devours me. I have no choice but to open my mouth and let him in. I moan against him as he ends our kiss. Still cupping my face, he drags his thumb over my lower lip.

"I want you more than I want to breathe," he says, his voice rough. "Don't ever question that. Keeping my hands to myself has been fucking torture, but you're not okay. You're exhausted, and I'm not an arsehole. I want more than a quick fuck to get my dick wet so you can finally sleep. No, baby. You deserve so much more than that. You deserve to have me worshipping you for hours when you're awake and alert enough to enjoy every bloody moment of it."

Shaking his head, he guides me into bed, then snuggles around me as I rest my head on his chest.

"You're going to sleep, and when you wake up, I'll make up for all our lost time. I'm going to consume every mouthwatering inch of you."

I grin and wrap my arm around his abdomen, toss my leg over his, and sigh contentedly as I burrow against him. There is *nothing* like this, right here, with this man.

"That sounds really nice."

He chuckles, the sound vibrating under my ear. "It's going to be better than *nice.*"

"I believe it." I can't stop the yawn that comes, and he drags his hand down my back. "Do you have to work tomorrow?"

"I told everyone to fuck off for tomorrow."

I lift my head and stare at him. "You took yesterday off, too."

"Aye. I didn't say they were happy about it."

"Connor, you don't have to do that. If you need to work, work."

"I need to spend the day with you," he replies, tucking me under his chin once more. "We may not leave this bed."

"In that case, yes, you're taking the day off."

There's more chuckling beneath my head. "It's glad I am that you approve."

Chapter Twelve

CONNOR

I hate that she's so tired. I also hate that this could have been us, this woman in my bed, for the past several months. Instead, I wasted so much time because I didn't get my head out of my arse long enough to see that not only is she an amazing woman but that she's also *mine*.

Her plump lips pucker in her sleep, and I can't resist brushing my finger over them, then up her cheek, forehead, and down the bridge of her gorgeous nose.

I'm permanently turned on whenever I'm near her. I always want her. The fact that she had to ask if I wanted to get my hands on her was so preposterous that I almost spread her wide and pushed into her right then and there. I want her so badly. That hasn't changed since that first time I saw her last year, and it's only gotten more intense since I realized who she is and how much time our families would spend together. The more I'm around her, the more I yearn for her. Her touch, her mouth, her pussy.

But it's not just about the sex. Not with Billie.

And that's new for me.

I love her sassy mouth, and I wasn't lying when I said her work ethic turned me on. She's a smart woman, and if I thought I could, I'd steal her away to work for me.

But she doesn't want to work for someone else.

She's her own boss.

And I'm damn proud of her.

Speaking of work, I do have some things to do if I'm going to take the day off with her tomorrow, so I press my lips to her forehead as I roll her onto her back and gently slip from the bed, careful not to wake her. Padding out of the room, I walk downstairs to turn off lights and lock up, set the alarms, and check in with Miller. Then I swing by my office to grab my laptop.

I'll work from bed so I can keep an eye on my angel.

After snatching a couple of bottles of Billie's favorite water from the fridge, I return upstairs and set the water at the bedside. I've just set my computer down and pulled my shirt off when I hear her whimper for the first time.

My gaze falls to her, and I furrow my brow when she shifts in the bed, a frown between her brows.

Quickly, I shed my sweats and climb between the sheets to gather her against me.

"Shh, it's okay." I kiss her head and hug her close, and she sighs. "I'm here, angel."

But she doesn't settle. She whimpers again, and this

time, she grinds her pelvis against mine, wrapping her leg over my hip, and my hand drifts down to her lush arse, gripping it firmly.

"Connor." She's awake now, kissing my bare chest, and every molecule in my body is fully awake and wanting her.

"Did you have a bad dream?" I murmur into her hair, and she shakes her head as she looks up at me with bright hazel eyes.

"Not a *bad* dream," she says as her hand moves down my side. "I have a question."

"Anything." I'm pulling my shirt that she's wearing up her back so I can touch her bare skin, and she stretches into my touch as if she can't get enough of it.

"Would you *please* fuck me into this mattress already?"

Her lust-filled eyes hold mine. She bites that lip, and all of my tightly reined self-control snaps.

With a groan, I roll her onto her back and work my shirt off her, toss it aside, and stare down at her in the soft lamplight. I pin one of her hands above her head as I kiss her. My free hand teases one of her nipples into a tight peak, making her squirm and moan against my mouth.

"You're so gorgeous," I say against her lips, and she bites my lower lip, then lets go and drags her leg up the outside of my own.

"I need you, Connor." She licks her lips, and my already hard cock swells at her breathy words. "I need you to fuck me until I can't walk tomorrow. I need you to fill me up, and tease me, and touch me until I'm begging for mercy."

"Christ." I lick and suck my way down her torso, stopping to pluck at her nipples with my teeth before I journey farther south. Her hands are in my hair, pulling as her head thrashes back and forth on the pillow. "Give me your eyes, angel."

She complies, and I keep kissing farther south until I'm at her already glistening pussy. "You want me to use my mouth on you?"

"Fuck, yes."

"Tell me. I want to hear you use your words, baby."

"Kiss me." She licks her lips and moans when I brush my tongue over her clit. "*Yes.* Oh God, yes. More, Connor."

"More of what?"

"More tongue. Move down just ... *yes.*"

I pull her lips into my mouth and devour her. My tongue pushes into her slit, into her core, and when I press my nose to her clit, she lifts her hips right off the bed.

"Connor!" She presses her heel into my shoulder for more leverage, and I bloody love it.

Christ, she went from dead asleep to this sensual goddess in less than ten seconds.

"Oh, please," she pants, her hands in my hair. I growl against her, and that's all it takes for her to cry out, fuck herself against my face, and fall apart. Her core is sopping wet as I replace my mouth with my fingers. Her walls tighten and hug them, and I kiss the inside of her trembling thighs.

"You're so goddamn beautiful when you come." I kiss over her hip and her belly on my way back up to her lips. Resting my cock in her slick, wet heat, I lean in and kiss her softly. "Do you taste yourself?"

"Mmm," she says, licking her lips. "Connor?"

"Yes, angel."

She shifts, and the crown of my cock rubs against her clit, making us both gasp. Her mouth opens in an O, and she clings to me, her nails digging into my shoulders.

"Please."

"Please what?" I kiss her chin, her neck, still dragging my dick through her folds. "Fuck, you feel amazing. Better than I remember, and that seems impossible."

"You're so damn big." Her grip moves down to my arms. "How did it fit last time?"

I laugh and catch her chin in my fingers, then nibble on her lips. "You just breathe for me, *mo rúnsearc*. I need to move away from you so I can grab a condom."

She frowns and, for the first time, looks vulnerable.

"Talk to me." I brush a lock of her hair off her cheek and kiss her lips. "Just talk, baby."

"I have the birth control handled." She holds her arm up and points at the skin over her inner biceps. "For another two years. There's been no one since you."

I can't help myself. I crash my lips to hers, wanting to consume her. "There's been no one since you either, angel. God, you're all I see. You're all I think about."

Her eyes fill with tears, and I shake my head.

"Nope. None of that right now. Later, bumble. Are you saying I can fuck you bare?"

A grin spreads over her breathtaking face, and she nods so smugly, it makes my chest tighten.

"Please do."

"Please do *what*?" I love her raspy voice, and when filth spills out of her fuckable lips, it's almost more than I can take. My cock is begging for her tight pussy.

"Please." She nibbles on my chin. "Fuck me." She kisses the side of my mouth and lifts her hips. "Until I'm so sore, you're all I think about."

I push inside her, all the way to the hilt, and she gasps as her walls tighten around me. I hitch her leg higher on my hip, drag my hand down to her arse, and hold on tight.

"You're so bloody snug."

"Holy shit." She takes a breath, those wide eyes on mine.

"Breathe." I rear back, pulling almost all the way out, and caress her sweet face. "Take a breath for me, beautiful girl."

She complies, and I push back in, and she moans now, her eyes almost rolling back in her head.

"There you go. God, you take me so well." I start to move in long, slow strokes, savoring every touch, every pulse, each quiver coming from inside her.

"I'm going to suck your cock later," she promises, then grins when I growl. "I'm going to swallow you down until I choke on you."

"Fucking hell." I'm fucking her hard now, unable to

hold back. Every dirty word coming from her mouth is fuel for my own lust to chase the climax I feel building in my balls. "I can't wait to fuck your throat."

"*Yes.*" She starts to shiver beneath me, then clutches me as if she can climb me from this position. "Oh God. Oh, Connor, I'm right there."

"Come for me. Do it, Billie." I bite her neck, marking her, and she arches her back and clamps down on me so tight, I can't help but let go and follow her over, spilling into her. "That's it. Feel the mess you just made, bumble?"

"*We* made that mess," she murmurs with a satisfied smile as she tries to catch her breath.

"You're a damn good dirty talker, angel," I mutter against her as I roll us both onto our sides, facing each other, still joined together.

I never want to pull out of her.

"I've never done that before," she admits and presses the sweetest kiss over my chest. "You must bring it out in me."

I feel the rumble in my chest as I growl and hug her closer. "I'm glad that this side of you is mine alone."

She's so sweet as she smiles and reaches up to push a piece of my hair off my forehead.

"It's never been like this before," she says, her eyes serious now.

"No," I confirm, dragging my hand down her spine to her arse and back up again to cup her neck in my palm. "No, it's never been like this before."

"It's not just me, then."

I shake my head and kiss her forehead. If she needs reassurances from me that this is special, I'll give them to her all day, every bloody day.

"I have to clean us up." I start to pull away, but she tugs me closer and cups my cheek.

"Why don't we go to the shower together this time?"

Without another word, I pull out of her, climb out of bed, and reach for her, tugging her with me.

"Great idea."

Chapter Thirteen

BILLIE

"I like this bathroom," I inform Connor as we slip into the steamy air. There is not one, not two, but *three* showerheads all doing their jobs, and it's great because that means that no one gets the *cold side* of the space.

He's already lathering up a washcloth with body wash, and then his hands are on me, soaping me up. Connor has strong, grade A hands, but add in the slickness of the soap, and all I can do is let my head fall back and sigh.

"You like that," he murmurs as he turns me so my back is to him and proceeds to wash my back and the globes of my ass.

"Of course, I like this. I like to be touched." I shrug and then his hands stall, and I glance at him over my shoulder. "Why'd you stop?"

He frowns and turns me back to him, skims the back

of his hand down my torso, ghosting over my breasts, and I press my hands to his chest.

Holy crap, the muscles on this guy.

"What's wrong?" I ask him.

"You like to be touched."

I blink up at him, wondering what I'm missing here. "Yeah. I think it's my love language, but I've never taken the stupid test. I don't get touched often, honestly, but it's okay. I make Birdie snuggle me whenever I need it."

His jaw firms at that, and I'm completely lost as to why he's gone cold all of a sudden.

"What did I say wrong?"

"Nothing." He shakes his head and pulls me in for a hug. "You didn't say anything wrong."

"I'm fine, you know. It's not a big deal. I wasn't trying to make you feel bad, not that *that* should make you feel bad. Geez, Connor, I'm sorry—"

He kisses me, stopping the mindless flow of words that I was spewing simply because I didn't know what else to say, and leads me under the spray, rinsing away the suds. When we're all clean and rinsed, he shocks me by lifting me under my thighs and bracing me against the tile. The cold makes me gasp, but then he's sliding inside me, and I wrap my arms around his neck and hold on as my body quakes around him.

"Jesus, how are you still hard? Hell, that's good," I moan as he kisses my shoulder and across my collarbone. He's moving in hard, jarring thrusts as if he can't get deep enough, close enough.

"You're the sweetest bloody woman," he growls next

to my ear, sending goose bumps down my whole body. "Christ Jesus, angel."

He speeds up, and his pelvis hits my clit, over and over again. I let my head fall back against the tile.

"Connor, I'm gonna ... I'm right ... ah, shit."

"Come." It's a hard command. "Look at me."

I open my eyes and stare into his bright, lust-filled gaze, and it tips me over into wonderland, falling apart in his arms.

"Yes, baby." With his gaze still on mine, he groans and follows me over. Watching him come undone is the most beautiful thing I've ever seen in my life.

We're breathing hard. My heart is in overdrive, and he keeps me here, up against the tile. His mouth rests against my shoulder as we try to catch our breath.

"You're so delicious, bumble." His accent is thicker during these moments, and it makes me clench around him.

"Still hate that nickname," I breathe, but push my fingers in his wet hair, enjoying the way the thick strands feel in my fingers.

"Do you want to know why I call you that?" He kisses my shoulder, then drags his tongue over my skin to my neck.

"Yes."

God, he touches me *so well*.

"Because you're strong."

He kisses my pulse point.

"A hard worker."

Kisses my throat.

189

"Always moving."

Kisses my chin.

"So bloody dedicated."

His lips touch mine, and we're breathing the same air.

"My bumble bee."

He's kissing me, and I'm melting into him, clinging to him. I feel him pull out of me, my feet find the tile floor, and he frames my face, kissing me so softly, so *lovingly*, it makes my heart catch.

He pulls back but doesn't release me, and I take him in. His biceps are bunched, showing off his *ridiculously* gorgeous arms. His chest and abs could be those of a Greek god. He's phenomenal in every way.

And he's here with *me*.

I'm a lucky fucking girl.

"It's funny," I whisper as I run my fingertip down the bridge of his nose. "When I think of bumble bees, I picture them covered in pollen, blissed out, and sleeping in a flower."

"That fits you, too," he says and lets his hands fall from me, and I already miss his touch. "Blissed out and covered in my cum, sleeping in my bed."

My jaw drops, then I wrinkle my nose and smack his arm. "That's ... *dirty*."

"There's absolutely *nothing* dirty about that picture." He kisses my nose and smiles down at me in one of those heart-stopping, full-on smiles that are so rare from him, and it makes me feel like I'm glowing. "Now come here and let me get us clean again. You distracted me."

Once we're clean and dry, he leads me back to the bedroom.

"Do you want a shirt?" he asks.

"Nah, I'll sleep naked. It'll just be easier next time."

I know I'm a plus-sized girl, but I'm perfectly comfortable in my skin. Connor doesn't seem to have any complaints, so sleeping in the nude doesn't bother me.

"I have to work for a while," he informs me as I climb into the bed, and I turn to frown at him. "I'm taking tomorrow off, so I have to get a few things done, but I'm going to work from the bed."

"Connor, I can go home, and you can—"

"Absolutely *not*." He's suddenly wrapped around me, holding me against him and pressing kisses all over my face, making me grin. "You're staying here, in this bed, with me. And I'll be right here with you. I just need an hour to tie up some loose ends."

I yawn and nuzzle my nose against his naked chest, enjoying the light smattering of hair there. I'm also relieved that he's not asking me to leave because I have a feeling I'm about to have the best night's sleep I've had in months. "Okay. Go ahead, just don't move a muscle."

He chuckles and kisses me again. I love that he always has his lips on me.

"I'm right here. Go to sleep."

I'm drifting off as I feel him move away, but he doesn't leave the bed. True to his word, he sits up and grabs his laptop. I curl up beside him, listening to the light *click-clack* of the keys as he types. Once in a while, he'll reach down and brush his fingers through my hair, making me sigh.

Yeah, this works.

And before long, I feel myself being pulled down into sleep.

He's passed out next to me, sleeping so soundly, I don't have the heart to wake him. There's light coming through the window, telling me that it's morning, but we're both taking the day off, so there's no hurry to get up.

Aside from the fact that my bladder is screaming at me.

I ease out of the bed, scoop up his shirt, and quietly pad into the bathroom, where I do my business, brush my teeth with his toothbrush—he's had his mouth *all over me* so if he has an issue with me using his toothbrush, I don't know what to tell him—and wash my face.

When I open the bathroom door, I see that he's still asleep, so I decide to go find coffee.

Snagging my handbag from the bathroom, I walk downstairs and pull my phone out and text Millie. The owner of the coffee shop will know how my guy takes his morning brew.

She knows everyone's orders by heart.

Hey girl! How does Connor Gallagher
take his coffee?

When I get to the kitchen, I startle and stare at a gorgeous woman standing at the island.

"Oh, hi there," she says with a bright smile. She looks like she should be on the cover of magazines. "I'm Cassie, Mr. Gallagher's cook. I'm just taking some cinnamon rolls out of the oven."

I'm standing here in just a thigh-length T-shirt because I don't have any clean underwear, my hair is a mess, and Cassie is fucking *beautiful.* Her auburn hair is tied up in a slick bun, she's fit and trim in her skintight tank and yoga pants, and her biceps flex as she takes the pan from the oven, showing that she clearly works out. Often.

And it occurs to me that the house smells amazing. How did I miss that?

"I didn't—" I have to clear my throat. "Do you make that every morning?"

"No, he requested that I make them today. Now I know why." She winks at me, seemingly unfazed by my appearance. "I just have to frost them."

"Is the frosting ready?"

"Sure, it's right here in the bowl."

"Do you mind if I finish up here? I'm going to make an executive decision and give you the rest of the day off."

Her eyebrows fly into her hairline, but I stand my ground. I'm sure she's a nice person, and she hasn't done anything wrong, but I don't love the idea of another woman in this house while Connor and I are having Sunday Fuckday.

I made that one up. I like it.

"Just let these cool for about fifteen minutes," she says, pointing at the pan. "Then spread the frosting over them and enjoy. You can also leave it on the side, if you prefer. They're pretty sweet."

"Thank you. And coffee?"

"It's a simple pod-style machine," she replies, pointing at the built-in machine in the walk-in butler's pantry, which makes my eyes bug out of my head. This pantry is bigger than my entire kitchen. "I know, right? Killer pantry. Makes my life so easy."

"Do you work here every day?" I ask.

"A few days a week. I do a lot of meal prep so he can eat whenever it suits him."

She doesn't have an accent, which I find intriguing.

"Do you travel with him?"

I've known Connor for months, and I've never even heard of Cassie.

"God, no. I should be so lucky. I live in Silver Springs, about thirty minutes from here. I'm a private chef for quite a few people, not just Mr. Gallagher. I usually have Sundays off, but he requested the cinnamon rolls, so I came in to make them." She grins at me. "You're a lucky lady."

"I know." I offer her a smile. "Thanks for these. They smell great."

"Oh, you're welcome. Tell him to let me know if you guys need anything."

And with that, she gives me a wave, and then she's off.

I have to take a deep breath.

I'm not typically the jealous type, but that ... yeah, I didn't like that.

I check my phone and see that Millie has responded.

> Millie: Just black. If you're making him coffee at seven in the fucking morning, that means that you spent the night together! Spill it. Tell me everything. Use the naughty words.

When I didn't reply to that, she sent a follow-up.

> Millie: Hopefully, your silence means he's got his face between your legs to thank you for the coffee. Fill me in later. Go get him!

With a laugh, I set the phone aside and get to work on our coffees as the cinnamon rolls cool.

Maybe I made a rash decision. Cassie isn't *my* employee, so giving her the day off might have been out of line. Hopefully, it doesn't piss Connor off.

With a cringe, I set the coffees on a wooden tray that I found in the pantry, then add two warm cinnamon rolls and a small bowl of frosting on the side. After putting the leftovers in the fridge and covering the rolls with plastic wrap that I also found in the pantry, I carry the tray upstairs and find Connor just coming out of the bathroom, sliding his glasses on his nose.

"You didn't leave," he says when he sees me.

I set the tray on the bed and look around. "Where would I go, and how would I get there?"

He tugs me to him and kisses my lips, then raises an eyebrow and gestures to the food on the bed.

"I have a confession," I say, climbing on the bed. "But we might as well enjoy these before they get cold while I make said confession."

His eyes narrow as he pulls on his gray sweatpants, and then he sits next to me and sips his coffee. "Tell me."

"I sent your cook home for the day."

He lifts an eyebrow but doesn't seem mad, so I take that as a good sign. "Go on."

"Okay." I let out a breath and stare at his chest for a second, trying to decide how I want to phrase this. "It was ... jarring to walk into the kitchen this morning and find a hot woman making breakfast."

Immediately, Connor sets his cup down, scowling, and I shake my head.

"No, let me finish. I'm sure she's a nice girl, and a good cook, if the smell of these cinnamon rolls is anything to go by, but I had no idea that I'd walk into that, and I walked down there like *this*"—I gesture to myself and wrinkle my nose—"although, she didn't seem to mind, or bat an eye, as if that happens all the time, and I—"

He scoops me into his arms and, with his hand on my throat, kisses the hell out of me, sending all thoughts of the chef right out of my mind.

"I'm sorry," he says against my lips. "I forgot to warn you that she was coming this morning."

"Your cook is not an old lady."

His lips twitch. "No, she's not. Would you rather she was?"

"Maybe." I chuckle at myself, feeling so silly, but I can't help myself. "Which is ridiculous."

"I like you jealous, angel."

I narrow my eyes at him and feel my cheeks heat. "I'm not jealous. I just don't like surprises when I'm mostly naked."

He nods, but his lips are still turned up on the side. "Right. Do you want me to fire her?"

I gape at him, panic searing through my chest. "No. Of course not. She didn't do anything wrong."

"Then how do you need me to fix this? Just tell me what you need."

With a sigh, I bite my lip and stare at his mouth. "I feel stupid."

"Well, stop that. Also, let me clear something up. Yes, Cassie is a pretty woman. *No*, I've never even considered fucking her. I met her after I met you, and I was already consumed by you, but even if that weren't the case, I don't pursue employees, *and* she's not my type. Second, I need you to be comfortable here. I want you here as much as possible. Bring a suitcase full of your things and move right in, as far as I'm concerned. So if having Cassie here makes you uncomfortable, I'll either make other arrangements, or we'll make do without a cook. You won't walk into another situation like that again, I can promise you that. There is nowhere in this house that's off-limits to you, and if you want to walk around as naked as the day you were born, by all means, do so. In fact, I highly encourage it."

I snort and lean my forehead on his shoulder as relief floods me. He's not mad. He wants me to be comfortable. And he wants me to *stay*.

He lifts my chin so he can look into my eyes.

"Understand?"

"Yeah, and thank you. I actually liked her. If you're happy with her, she's fine, but not on Sunday Fuckdays."

He barks out a laugh at that, and I grin at him.

"Deal. Sundays are just for us, then. Also, you'll want to talk with Cassie so she knows what your preferences are."

"My preferences?"

"For meals. Snacks. That sort of thing."

"How often do you plan on me being here, billionaire?"

"Like I said, I'd be happy if you were here all the time."

I stare at him, skimming my fingertips down his cheek as I take a long, deep breath. "I guess it's not exactly *fast* since we've known each other so long, but when you decide to get swoony, you really go for it, don't you?"

He frowns at me. "What does that mean?"

"We went from *Connor barely speaks to me and only kisses me at family functions* to *move your shit into my mountain mansion and tell the sexy cook what you like to eat* in about ten minutes flat."

"I know what I want," he replies, setting me aside so he can reach for his now tepid coffee. "If you prefer we stay at your place, that's fine. I'll bring a bag over later today."

I blink at him, then reach for my own coffee. "Maybe we bring things to each other's places."

He grins, that full smile that takes my breath away, and I feel like I just won the lottery. "Deal."

Sunday Fuckday was a success, and now that it's Monday, my body feels loose from all the amazing sex. I'm well rested after two full nights of blissful sleep, and I'm ready to get back to work.

I have four interviews first thing this morning. Once the fourth is finished, I join Tiffany at the checkout counter and grin at her.

"Which ones do you like the best?" she asks.

"All of them. There's no way to choose. I'm hiring all of them."

"All *four*?" Tiffany questions. "Holy shit, that's awesome."

"Gina said she loves working with online orders, shipping and packing, that kind of thing, which is so great because our online store is starting to go bananas. I think all of them will be assets to the team. And they can all start this week."

"This is *amazing*." Tiffany grins. "I love it here, Billie. The store is so inviting and cozy, and hell, I would live here."

"You already come in on your days off to read," I remind her with a laugh. "You're almost too dedicated."

"Never." She loops an arm around my shoulders and gives me a squeeze. "Tonight is Spicy Girls Book Club?"

"Yep. Are you coming?"

"I can't. I have other plans, but I'll be there next month for sure. What's the next read going to be?"

"I think we're looking at dark hockey romance. *The Pucking Wrong Number* by CR Jane. I hear it's super sexy and more than a little unhinged."

"I *love* hockey romance. I'm in."

"I need to finish this month's book," I reply with a frown. "Maybe I can take a couple of hours this afternoon if things slow down."

"I don't see why not."

The bell over the door dings, and I turn to welcome the customer, then freeze.

"Juliet?"

My heart thumps, and I rush around the counter to run to the woman I considered a big sister for so long. I wrap my arms around her, hugging her tight.

She sniffs next to my ear, clinging to me.

"Hey, bug," she says, calling me the nickname she gave me as a kid. "God, you're fucking gorgeous, you know that? I missed you so much."

"I missed you, too," I whisper as I let the tears flow. "I'm still mad at you."

"I know. I'll make it up to you. I promise."

I pull back, and she brushes my tears from my face.

"Is it true? Are you really moving back here and opening a restaurant?"

She wipes at her own tears and nods. Her dark hair is a riot of curls, just the way I remember it. She's not wearing any makeup and dressed casually in a pink tank top and shorts. It's *so good* to see her.

I always thought she was the most beautiful girl in the world. I was so lucky that Brooks loved her, and I got to have her as my big sister.

Then the world blew apart, and them with it, and she was just ... gone.

"It's true," she says. "And you own a whole book-store, which is so fucking badass."

"Check it out," I say, gesturing to the shelves. "It's mostly all romance, with a little women's fiction and thriller thrown in. Do you still like to read?"

"Are you kidding? Of course, I do."

"Good."

Juliet used to sneak me her romance novels when I was much too young to be reading them, but she's why I love books so much.

And she's back.

"What do you recommend?" she asks.

"You need Laura Pavlov in your life, my friend. Brandy Hynes. Marni Mann. Adriana Locke. Come on, I'll hook you up."

For the next hour, we talk about books, and Jules builds a stack that she wants to leave with, making me laugh.

"I didn't expect you to buy me out," I tell her while I'm ringing her up.

"Are you kidding? I'll be your best customer." She winks at me and taps her card to the screen. "How's your brother?"

And just like that, my smile falls.

"Jules, I can't—"

"I just need to know that he's okay." Her voice is quiet, her eyes pleading with me, and I let out a breath.

"He's okay."

"Thank you." She holds up her hand. "I know that if I want to know more, I should seek him out. And maybe once I've had enough liquid courage one day, I will. But today is not that day, so I'm going to bury my nose in one of these stories, satisfied with the knowledge that there will be a happily ever after in them."

"Come back often and keep me posted on the restaurant."

"Will do, bug." She smiles and walks out, and I rub the spot over my chest.

God, I've fucking missed her.

Seeing that there's no one else in the shop, I fetch my Kindle from my handbag and take a seat in one of my plush lounge chairs.

Good God, my glutes, my inner thighs, and my core are all so ... *tender.*

I can't help the smug smile that comes at the thought.

"Goddamn, your mouth looks so fucking good wrapped around my cock," he said as I worked him over in the kitchen, unable to keep my hands to myself while we made lunch.

And later, in the lounge area off the bedroom, we snuggled up watching a movie when Connor slipped his hand between my legs.

"I need to make you come again."

His fingers pressed inside me, all the way to the first knuckle, while his thumb brushed over my hard clit, and I saw stars as I came apart, my climax rolling through me in waves.

"You're so bloody beautiful when you come."

With a happy shimmy of my shoulders, I open my book.

This month's read is *Crossroads* by Devney Perry, and it's *brilliant.* I've cried so much while reading it, so swept up in this beautiful second-chance story, but I only have about 15 percent left, so I hope the tears are finished for this tale. It should be a happy ever after from here on out.

Fifteen minutes later, I couldn't be more wrong.

I have to set the device aside and bury my face in my hands as I sob, not even caring anymore about the state of my makeup. Suddenly, I feel a hand brush down my hair, and I open my eyes to find Connor squatting before me, his concerned eyes so full of worry as he cups the side of my neck.

"Who hurt you, angel?"

I shake my head and brush away the tears, taking a deep breath. "No one."

"Just tell me, and I'll take care of it."

I can't resist taking his hand in mine and kissing his palm. "No one hurt me. I'm finishing my book for tonight's book club meeting, and it's so good, and *so fucking sad*. This author has such a brilliant way with words, and I just fell apart."

My breath is choppy. Connor stands, pulls me to my feet, then sits and tugs me onto his lap. He holds me against him, and it feels like I belong right here, snuggled up to him.

"In the book," I continue, resting my head on his shoulder as he presses kisses to my forehead, "she loses her dad, and it's so sad, and it made me miss my dad because they didn't come home this summer. Mom's been volunteering for a lot of stuff in Florida, and I don't have time to go see them. Anyway, it's silly."

"It's not silly." He tightens his hold on me and kisses my forehead. "Would you like to go visit them tonight, then?"

I frown and pull back so I can stare up at him. "What in the hell?"

"I have the jet. We can leave after your book club meeting, and you can join them for breakfast tomorrow."

Holy. Fucking. Shit.

"Okay, billionaire, take the rich-guy thing down a notch. That's crazy."

"It's not crazy, *mo rúnsearc*." He kisses my forehead

and then my cheek. "You miss them. I can make sure you see them."

This man likes to fix things. And I love that he wants to do this for me, but it's a little over the top.

"Thank you." I kiss his lips softly as I wrap my arms around his neck. "I know you're not kidding, and you'd make it happen."

"Just give me the word."

"But I can't leave tonight. I have new employees to see to."

He narrows his eyes at me. "You hired them, then?"

"Yes. Four new girls, and I'm excited."

He tilts his head and nods. "Good. It scared me when I walked in and saw you upset. I don't like it when you're unhappy. It doesn't sit well with me."

"You're sweet."

Connor laughs at that. "I don't think anyone has ever accused me of being sweet a day in my life, angel."

"Then they're wrong." I kiss his cheek and breathe him in. "I'll be late tonight. I'll just crash at my place."

"I'll meet you there," he replies.

"You don't have to—"

"I'll meet you there, bumble. No arguments."

With a smile, I hug him back. "Okay, billionaire. No arguments."

Chapter Fourteen

CONNOR

"Take me home, Miller," I say as I exit the bookshop and get in the back seat of the SUV.

I have calls to make, work to do, and I need to pack a bag to take to Billie's house this evening.

Speaking of that, Miller's not going to like this news.

Not that it matters.

"I'll be staying at Billie's tonight," I inform him as he pulls onto the road. I don't miss the way he frowns at me in the rearview, and I raise an eyebrow at him. "Problem?"

"Her security is shit."

He's not telling me anything I don't know.

"Doesn't change anything about where I'll be spending the night."

Miller simply sighs and keeps his mouth shut, which is wise.

My goal is to get Billie moved in with me sooner

rather than later. Not because there's anything at all wrong with her home—aside from the security. I just want her in mine.

Permanently.

My phone rings, and I smile when I see the name of an old friend on the screen.

"Kane," I say in greeting. "So nice of you to return my call. From four bleeding days ago."

"I don't answer the fecking phone," he reminds me, sounding as cheerful as ever. "If my wife didn't remind me to look at it once in a while, I wouldn't even have it."

"And how is Stasia?" I ask him. "Does she miss me? I bet she pines."

"Go feck yourself," he mutters, making me grin. "She can't stand you, and you know it. Why are you bleedin' calling me, boyo?"

"Are you on your island these days or in Galway?"

Kane and I grew up together as boys in Galway. He and his family moved to an island off the coast of Seattle before we were teenagers, but we stayed in touch. I went into the family business, but Kane became a world-renowned glass artist, with museums dedicated to his work in several major cities across the globe.

His pieces are owned by royalty, celebrities, and anyone willing to pay a lot of money for them.

"We're on the island right now," he says, "but we'll be headed over to Galway in about a week. I have a show opening in the Galway gallery in two weeks."

I narrow my eyes. "You don't say. What might an old mate of yours have to do to get two tickets to that?"

"Buy one of my pieces that night, and we'll call it even."

"I can do that. I also want to talk to you about a commission."

Miller pulls up in front of my house, and I walk inside and straight through to my office, where I put the call on speaker and set the phone on my desk.

"What do you want?" he asks. I can hear the scowl in his voice, and it makes me chuckle.

"You know, for someone who charges a feckton of money for his art, you sure complain about making it."

"That's part of the job," he says easily. "What are you after then, mate?"

"I want a piece for my Montana home, but it's a gift for my girl."

He's quiet for a moment. "Say that again."

"Shut up."

"No, did you just say that you have a girl? Wait, this *is* Connor Gallagher, and I didn't dial the wrong bleeding number, right?"

"You're a prick," I inform him, finally making him laugh. "I want blues and greens, inspired by the mountains. I can send you pictures of the scenery around here. Or you can swing through here on your way to Ireland if you have time."

"It's always better to see it in person," he murmurs, and I can tell the wheels are turning. "But I don't think I can make it work before Galway. I could do it on the way back."

"I can make that work," I confirm. "I'd like the piece here in a few weeks."

There's another heavy pause. "Are you an eejit? I don't dance on command, and you know it. That timing is impossible."

"Kane—"

"However," he continues, "I have a few pieces already done that aren't coming with me to Ireland, and I have one particular in mind that might work. I'll send you a photo now."

I pick up my phone, and when the image comes through, my eyebrows lift. "Aye, that's beautiful, mate. I'll take it."

"It was meant for the museum, so it'll cost you."

"I'll pay double your standard fee."

He growls in my ear, and I laugh because Kane never passes up extra money, despite being good and wealthy in his own right.

"Fine. We'll make it work. Tell me about her."

I shove my hands in my pockets and stare out at the mountains I've grown to love over the past year.

"She's everything, mate. That's the long and the short of it."

"Welcome to the club," he says, sounding cheerful for the first time. "I'll see you soon."

He hangs up, and I sit at the desk and dial another number.

"This is Cassie," my chef answers. "How can I help you, Mr. Gallagher?"

"I'd like to make some changes to our arrangement."

I outline exactly what I expect of her moving forward. When I'm finished, I can hear the smile in her voice.

"Oh, this is no problem. I thought this call might be coming. I'm sorry if I made Billie uncomfortable in any way."

"It's not your fault. I'll give her your number so she can call you and inform you of her preferences."

"I look forward to that. Thanks, Mr. Gallagher."

I end that call, then check the time and make one more.

"Anderson," my architect barks in my ear.

"I want you to build me a library. Today."

He laughs. "Of course, you do. I can't do it today."

I grind my molars together. "When?"

"First, I need information. How big? Are we remodeling existing rooms or adding on to the house? Is this for you?"

I close my eyes. I don't want to explain any more. I just want it to *happen.*

"I'll get more information and call you back. I want this project to move fast, Anderson."

"When the hell *don't* you want it to move fast?" He snorts. "Get me more info, and I'll see what I can do."

I should pass this along to an assistant, but I want anything I plan for my angel to come from me. Strangely, for me anyway, this isn't about control. I've learned to delegate well over the years and have built skilled and trustworthy teams across several countries. *But for Billie?* For the woman who has become my everything? Only I can design what I want her to luxuriate in. Only I can ensure every chair is as comfortable to read in as the ones in her shop. And only I can guarantee that when she walks into *her* library, she feels ... cherished. Adored.

Loved.

After two more hours of work, I meet Miller at the car, where he's waiting with the back door open.

This man knows my schedule better than I do.

Ten minutes later, we pull up to my sister, Skyla, and her boyfriend's farmhouse.

Beckett Blackwell owns this ranch and the dairy farm on it and does well with the business. He also built eight small cabins in the woods with an incredible view of the mountains to use as vacation rentals, and although they rent well enough, Beckett has discovered that dealing with guests is his least favorite thing in all the world.

So he's taken them off the rental market, and we're working to offer them to families with sick children who want to come here on holiday.

I'm providing the charity and the money, and Beckett's providing the cabins—for a fee of course—and we're going to build a lodge for more guest suites, a kitchen, and a common area.

"You're the only bloke I know who would come out to a ranch in a suit," Skyla says as she steps out onto the porch and grins at me.

"I've been working," I inform her and pull her in for a hug. "No time to change. Where's your man, then?"

"He's coming over from the barn," she replies as her dog, Riley, steps outside with her.

I scratch his head between his ears, and he leans into

211

me, reminding me of my bumble bee and how much she loves to be touched.

I like to be touched.

When she said those words to me in the shower, I felt … shame. Because everything slipped into place at that moment.

She loves sex, but she blooms when she's snuggled.

She leans into my hand when I cup her cheek.

She can only sleep well when I have my arms wrapped around her.

It made me feel so much shame that I hadn't picked up on it sooner, and I'll spend the rest of my life making sure she's treasured, if she'll let me.

"I'm looking forward to getting this project off the ground," she says as I hear Beckett walk up and join us.

We pile into a UTV with Riley and head over to the cabins on the other side of the property. Just as every time before, when we come around the bend and the mountains are revealed from behind some trees, my breath catches.

The mountains are spread out before us, with a pretty meadow full of wildflowers in the foreground, and it's simply stunning.

Yes, it's going to be perfect for our charity.

"We're thinking about building the lodge over here," Skyla begins, pointing to just behind the cabins. "The first floor won't have much of a view, but the second floor, where all the suites would be, will have a great view of those mountains."

We walk the space, making plans and taking notes,

and when we're finished, I prop my hands on my hips and turn to the man my sister loves.

"You're sure about this, then?"

"I am," he says as he wraps his arm around Skyla and tugs her into his side. "I'm still surprised that you want to use *my* ranch for this, but I love the idea of offering it to families who want some special time together. My guys and I are already planning ahead to horseback rides, lessons, and tours of the dairy operation, if people want it. And we can put together information for fishing and rafting guides, hiking excursions, all kinds of things."

"I think that's excellent," I reply with a nod. "We'll finish the plans for the lodge, and if all goes as intended, we should open by spring. In the meantime, you're losing revenue because you've stopped offering nightly rentals here."

"It won't break me." He shrugs.

"I'm going to pay you what your normal average monthly revenue would be from now until we're able to open next year."

"No." Beckett shakes his head, and Skyla clamps her lips closed, holding back a grin. "I don't need the money."

"You told me last year that you depend on that money."

"The dairy's doing well enough to make up the difference."

"I don't fecking care." I shake my head. "You don't need to struggle while we're gearing up for this. Consider it coming from Skyla if you don't want it from me."

"I don't want it from her, either."

I raise an eyebrow, and now Skyla snorts.

"It's fun to watch the pair of you spar back and forth," she says. "You're both so bleeding stubborn, I'll be interested to see who wins."

"I'm not with your sister for her money."

"No one thinks you are," I reply. "I never said that."

We stare each other down for a couple of minutes, and then Beckett glances down at my sister.

"No."

"We'll revisit this conversation," I reply. "Changing the subject, I'd like to fly your parents here in time for Sunday dinner this weekend."

Beckett scowls. "Why?"

"Because Billie misses them, and I caught her crying this afternoon because of it, and I can fix that. Billie doesn't need to be crying over anything at all."

Skyla's smile is a mile wide.

"Are you going to tell me what the fuck's going on between you and my sister?" Beckett asks.

"I'm falling in love with her."

He blinks at that, and Skyla's eyes fill with tears.

"Oh, Connor." She sniffles and wipes her cheek. "Oh, that's lovely. She's my best friend, and—"

"Whoa." Beckett holds up a hand. "That's romantic and all, but isn't it fast?"

"I've known her longer than you've known Skyla." I cross my arms over my chest. "What else do you have to say?"

"I—" He shakes his head. "Well, hell. Billie has a soft heart, and she's smart as fuck, and—"

"I know." My voice isn't as hard when I interrupt him. I know what it is to love a sister and be worried about her. Mine is standing right next to him. "She's the best woman I've ever met, and that's the truth of it, Beckett. She misses her da, and it made her cry today, so I'm going to make sure she sees him and your mum. Do you want to call them, or do you want me to handle it?"

"Just send me the information, and I'll forward it to them," Beckett says. "We'll get them here."

I nod and tug my sister to me so I can hug her and kiss her wee head.

"Stop crying, *a stór*."

"It's not a sad cry." She sniffs. "It's a happy one. I have to get ready for our book club."

"Don't tell her about her parents coming for a visit," I say. "It's a surprise."

"I can keep a secret." She bites her lip, then bounces on her toes. "But thank the gods I don't have to keep it for long."

"You're *not* good at keeping a secret."

"Uh, yes, I am. I didn't tell Ma and Da that I was being stalked for *three years*."

"That's because you're a bloody moron," I counter.

"While I don't disagree that that was a mistake," Beckett interjects, "I can't let you call my woman a moron, man."

"I'm her brother."

"Still." He shrugs. "Can't do it."

215

"Fine, I'll do it when you're not around."

Skyla snorts, and we head back to the house. Before she runs inside to get ready, Skyla wraps her arms around me again and hugs me tight.

"I'm really happy for you," she says. "Be nice to her, or I'll make your life a living hell."

"Thank you." I kiss her cheek, and then she's off, leaving Beckett and me standing in the driveway. "Are you going to warn me as well, then?"

"Nah, Skyla can make you suffer more than I can," he says. "And you already know that if it got too bad, my brothers and I would simply kill you and feed you to the goats."

I blink at him. "I thought goats were vegetarians."

"Goats will eat anything." He smiles at me and pats me on the back. "Wanna stay for dinner?"

"No thanks. I have work to do. I'll be in touch about everything."

I get in the back of the SUV, ready to go home. After packing a bag for tonight, I'll work until it's time to go get my angel.

Because even a few hours without her are too bloody long.

Chapter Fifteen

BILLIE

"**B**ook club time is the *best* time," Polly Wild announces before taking her final bite of a cherry tart that Jackie brought from The Sugar Studio. "It's my favorite night of the month."

"Absolutely," Dani agrees with a nod.

It makes me so happy that these ladies love this time together as much as I do. My staff and I work hard to make sure everything is ready for our book club nights, and it's honestly my favorite thing, too. Not to mention, I love that Skyla, Dani, and I came up with it one day.

Best spontaneous decision ever.

Once everyone is armed with next month's read, and the crowd has thinned down to our core group of besties, Millie, Alex, Dani, Skyla, and I sit with a glass of wine and grin at each other.

"That was fun," I say.

"Best one yet," Millie agrees. "Our group keeps growing."

"Yeah, yeah, we love spicy books, blah blah blah," Alex says, waving us off. "I want to hear about Billie and Connor because I have sources—who I'll never disclose—who have seen them all over town together, looking super cozy and mushy and cute, and we haven't had a girls' night since the night of the bar, and you need to spill it, girl."

"Hold up." I raise a hand and shake my head. "You're skipping something *very* important, friend. We need to know about the two dudes you went home with that night."

"*Excuse me*?" Millie interrupts. "What in the actual fuck? Why do I always miss the good stuff? You left with *two* men? Alex Lexington! Wait until I tell your brother."

"You will absolutely *not* tell my brother," Alex says with a smug smile. Millie is married to Dani and Alex's older brother, Holden, and the siblings are super close to each other. "I forbid it. Anywho, yes, I met two amazing men at the bar that night, Adam and Gabe, and *yes*, I'm still seeing them both, and the sex is off the charts, and you're all jealous of me."

"Wait, you're having sex with *both* of them?" Skyla demands. "On the regular, and you haven't told us?"

"Oh girl," Alex replies, fanning her face. "Hell to the yes. And they have sex with each other, and it's a whole magical thing."

We're all quiet as we stare at our friend. Dani frowns at her twin as if she's grown a second head.

"Why didn't you tell me?" Dani demands, hurt coating her voice.

"Well, at first I thought it was just going to be a drunken one-night thing, but now it's sort of ... *not.*"

"What does that mean?" I ask her.

"It's kind of turning into a relationship. A *throuple*, if you will. It's new and different, and I don't even know how things will shake out because it's so outside of societal norms, but ... they're both incredible. There's no way I could choose between them, and I don't have to."

I don't know my cousin Gabe well, but I've known for a long time that he's bisexual. He's a good guy, and I'm happy that he's moved here so I can get to know him better.

"I mean, they're sexy as fuck," I add. Alex blushes, which is so unlike her, and I can't help but laugh. "Millie, one of her new men is my cousin Gabe. His family is from Silver Springs, but he recently moved over here to work for Brooks at the garage."

"Reeeeeally," Millie says, drawing out the word. "I've met Gabe a few times. That man is *sexy.* Who's the other guy?"

"His name is Adam." Alex tucks her hair behind her ear, still blushing. "He's only been living here for about a year."

"And what does Adam do?" Skyla asks. "Besides you and Gabe."

I can't help but snort at that. *God, my friends are funny.*

"He's in finance." Alex shrugs a shoulder, and we all stare at her. "What?"

"Let me get this straight," Dani says, leaning in.

"You're currently in a *situationship* with two hot dudes. One is a blue-collar grease monkey and one is a rich, wears-a-suit, white-collar guy?"

"I didn't say he was rich," Alex says, then nods when we all just keep staring at her. "Okay, he's loaded. Like stupid rich. Maybe not as wealthy as Connor or Ryan, but he's doing better than most."

"Wow." Millie holds up her glass of wine. "Cheers to you, girl."

"We just want you to be happy," I agree with a nod. "And based on what I saw that night, they're both nice guys. I already knew that about Gabe, but you know what I mean."

"It doesn't suck to be worshipped by two hot men at once," she admits with a smug grin. "Anyway, I'll keep you posted on that. Now, Bee needs to spill the beans."

"My beans are not as spicy as the ones you just shared," I reply. "Although, to be fair, Connor *is* damn fucking spicy in his own right. Things are good, guys. I asked him for more than sex, and he's delivering. There is swoon *and* sex, and it's awesome."

Dani's head tilts to the side as she examines my face. "What aren't you telling us?"

"Nothing."

Do I sound defensive? Yeah. Dammit, I do.

I smooth out the skirt of the Louis Vuitton dress I'm wearing, then sip my wine, but they're still silent, waiting for an answer.

Why do I have besties who know me so well? It's fucking inconvenient.

"It scares me," I admit in a low voice. Dani immediately reaches out to take my hand, giving it a squeeze. "And you know that I'm not self-conscious about how I look, and I know I'm badass, but part of me is doing the whole *why me* thing. Like is he only giving me *more* because he also wants the sex? Did I twist his arm? And when he's decided that he's over it, will he move on to someone richer? Prettier? Smarter?"

"Whoa," Skyla says, shaking her head. "I can tell you that none of that is true. If he's giving you *more*, it's because he wants to. My brother doesn't do relationships. He always said that it caused entanglements he didn't want to deal with. And I've spoken with him, Bee. You can relax and enjoy him because I don't think he'll be *over it* anytime soon."

I take a deep breath at that and sip my wine. In safe spaces like this, I'm comfortable having a little alcohol again.

"You think?"

"I know," she replies. "Also, Connor's levelheaded. When you start to feel insecure, talk to him."

Talk to me, angel.

He says that all the time. Maybe I need to be bolder about asking for what I want. I asked for *more*, and he gave it to me.

"Maybe I need to trust him more," I murmur. "Sometimes he can be a little intimidating, you know?"

"No, not a sexy-as-hell billionaire." Alex chuckles. "I'd be shocked if you *didn't* have moments of being intimidated."

"I guess that's true."

The bell over the door dings, and in walks the man himself. He's changed from his suit to black jeans and a short-sleeved black button-down. I'm pretty sure my vagina just started to drool, thanks to the way those short sleeves hug his biceps.

He walks straight for me, pulls me out of the chair, and tips my chin up so he can kiss the hell out of me.

"Get it, girl," Millie calls out while the others whoop and clap, and I can't help but laugh against his lips.

"I missed you," he says, kissing my forehead.

"And that's our cue to leave," Dani declares. "It was fun tonight, ladies. Next month, it's unhinged dark hockey players for the win."

Connor's eyebrows lift in surprise, and I laugh as I pull away and walk my friends to the door.

"Drive safe, guys."

"See you," Dani says, giving me a hug. "Call me if you need me."

"Same goes, always." I kiss her cheek. When they're all gone, I lock the door behind them. When I turn, Connor's watching me, his hands in his pockets. "You didn't have to pick me up here."

"It was on the way to your house," he reminds me. "What do you need me to do?"

"It's all done," I reply and cross to him, smoothing my hand up his chest to his cheek. "I just have to turn off the lights."

He takes my hand and kisses my palm, sending a spark down my arm.

With a grin, I walk away and into the back of the store, where the electrical box is. I've just shut off the light switch when I feel him behind me.

"I don't think I can wait to do this until we get to your place." He pushes my hair to the side, exposing my neck, and brushes wet kisses up to my hairline, making me lean back into him.

"It's only five minutes from here." My voice has gone rough and breathy. He's gathering the skirt of my dress up until it's around my waist, and his hand is between my legs, brushing over the tiny scrap of my thong.

"Too far," he growls. "Bleedin' hell, you're so wet for me."

One finger slips through my folds and plunges inside me, and I whimper as I lean my forehead against the wall in front of me.

"Connor."

"So tight," he whispers against my skin as he peppers kisses along the slope of my shoulder. "So bloody *everything*. I can't keep my hands to myself."

"I don't want you to." He adds a second finger, and I quiver around him. "Fuck, I'm gonna—"

"Not yet," he growls next to my ear. "My greedy girl, you're not going to come quite yet. All I've thought about today is you. When I'm supposed to be working, you're in my head. Your smart mouth and your sweet smile and the way this pussy tightens around me."

"Oh my God."

I hear his zipper behind me, the rustle of fabric, and then the crown of his cock is *right there.*

"Tell me."

"I want you," I moan, pushing my ass back at him, practically begging him to fuck me already. "Please."

"That's my girl." He pushes inside me all the way, and he's so big. I'm so full, I can't help myself from crying out. "You take me so well, *mo rúnsearc*. Christ, you're so fucking beautiful."

With his hands on my hips, he sets a punishing rhythm, his hips slapping my ass with every thrust.

"Connor ... ah, hell. Fuck, I'm going to come. I can't—"

"Do it," he says, fisting his hand in my hair at the nape of my neck, and when he tugs, there's no stopping the climax that consumes me. "That's it. That's my girl. God, you're so bloody gorgeous when you let go like that."

He pumps into me three more times, and then he's grinding against me as he groans, filling me up as he comes, his forehead resting on my shoulder.

After a moment, he pulls out, and I can feel the mess of us run down my thigh, but it just makes me laugh in surprise. He just railed me against the wall because he *missed me.*

That doesn't suck.

"I'll be right back." But first, I turn around and pull him down to kiss me. "And for the record, I missed you, too."

He flashes that sexy-as-all-get-out grin before I pull away and go clean myself up in the bathroom.

When I walk back out, mostly cleaned up, I find him

leaning against the wall, his arms crossed over his chest. He's a sight to behold.

"We're walking to your place from here," he informs me, surprising me.

"We are? Won't Miller be mad?"

"Miller works for *me*, not the other way around, and it's a lovely summer evening. I want to take a stroll with you, angel."

I can't help but smile at him.

"Unless your feet hurt in those death traps you call shoes."

"My death traps are perfectly comfortable," I reply as I take his offered hand, and we walk out the front door. "Oh, but my car is parked out back."

"I'll have Miller handle it."

"Poor Miller. He shouldn't have to do that."

Connor laughs and kisses the back of my hand. "Trust me, Miller's just fine."

I lock the door, set the alarm, and then, with my hand clutched in his and our fingers laced, we walk side by side down the sidewalk toward my house.

"Tell me about your ideal home library," he says, making me frown up at him.

"What do you mean?"

"If you could dream up any library you'd have in a home, what would it look like?"

"I mean, there are factors here. How big could it be? How much light is there? I used the formal dining room in my house and converted it into a small library, and I like it, but it's really small."

"It could literally be *anything* you want, bumble."

I blink at that, thinking it over, then I pull my phone out of my cross-body handbag.

"I just so happen to have an entire Pinterest board dedicated to this topic." I tap the screen, select the app, and once I've found what I'm looking for, I show it to the sexy man walking next to me. "I love the idea of a room with a monochromatic design. Personally, I'd love a sage green or a pretty blue, like this one. So the walls, the trim, and the bookshelves are all the same because I'd want to showcase the books. I'd want brass hardware and light fixtures, and I'd have these super deep, comfortable chairs with ottomans. Little tables at the side to hold a drink and maybe a snack."

I glance up to see if he's listening, and he's staring down at my phone intently as if he's taking mental notes.

"Send that to me," he says.

"I'm not done." I flip to another photo. "See how the shelves are floor to ceiling? That's a must-have. I don't want to waste any space at the top of the bookcase."

"Send it all to me, bumble."

I shake my head and close out of the app, but before I can pop the phone back in my purse, a text comes in from my cousin, Gabe, and the notification shows the beginning of his message.

> Gabe: Hey, beautiful, I have a question ...

Connor stops walking, and I look up at him. "What's wrong?"

226

"Who in the bloody fucking shite is *Gabe*?"

I blink at him, then look back down at my phone and open the message so I can read the whole thing.

> Gabe: Hey, beautiful, I have a question. Do you happen to know when Alex's birthday is? Adam and I want to surprise her with something, and I need to know if I can make it a part of her birthday present or if that's too far away. Help a guy out.

I turn the phone up to show him the screen and watch as Connor's eyes narrow. He reads the text, then his eyes jump up to mine.

"Gabe is one of the guys Alex went home with that night at the bar. He's also my cousin. That's how he has my number. Alex and the guys have decided that that wasn't just a one-night deal, and they're in a relationship, all three of them. She told us about it tonight."

I slip my phone into my purse, then close the distance between us, wrap my arms around Connor's middle, and press my face to his chest, hugging him close. I both love and hate his jealousy. I don't have anything to hide from my amazing billionaire.

"I'm sorry," he whispers before he kisses the top of my head and wraps his arms around me.

"Don't be." I press my lips over his heart. "I'd have been jealous, too. I don't mind if you get a little jealous now and then."

I tip my head back to look up into his face, and I have to take a breath because his eyes burn with intensity.

"But you need to know that you're the only man in my life, and when you told me that I'm all you see, it works both ways, Connor. You can go through my phone if you want and put the tracking app on it so you always know where I am. I don't care because I will never betray you like that. I—"

Before I can get another word out, he's framed my face, and his lips have crushed mine in a hot, desperate kiss that feels so different from any of the kisses we've shared. My head spins, and I moan against him. When he pulls back, we're both breathing hard as he brushes his thumb along my lower lip.

"I don't want or need to go through your phone, angel. I trust you implicitly. I simply don't take kindly to seeing another man's name call my woman *beautiful*."

"I am beautiful," I remind him, making the edges of his lips tip up. "So you'd better stay at the top of your game, billionaire."

"Is that so?"

I laugh and turn to continue walking to my house. "I love summer because it stays light out so late. It's almost ten, and the sun hasn't even set yet. Is Ireland far enough north to still be light out this late?"

"Aye, it is," he replies. "The days are long in the summer and short in the winter, just like here."

"Does it snow?"

He smiles down at me and tucks my hair behind my ear. "Mostly just in the high country. For the most part, winter is rainy and dark. Dreary."

I nod as we turn down my block. My house is just three doors down.

"That must be why Skyla loves the snow so much here. She's trying to talk me into going skiing this year." I make a face at that as we walk up to my front door.

"Not a skier then, are you?"

"No. Hell no. It's too cold for that. This past winter, the day after I met you, in fact, Birdie and my brothers talked me into going up to the resort for sledding since it had snowed so much."

I push inside my house and toss my keys on the table next to the door, then immediately kick out of my shoes.

"I went up there, but no. I didn't sled. I watched and drank hot chocolate. Took pictures. Threw snowballs at my brothers. Then we relaxed in the lodge."

"If you don't like to sled, why did you go?"

"Because my family wanted me there, and I love watching Birdie play."

I sit on the couch and wiggle my toes, thankful to be off my feet. Connor sits on the coffee table in front of me. He lifts my foot into his lap and starts to massage it, making me moan.

"You never should have shown me that talent you have there." I lean my head back and moan.

"And why is that?"

"Because now I'll expect this kind of treatment on the regular."

"And you'll get it." He lifts my foot and kisses the pad of my big toe, making me scrunch up my nose.

"Ew. I've been on those feet all day, you know."

"It doesn't bother me." He digs his thumb into the arch of my foot, making me moan again. "Keep making that noise, and I'll have to get you naked again."

I open one eye and stare at him for a second, then moan.

Suddenly, I'm in the air, on his shoulder, and he's marching down the hallway to the bedroom.

"Connor!"

"I warned you." He drops me on the bed, his smile feral as he unbuttons his shirt. "Now you pay the consequences."

"Consequences of what?"

"Being sexy as fuck."

He sets me on my feet next to the bed and pulls my dress over my head in one swift motion. I'm in a simple bralette and thong, and I'm pulling his shirt out of his jeans, exposing the abs that make me lose my mind.

"Christ Jesus, you've a body that would make the gods weep," he says as his hands drift down my chest to my breasts, almost reverently.

"Naked." I'm pushing at his clothes. "Get naked, Connor."

He complies, then we're on the bed, and he's pulling my panties down my hips and pressing them to his nose. His eyes close, and he hums, then sets them aside before spreading my legs wide and leaning in to lick my entire slit, making my hips buck.

"So bloody wet," he mutters in a rough voice before diving in and sinking his tongue inside me. "Look at this needy pussy. I can taste both of us down here, baby."

His fingers replace his tongue, and now he's sucking on my clit, and I'm writhing on the bed. Is that my voice, whimpering, begging, crying out?

"Connor."

"What do you need, angel?"

"You. Please."

"Tell me, *a ghrá*. Use your words."

I don't know what the Gaelic means, but it sounds so fucking sexy, it sends me closer to coming apart.

"Inside me." That's all I can get out. My hands are in his hair, pulling on him. "Please. I need you inside me."

He moves fast, covering me, and his mouth slides over mine, so gently this time that it almost brings tears to my eyes. "You're all I see, angel."

I hitch my leg up higher on his hip as I reach between us and take his thick, hard length in my hand. I lead him to me, moving the crown through my wet folds, making his eyes close on a sigh.

"Connor. Please."

Those gorgeous eyes open, and he sinks inside me, making us both moan with it.

He starts to move, watching me as he pushes in and out of me. "Do you feel how wet you are?"

"Yes." Reaching between us again, I cover my finger in the wetness, then brush it over my clit, making me clench harder, and his jaw tenses.

He pushes the bralette up, freeing my breasts, and clenches his mouth around one nipple, pulling hard, and my back arches up off the bed.

"Connor."

"That's right." He's moving harder, faster, and it's the perfect tempo.

"I'm right there."

He doesn't change a *thing*, which is exactly what I need.

"Come for me, *a ghrá*. Come all over my cock." He nibbles my neck and grinds his pelvis against my hand, pushing it harder against my clit. That's all it takes to send me careening into a climax.

Before I'm down from that high, Connor pulls out of me, flips me over, tugs one of my arms behind my back, then plunges right back inside me.

"Holy shit!"

He's a man possessed, slapping his hips against my ass as he holds my arm, pushing it into my back. "Fuck, baby, you're so tight. So goddamn perfect."

I moan as I manage to push back against him, despite his tight hold on me, and with only two more thrusts, he's coming inside me, rutting into me so hard and for so long, it doesn't feel like it'll ever stop.

But when it does, he pulls out, lets go of my arm, and collapses next to me, pulling me against his side.

"Christ, did I hurt you?"

I shake my head and brush the hair off his forehead.

"Absolutely not."

Chapter Sixteen

BILLIE

"**I** think your thumb is clean."

I hear Blake, but I'm not paying attention to him because right now, I'm hyperaware of the sexiest man I've ever seen in my life standing across the room from me, smiling down at my adorable niece, and my ovaries are sparkling like it's the Fourth of fucking July.

"Bee."

"Huh?" I let my thumb fall from my mouth. I was licking off some mayonnaise when I glanced over and caught the view of Connor in that sexy-as-hell plain white T-shirt. *His arms do things to me.*

We're at the ranch for Sunday family day. We spent the day with the horses, much to Birdie's delight, and now we're all in the house. I'm helping with dinner, but everyone's in the kitchen/dining space, talking and laughing.

Our family has grown so much, with Skyla's best

friend, Mikhail, and his husband, Benji, joining us, along with Millie and her husband, Holden. My brother might have to consider adding on to this kitchen.

But I'm only paying attention to my man.

Mine.

His gaze lifts and finds mine, and he graces me with that sexy, knowing smile, just as his eyes rake up and down my body. Heat spears through me. He doesn't even have to touch me, and I'm a live wire.

"For fuck's sake, Bee," Blake says next to me. "Take him home and screw his brains out or pay attention already."

I blink and frown at my brother, who's trying to thrust a platter of cheese, meat, and crackers at me.

"You can't put this on the counter yourself?" I demand as I take the platter and roll my eyes.

"You're supposed to be helping," he reminds me. "So either help or get the hell out of this kitchen."

"Brooks!" I call out, my eyes pinned to Blake's, and he scowls at me. "Blake is being mean to me!"

"You're such a fucking brat," Blake spits out just as Brooks clomps into the kitchen.

"What the hell is going on in here?" And there he is, the oldest brother who will come to the defense of his baby sister—me—on command.

It's handy, really.

"Blake's being mean."

Brooks raises an eyebrow at Blake. "*Are* you being mean?"

Blake just rolls his eyes, mutters something about me

being a pest, and goes back to what he was doing. It's funny how here, Blake Blackwell is just an annoying big brother, despite the fact he's more educated than the rest of us siblings and is a well-respected doctor in the area.

With a grin, I hug Brooks around his waist, and he pats me on the back.

"Thanks." My gaze catches Connor's again. His arms are folded over his chest, and he's shaking his head. He clearly witnessed the entire scene, but he's smirking.

Because I'm damn funny.

"I'm so glad you guys came for dinner," I say to Millie as she slings her arm around Holden's waist.

Holden and his sisters have always been welcome at our ranch. Well, *everyone* is welcome here, but our home was a haven for the Lexington siblings when their abusive father got to be too horrible. Holden would bring his four younger sisters here, and we'd all hang out together. I've always thought of him as another brother, and as he leans down to kiss his wife's head, he winks at me.

"Hey, brat. How's it going?" he asks me.

"It's going well. Or, it was, until your ugly face showed up here. Did you know that you smell, too?"

Holden smirks, and then like a shot, he lets go of Millie and runs after me. I squeal and run away, around the kitchen island, but he's way faster than I am and catches me by the waist, turning around in a circle with my feet off the floor.

"Help! Help! I'm being manhandled!"

"Take it back," he demands and swiftly puts me in a

headlock. Geez, what's up with all the big biceps on these guys? He's going to choke me out with those things.

"You're so fucking old," I tell him, out of breath. "How do you move so fast?"

"I'm old *and* smelly?" he demands.

"And ugly," I remind him, giggling. Holden is the opposite of ugly. The man is way too sexy for his own good.

In fact, I can objectively say that every man here is hotter than Hades. Even my brothers.

"Beg for mercy," he says as he rubs his knuckles in my hair.

"Brooks!" I call out.

"I'm not helping you this time," my brother replies from across the room. "You deserve it."

With another hysterical laugh, I shove my elbow into Holden's side, making him wheeze out a breath.

"Connor!" I'm still wiggling, but Holden's too damn strong. "Connor, help me!"

Suddenly, I'm yanked out of Holden's arms and wrapped up in an embrace I know all too well.

"Was the bad man bothering you, angel?" Connor growls against my ear, making all of my lady bits stand up at attention.

"Yes. Kill him and discard the body."

"Harsh," Beckett says, shaking his head as Connor chuckles and gives me a squeeze.

"From now on," Connor whispers so only I can hear, "when you need help, you ask for *me, mo rúnsearc*, no other man, not even your brother. Understood?"

I lean back to look him in the eye and grin at the heat there.

"I hear you."

"Good." He kisses my forehead, then walks away, and I have to clear my throat.

Holden winks at me before he steals a piece of cheese, then walks over to chat with Beckett, Mik, and Benji.

"Okay, what do you need me to do?" I ask Blake, who just shakes his head.

"Nothing."

"What's for dinner?"

I whirl at the voice coming from the doorway. *I know that voice!*

"Mama!"

Our parents are standing thirty feet away, grinning at all of us. Mom's eyes fill with tears as we rush them, taking our turns with hugs and kisses, and when Birdie starts to cry because she's so happy to see her grandma and grandpa, I can't help but cry, too.

"God, I missed you," I whisper, clinging to my daddy as he wraps his arms around me, holding me in the bear hug that I've loved for as long as I can remember.

"I missed you too, baby girl." He pulls back to brush the tears from my cheeks. "No more tears."

I nod and move on to my mom, hugging her so tight, I'm afraid I might bruise her ribs.

"How?" I ask. "I thought you were busy in Florida."

"We are," she confirms. "So we're only here for two days, but Connor assures us his plane is ready for us anytime, so we don't have to go by the commercial flight schedule."

I whirl, scanning the room for my man, then I rush to him, throw my arms around his neck, and hug him close.

The damn tears are back.

"You did this for *me*?"

"You cried, angel," he reminds me, his hands moving up and down my back soothingly. "And that was unacceptable."

God, I love this man.

Holy shit.

I'm in love with him.

This isn't a crush.

It's not simply incredible sex.

I'm in love with him.

Chaos reigns around us, but I frame his face in my hands and gently lay my lips over his, and suddenly, everyone has gone quiet.

"In case anyone hadn't heard," I say, not raising my voice and not tearing my gaze from Connor's, "we're a thing. I'm not taking suggestions or concerns about it at this time."

Connor's smile spreads, then he laughs as he kisses my forehead.

"We figured," Mom says with a wink. "Now, really, what's for dinner? We're starving."

"We're grilling," Birdie informs her. "I'm going to flip the burgers."

"No," Bridger says, shaking his head. "You're not. It's too hot for little girls."

"I'm not little. I'm going to be a big sister, so I'm a big girl."

Dead silence.

My gaze whips to Dani, who's biting her lip and fighting tears.

"Do *not* play with my emotions," I say, pointing at her, but she just smiles at me. Then I run to *her* and hug her harder than ever. "Really? A baby?"

"Yeah," she says with a giggle as Skyla crashes into us in a group hug. "Next spring."

There's more chaos. More hugs.

I glance over in time to see Holden, with tears in his bright blue eyes, pull his sister in for a tight hug, holding her close. He whispers something in her ear, and it makes her break down, and now I'm a blubbering mess, too.

Goddamn emotions.

"Here, angel." Connor's suddenly right next to me, holding out a handkerchief.

"You're so fancy," I say through my tears as I dab at my eyes. "Wow, this is the best family dinner *ever.* I can't believe you did this. Did you know that Dani and Bridger had this announcement, and that's why you flew Mom and Dad in?"

"There's not much in this life that I wouldn't do for you. But, no." He kisses my head, wrapping his arms around me as we watch the others hug and laugh. "That's a happy coincidence."

"The happiest." I sigh and wink at Bridger when he

finds my gaze. "He's such a good daddy. I'm happy for them."

"Do you want kids?" Connor asks me.

"Maybe. Probably." I shrug and glance up at him. "You?"

"I didn't think so." He frowns, and his eyes scan the room, taking in this big, loud family surrounding us. "Now, maybe. Probably."

My gaze finds his, and he skims his knuckles down my cheek. "Go love on your family, bumble. I'll be right here."

"You're pretty great. I mean, I don't want to feed your ego too much, but you're pretty fucking great, Connor Gallagher."

He chuckles as he loosens his hold on me and steps back. "Go on then."

"I'll show you my appreciation later."

"Looking forward to it."

Chapter Seventeen

CONNOR

"She's a headstrong girl," Brandon, Billie's da, says as we walk down the driveway. He asked me to join him on a wee walk, and I knew something like this was coming.

Especially after the way my angel kissed me in front of her family and staked her claim. For so many years, I've hated when people have ostensibly *staked their claim* on me. It's always been for an agenda or to propel the other person's status.

Not this time.

Billie Blackwell *showed* her entire family that I'm hers. I honestly wasn't sure she'd ever get to the same point that I'm at, so I'm floored. I love this gorgeous woman.

I also almost hauled her off to the closest bedroom so I could fucking devour her.

"She's a woman, not a girl," I reply, and Brandon

nods slowly next to me. "I mean no disrespect when I say that, sir."

"None taken," he replies. "You're right. She's going to be twenty-eight soon. She's not a girl. But she's *my* girl. And even though I appreciate the fancy ride home and the chance to see my family, I'm still going to put you on the spot and ask you what you feel for her. It must be strong if you're sending your jet off to pick up her folks."

I shove my hand through my hair and take a deep breath, enjoying the scent of pine and wildflowers hanging in the air. "I've never known anyone like Billie Blackwell, and that's the truth. Yes, she's stubborn. So bloody stubborn."

He smirks at that and claps me on the shoulder.

"The best ones always are, son."

"But she's also sweet and kind. Smart as hell. Knows her mind when it comes to business, and it's proud I am that she's made such a success out of her bookshop."

"And do you love her?"

My jaw firm, I stop walking and turn to face him.

"Listen," he says as he rubs his hand over his mouth. "I don't really care about the age thing. You're both adults. I don't give two shits about your money. Our family does fine, and Billie's doing her own thing, like you said. But my girl is softer than she lets on to anyone. She's strong and determined, and doesn't show weakness often, but she's a softhearted person, so if she's just a good time for now until you find someone else who catches your attention, well, I'm going to tell you here and now that I'm not okay with that. I don't care what your last name is."

I see where his sons get their integrity. It also affirms my respect for this man and how he's raised his family.

"No, she's not a distraction or a good time for now. Christ." I push my hand through my hair again. "It's not that I have an issue admitting how I feel about your daughter, but I haven't even told *her* yet, and I think, out of respect for her and our relationship, I'd like to have that conversation with Billie first."

He narrows his eyes on me and nods, looking down at the ground. "That's fair. And it tells me everything I need to know. Now, we'd better go make sure they're not overcooking those burgers. Blake's amazing in the kitchen, but he's not great at the grill. Although I'll deny I said that if you ever tell him."

My phone rings, and Brandon nods.

"You take that. I'll see you over there."

He wanders over to the house, and I answer the call.

"Christ Jesus, it's Sunday. Don't you ever take a bloody day off?"

Ronan scoffs in my ear. "I take as many days off as you do, boyo. We need you in New York late this week. There's a meeting regarding the new boutique hotel in Manhattan, and I'd feel better about it if you were there."

I start to argue but then pause.

I'm planning a trip with my angel anyway. I'll extend it and show her New York. Take her shopping and to a show.

Because I'm not going anywhere without her.

"Aye, okay. I can do that. Send me the details."

I end the call and walk to the house, finding all of the brothers, plus Holden and Brandon, on the deck, hovering around the barbecue the way American men seem to do. But in the middle of them is my angel, holding a beer and laughing with them.

"How's business?" Brandon asks her, and everyone turns their attention to her. They're truly interested, not simply humoring her, and I love the way Billie squares her shoulders at the question, like the boss she is.

Good fucking girl.

"It's really great," she says. "I just promoted Emily to general manager of the store, with Tiffany the assistant manager, *and* I hired four new employees, one of whom is going to kill it with our online sales."

Good. This means she'll be able to leave for a little while and not worry about the business running fine without her.

"I've started working with publishers and PR companies on in-store signings, and I'd love to find some graphic designers to start offering special editions that readers can only get from our store. Incorporate it into our monthly book club, and then I could eventually include an online book club."

She's so bloody smart. Billie turns me on in every way, always. But when she's in boss mode, she slays me. Intellectually. Physically. She's lucky she's surrounded by her brothers at a family event right now, or I wouldn't be keeping my hands to myself.

Today, she's in those jeans that show off her sexy arse,

and a tank top, showcasing her strong shoulders. Her hair is up in a thick ponytail, just begging for me to wrap it in my fist. Her makeup is simple and flawless despite being out all day with the horses.

And now she's talking business, and I've never wanted her more.

Her father asked me if I loved her. Fuck, yes, I love every inch of her. Every bit of her. I can't breathe unless I'm with her, and I'm never letting her go.

I just have to find the right time to tell her because there are still moments when I swear she's nervous or holding back on me.

And we need to talk about that.

I climb the stairs to the deck, and when Billie notices, her smile spreads, making me feel welcome.

Making me feel at home.

"Everything okay?" she asks, and I tilt my head in question. "Your phone call. It's Sunday."

"Ah, yes. Everything's just fine, bumble." I kiss her cheek and take the offered beer from Bridger.

"Bumble?" Bridger asks.

"I'm a worker bee," Billie says before I can tell him it's none of his business. "You know, always busy. Always fuzzy and cute."

Bridger snorts at that, and I shake my head at her.

"Always sassy," I counter.

"I'm going in with the girls." Billie kisses my cheek and saunters inside, closing the door behind her.

"Congratulations on the wee babe," I say to Bridger.

"Thanks." His face softens as he looks toward the door, where the women are beyond. "It was a surprise."

"You don't know how babies are made?" Blake asks him, wielding a spatula. "Medically speaking—"

"Stop," Holden says. "It's my sister, man. Don't make me fuck you up."

"It wasn't *planned*," Bridger amends, rolling his eyes. "But we're thrilled. Birdie is ready to shop for baby clothes and stuff."

"Your mother and I have some news of our own," Brandon says, eyeing the door. "We were going to wait to say anything until things were set in stone, but we're moving home."

"What?" Beckett asks. "Holy shit, that's great. Skyla and I can find another—"

"No," Brandon says. "We're not moving *here*. This is yours, and I'm happy for you to keep it. I'm done being a farmer, and I'm not coming out of retirement. But we're moving back to Bitterroot Valley. We're under contract for a house in town, and the condo in Florida is on the market."

"Why?" Brooks asks his father.

"Because our family is *here*. Our kids, who we're so damn proud of, are here, and we want to spend more time with you guys. We miss Birdie and all her funny antics, and now there will be a new baby to love on. We don't like missing out on your lives."

"But Mom hates the snow," Blake reminds him. "It's not good for her arthritis, and it still snows here."

"We can take a long vacation in the winter after

Christmas," Brandon replies. "Our minds are made up. It's the right thing to do."

"This is great," Bridger says. "Lots of amazing news today."

"Did you really bring our parents here because Billie cried?" Blake asks me.

"Aye. I don't like seeing her cry."

"She doesn't. Not often, anyway," Brooks replies. "That mean you're sticking around?"

"Aye," I say again, nodding as I lean back against the railing. "I'm sticking around."

"Good." Beckett passes me another beer. "Your sister's thrilled, you know."

"God forbid Skyla not be thrilled."

Beckett grins. "Exactly."

"Oh God, not again. I can't do it again."

She's spread out for me, gloriously naked and writhing on the bedsheets, her head tossing back and forth as another orgasm builds. Her pussy quivers around my soaked fingers, her clit pulses against my tongue, and she's so bloody beautiful.

"Yes, you can. Breathe, baby."

"Can't," she whimpers as her hands fist in my hair, and every muscle tenses as her pussy pulls my fingers farther inside her. Her climax is spectacular, and my girl cries out. "Connor!"

Before she can come down from that high, I cover her, nestle myself between her thighs, and push inside her, making us both groan.

"That's right, angel," I growl as I start to move. "Say my name."

"Connor." It's a whimper this time.

"Fuck, you're incredible." I can't go slow and easy. I'm pounding into her, one hand holding hers over her head, the other gripping her arse, pulling her to me. "It's never bloody enough."

Her teeth latch on to my shoulder, but I revel in the pain of it and push harder. Faster.

"You're mine," I growl against her ear. "Do you understand me?"

"Yes." Her voice breaks around the word, and she's holding on to me for dear life.

"Say it."

"Yours." She swallows hard and cups my face. "Look at me."

My eyes find hers, and she lifts to cover my lips in a sweet kiss.

"Only yours."

The climax is swift and feels like a nuclear bomb detonating in my soul. I roar as I grind against her, spilling inside her, and then I can't help but pull out and fist my dick and come all over her.

Marking her.

Fucking mine.

I've never wanted to claim someone the way I do Billie. *Never.* But the mere thought of another man touching her, thinking of her like this, makes me feel unhinged.

"Connor." She's running her fingers up and down my arms, her legs wrapped around my hips, and I know without a shadow of a doubt that this is exactly where I want to be for the rest of my life. "Baby, are you okay?"

"Never bloody better," I murmur before pressing my lips against her collarbone and chin. "Why?"

"I don't know if I've seen you quite that ... intense." Her face softens in a smile, and her fingers ghost down my cheek. "And I feel guilty as fuck."

"Why?"

"Because I was supposed to be thanking *you* for bringing my parents to me, and instead, I'm the one who had three orgasms."

"You deserved three orgasms," I inform her before rolling off her and pulling her against me.

"We're a mess, Connor."

"Don't care." I kiss her temple, hugging her close, and I grin as she links her legs with mine.

Billie wasn't kidding when she said she likes to be touched. But more than that, she likes to be *held.* Cuddled.

And I'm more than happy to oblige her any chance I get.

"We need to talk, bumble."

She moves back far enough to look up at me. "Am I in trouble?"

I keep the smile off my face as my fingertip drifts down the bridge of her perfect nose. "I don't know, what did you do?"

"Oh, the list is vast." She draws shapes on my chest and narrows her pretty eyes as if she's thinking it over. "My car is due for an oil change, but don't tell Brooks because he'll yell at me. Actually, it's probably also due for new brakes."

I scowl at her. "What the fuck do you mean, it needs new brakes?"

"They squeak now and then." She shrugs. "I don't go very far, so it's not a big deal."

"Brakes are a big deal." Fuck, I'll just buy her a new car and have it delivered tomorrow. "What else?"

"I've been busy and forgot to change the filter in my furnace for about two years. I mean, who can even remember that there are filters in furnaces?"

I close my eyes and pinch the bridge of my nose.

She's going to be the end of me.

"Baby, your house could burn down."

"My brother's a fireman, so at least I know someone who can put it out."

"Billie."

She chuckles and kisses my chest. "Kidding. Anyway, the furnace is under the house, in a crawl space. Do you know how many spiders are down there?"

"You're moving in here. With me. Immediately."

Billie laughs, and when I don't laugh with her, she blinks at me. "You're not joking."

"I don't find the idea of you living here with me funny, bumble."

"It's just a furnace filter."

I roll her onto her back and cage her in, my elbows on either side of her head. "It's not about the filter. I just want you here. I'm a selfish man, and we're already busy enough with our own businesses. I don't want to have a conversation every day about whose house we're going to stay at. I want you *here*. Every night after work. Every morning. Every goddamn minute that I can have you."

Her gaze drops to my lips, then flicks back to my eyes, and she rubs her lips together.

"What would I do with my house?"

"Whatever you want. Sell it. Rent it. Use it as storage. I don't care, angel."

She tips her head to the side. "You're serious."

"As fuck."

"I'm not an easy person to live with, you know." Panic starts to creep into her beautiful eyes, and I brush my thumbs over her temples, trying to soothe her. "I'm moody when I'm on my period, and I can be a brat, and sometimes I play my music too loud."

"None of those things scare me." I kiss her softly, sinking into her. "You're not going to talk me out of this."

"What if you change your mind?" The question is a whisper, and there's so much vulnerability in her words that it makes my heart ache.

Quickly, I sit up and pull this incredible woman onto

my lap, covering us both with the blankets. She's staring at my chest, so I lift her chin.

"I'm not going to change my mind."

"I know you believe that *now*, but—"

"Stop, *mo rúnsearc.*" I kiss her lips again and feel her soften against me. "Have I given you a reason to think I'll change my mind?"

She lifts an eyebrow. "Were you privy to the first eight months or so that we knew each other?"

"Since we've been seeing each other. Since our day in the Jeep and every bloody night we've spent together since."

"No." She takes a deep breath and cups my cheek. "No, you haven't."

"Good. It's decided. You're moving in. But it'll have to happen when we get back."

"Back from where?" She frowns up at me, but I'm reconsidering.

"You know what? I'll hire movers, so it can still happen tomorrow."

"Connor. Where are we going?"

"Oh, that's what I wanted to talk to you about. I have to be in New York by Friday morning. We'll leave Thursday on the jet, and we won't be back here for about ten days."

Her mouth drops open, and then she slowly shakes her head.

"Ten days in New York sounds incredible, but—"

"Three." She blinks at me. "Three days in New York, seven in Ireland."

That has her blinking fast as if she's fighting tears.

"Okay, that sounds ... I can't even find the words, but I just hired new people, and I can't leave them yet."

"Hey." I kiss her forehead and drag my hand down her back. "This isn't supposed to upset you, angel. You already said that you promoted Emily and Tiffany. You'll have four full days with your new hires, and then Emily and Tiffany can take over. You said yourself that you can work from anywhere."

She nibbles on her bottom lip, and I tug it free with my thumb, then smooth it over.

"You'll work from my plane, from my penthouse, from my house on the cliffs."

"You have a lot of houses," she whispers, and I simply smile at her.

"I'm not willing to go without you," I add. "I won't be away from you for that long. So we'll figure this out. Because you'll be on that plane with me on Thursday afternoon."

"Do I have a choice?"

I tilt my head. Am I reading her wrong? Would she rather stay home than travel with me?

"You always have a choice. I apologize if I over-stepped."

I move to pull away, but she wraps her arms around my neck and pushes her face against my skin, holding on tight.

"Don't pull away from me," she says, her arms tightening. "That's not what I meant."

"Then I need you to tell me what you meant."

"I just ... of *course*, I want to go. I don't want to be away from you, either."

"Spell it out for me, angel."

"I told you before that I'm not good at taking orders, and I'm a brat. My mouth ruins things when I'm nervous."

Now, my arms circle her, and she relaxes against me.

"Why are you nervous, *mo rúnsearc*?"

"Because ..." She sighs. "Because this feels like a big deal."

"It's a trip. It's not brain surgery. We're not buying and selling countries. We're not curing diseases or ending world hunger."

"No, but between talks of me moving in with you and this vacation you want to take me on, it's a lot. And for a minute, it made me feel like decisions are being made *for* me rather than *with* me."

"Ah, there it is." I kiss her cheek, then tug her back to kiss her lips. "You just have to tell me that, angel. Just talk to me. But you need to know, I'm an overbearing man who gets what he wants, and what I want is you."

She bites her lip once more. "Okay, overbearing man, I need a shower, and then I need to work because my super bossy and generous boyfriend is taking me on a trip."

Boyfriend.

Oh, bumble, we can do better than that.

But rather than argue, I nudge her out of my lap, then take us to the bathroom to clean up.

We have plans to make.

Chapter Eighteen

BILLIE

"Ready?"

I feel frazzled, but I let out a breath, staring at my side of this massive closet, and hope that I remembered everything for this trip.

"I hope so," I reply. "What if I forgot something? What if the outfits I chose aren't what I really want to wear?"

Connor wraps me in his arms from behind and kisses the top of my head.

"Then we'll get whatever you need when we're there."

"I feel a little unorganized." I fidget with the shamrock necklace at my throat.

No moving boxes remain after the whirlwind move into Connor's house earlier this week. The movers came to my house Monday morning. I pointed out everything that had to come with me right away, and we'll get the rest when we return from this trip.

I managed to unpack my clothes and bathroom stuff Monday night. Everything else is in boxes stashed in a guest room for now until I have time to deal with it.

"Breathe, angel."

I lean against him and take a long breath. He's so warm, so solid behind me that he soothes me. "It's been a crazy week."

"I know. Do you feel okay leaving the shop?"

I turn in his arms so I can wrap myself around him. "Actually, that's the least of my worries. I've spoken with Emily, and she's feeling super confident in her new role. We've scheduled plenty of check-ins while I'm away, and the new hires are already doing great. The girls have it handled, and I have plenty to work on remotely. It's going to be just fine."

"Good." He presses another kiss to my head. "The jet's waiting, but if you need another minute, take your time."

"No, I'll overthink it." I step away, and grab my computer bag, which Connor takes out of my hand. I follow him downstairs to where Miller's waiting at the SUV. "Are you going with us, Miller?"

"Of course, miss." He waits for me to hop in the back seat before closing the door for me.

Just as he puts the vehicle in gear, I yell out, "Shit! Wait."

I rush out of the car, back inside and up to the bedroom to grab my reading device, then run back outside.

"That was almost catastrophic."

Connor lifts an eyebrow.

"My Kindle." I wave it in front of him. "I'm going to read to you later."

"Is that so?"

I laugh and slip the device into my computer bag. "Sure, why not? This one is spicy."

"Is it the unhinged hockey player?"

"No, I finished that one. And unhinged doesn't even begin to describe that guy. It was hot as fuck."

Connor barks out a laugh, and I grin at him.

"You have a great laugh."

He smiles and lifts my hand to his lips, and we sit in relative silence on the short drive to the airport.

I rode on Connor's private jet earlier this summer when he took our whole family to London to watch Skyla and Mik dance for the coronation of the new king and queen, so I'm not new to private flying, but it's still exciting.

This plane is *wow.* The opulence is incredible, with rich, buttery leather seats, televisions, tables to eat or work on, and a bedroom with a king-sized bed in the back of the plane. The bathroom has a full shower.

I take a seat in the middle of the plane, set my bag on the seat next to me, my sweatshirt on the other side of me, and sigh in happiness.

"Are you comfortable, then?"

I grin at my billionaire. "Hell yes, I am. I'm spreading out. Don't even think about trying to crowd me."

"I'll sit across from you," he replies with a smirk, watching me. He's in navy slacks and a white button-down, which is his work-casual look when he doesn't go with a full suit. His sleeves are rolled up to his elbows, and the muscles and veins in his forearms make me salivate. "What are you looking at, angel?"

"Your arms," I reply honestly. "They do things to me."

His eyebrow lifts in surprise. "What kinds of things?"

"Sexy things." I bite my lip just as Miller climbs on board and walks between us toward the back of the plane, and I grin at Connor.

The flight crew is already here. The pilots are in the cockpit, the door open as the flight attendant prepares us for the flight. I don't like how she keeps looking at my man. She's probably thirty-ish, pretty with blond hair tucked back in a low bun, her slim figure showcased in a red uniform.

She glances over at Connor and licks her lower lip, and just like that, I've had enough.

"Be right back." I stand and cross over to her. "Hello, I'm Billie."

"Oh, hi." Her smile is as fake as my acrylic fingernails. "How can I help you?"

"What's your name?"

"Uh." She frowns and glances over my shoulder, but I block her view of Connor. "I'm Bethany."

"Are you new, Bethany? Or have you worked on one of Mr. Gallagher's flights before?"

"This is my first flight with this crew." Her face has gone to stone. She doesn't like me.

That's okay because I now don't like her either.

"Listen, Bethany, I'm going to need you to stop eye-fucking my man. We have a long flight ahead of us, and I find it *incredibly* unprofessional that we've been on board for roughly six minutes, and you already have him down to his skivvies in your brain. So here's how it's going to work. Either you keep it professional or we replace you. What do you think?"

"I ... I didn't ... I'm so sorry that you thought—"

"What's it going to be, Bethany?"

"Of course, I'll be completely professional."

"Great." I give her a toothy smile. "I appreciate it. Whenever you have a moment, I'd love some ginger ale, please. Sometimes my tummy gets a little off from the bumps."

I wink at her and return to my seat, and Connor is lounged back in his seat, his hand over his mouth, watching me with hot, intense eyes.

"I didn't like that," I inform him.

"I heard," he replies. "Come here, angel."

Without hesitation, I move across the aisle, and Connor tugs me into his lap, cups my face, and kisses the hell out of me.

When I come up for air, I rest my forehead against his.

"What was that for?"

"I love your backbone," he growls against my lips.

"She was being rude, and she's an employee. That doesn't fly, no pun intended."

He smiles, then brushes his lips over mine again, gently this time, as if he's soaking me in.

"I always want you to speak up for yourself."

"Good." I kiss his chin. "Because I will."

"The cabin door is closed, and we're getting ready to take off," the pilot says through the speaker. "Should be a smooth five-hour flight to New York City this evening. There might be a few bumps as we climb to our cruising altitude of thirty-six thousand feet, but we'll be quick getting through them. Enjoy your flight, Mr. Gallagher and Miss Blackwell."

"I'd better get buckled in." But instead of moving off his lap, I wrap my arms around his neck and hug him close, bury my nose in his neck and breathe him in. His arms tighten around me, and he whispers in my ear.

"Are you okay? Did she upset you that badly? We haven't taken off yet. I can have them stop, and we'll replace her."

"Oh no." I shake my head. "I'm not upset. I'm just enjoying you. Snuggling you is my favorite hobby."

I feel him smile against my hair as he presses a kiss there. "You're so sweet, bumble."

"I don't think Bethany would agree with you."

He chuckles, making me smile. "Who gives a fuck?"

"Not me."

I'm not lying. Snuggling up to this man *is* my favorite thing in the world. It's even better than reading. Since we've been together, I've slept better than I ever have in my life. Nothing brings me peace like being held by Connor.

"Okay." I kiss him once more, then climb off his lap, sit in my seat, and buckle the belt, relieved I don't have to ask for an extender. I usually don't, but sometimes airlines like to fuck with big girls and their self-esteem, and the belts wouldn't fit a toddler.

"Before we take off," Bethany says, carrying a glass of ginger ale on a tray, "I wanted to make sure you have this in case we have bumps like the pilot said."

"Thank you," I reply with a genuine smile this time. "I appreciate it."

"Would you like anything, sir?" Bethany asks Connor, keeping her face perfectly bland.

"No, thank you," Connor replies, not even looking her way.

Bethany nods and returns to the front of the plane as I happily sip my drink and eye-fuck my man.

He really *is* gorgeous with all that dark hair, those green eyes that burn right into me, and a body made for sin.

An hour later, with a bowl of popcorn at my elbow and more ginger ale, I'm typing away on my computer, deep in thought. I reached out to a few graphic artists this week to see about working together on special edition hardcovers for some upcoming books, and I'm glancing through samples they've emailed when my screen goes black.

I narrow my eyes and hit the keys, but nothing happens. So I pick it up and shake it.

Still nothing.

Maybe the battery died? I pull out the cord, plug it in and connect it to the laptop, but still nothing.

"No." I drop my face in my hand and whine. "You've got to be kidding me."

"What's wrong?"

"My computer died."

"I can keep you occupied while you give it time to charge."

I lift my eyes to Connor, who's working on his own computer, looking sexy as hell in his glasses, but I don't return his smirk.

"No, I mean, it *died*. I've only had it for three years, dammit." I slam it shut and lift it over my head like I want to throw it, but instead, I slip it into the bag and flag down Bethany. "I need a glass of wine, please. White is good."

"Of course." She nods and heads to the kitchen.

My gaze returns to Connor. "I'm going to assume that Bethany isn't going to drug me and indulge in one glass of wine so I can mourn the computer properly. Thank God everything on that laptop is also on my desktop at the store."

He hides his smile behind his hand. "I'm quite sure there are about sixty Apple stores in Manhattan alone."

"Yeah, but I can't migrate my information over if this laptop is dead. It's a huge pain in the ass."

I pout for a minute, and Bethany delivers the wine. I eye it for a minute. I didn't make a friend with the flight attendant, but I'm pretty sure she didn't slip anything into it.

I shrug and take a sip, and notice that Connor's still grinning at me.

"Am I amusing you, billionaire?"

"Always."

My phone pings with a text. Thank God for billionaire Wi-Fi on this flight.

> Brooks: Your car is ready. Changed the brakes.

> You're the best brother ever! Don't tell the others.

With a smirk, I put my phone away and Connor lifts an eyebrow.

"It was Brooks. He changed the oil and brakes in my car today." I hold the bowl of popcorn out to him. "Want some?"

"No."

Connor has grown quiet. Slightly more intense.

"Something wrong?"

"Yes."

He pushes his glasses up the bridge of his nose, stands, and holds his hand out for me. After unbuckling my belt, I take his hand and let him pull me to standing, and he leads me to the back of the plane.

"Go to the front, Miller," Connor says as he opens the bedroom door and ushers me inside. He closes the door and pushes me back onto the bed. Crawling over me, he kisses me silly.

"I'm hungry for something," he says, "but it isn't popcorn."

"No?"

"Mm-hmm." He kisses down my neck. "I want *you*."

"Isn't it handy that we have this bed at thirty-six thousand feet in the air?"

He works my top over my head, unfastens my bra, then feasts on my breasts, nibbling and biting the nipples, and then he gets to work on my jeans. I took my shoes off not long after we boarded to get comfy, so he's able to slide my pants and underwear right over my feet, laying me bare for him.

"Now, I need you to be quiet, bumble. Because I'm going to have to kill anyone who hears you come, and I'm rather fond of Miller."

I stare at him as he lowers his face to my pussy. "*Connor.*"

"Yes?"

"I can't be quiet."

"You will be," he says with way more confidence than I feel. He drags his fingertip through my already soaking slit and grins up at me. "I fucking love how wet you get for me."

"I can*not* be quiet."

Not looking concerned in the least, his tongue follows the path his finger just took, and I have to bite my hand.

I'm going to die.

Or Miller and Bethany will because once Connor gets going on me, I can't keep it in. I am not quiet when he's having his way with me.

And he knows it.

He presses a finger inside me, and I moan.

"Shh," he says and bites the inside of my thigh *hard*.

"Ouch."

"Do you know how delicious you are?" He licks me again, and his finger continues to move slowly in and out of me, up to spread my own juices over my clit, and then back inside, making my hips move in circles. "You taste so sweet."

"Connor," I whisper, hearing the need in my rough voice. "I need you."

"You'll have me when I'm ready."

He presses kisses to the crease where my thigh meets my center, another to the top of my pubis, and then over my clit, and I start to see stars.

"You're not allowed to come yet, *mo rúnsearc.*"

"Then stop touching me," I growl, and he chuckles, his voice rough with lust and need, before kissing my clit again. "Connor, I'm telling you right now, I need you inside me. God, please, fuck me on this bed."

"Aye, I like it when you beg." He kisses up my stomach, but his fingers don't leave my core. "I like it very much."

"Please," I ask again, my hands diving into his hair as he kisses up my torso. When his lips are against mine, and I can taste myself on him, I whisper again, "Please."

His fingers pull out, and suddenly, I'm flipped onto my stomach.

"Bite the bloody pillow, angel, because I don't want you to make a fucking sound, and I'm not going easy on you."

His cock slams in, and I bite the pillow, stifling my cries as I immediately come apart around him.

He's pounding into me, so hard and rough it makes my nerve endings sing, my toes curl, and every atom in my body do the cha-cha.

I press back against him, and he moves his forehead against my shoulder, groaning as he comes, grinding into me so hard, it's just this side of painful.

"Christ Jesus, you're incredible," he whispers at my ear.

He rolls us, tugs me on top of him, and kisses me long and slow.

"Holy shit." I push my hair off my face and stare up at him. "What brought that on? My computer dying?"

"The second you told that flight attendant off, I wanted to fuck you raw," he growls. "Then you spent an hour with your nose to the grindstone, working, murmuring about ROIs and quantities and bloody sprayed edges—"

"The sprayed edges are pretty."

"—and I've been hard for you for hours. Enough was enough."

"Hmm. I'm glad I didn't make you mad by telling her off. Why do you have so many attractive women working for you?"

He frowns, staring at the ceiling.

"Do I?"

"Yeah, billionaire, you do."

"It's not a conscious thing, I simply hire those who are qualified. I don't fuck employees, Billie."

"You'd better only be fucking me." The words are out before I can stop them, and then he rolls me over, caging me in, and glares down at me.

Glares.

This is Connor from a few months ago. Intense and broody.

"Don't make me spank your excellent arse," he growls. "I'm not a bloody cheater or a liar."

"Hey." I cup his cheek and boost up to kiss him. "I'm sorry. I know you're not, and I would *never* imply you are. Honest, I'm not upset, and I'm not saying that I think you employ hot girls so you can get in their pants."

"Jesus fuck, Billie."

"You're a man of integrity, and I know you're obsessed with me."

He narrows his eyes, and I offer him a big smile.

"And I know that because I recognize the signs. Because I'm obsessed with you, too." *I love you so much it makes my chest hurt.* "It was just a remark, a thoughtless one, and I won't do it again because I don't want to upset you, and I don't believe you'd ever hurt me that way." *And, God, I hope you love me too because if you don't, it might destroy me.*

He still looks ready to fight, but then he sighs, kisses me hard, and rolls to my side, pulling me against him once more.

"This is a really comfortable bed for an airplane," I inform him.

"Have you slept on many beds on airplanes?" he asks, pushing my hair away from my face.

"This is the first," I reply. "And I don't call this sleeping."

He smirks in that sexy way he does when he's amused by me. "Why don't we have a wee nap? Since you can't work right now, get some rest."

"Only if you'll stay with me."

"I've nowhere else to be," he replies as he covers us with the blanket.

"In case I forget," I whisper to him as I thread my leg through his and wrap my arm around his middle, tucking my hand between his side and the bed. "Thank you for everything. I had the best time."

He kisses my forehead, his hands rubbing up and down my back.

"Go to sleep, Billie."

I can't resist him. Between that mind-numbing orgasm and the stress of the week, I'm exhausted, and quickly fall into sleep.

Chapter Nineteen

CONNOR

"So you had someone drop this SUV, which looks exactly like the one in Montana, at the tarmac so Miller could drive us to wherever we're going when we got off the plane?" Billie asks as we travel through the city on the way to my penthouse.

"Aye." I reach over to brush my finger down her cheek. Christ, she's magnificent. Watching her put the flight attendant in her place was such a fucking turn-on. I didn't know whether to laugh or strip her bare and fuck her. She didn't even raise her voice. She simply kept her chin up and made it clear she wouldn't tolerate being disrespected like that.

I wasn't aware the attendant was paying any attention to me. Why would I? I'm always too consumed with the woman next to me.

She slept through the rest of the flight, curled up around me, and surprisingly, I was able to sleep almost as long. So despite landing in New York at about midnight local time, we're both wide awake.

And Billie is staring at the lights out the passenger window.

"Have you been to New York City before, angel?"

"No." She shakes her head but doesn't turn to look at me. "I haven't been east of the Mississippi very much. It's so ... bright."

"It is that." I link my fingers with hers as Miller drives us into the Upper East Side of Manhattan.

Miller pulls into the parking garage under my building, and Billie turns to me with a scowl.

"What's wrong?" I reach over to brush her hair over her shoulder.

I can't stop touching her. Ever.

How did I stay away from her for all of those months?

"This doesn't look like a hotel."

I glance out the window, then back at her. "That's because it's *not* a hotel. Did you want to stay at one? I can arrange it."

"Oh, no, I assumed we'd be—" She bites her lip and frowns, and now that we're stopped, I unclip her seat belt and pull her against me.

"Talk to me, *a ghrá*."

"That's a new one," she murmurs. "I shouldn't assume things. So you have a place in this building?"

I smirk and press a quick kiss to her pouty lips. "I have the building, baby."

Her mouth gapes, and I push out of the vehicle and

walk around to open her door. When she hops out, I take her computer bag from her, carrying it myself.

"Come on, we're on the top floor."

"Of course, we are," she whispers, but I catch it.

"Simon and I will bring everything up in a few," Miller says, and I nod his way as I escort Billie to the private elevator that leads to the penthouse.

"Breathe." I rub her back in big circles. "It's just an apartment, you know."

That makes her bark out a laugh. "Right. I'm sure it's similar to the apartment I had in college."

I can't help but wink down at her as the doors open into the foyer of my place. Linking her hand with mine, I lead her out of the elevator.

"Wow," she whispers, dropping my hand and immediately going for the windows that offer stunning views of Central Park. I set her bag on the sofa, watching her. She's full of nervous energy, and I don't like that. "You own the *building*."

"I do, but I lease the other floors." I shove my hands in my pockets as I stand back and watch her take in my place. It's not similar to the Montana house in any way. This has a more luxurious feel, and for the price tag, it should. The living room is expansive, open to the kitchen, and everywhere you look is glass because it's been designed to let in the views of the park and city around us.

I don't like how quiet she is.

"Talk to me."

"I mean, it's—" She props her hands on her hips,

takes another look around, and blows air out of her mouth, making a raspberry with her lips. "Gorgeous. Smart. Welcoming. Fucking intimidating."

"Funny, I think you just described yourself."

She turns to me with a half smile. "How long have you owned it?"

"About ten years. I don't know how much longer I'll keep it."

"Why?"

"I'm never here. I haven't been here in months. If I do come to Manhattan, there are four resorts, with another on the way, that I own and can stay in."

She nods slowly, and I move to the dining table.

"This is your new computer," I inform her.

"Wait. What?" Billie marches over and opens the laptop, then spins to pin me with a shocked stare when it's exactly as her old one was. "How did you do that?"

Gliding my hand around her waist, I tug her to me. "You're cute."

"Seriously, Connor, how did you get me a new computer and get it already set up for me? We've been asleep on an airplane."

"I know people, bumble. Now, are you hungry?"

"Holy shit," she whispers, her fingertips ghosting over the gleaming keys. "Yeah, I'm hungry."

"What would you like? The fridge and pantry are stocked, but we can also order something in if you want."

"After midnight?"

I grin at her again.

"We're not in Montana anymore," she says.

"No, we're not. We can get food any hour of the day. What'll it be? There's a good pizza place around the corner."

"That sounds good," she says, kicking off her shoes. My shoulders relax. If Billie's kicking off her shoes, that means she's comfortable. "I need a shower and comfies. I'm stealing your clothes tonight."

"Come, I'll show you the primary suite, and then I'll order while you're getting cozy." With her hand in mine, I point out the kitchen, a laundry space, my office, a media room, two guest rooms, and then we make it to the stairway.

"Jesus, billionaire, I'm going to need a map for this place."

"It's not that big."

She snorts and hangs on to the bottom of my shirt as I climb the stairs ahead of her.

"Another guest room is up here as well as the primary suite."

When I lead her into the bedroom, she gasps.

"Holy shit, the view." She crosses to the windows that look out onto Manhattan. "This is incredible, Connor."

"It was that view that sold me on it," I agree. "I like seeing you here, in this spot, *mo rúnsearc.*"

She turns to look at me. "How many—"

"None." I saunter to her and drag my thumb over her lower lip. "Just you. You're the only woman, besides my sister and the housekeeper, who've been here."

"I shouldn't have asked."

Closing the gap between us, I palm the back of her neck and lower my lips to hers, brushing them back and forth twice. "You can ask anything."

She swallows, watching my gaze.

"Connor?"

"Aye, Billie."

"How did you get that computer here like that?"

"I have a security and tech specialist in the building, and they handled it. Former CIA."

She blinks twice, then leans her forehead against my sternum.

"I think I ask too many questions."

"Never." I kiss her forehead and lead her to the en suite. "Everything you need is in here."

"Why did I bother bringing my bathroom stuff if you already had it brought in for me?"

"You didn't ask me if you should pack it," I remind her. "I have no idea what's in your many suitcases."

Her favorite shampoo, conditioner, body wash, and even the razor she prefers are in my walk-in shower.

"Do you have elves?" she asks, then gasps when she opens a drawer at the vanity and discovers her skin care regimen, all waiting for her. Another drawer reveals the makeup she uses the most. "Jesus, Connor."

"What? Did they get the wrong thing?"

"No." With her eyes wide, she turns to stare at me. "This cost a fortune."

I boost her up onto the vanity and lean my palms on the marble, stepping between her legs so I can crowd her.

"It's nothing to me."

"It's not nothing to me," she whispers and glides her fingers up my chest to my face. "Thank you."

"You're welcome. You'll find the same setup in Ireland."

She frowns. "Connor—"

"No arguing." I kiss her lips softly, still not touching her. "I need you to be at home. I need you to be comfortable."

"Why?" she whispers against my lips.

Because I love you, and you've become my world, mo rúnsearc.

But given she's overwhelmed by the largesse of my life, I'm waiting to tell her that.

"Because I need you with me." After one more kiss, I back away. "Have your shower. Fresh towels are over there on the warming rack. I'll set some clothes on the bed for you."

"Thank you."

Before I can leave the room, she hops down and rushes over to wrap her arms around me.

"Thank you," she says again, and I plant my lips on her head.

"You're more than welcome. If you need anything at all, don't hesitate to tell me."

"I think you already thought of everything."

"That was the goal. Get cozy, and I'll order some food."

I set out an old T-shirt for my girl, and when I get downstairs, Miller and Simon have delivered the bags. I find Miller in the kitchen, drinking a bottle of water.

"Do you want pizza?" I ask him as I pull my phone out to order. "We're hungry."

"I won't turn it down," he replies. "Simon's settled in downstairs. He'll be Billie's detail while we're in New York. Do you want him in Ireland?"

"No, she'll be with us most of the time in Ireland. I knew she'd be on her own a lot here, and I want someone with her." I finish ordering online and pocket my phone. "Why do you look more uptight than normal?"

"Someone's not happy about the new build in Sweden."

"Lots of people aren't happy about that build." I rake my hand through my hair. "We should have pulled out of that project. It's done nothing but piss me the fuck off."

"They're pissed enough that they decided to send you a threat."

I narrow my eyes on him. "What kind of threat?"

"Stop the build immediately, or they'll kill you."

I shake my head. Death threats happen frequently, but this time, Miller's face doesn't change.

"This isn't an idle threat," he says. "It came from an extremist group that's been on the watch list for a decade. They mean what they say."

"I want Simon in Ireland," I decide, changing my mind. *Nothing is ever going to touch my girl.* "And back in Montana. If he's willing to relocate, he can be a permanent part of the detail."

"He's willing," Miller replies. "I think it's smart."

We talk for another thirty minutes. The pizza arrives just as Billie's coming down the stairs.

"Pizza's in the lobby," I say to Miller.

"I'll get it," he replies and crosses to the elevator.

"Does Miller ever sleep?" Billie asks when she reaches me. She wraps her arms around me for a hug, the way she always does when she greets me.

"I assume so." I kiss her lips and skim my fingers over her neck. "How was your shower?"

"Heavenly. I think that whole bathroom is a religious experience. I might just live in there for the rest of my life. Toss food at me and I'll be fine."

I chuckle and brush my nose over hers. "You're funny, bumble."

The elevator opens, and Miller walks in with the pizza.

"Let's eat," she says.

"Wake up, angel." I love seeing Billie in my bed. Her dark hair and golden skin against the white linens, sleeping peacefully as the sun shines in through the wall of windows makes my chest ache.

I love her so much, I don't know what I'd ever do without her.

"Time is it?" she murmurs, not opening her eyes.

"It's about seven." I kiss her cheek. "I have to go to the office, and I need to talk to you before I leave."

She stretches and the covers pull down, revealing her hot-as-hell breasts. She didn't last long in my clothes once we came to bed just five hours ago.

"Okay, I'm awake."

But she burrows down into the pillow, hugging it to her.

"Just give me five minutes, and you can go back to sleep, baby."

She moans, then turns onto her back and pries one eye open. "Hi."

"Good morning, beautiful."

"Okay, I forgive you for waking me up." She grins up at me. "I wouldn't want you to leave without saying goodbye anyway."

"And I wouldn't do that. I left my credit card on the table right there. Go use it today. Shop and have fun."

She frowns and glances over to the table, and then those eyes blow wide. "Connor, that's a black AmEx."

"I'm aware."

"You're such a rich guy." She blinks, then sighs. "Not that there's anything wrong with that. Cool, I'll do some shopping."

I push my fingers through her soft hair. "Good. You'll have a driver today. His name is Simon, and he'll take you wherever you want to go."

"I can take a cab or an Uber."

"No. That's not negotiable. I'm not asking you, Billie. I'm telling you."

She bites her lip. She likes it when I get bossy. But then I think back to our discussion last weekend and reconsider my answer.

"I know you don't love having decisions made *for* you rather than *with you*. I heard that, angel. But there will be times when I need you to adhere to my demands without question, especially when we're in a city that's strange to you and you're outside your comfort zone. Accept the ride. For me."

"Thanks for the ride." She sits up, unconcerned about being mostly naked, and wraps her arms around me. "And for the computer and shopping. Seriously, I don't need it."

"I do." I kiss her shoulder, then her neck. "Now, I have to leave this room before I say fuck it all to work and pound you into the mattress."

"I'm still sore from last night." She chuckles and drags her hand down my cheek.

"Excellent. I want you to feel me there all day." Unable to resist, I kiss her once more, then walk away. "Have fun, bumble."

"I plan to," she yells after me, making me smile.

"The facade of the building has to remain the same because it's a landmark," Julie says as she shows us renderings of the new boutique hotel we're about to break ground on. "But we can change the interior however we see fit."

My phone rings, startling the people at the conference table, and when I see it's Simon, I stand and excuse myself from the room.

"Update," I bark into the phone as soon as I'm in the hallway.

I'm irritated as fuck. Why the fuck is Julie bringing this up again that we can't change the facade? Of course we fucking can't. That was known before we signed the goddamn contracts *after* we'd filed for developmental approval. *This is such a waste of my time.* I'd much rather be with my angel, buying her anything she wants, than sitting in this goddamn meeting rehashing irrelevant information on a new boutique hotel we signed on for twelve months ago.

"She's in her third store of the morning," he says. "She asked me to drop her off at a place called *This & That* in Downtown."

My stomach drops. "What the hell do you mean, you're in *Downtown*? Why aren't you on Fifth Avenue?"

"She didn't want to go there," he replies, with no change in his voice. "She wanted to come Downtown, to these specific shops."

"What is she doing right now?"

"I assume she's shopping. I'm parked around the corner."

What. The. Fuck. "I didn't hire you to be a goddamn taxi. You're her fucking *detail*. I want you with her, eyes on her, every minute I'm not with her. Get to her, *now*, and send me a photo."

I hang up and immediately dial Billie's number, but she doesn't answer, so I send a text.

> Answer your phone, angel.

I wait ten seconds and try once more, but it goes to voicemail again.

> Billie, I need you to answer your fucking phone. Now.

Before I can call her again, Simon shoots through a text, and it's a picture of Billie.

She's grinning ear to ear, holding up a handbag, and it looks like she's having the time of her life.

I dial Simon's number.

"Yes, sir."

"Let me talk to her," I growl at him.

I can hear her voice in the background as he approaches.

"Miss Blackwell, I have Mr. Gallagher for you."

"Oh! Thanks, Simon." Her voice is closer when she says, "Hey there, handsome."

"You're not answering your phone."

"Oh, I'm sorry. The ringer's off, and I've been so busy finding fun things, I didn't look at it." I close my eyes as my heart settles, knowing she's okay. "Is everything okay? Did you get a message from the credit card company? I only spent a couple of thousand at that last store, but if that's more than you'd planned, I'll totally pay you back. Sorry about that."

I take my glasses off and pinch the bridge of my nose.

"No, *a ghrá,* spend whatever you want. Spend a million dollars. I don't care. Why are you in *Downtown*?"

She's quiet for a second, and then, "Because this is where the fun consignment shops are. I found a Chanel bag from 2022 that is *impossible* to get, Connor. And it wasn't crazy expensive. There was an incredible pair of Dior slingbacks, *in my size,* never worn, and I had to have them. And then—"

"Billie."

"Yeah?"

"I love that you're having fun. But why aren't you shopping on Fifth Avenue for new things?"

"Do you even know me? I *love* the hunt, and you know it. I'm in New York City, where people consign everything. Do you know that they have a Birkin in here, in my dream color and size? But I would *never* pay that much for a bag. I'm like a kid in a candy store, Connor. You can't take this away from me."

"I'm not trying to take anything away from you, *mo rúnsearc.* I'm glad you're enjoying yourself. Buy the Birkin."

She giggles. "Absolutely not."

"Let me talk to the manager."

"No. You're not buying me that bag, billionaire."

"Billie. Give the phone to the fecking manager or salesperson or whatever."

I hear her sigh, and then there's jostling, and a woman says, "Yes, this is Olivia. How may I help you?"

"When the woman who passed you this phone checks out, she leaves with the Birkin she wants. If there are other things you think she'd enjoy, send them with her."

"Yes, sir. I'm happy to help."

After more jostling, Simon's voice comes over the line.

"I'm back, sir."

"If you want to keep this job, you won't let her out of your sight again. She's the most valuable thing in this world, and I want you to guard her like your goddamn life depends on it. Do you hear me?"

"Understood, sir."

"Check in with me every hour."

I hang up and walk back into the conference room. I want this day over so I can get back to my angel.

"Do you even know me? I love the hunt, and you know it."

Fuck, I love that woman.

Chapter Twenty

BILLIE

Two things. One, I've never spent so much money in one day. And two, holy shit, shopping should be an Olympic sport because it is *rigorous.*

I'm exhausted after today's gold medal performance, but Connor texted me thirty minutes ago to tell me he's on his way back to his penthouse, and I'm making him dinner. I'm excited to go with him to Ireland so I can see his favorite things to eat firsthand, and maybe I can learn how to make some of them. But tonight, he's getting spaghetti with salad and garlic knots, all from scratch except for the pasta. As of now, everything's ready and just waiting for him to get back.

I whirl around when I hear the elevator ding, and when Connor walks through the doors, he looks ... *pissed.* He's scowling, every muscle in his impressive body tight, and the energy is intense.

"Hey, are you okay?"

"Hold on, angel," he says, holding up a finger as he dials his phone. "Get up here, now."

He hangs up, slips his phone into his pocket, and pulls off his tie, tossing it on the couch. As he walks through the room, with those intense green eyes pinned on me, he unbuttons the top two buttons of his shirt and rolls his sleeves. The frustration and anger are rolling off him in waves.

I've never seen him like this. I'm not afraid of him, but I'm worried about him.

"It smells good in here," he says. His voice is rough but gentle because he's speaking to me, but something is *not* right.

"I made dinner. What's going on, billionaire?"

"Don't worry about it." He kisses my forehead, then the elevator doors open, and Simon strides inside. His face is impassive, showing no emotion, but his hands are in fists, displaying the tension he's feeling.

What in the world is going on?

"My office," Connor says, setting off down the hall, and Simon follows him.

I spent all day with Simon. He's a handsome guy in his mid-thirties, built like a professional wrestler, with tattoos all over the place, even down his fingers and up his neck to his jawline. He doesn't ever smile, and I tried hard to get him to grin at me.

He never did.

Simon's kind of scary.

But he was also kind to me, and I'm worried he's in

trouble. So I do what any curious person would do, and I walk down the hall to eavesdrop.

Connor should have shut the door behind him if he didn't want me to hear this.

"What the *fuck* were you thinking?" Connor barks, his voice menacing. I've never heard that tone from him, and I don't think I ever want it directed at me.

"Miss Blackwell asked me to drop her off so she could shop. She told me not to hover. My orders were to give her whatever she wanted, so that's what I did."

He's in trouble because of me.

But he's just a driver.

"Miller briefed you on everything going on, and you know you were hired as her personal security. If I want a driver for her, I'll hire her a motherfucking driver. She's the *only bloody thing* in this world that matters, and you dropped her off in Downtown New York City and parked around the goddamn corner?"

He continues to rail on Simon, completely unhinged, and I decide I've had enough and walk back to the kitchen.

She's the only bloody thing in this world that matters.

Wow.

As I check and stir the sauce, I can still hear him yelling, and then things quiet, and the men walk through the penthouse again.

Simon nods at me before he calls for the elevator and leaves. Connor sighs, takes his glasses off to rub his eyes, and crosses to me.

He wraps his arms around me from behind and

kisses my head as I turn the burner under the sauce way down and cover it with a lid.

"You had fun shopping today?"

I turn in his arms and blink up at him. "Are you kidding me right now?"

He scowls. "What are you talking about?"

"Okay, back up." I scoot away from him so I can pace and breathe, pausing by the dining room table to take a sip of the wine I poured when I sat there with my new laptop, working earlier before he texted me. "You get home and immediately verbally beat the shit out of Simon, all because of *me*, and now you're going to pretend that doesn't matter?"

"You don't need to worry about it."

My eyebrows climb, and I take another sip of wine. Connor sighs, bracing his hands on his hips.

"You told me I had a *driver*, Connor. No one said a fucking word to me about him being security or that you wanted him with me all of the time. It was my fault that I asked him to wait for me and to stop hovering because *I didn't know.*"

"It's not your fault," Connor counters, shaking his head. "He's a fucking professional, and he knew what his job was today. He works for *me*, not for you. I need to trust that he's doing that job and keeping you safe."

"Why wouldn't I be safe?" I demand. "I'm just a girl from Montana, Connor. I'm not rich. I'm not famous. I'm nobody. I'm just a tourist, wandering around the city, spending money that doesn't even belong to me."

Connor's jaw clenches, the muscles bunching as his

eyes gleam with rage. He stalks to me, palms the back of my neck, and pulls me against him, lowering his face to mine.

"You're not *nobody*, and you're not *just* anything. Do you understand me? You're fucking everything in this world to me. And you're mine. And that makes you a target. If someone has been watching my comings and goings here, they've seen you with me, and that means that if they want to hurt me, they could try by hurting you, and I will not, today or any other goddamn day, let that happen."

"*You're* hurting me," I whisper.

He drops his hand, but he doesn't walk away. His brows pull together. I can see the emotion raging through him, the frustration, the anger, and the ... *love*?

"Christ, I'm sorry. I'd never hurt you, angel."

"I know you wouldn't. I'm okay. You're upset."

"That's no excuse."

"Hey, I'm fine. We just need to talk this out. You're always telling me to talk to you." I want to reach for him, to touch him, but we're both so damn angry with each other. "It goes both ways. I didn't *know* he was there to protect me. I didn't know there was a threat to you and, therefore, me. I. Didn't. Fucking. Know. And I don't want Simon to be in trouble or lose his job just because things happened a certain way because of choices I made out of ignorance."

"Why are you sticking up for Simon?" he demands, then his whole face changes. "Unless—"

"Do not fucking go there." I stomp to him and take

his hands in mine, holding on tight. "We're not doing that, Connor. Are you crazy? You didn't like it on the plane last night, and I won't tolerate that now."

He sighs and closes his eyes. "Feck."

"I simply know when to own my own shit. Yes, he knows his job, but it was also on me for sending him away because I didn't know better. So I guess you should yell at me, too."

"Goddammit, I was fucking terrified!"

He paces away from me, fisting and un-fisting his hands before he wipes his hand over his mouth and then turns and pins me in his stare.

"You know, I think I'm going to change and give you some time to calm down."

I walk away, headed for the stairs, and then suddenly, I'm airborne, in Connor's arms, and he's carrying me bridal style to the couch.

"You won't walk away from me in anger," he says, sitting and keeping me in his arms, holding me against him. "Never. We'll have this out and move on with it."

"Did you fire him?"

"No."

"Did you threaten to?"

"Fuck, yes."

I wiggle and straddle him so I can see him better. "Why didn't you tell me that he's security and not just a driver?"

"I didn't think about it. I put him with you to act as another Miller, and it didn't occur to me to spell it out to you because *I don't ever explain myself*, Billie.

I'm the boss. I make the rules, I give the orders, and everyone else follows them to the letter, or they're gone."

"But I'm not an employee."

"No, you're everything." His voice is rough, and he looks so fucking tired when he closes his eyes for just a heartbeat, then he pins me with his gaze again and skims his fingertips down my cheek to my neck, holding me so tenderly, it makes me swallow hard. "I'm not used to relationships, angel. The one I had ended in divorce, and there hasn't been another since. So far, I think our communication has been pretty good."

"Pretty good," I confirm. "Once you pulled your head out of your ass."

His eyes narrow, and his hands rub up my thighs and around to my hips, and I continue.

"I'm not asking to be privy to every decision you make because that's ridiculous, but if it involves me, I need to know, Connor."

"You're right." He licks his lips, his eyes on my mouth, his hands firming on my body, as if it's getting harder for him to keep himself under control, and it makes my nipples tighten against his chest. "I apologize. I *won't* apologize to Simon because he fucked up. He's going to be your personal security detail for the foreseeable future."

"Like on this trip?"

"All the time. Even after we get home."

I frown, slowly shaking my head. "I don't need—"

"*Mo rúnsearc.*" He takes a deep breath and cups my

face so gently, so in contrast to the anger he clearly feels. "I'm. Not. Asking."

I narrow my eyes at him. "I don't see why I need to be protected at my shop."

"Why are you so bleedin' stubborn?"

"I could ask you the same thing." I move to get off him, but he holds me in place.

"I protect what's mine," he says, his jaw clenched. "I protect what I love, and goddammit, I'm so in love with you, I ache with it. Living without you at this point isn't an option for me. You're the reason I open my bloody eyes in the morning, and the thought of someone hurting you, *touching* you in any way because of me, brings me to my knees. You were in a part of the city known for not being the safest today, and then I learned the man I hired to keep you safe when I can't be with you walked away from you. *All* I could think was that you could be in danger, that I could lose you, and that would end me, Billie."

God, his eyes are on fire as he stares at me. He grips my arms so tightly, they might have bruises later, but I can't bring myself to care.

Because he loves me.

He loves me.

"You wanted more," he says, softening slightly, as he tips his forehead to mine. "And because I needed to be with you, to touch you and spend time with you, I gave it to you. I'm doing the work, learning you, caring for you, and giving myself to you in ways I never have with anyone else before. You've become the center of my universe, and in giving you the *more* you needed, I've lost my entire heart and soul to you. I'm yours. Everything I have is for you. So yeah, *a ghrá,* today terrified me, and I took that out on Simon, and I won't fecking apologize for it."

My throat and nose sting as tears come to my eyes, and I try to swallow them down, but it's no use.

"God, I'm so sorry you were scared." I wrap my arms around his neck and hug him close. Connor buries his face in the crook of my neck, his arms locked around me as he takes a deep, shaky breath. "I didn't mean to scare you. I would never do that to you."

"I know, it's not your fault, *mo rúnsearc.* But it can't happen again."

I shake my head, still holding on. "It won't."

We're quiet, clinging to each other, and then I whisper in his ear, "I love you, too, you know."

He releases a shuddering sigh, as if hearing the words is a huge relief, and then his lips cover mine, kissing me so tenderly that more tears fall from my eyes.

"Say that again," he says as he changes our position. Laying me on the sofa, he kneels between my knees, bracing himself over me.

"I love you." I bite my lip as he makes a grab for my khaki pants, pulling them down my legs, along with my panties, and tossing them aside. "You're so damn smart and kind, and you love your family."

His eyes warm as he works my blouse off, along with my bra.

"You're thoughtful." I help him get his shirt over his head. "And gentle. I can sleep when I'm with you."

His gaze whips up to mine and narrows. "What do you mean?"

"I've never slept as well as I do when I'm with you. I joked with the girls that I wish we'd have nap dates."

The corner of his mouth tips up. "Nap dates?"

"Yeah, just let me curl up around you and sleep. Jesus, it's heaven. I've spent a decade exhausted because I can't sleep, so if you dump me and I have to start sleeping alone again, I'll have a nervous breakdown. No pressure."

Now, that smile spreads all over his face. "Oh, I'm not letting you go anywhere, bumble."

I raise an eyebrow. "Good. Because I'm also addicted to your body. These muscles are *crazy pants*. Your body is insane. I've never met anyone with such an incredible physique. And when you're inside me—"

He does just that, slipping right inside me, making me gasp and hold on to him.

"What, baby?" he asks, dragging his nose up the side of my neck.

"It feels like I finally have my person."

His eyes drift closed, and he rests his forehead against my own as his hips slowly start to move.

"You're *my* person," he whispers before kissing me sweetly. "I'm taking you shopping tomorrow. On Fifth Avenue."

"You don't—"

"Let me. Let me dress you from head to toe *for my enjoyment* and then take you out somewhere special." He picks up the pace, grinding against my clit, and I start to see stars. "You don't get to come until you agree."

"That's blackmail." I have to lick my lips. "Or entrapment. Or treason. It's something."

He chuckles, brushing his nose against mine. "Say yes."

"Connor, shit, I'm so close."

"Don't you do it. Not until you agree." He pulls out halfway, holding himself away from my clit, and I scowl at him. "Say yes."

"Fine. Let's go shopping."

He slams in but pulls back out again, and I groan in frustration.

"Say it again."

"I said we could go shopping."

He shakes his head. "Not that."

Cupping his cheek, I urge his mouth down to mine, and against his lips, I whisper, "I love you so much, billionaire."

"*A ghrá*," he whispers, his eyes closing. "*Mo rúnsearc. A chuisle mo chroí.*"

I don't know what any of the Irish words mean, but I'm so close to tumbling over the edge that I can't ask. His name is on my lips as I explode, and when the storm is over, he's brushing his fingertips down my cheek, peppering my face with kisses.

"What did it mean?" I ask. "I've never asked what the Irish words mean."

"*A ghrá* is my love." He swallows hard. "*A chuisle mo chroí* is you are the beat of my pulse."

Wow.

"And the other? The one you've used for a long time?"

He tilts his head, watching me intently. "*Mo rúnsearc* means my secret love."

I feel my eyes widen in surprise. "You've been saying that for *months.*"

"Aye." He kisses me, then skims his knuckles down my cheek. "I've known for a long time, even if I couldn't tell you quite yet."

My stomach growls, making us both laugh.

"Come on, bumble. Let's feed you, and then we'll go up to bed for round two."

"I'm not going to argue with that."

Connor has my hand in his, and with Miller and Simon walking behind us, he tugs me toward yet another store.

"Okay, this has to stop."

"What?"

"The shopping. Connor, you already bought me a *killer* dress, shoes, underwear, and a clutch to go with the dress even though I have plenty of bags at the penthouse. We're done."

"Not quite yet, we aren't."

I gasp when I realize where we are. "This is *Cartier*," I whisper-shout at him.

"I'm well aware." He stops abruptly and presses his lips to my ear. "I was balls deep inside you last night when you agreed to let me dress you from head to toe. That's what I'm doing. Do we have a problem, angel?"

That firm tone in his voice sends a shiver down my spine.

"No. No problem."

"Excellent." He nips my ear. "I love you, you know."

I can't help but grin at that. He's told me no less than ten times today that he loves me, and it never gets old.

"Yeah, yeah, I guess I love you, too."

"That's so precious, darlin'." He winks at me and leads me to the salesman who looks like he might have a heart attack.

"Hello, Mr. Gallagher. How can I assist you?"

Of course, he knows who Connor is.

"Diamond earrings," Connor replies. "Let's see what you've got."

The man is certifiable.

But he's had so much fun today, I can't tell him no.

An hour later, we walk out with not just the sexiest pair of pear-shaped diamond earrings I've ever seen but also a matching necklace.

Because of course, we did.

"Okay, billionaire, that's all I have in me. I'm wiped out. I need food and a massage, STAT."

"We're going home," he says. "For a snack, and I'll rub your feet. And then, we'll have to get ready for our night out."

"Are you going to tell me where we're going?"

"No." He brushes his lips over my forehead. "It's a surprise."

Gazing in the mirror, I take stock.

Hair done, check.

Makeup, check.

I haven't put the dress on yet, but it's hanging behind me, ready, when my phone pings with a text in our Spicy Girls Book Club text thread from Dani.

> Dani: Earth to Billie! We haven't heard a word from you since you landed in New York. How's it going? Did you shop? Tell us things!

I giggle and hop up on the vanity, letting my feet dangle as I take a quick selfie, then type out a response.

> Hi, guys! Sorry, things have been kind of busy.

> Skyla: Tell us everything.

> Alex: Is BUSY code for full of sexy time?

Millie: Why are you projecting all of your amazing threesome sex onto Bee, Alex?

I snort at that. It's only been a couple of days, but I already miss my girls.

There has been sex and shopping and food. So much food.

Skyla: Make Connor get you pizza from that place around the corner from his penthouse. It's my fave.

We had that the first night!

Dani: You look so pretty tonight! Where are you going?

I don't know. He hasn't told me. It's a surprise. You guys, I have to tell you something BIG.

Alex: Spill it.

Millie: Tell us.

Dani: Are you already engaged?

Millie: Oh shit, I didn't go there! Wait, are you?

With a giggle, I type out my response.

> No, def not engaged, but we've said the I love yous. We were arguing, and it just popped out.

Alex: Who said it first?

Dani: Why does that matter?

Skyla: This makes me so happy!

> He said it first.

So many heart, kissy, and celebration emoji come through that it makes me burst out laughing.

> Okay, I have to finish getting ready. I'll text more from Ireland.

Dani: Send us a pic of the two of you together tonight. We'll want to see.

> You got it. Love you all! xo

With a happy sigh, I take the red dress off the hanger and slip it on, then turn back to the mirror.

I'm going to make my billionaire swallow his tongue.

Chapter Twenty-One

CONNOR

I'm leaning against the kitchen island, sipping two fingers of Macallan, when Billie descends the stairs. All the air leaves my body.

Christ Jesus, she's bloody staggering.

Her dark hair is glossy and curled in loose waves around her shoulders. Her makeup, as usual, is flawless, and she's added a darker eye along with raspberry-red lips. Her diamonds sparkle at her ears and around her neck, and as my gaze lowers, my cock joins the party.

Because every delicious curve is showcased in a red dress that has my mouth drying up. Off the shoulder, the sleeves are long, ending just before her wrists. The bodice crisscrosses over her breasts, and then the dress falls in a billowy skirt with a slit that shows off her incredible leg as she walks.

With black heels to complete the look, I've never seen anyone more beautiful than my angel looks tonight.

At the bottom of the stairs, she lifts an eyebrow and turns a circle, and I feel the smile spread over my face.

"We can't go," I declare.

"Oh, we're going. Do you know how long it took me to look like this?"

I cross to her, and she slides her hands up the lapels of my tux, smiling at me.

"If we go," I say as I lean in to press my lips to her forehead, "I'll have to make Miller kill every man who ogles you, which means there will be a lot of deaths tonight, *a ghrá*."

"You promised me a night on the town." She lifts an eyebrow in that sassy way she does that makes me want to devour her. "So if people have to die, it just is what it is."

I chuckle and kiss her hand, then tuck it in my arm and escort her to the elevator. "If we don't leave now, I'll mess you up."

"You can do all of the messing later."

It's our last night in New York City, and I want her to enjoy every minute of it.

"Wait," she says, stopping me before we can step onto the elevator. "Let's take a quick selfie. I promised the girls I'd send one."

Unable to keep my lips off her, I kiss her forehead and then call down to my men.

"I need you up here, please."

"On our way," Miller says.

Bee raises an eyebrow.

"You're too fucking gorgeous for a *selfie*. We'll take a proper photo, *a ghrá*."

When the elevator doors open, Miller's and Simon's eyebrows lift in surprise as they step out of the car.

"You look lovely, miss," Miller says to Billie.

"Beautiful," Simon agrees with a nod. "We'll be extra vigilant tonight, boss."

I smirk down at Billie. "Told you."

Billie passes her phone to Miller, who immediately passes it on to Simon, making Billie laugh.

"We need a photo," Billie says.

"In front of the windows," I add and lead her to the glass. The sun is almost down, and the view is beautiful right now, with Central Park spread out behind us.

Simon snaps a few, then passes the phone back to Billie, and we make our way down to the garage.

"Oh, these are good," she mumbles as she sends them in her group text. "Aw, look at this one, where you're looking down at me."

She shows me her screen, and I immediately know I need that photo.

"Please send it to me, angel."

"Okay."

She sends the text and then climbs into the SUV.

"Okay, where are we going?"

"First up is dinner at 220 Park Ave South," I reply. "It's an exclusive restaurant not far from here."

"Is it on Billionaires' Row?" she asks, surprising me.

"Where did you hear that term?"

"One of the salesladies and I were chatting yesterday, and she said this part of the city is called Billionaires'

Row. Because it's full of the fanciest of the fancy, which makes sense because you're here. So?"

I grin and take her hand in mine, pressing my lips to her knuckles. "Yes, it is. It's an exclusive restaurant that you have to buy a membership for. But the food is incredible."

"I'm so glad I wore my pretty dress," she says with a wink.

Tonight is going to be bloody brilliant. Billie is charming and funny, and she fucking loves me.

Loves me.

"Okay, what's happening after dinner?"

"That's all I'm telling you for now, bumble."

Miller laughs behind the wheel, and Billie narrows her eyes at me.

"Okay," she says, squeezing my hand. "I can be surprised. Just give me a hint."

"No." I chuckle and shake my head at her. "Trust me."

"I do."

She looks out the window as we maneuver through Manhattan, and I can't look away from her.

I've never had a woman come with me on a business trip, and despite the initial day's hiccup, it's been an amazing few days. We both managed to get a lot of work done, the meetings I've endured have been fruitful—even if another board member could have handled them—and I've smiled more than I thought possible. My life feels so … complete. And if I can do one thing well for this woman, it's spoil her to distraction.

That includes tonight, when I'm determined to give her the best night of her life.

"It's too early, baby," Billie moans the following morning, scowling as I try to wake her up.

"I know, *a ghrá*. But we have to get to the airport. You can sleep on the plane." I brush my fingers through her soft hair. "It's another long flight. You can even shower on the plane if you want to."

She sighs and turns onto her back. "I think I'll miss this place."

"The penthouse?"

She nods and stretches, and I can't resist reaching out to glide my hand down her chest, between her breasts. "I like it here. It's ridiculously over the top, but it's also comfortable."

"Then I'll keep it."

If she wants it, it's hers.

"You could probably make a killing if you sold it. What's it worth, about ten million?"

I lean down and kiss her lips, then her cheek. "Two hundred million," I whisper in her ear, and then I laugh when she simply gapes at me.

"You ... I ... for fuck's sake." She pulls a pillow over her face, making me laugh more as I pull it away.

"Come on, we need to get going."

"You're already dressed," she says, looking me over. "Get naked and snuggle me. I need some skin-on-skin contact."

"No distracting me. You need to get dressed because no one gets to see you naked but me, and we need to get going. Let's go, bumble."

She sits up, yawns, and then climbs out of the bed, headed for the bathroom.

"It's not my fault someone kept me up all night, screaming his name," she says as she walks away, her bare arse in full view, making me hard all over again.

"It *is* your fault," I call after her, "for looking like that. Now, let's go. I won't tell you again."

While she gets dressed and finishes packing, I cross to the hidden coffee station here in the bedroom and brew her a cup of coffee.

"Has that been here the whole freaking time?" she asks as she pulls on a pair of leggings and a flowy tank top that looks sexy as hell. She tosses a jumper on the bed that she plans to wear on the plane.

"Aye," I reply, passing her the mug. "I forgot it was here, honestly."

"That's handy. We need that at home in Montana."

Home. I fecking love that she considers the Montana house home even though she's only technically lived there with me for a week. "Consider it done."

"Thanks." She smiles softly and, with the mug in hand, turns to finish gathering her things. "I don't know how I'm going to pack all of this."

"You don't need to," I inform her. "I'll have it all handled and shipped to Montana. It'll meet us there."

"Thank God. Your elves are handy. Okay, I want to take a couple of things to Ireland that I'll switch out with things I brought from home." Her voice is muffled as she digs through the bags in the closet. When it looks like she has her things sorted, she lets out a sigh. "Packing is cardio. It's science."

"How can I help, *mo chroí*?"

"Can you just zip this suitcase? It's going with us. The rest can go to Montana."

Ten minutes later, we're walking through the penthouse to the elevator. My girl's face is makeup-free, her hair is up in a messy bun, and she looks comfortable.

She's as gorgeous right now as she was in that red dress, styled to the nines.

"Thank you again for last night," she says, leaning into me as we ride down to the garage. "It was incredible. Every second of it. From the moment I walked down those stairs until the last orgasm a few hours ago."

"I'm glad." I kiss the top of her head, enjoying her warmth against me. "It was the same for me."

Her eyes are still heavy with sleep, and when we're in the SUV, I pull her against me and clip her into the middle seat belt so she can lean on me and sleep.

Thanks to traffic in New York that never really dies down, it takes almost an hour to get to the plane, and then it's time to wake her up again.

Once we're in the air, I take my girl to the plane's bedroom and help her get cozy in the bed.

"You're not going to sleep?" she asks me groggily.

"I have to work, *a ghrá*. But I'll bring the laptop in here so you can sleep."

"You don't have to," she says with a frown. "I'm sure I'll sleep fine. You'll be more comfortable in the seats out there."

I narrow my eyes at her. "You're sure?"

"Let's give it a try. I know you're nearby." She gives me an encouraging smile.

"Come get me if you can't sleep."

She nods, and I walk out, closing the door behind me. Although the bed on the plane is comfortable for sleeping, I can tell that it wouldn't be great to sit up and work in, not like our bed at home. But if she needs me, I'll go be with her.

"Is she okay?" Miller asks, looking up from his iPad. Simon's a few rows up, typing on his computer. One of the reasons I hired him is because he's excellent with tech, with tracking, and he's smart as fuck.

"Aye, just tired." I sit and pull out my laptop, and within minutes, I'm absorbed in emails, projections, reports, and more decisions than most people make in a year.

But then, the air shifts, and I know my angel has come out of the bedroom.

I glance down the aisle and see her walking toward me. She doesn't look particularly refreshed, which tells me she never fell asleep. *Fuck.*

"Hey," she says as I set my laptop aside, and she climbs in my lap, straddling me, wraps her arms around my neck, and hugs me, burying her sweet face in my neck.

"I'm sorry. I should have stayed with you."

"It's fine. I don't think I would have slept more anyway. I should work, too. I have a bunch to do since I took a couple of days off to shop."

I feel her smile against me.

"Not that I'm complaining."

I chuckle and rub my hands up and down her back. "I understand. Want to go cuddle for a wee bit before we get back to work?"

She sighs, and I know I just hit the nail on the head. She didn't want to ask, but she needs to be touched, and I will *never* turn her down. I love that she craves my touch.

Billie's needs always come before anything else.

I nod at Miller as I stand with Billie in my arms. She wraps her legs around my waist, and I carry her to the bedroom, and we get comfortable on the bed. I pull her against me, and she tucks her face against my chest.

"I know I'm needy," she says, hugging me close. "And I'm not sorry."

"Nor should you be." I tip her chin up and kiss her softly. "I enjoy cuddling you, *a ghrá.*"

"Something occurred to me while I was lying here, and I want to talk to you about it." She's still looking up at me and raises her arm to brush her fingers through my hair. "If you don't want to talk about it, it's okay."

I ghost my fingertips down her smooth cheek. "What is it? I'll tell you whatever you want to know."

"I was just thinking about the other day, when you were so upset, just sort of replaying it in my head—"

"I'm sorry I was an arse."

"No, that's not what I was thinking about. I was just contemplating the events, and then I realized why you might be extra overprotective. Because of Skyla and everything she went through at the hands of that piece of shit who stalked her and tormented her. I know that had to have impacted you because the two of you are so close."

I frown and kiss her forehead, breathing her in, so fucking grateful that she's so perceptive.

A psychopath stalked my baby sister for three bloody years, and every day of those was a torment I don't wish on anyone.

"I felt incompetent," I finally say. Our voices are quiet, and lying here with her intimately, I'd confess anything she wanted to hear. Her compassionate eyes hold mine as she gently brushes her hand up and down my arm. "No matter what I threatened or bribed him with, nothing mattered. He wouldn't stop. Every day, I watched Skyla's security cameras, checked in with her, and kept an eye on his comings and goings. It was always easier when he was out of the country."

"Who was he?" she asks with a scowl. "I mean, I know his name, and that he was wealthy, but as you said, most people do exactly what you say, especially if you threaten them. So, why didn't he fear you?"

"He was a senator's son," I reply. "He had people in his pocket, and he wasn't afraid of anything. I had Miller threaten him. I called the IRS, but nothing came of it. Anything I did, aside from kill the motherfucker, bounced right off him. It was incredibly frustrating, and it terrified me. Because he would have killed my sister."

Her arms tighten around me. "No, he wouldn't. Because she has you."

"I didn't do her any good in that situation, angel."

"Yes, you did. You made her feel safer. She loves you. You're her big brother. With four big brothers of my own, I know how that feels, and the fact that you took care of the security, that you helped her move to Montana and settled her in, and came to visit so often, helped her."

"Nothing like that will ever happen to you." I'm squeezing her so tightly, I'm surprised she can breathe. "You're the blood in my veins, and I will *not* allow you to be hurt. Aye, I likely have anxiety from the experience with Skyla, and that could trigger some of my reactions, but at the end of the day, you're the most important thing in my life, and there are no lengths I won't go to keep you unharmed. I want you to keep Simon with you when I can't be there when we're not at home."

"Which home?" she asks, her lips tipping up in a sassy grin.

"Any of them." I nip at her lips. "There's a new property that Gallagher Hotels is working on in Sweden that has garnered some attention from extremist groups who don't want to see any building on the site we've chosen. We're getting some threats, and I want to make sure you stay safe."

"Thank you for telling me." Her voice is soft, her hand still roaming over me. "I'll stick with Simon and won't do anything stupid."

"Thank you."

"And you have to promise me that you'll stick with Miller."

I smile down at her. "Worried about me, angel?"

"Of course, I am. I'm in love with you."

Rolling over her, I kiss her with everything in me, my entire world knocked off its axis at her words. I'll never get tired of hearing them. I'll never lose this feeling of possession, of obsession, whenever I merely think of her.

"I'm so fucking in love with you, *mo chroí*," I growl as I reach between us and rip her leggings away, making her gasp, her eyes widen. "I never get enough of you. It's like a fever I can't shake, and I don't want to. You need to be quiet now."

Her hands fumble with my pants, and finally, my cock springs free, and I push inside her, both of us gasping at how wet, how hot, how goddamn *perfect* she is.

"I need you," she whispers against my lips. "And it scares me. Because I don't need anybody."

"You don't have to be scared, *mo rúnsearc*. Because I'm right here, and I'm not going anywhere."

Linking my fingers with hers, I pin her arms over her head and move in and out, almost coming undone by the way her inner walls squeeze my cock.

"It's so good," she moans, lifting her hips with every

311

thrust and squeezing around me as her orgasm gathers. "Fucking hell."

"Shh. Go over, baby." I lick over the seam of her lips, then kiss her mouth as she cries out, quivering around me and pulling me into my own climax.

As we catch our breath, I brush her hair back from her face, murmuring, "You're so beautiful. So damn sweet."

With a happy smile, she presses her lips to mine. "You're so sexy. And for as long as I live, it'll never be long enough with you."

"Christ." I lower my forehead to hers. "You undo me, *a ghrá.*"

She makes me feel special. Not because of my name or the money but because she sees *me.* And she loves me.

And I will treasure her until I take my last breath.

"Do you want to go to the office first or the house?" Miller asks me once we're in the SUV leaving the plane.

"The office," I reply. "We'll go straight to Galway from there tonight. I don't want to stay in Dublin."

Miller's eyes meet mine in the rearview.

Yes, I'm changing the plan, but I only get one more week alone with my angel, and I'm going to spend it in my favorite place with her, *not* at work.

I lift an eyebrow.

"Yes, sir."

I feel Billie's eyes on me, and I turn to look at her.

"I take it you were supposed to be in Dublin longer than a few hours?"

"The best thing about being the boss is, I make my own rules, angel. I'll be in Dublin as long as I wish to be, and right now, that's not long. I want to show you my home on the cliffs and spend time with you there, so that's exactly what we're going to do."

"Sounds great to me." She squeezes my hand and leans over to press a kiss on my shoulder.

Thirty minutes later, Miller pulls into the car park under my building, and we're headed up to my office.

"You're welcome to work in my office," I offer her. "I have to sit in on a couple of meetings."

"Perfect." She smooths her hands down her Dior blouse. After we made love and slept for a couple of hours, we each had a shower and changed clothes. Billie is once more impeccably dressed, her hair and makeup flawless.

I know she prefers luxury fashion labels, but it seems her favorite is Dior. I'll have to take her to the flagship store in Paris for Christmas.

When we arrive on the top floor, where my offices are, we step out of the elevator, and Billie takes it in. The building is several centuries old, but this space has been decorated with sharp lines. The color palette is black and white, with splashes of color here and there.

Her heels clip on the hardwood floor as I lead her to my office. Once I've unlocked the door, I gesture her inside, and she sets her bag on the couch on the far wall.

"This is a big office," she says, her eyes touching on everything in the room. "How often are you in it?"

"Before I started the Montana property? At least once a month. Now? Quarterly."

She nods, and I cross to her. Taking her chin in my grip, I lower my mouth to hers. Her hands land on my sides, holding on to my jacket as I devour her mouth, and when I pull back, her eyes shine with lust.

"What was that for?" she asks.

"You look sexy in my office. Pity we don't have time for me to fuck you on my desk before we leave."

That has her blinking rapidly, and before I can kiss her again, there's a knock on the door.

"You're here."

I tuck Billie into my side as I turn to my ex-wife and smile at her. "Hello, Fiona. This is Billie Blackwell."

Billie tenses beside me, only enough for me to feel it, but then she immediately walks forward, offering her hand to my ex.

"Pleasure," Billie says, shaking Fiona's hand.

Fiona raises an eyebrow and looks at me over Billie's shoulder, and I know she's about to underestimate my girl.

"How lovely to meet you," Fiona says. "And a beautiful girl you are at that. That's a lovely blouse."

Billie stiffens as she steps back. "Thank you. If you'll excuse me, I have a lot of work to see to."

She smiles at both of us, then crosses to her computer bag and pulls out her laptop.

"Connor, can I sit at your desk, or should I—"

"Make yourself comfortable, angel," I reply easily, still watching Fiona. "I'll be a couple of hours. If you need anything at all, Scott is at his desk, and he can help you. He's Fiona's and my assistant since I'm not in the office often."

"Thank you," Billie says with an easy smile. "I'm fine for now."

"Everyone is in the conference room," Fiona says, waiting for me.

I nod, but I don't move toward her. Instead, I cross to Billie and press my lips against her forehead, then lean down to her ear and whisper, "I love you to distraction, *a ghrá*. Make yourself at home."

She smiles up at me and doesn't bother to whisper when she replies, "I love you, too."

With that, I walk toward Fiona, not missing the way her eyes have widened, and when we're in the hallway and my office door is closed, she immediately starts asking questions.

"This is serious, then? And how old is she, Connor? She looks like a bleedin' uni student."

I stop and turn to her. "You'll want to be careful how you talk about her. I won't warn you again."

She scowls, but I keep walking into the conference room. She's my friend, but she's also my ex-wife, and I won't confide in her about my relationship with Billie. I know that'll piss Fiona off, but I don't care.

I want to get through these meetings quickly so I can take Billie home.

The sooner I get out of here, the better.

Chapter Twenty-Two

BILLIE

So that was Connor's ex-wife.

Sitting behind his desk, staring at the black screen of my laptop, I nibble on my bottom lip until it's swollen. I saw the way her eyes moved over me, assessing me. I felt the cold judgment and could almost hear her thoughts.

This girl is too young and definitely not good enough for the likes of Connor Gallagher.

At any point since he told me he'd been married and who his ex-wife was, I could have searched for Fiona online, to look at photos, to dig into her life a little, but I purposely didn't do that. However, after being blind-sided today, maybe I should have.

Fiona is beautiful. There's no denying it. Long blond hair cascades down her back, her blue eyes are sharp and don't seem to miss anything, not to mention, she has a figure to die for. Perfectly hourglass, that woman is the epitome of *bombshell*.

And he hasn't been with her in a dozen years.

I'm not jealous of his ex. Connor has made it abundantly clear that I'm the center of his universe, and that didn't change when Fiona came into the room. I have no reason at all to feel insecure when it comes to my relationship with Ireland's most eligible bachelor.

But something there made me uneasy.

Something I can't put my finger on, but I learned a long time ago to trust my gut.

"I'll just keep my guard up," I decide as I wake up the computer and get to work. It's late enough in the day now that most of the United States is awake, so I can send emails, texts, and check in with my girls at the shop.

> Hi, Emily! How is everything going there?

As I wait for a reply, I toggle over and shoot out some emails to a designer and a couple of authors who want to collab on some work in the coming months.

> Emily: All is well here, Bee! I'm emailing over the list of things that need to be reordered ASAP because we keep selling out. The dark romance section is starting to look sparse.

She goes on to tell me about all four new hires and how well they're doing. Finally, I simply call her.

I'll pay the roaming fees.

"I think this is easier than texts," I say when Emily answers.

"Definitely, I just didn't know if you're still in the country."

"I'm not. We're in Ireland, but I'm available any time. You know that. So the new girls are doing well?"

"They're great, Billie. I can see why you couldn't choose between them. The best thing is that their schedules are flexible, so all of the shifts are covered. And they're fun to work with. We approve."

"That's good news. I was so nervous about leaving for this long so soon after they started."

"No need," Emily assures me. "They caught on quickly, and we're a well-oiled machine now. It helps that they all love to read and enjoy talking about books, too."

"That's a huge bonus," I agree. "And it wasn't a prerequisite, but I'm glad it worked out that way. I'll be sure to put in a restock order when we get off the phone. What else do we need? Stickers? Bookmarks? I saw some really cute Kindle covers that we should stock."

"That's a good idea. And what about notebooks, candles, even blankets? Who doesn't love to be cozy when they read? Fall will be here before we know it."

"You're so right. I'm on it. Good idea, Em."

"I aim to please."

"As you think of other things, text me. I'll be ordering stuff for the next couple of hours."

"I'm going to talk to the other girls, and I'll shoot you ideas as we think of them," she promises. "This is *so fun*. It's like shopping, but not with my own money."

With a chuckle, we end the call, and I check my email to see what Em has suggested we restock.

"Oh, she's good. She was absolutely the right choice to manage the store."

I get to work ordering new books for the shop. After checking upcoming new release schedules, I get those preordered so they're available on release day as well. In the meantime, my phone pings with all kinds of ideas from my girls.

I'm in the middle of ordering new stickers with things like *Smut Reader* ... and *Beg, Baby Girl,* and other things that never fail to make me giggle.

Just as I've moved on to bookmarks, the door of the office opens, but I finish double-checking my cart before I greet Connor.

"Sorry, I just need a minute to make sure this is right."

"Take your time."

My head jerks up. That's not Connor's voice. That's Fiona.

"My apologies," I reply. "I was expecting Connor."

And I expect anyone else to knock on the goddamn door.

"He's still in a meeting with Ronan," she says with an easy smile as she sits in the visitor's chair across from me. She crosses her shapely legs, smooths her black skirt, and pins me with her stern gaze.

Why do I feel like I've been summoned to the principal's office?

"Can I help you?" I ask, not willing to cower or give her the upper hand.

This woman will be sorely disappointed that she can't bully me.

"I thought I'd swing by and get to know you a wee bit better," she says as if we're about to be good friends.

I don't think we are.

"Great," I reply with a wide smile. "What do you do here for Gallagher Hotels?"

She looks surprised as if I should already know.

"I'm an attorney," she says simply.

"I see. Does this organization fend off many lawsuits? Given how vast it is, with so many properties, I would think it does. I'm sure people often fall or are unhappy with the chocolate on their pillow at night."

"Are you planning to sue us?" She lifts an eyebrow.

"Right." I snort and shake my head.

Fiona blinks at me slowly. "And what do *you* do, Miss Blackwell?"

"I'm a business owner," I reply, holding her gaze head-on.

"Interesting." She flicks a microscopic piece of lint off her skirt. "What kind of business would that be? Are you a social media influencer? A photographer? A travel blogger?"

I don't flinch. I don't show any reaction to Fiona's effort to be condescending and make me look like a fool.

This bitch.

"No, actually, although I think that any successful business or endeavor is valuable, as long as the person doing it is fulfilled, I own a brick-and-mortar independent bookstore in Bitterroot Valley."

Fiona's eyebrow lifts in surprise. "And what kinds of books do you sell?"

Why are you interviewing me?

"We primarily sell romance, along with women's fiction and some thrillers."

Fiona snorts. "I see."

"Do you?"

That eyebrow lifts once more.

"Did you know that romance accounts for one-point-four billion dollars worth of business every year, and it's climbing? That's almost double the next highest-selling genre, which happens to be thriller. Romance continues to grow each and every year in sales, and I would be ridiculous if I didn't capitalize on that. Besides, I enjoy it myself."

"I didn't say anything derogatory about it," she insists.

"Not with words, but your smirk did." I sit back in the chair and cross my arms over my chest. "You have already decided that you don't like me."

"You seem to have a habit of putting words in others' mouths."

I smile at her, not backing down at all, and Fiona finally shifts in her seat.

"I'll cut to the chase," she says, leaning forward. "I don't dislike you, Billie."

Oh, now we're on a first-name basis.

"Not at all," she continues. "I don't know you well enough to make such a decision. But I did want to warn you that as charming and handsome as Connor is, he'll never commit to you, no matter how much you beg him to."

I lift an eyebrow, but she keeps talking.

"He's a good man. Kind. Smart. But he's not great at being in a relationship, and he will never confide in you, be truly intimate with you, and I don't mean that in a physical sense. He's excellent in bed."

I narrow my eyes, and still, she continues.

I would like to scratch her eyes out.

"You're young. *So young.* Fresh and new, and I can see the appeal. But you have so much life ahead of you. Do you really want to spend it with someone who has so much more life experience than you? Of course, he *is* wealthy."

I'm so fucking angry. This woman is one of Connor's best friends?

"I'm sure it was exciting when he took you shopping for those clothes. Connor has excellent taste, and he's generous almost to a fault. As long as he's still enamored with you, he'll continue to shower you with expensive gifts. He'll likely even let you keep them when he's through with you."

Fuck, she sounds bitter. Connor led me to believe that they were good friends because the divorce had been wanted on both sides.

I'm wondering now if Fiona was not as agreeable as Connor believed. *Is she angry that she no longer has access to him?*

"Is that what he did to you?" I ask, my voice even. "He let you keep the gifts?"

"He didn't *let* me do anything," she says, finally showing her frustration. "Those items were mine."

"Of course, they were," I reply. "They were gifts, so they were yours."

"Connor—"

"I'm going to stop you there." I hold up my hand. "I can't stomach listening to you disrespect the man I love any longer. I don't care what you think of me. Yes, I'm a lot younger than him. That's just ... time. Completely out of anyone's control. I'm not a child. I'm a successful businesswoman who comes from a nice family in a small town in Montana. I'm not wealthy. And honestly, who the fuck cares?"

Her eyes widen at that, and I continue, keeping my tone even because I refuse to raise my voice in this office. She's not worth it.

"You don't know us. You have no idea what happens in our relationship. But I can guarantee you this: what Connor and I share is not at all the same as what you had with him all those years ago. I know that because we're different people. Connor's not the same person as he was back then. He claims that you're one of his closest friends, but I'd disagree. I suspect, based on this conversation and the way you greeted me today, that your divorce was not as amicable as you let him believe it was. Sure, *my* good friends might ask questions and even warn him that hurting me means they hurt him in turn. But they wouldn't deliberately try to destroy something important to me."

"I'm not—"

"You are. You're trying to hurt *him*. Because scaring me off, talking me into running away from him, would only hurt him."

I plant my hands on the desk and stand, and she also rises out of her chair, glaring at me now.

You picked the wrong girl to fuck with, Fiona.

"Nothing you could say would make me leave him. I don't give two fucks about his money. Oh, by the way, he didn't buy me this blouse. I bought it. Me. If I want pretty things, I can buy them. I don't need a billionaire boyfriend for that. I'm not sure where this jealousy is coming from."

Fiona's jaw drops, but she doesn't say anything.

"From what I understand, you're happily married with two children."

"I'm simply looking out for a friend."

"Right." I snort and shake my head. "And I'm a flamingo. I'm in love with that man, and I will *never* sit back and let anyone speak about him the way you just did. He's so much better than that. If you don't like me or approve of me, or whatever, that's okay. It honestly doesn't bother me. I'm not everyone's cup of tea, and at the end of the day, you don't matter to me. But you walked in this room today with a *huge* chip on your shoulder, and that's bullshit."

Practically shaking, I straighten up and look Fiona up and down.

"You should be ashamed of yourself."

I have to get out of here. I'm so angry, I want to deck

that bitch, so I march to the open door but stop and look back at her.

"And the next time you walk into this or any other of Connor's spaces, you'll fucking knock or you won't come in at all."

I stomp out, running into a hard chest, and when I look up, I find Connor, whose green eyes are on. Fucking. Fire.

"How much of that did you hear?" My voice is starting to shake from the adrenaline, and I hate it.

I can't catch my fucking breath. My hands are in fists. I'm going to lose my shit, so I need to get somewhere private.

"From the minute she asked you what you do for a living. Angel, I—"

All of it.

He heard all of it.

"That's some friend you have there." I storm away, my heels clicking on the floor.

"Billie—"

"I need the ladies' room," I reply, without looking back at him and push through the door, walk to the sinks, and lean on the granite, staring at my reflection.

My cheeks are pink with anger. My eyes are flashing. My jaw is tight.

I look like I want to burn the world to the ground.

Because I do.

How dare she?

"She doesn't know you," I remind myself. "And she sure as fuck doesn't know him."

Chapter Twenty-Three

CONNOR

I want to run after Billie and make sure she's all right.

Aye, her backbone is something to behold.

I've never seen her so angry, and as much as it's a turn-on, I'm also worried that Fiona has pushed her beyond what she can bear.

Or is willing to tolerate.

And that would be unforgivable.

I cannot lose this woman. My heart. How many unwanted situations will Billie have to contend with by being in my life? I want to reassure her that nothing Fiona said was true. Not for us.

But before I can do any of that, I have to talk to my ex-wife.

Calmly, I stride into my office and close the door behind me. Fiona's standing before my desk, breathing hard, but when she sees me, she pastes on a smile.

"You just missed Billie," she says.

"I saw her," I reply and stop ten feet from her, shove my hands in my pockets, and rock back on my heels, watching her. She stares me dead in the eyes. "She didn't look happy."

"Oh, you know how young people are," she replies, waving me off as she strides toward the door. "So emotional."

"Especially when their man's ex-wife tries to warn them off the relationship."

That has her coming up short, and she turns to stare at me with a frown. "Pardon?"

"You heard me, Fiona. I heard every bloody word you said to her."

"It's not like you to eavesdrop."

"I didn't realize it was like *you* to be a condescending, coldhearted bitch, but here we are."

Fiona gasps, clutching at her very real pearls. "You can't speak to me like that."

"Oh, aye. I can. That woman did *nothing* to you. She's not the reason our marriage failed. She's not trying to take anything from you. So would you like to explain to me what in the actual feck your problem is?"

"I didn't *try* to be cruel," she says, her shoulders drooping in defeat. "I honestly wanted to make sure she understood what she's getting herself into with you because I know from experience that the aftermath can be devastating. She's *so young*, Connor. And she's so desperately in love with you, she might as well be walking around with heart eyes, and we both know that you don't *do* love."

I shake my head. I don't want to hurt her, but she took a shot at my angel, and *no one* in this world gets to do that without consequence. "I'm in love with her. Desperately. Completely. Irreversibly, and I've told her so. Often."

Fiona's eyes register hurt before she schools her features and clears her throat.

"I see." She swallows hard and nods. "Do you know that in the five years we were married, you never *once* said those words to me? Not one time."

I lift an eyebrow. "No, I didn't."

"So it's not that you're not capable, just that you weren't able to love *me*."

"Fiona." I sigh and push my hands through my hair. "What in the actual— Where is this coming from after a dozen years, another marriage, and two kids? None of this is news. I'm not *cheating on you* because it's been over for what feels like a lifetime. If you're half the friend you claim to be, you'd be happy for me, with maybe a *hint* of concern. You don't attack the woman I love in my own bloody office."

"It has disaster written all over it. Besides, what am I supposed to think? The age gap is significant, Connor, and she comes from a family with such meager wealth, it screams gold digger."

"If you want to keep your position with this company, you'll watch your goddamn mouth."

Her mouth opens and then closes again.

"Like Billie told you, you don't know us, and what's between us is none of your fecking business. I don't care what you think about my relationship with Billie. If you think I'd choose you and our friendship—which is hanging on by a bloody thread—over the love of my life, you don't know me at all. But I'm going to give you a piece of advice."

I cross to her and sense that the rage boiling inside me is written all over my face. Her eyes widen.

"Upset her again, and you'll regret it. If you can't handle seeing me with her, you need to find another position elsewhere. Because she's not going anywhere."

"Ronan—"

"Agrees."

Both of our heads turn to see my best friend standing in the doorway, his blue eyes fierce as he stares at his wife.

"I don't know what you did," he says, his voice hard, "but you were wrong. And if you're still in love with him, you should have said so a long time ago."

"No, that's not it at all," she says, shaking her head, looking desperate now. "I'm *not* in love with Connor. I don't know if I ever truly was. How can you love someone like that when they don't return the feelings?"

Ronan's eyes soften slightly, but I can see the hurt there, too, and it makes my stomach clench.

Jesus, Fiona.

She sighs, shakes her head, and throws her hands up at her sides. "I had good intentions. Warn the girl that Connor Gallagher is emotionally unavailable. Then I discovered that there are real feelings there, and yeah, it bruised my pride because once upon a time, I wanted those feelings from you. It doesn't matter that I don't want them now. It still gave me a jolt."

"We need to have a private conversation," Ronan says, suddenly looking tired, and I nod.

"And I need to find my angel and make sure she's okay."

I breeze past Fiona, but when I get to Ronan, I lay my hand on his shoulder.

"I'm happy for you," he says to me. "And that's the truth of it, mate. You deserve to be happy."

"So do you," I remind him before I walk out of the room and head for the restroom that Billie walked into ten minutes ago.

When I walk inside, I find her standing in front of the sinks. Her arms are crossed over her chest, and she's scowling at her own reflection.

Without a word, I wrap my arms around her, capturing her arms between us, and hold on tight.

"I wasn't prepared for that," she whispers against my chest.

"Of course, you weren't, and it's sorry I am that you had to deal with it. She's so out of line, *a ghrá*."

"I know."

"I'm sorry that you're upset."

"I'm not." She looks up at me, and I see a fire raging in her eyes.

She stood up for me to Fiona. Like a goddamn warrior.

"She doesn't *ever* get to say those things about you," she says, her voice hard, not shaking in the least. "I had to leave before I decked her."

"God, you're bloody incredible, Billie Blackwell."

"I'm questioning your judgment in friends right now," she says, still scowling at me. "I haven't even met Ronan yet, but if he's anything like her—"

"Listen to me." I frame her face in my hands, and she wraps her arms around my waist, leaning into me. Her body is tight with anger, and the fact that it's on my behalf is humbling. "I spoke with her and made it clear that if she has a problem with you and me, she needs to go."

Billie blinks fast. "Go ... where?"

"Find another job. I don't fecking care. Because *you're* my heart, and if she can't be happy for me and accept you, then she's no bloody friend of mine."

Surprise flashes through her amazing eyes. "You'd give her up because I had a fight with her?"

I can't help the chuckle that escapes me as I brush my lips over hers. "I'd do *anything* for you. You are priority number one, and if they don't approve, they can go. Because you're here for the long haul. I heard you in there, your magnificent spine in every bleeding word you handed her. It was the sexiest thing I'd ever heard."

"She pissed me off," she admits. "I know she was trying to be a mean girl, maybe bully me a bit, certainly let me know that I'm far beneath her shiny Louboutins, but she messed with the wrong fucking girl. I'm not a shy wallflower who will cower to her or anyone else. You're mine, and I stick up for what's mine."

"*Mo chroí.*" I pull her in and kiss the top of her head, then I pick her up in my arms. She wraps her legs around my waist, her skirt bunching up around her hips, as I carry her to the door and flip the deadbolt, locking us in.

"I'm not having sex on that sink. Public restrooms are *gross.*"

I grin against the curve of her neck and hitch her up higher, then pin her against the opposite wall so no one can hear us.

"This works," I growl against her ear. "God, you're so goddamn strong and sexy and perfect for me in every way."

I get my pants undone and my cock freed. Sliding her panties aside, I run my finger through her slit, groaning when I find her wet.

"Inside me," she breathes. "Please, Connor, I need you inside me."

"Such a good girl," I whisper against her ear as I push inside her, pausing when I'm balls deep to nibble on her neck.

She squeezes around me. She loves being praised, and I love doing it.

With my hands planted on her arse, I start to move, long and slow strokes at first, but then I pick up the pace until I'm driving her into the wall, her back hitting it with every thrust, and she starts to unravel against me.

"Yes," she breathes, her hands clenched in my hair. "*Yes*, baby. Oh God, it's so good."

"So bloody good," I echo. "I need you to come for me, bumble. Come apart for me, good girl."

She gasps, lets her forehead fall to mine, and then she's quaking around me, her pussy clenching me so tightly, there's no way to hold back my own climax. Eyes pinned to hers, I empty myself inside her.

"Thank you," she whispers against my lips as she continues to cling to me, and I brace her against the wall.

"You never have to thank me for this."

She grins and brushes her nose against my own. "Not for *this*, billionaire. For being you. For giving me more. For showing me how you feel about me."

"It's entirely my pleasure. Every minute with you is an absolute *pleasure*, and that's the truth, *a ghrá*."

I capture her mouth with mine, showing her how much I love her before I set her down and we both clean up. I unlock the bathroom, and we walk out.

No one looks at us. No one even hints that they might know what was happening behind that door.

Good, I don't have to fire anyone today.

"Are you finished with your meetings?" she asks me.

"Aye. Did you get everything done that you needed to?"

"No, actually, I was interrupted." *Dammit, Fiona.* "But I can finish on the plane or in the car or whatever mode of transportation we're taking."

"You get motion sickness, baby."

I brush my hand over her hair as we walk toward my office.

"I'll probably be okay."

"No, you'll sit at my desk and finish up. We can leave any time. There's no hurry."

"You're sure?"

"Yes. Are you hungry?"

"Actually, I'm starving."

"Then I'll order in some food, and we'll leave in a couple of hours."

She bites her lip as she sits behind my desk.

"What is it, bumble?"

"My work isn't as important as yours. It can wait if you want to go."

I shake my head at her. "I don't know where you get the idea that what you do isn't as important as what I do. You run a business, same as me. They're equally as important. Do what you need to do, *mo chroí*."

"Okay." She smiles and wakes up her laptop. "I'll be done within the hour."

"Perfect, I'll go order the food."

I walk out to Scott's desk, and he looks up at me expectantly.

"Aye, sir, how can I help ye?"

"I need you to order in fish and chips for two, along with some Bailey's cheesecake."

"The whole cheesecake, sir?"

"Aye. Within the hour."

Walking back into my office, where Billie's already hovered over her computer, her brows pulled together as she scans the screen, I fetch my laptop, sit on the other side of the desk from her, and dig into my own work while we wait for the food.

"You can have your chair back, and we can switch sides," she offers.

"No need," I reply. "I'm happy where I am, bumble. I like watching you be the boss."

She smirks, flashes me a sassy wink, then gets back to work. Sometimes she mumbles when she makes notes on her iPad. Sometimes she grins when she sees something that pleases her.

I hear texts come in on her phone, and she easily shifts focus to handle those, then returns to her computer.

Unable to help myself, I send her a text from my computer.

> You're fucking beautiful, a ghrá.

Her eyes dance up to the corner of her screen when the message comes through, and she grins as she types out a reply.

> Angel: You're the sexiest man I've ever seen. From the minute I saw you in my bookstore all those months ago, I knew I wanted to climb you like a fucking tree. And you are way better than any fantasy I could have conjured up.

Before I can round the desk and fuck her into next week, there's a knock on my door.

"Come in," I bark.

Scott pokes his head in. "Delivery, sir."

After my nod, Scott walks in and sets two bags of food on my desk.

"Let me know if you need anything else," he says before he leaves, shutting the door behind him.

"It smells good," Billie says, her eyes full of mischief.

"We need to eat and finish working so we can leave."

"I didn't think we were in a hurry." She pulls two boxes out of the bag, one for each of us, and passes one over to me.

"That was before I decided that I need to get you home, naked, so I can fuck you into next week."

She licks some salt off her thumb, her gaze pinned to mine. "I could eat this on the plane."

I bark out a laugh and open my own meal. "How are you feeling now?"

"After earlier?" she asks, and I nod. When she takes a mouthful of her fish and her eyes close, she hums with appreciation. I have to adjust my dick, who always twitches when she makes that sound.

It's not for you, mate.

"I'm still mad at her for what she said about you."

"What about what she said about *you*?"

Billie shrugs at that. "Meh, whatever. I let a lot roll off. I'm not one of those people who needs everyone to like them. I mean, I'm kind to pretty much everyone, and I'm a total hype girl when it comes to other women, and my friends, and people I love. But I didn't lie when I said I'm not for everyone, and that's okay with me. I've been judged my whole life, Connor. So if your ex-wife has an issue with me, I guess that's not my problem. I'll always be cordial to her because she's your friend and your very best friend's wife, but I don't think I'll be inviting her to my book club meetings. I get the feeling romance novels are *beneath her*. Whatever, she's missing out."

Fiona thinks this amazing woman is too young for me, but Billie has more maturity, more integrity than most people I know, regardless of age.

"But I'm warning you right now." Her hazel eyes flash over her fish. "If she says one more fucking word about you that I don't like, I'm taking her down."

"I don't need you to protect me, angel."

"Need? No. Gonna get it? Yep. Because you'd do the same for me, and this relationship works both ways."

It's said so simply, I can only blink at her.

I'm going to marry this woman.

Chapter Twenty-Four

BILLIE

I t was dark when we arrived in Galway last evening, so I didn't get to see the view from Connor's mansion. But I could hear the water crashing against the cliffs, and the air was heavy with salt and sea, so it made me long to take in the view.

Connor's still sleeping beside me when I wake and discover that the sun is just starting to come up. His arm is wrapped around my shoulders, holding me against his side, but he lets go when I gently move away.

After quickly using the bathroom, where he was true to his word, and all my toiletries were waiting, I make my way into the closet that rivals the size of the ones in New York and Montana, and tug on some leggings, a T-shirt, and because the air was so chilly last night, I borrow one of Connor's hoodies.

The material is well-worn and soft, so it's obviously one he's had for a long time, and when I pull it over my head, I'm surrounded by his cedarwood scent.

God, he smells good.

I wonder if he went to Cambridge? Or was this a souvenir?

Something tells me he wouldn't buy a hoodie like this unless it was his school.

With a shrug, I slip into sneakers and head downstairs, where I brew myself a cup of coffee, then slip out the sliding glass doors off the massive kitchen onto the expansive grassy area that leads to a path overlooking the sea.

When I reach the end of the path, roughly twenty yards from the side of the cliffs, I take a long, deep breath and stare out at the ocean.

It's fucking gorgeous here.

Birds fly overhead, floating on the wind. The water crashes on the rocks below, sending up a symphony of sound that drowns out everything else. For the first time since I can remember, there's no traffic in my head. The white noise from the ocean drowns it out, and I can just ... *be.*

The sun has barely crested over the green hills, casting the sky in light pink, and I take another long, deep breath, pulling it all in.

I don't know if I've ever seen anything more beautiful. I've heard stories of Ireland being green, but it's ... *green.* As if it invented the word. And it's the same color as my man's eyes.

I turn to look at the enormous stone mansion and see Connor walking toward me in black joggers and a hoodie similar to the one I'm wearing, holding his own mug of coffee, those Irish eyes smiling at me over the rim.

He's happy here.

"I needed to come see it," I say when he reaches me and wraps his arm around me to pull me into his side. "I couldn't wait."

"You should have woken me, angel."

I wrinkle my nose at him and sip my coffee. "Did you grow up in this house?"

"No. Ma and Da still own that house. It's about fifteen kilometers from here. Unless you have objections, we'll be going there this evening for dinner."

"I don't have any objections. I like your parents."

I was able to spend some time with them in London when we were there for Skyla and Mik's performance, and Connor's parents have been to Montana several times.

They've been nothing but nice to me. Of course, that was before their son and I were a couple. I wonder if they'll be as welcoming, knowing that we're in a relationship.

"Don't overthink it." He kisses my head, and we turn back to the ocean. "It's going to be fine. What do you think of the view?"

"Meh, it's fine."

I feel him staring down at me, and I can't hold back the laughter.

"Are you kidding me? Holy shit, Connor, this is gorgeous."

He grins, and his eyes drift down to the hoodie, and they narrow. "I like that."

I sip my coffee. "The fact that I stole your sweatshirt?"

"You wrapped up in my alma mater," he says, those blazing green orbs returning to my face. "Fascinating."

He's more relaxed here. I noticed it the second we stepped off the plane last night. It's like he's in the one place where he can drop his guard, and although I love him every day, this side of him is dreamy, too. And we all know how much I love his casual side. Connor is as sexy as sin in a suit, but Christ on a cracker, the things he does to me when he's let his proverbial hair down and is in relax mode?

My vagina is weeping with joy.

"I have a question," he says as I sip coffee and breathe in the sea air and ogle my man.

"Right now, dressed like that, I'll give you anything you want, billionaire."

His lips twitch, and he ghosts his fingertip down the bridge of my nose. "It's just lounge pants, bumble."

"It's not *just* anything. Okay, focus. What's your question?"

"What's your favorite book?"

I pause, then frown up at him. Christ, he's *tall*.

"Like my favorite book this year so far? Or my favorite broken down by trope or genre?"

"Of all time," he replies, skimming his hand up and down my arm.

"I don't know if that exists for me," I reply honestly.

342

"I've read thousands of books, I'm sure. If you want to talk classics—"

"Start there," he agrees.

"Well, there's a list. *Little Women*, of course. *Jane Eyre*. *To Kill a Mockingbird*, *Anna Karenina*, *The Count of Monte Cristo*. I read *Wuthering Heights* every year at Christmas."

"You do?" He kisses my forehead and smiles down at me. "Why?"

"Because it's heartbreaking and wonderful and like visiting an old friend. It's an interesting story about greed and family, and well … I like it. Finding a first edition is almost impossible."

Now his gaze tightens, obviously interested in what I'm telling him.

"Why?"

"Well, it was originally published under the name Ellis Bell rather than using her real name, Emily Brontë. It was also her only novel. She died at just thirty years old. Anyway, finding a copy of *Wuthering Heights* with Ellis Bell listed as the author isn't easy to do and quite expensive."

He takes my hand and leads me down the path that seems to meander by the cliffs, away from the house.

"Aside from the classics, I also enjoy *Outlander,* yet among modern work, I don't know. It's so hard to choose."

"Favorite authors, then?" he asks, and again, I have to bite my lip and think.

"I'd have to narrow it down to about ten." I shrug

when he laughs. "You don't understand. There are so many gifted authors, and I consume a lot of books. Devney Perry and Monica Murphy are two of my favorites. They're auto buys for me."

He nods, and now I'm curious.

"What about you? What do you like to read?"

"I don't have a lot of time to read for pleasure."

"Bullshit." There's no sting in my words as I nudge him with my shoulder.

He kicks up an eyebrow, and I shrug. "We all have time. We just choose to use it in different ways, which is totally valid. And you *are* a busy man. But you're not working twenty-four seven."

"I'd rather spend any free time I might have with you," he says.

"And sometimes, I'm reading while you're spending time with me." I chuckle and lean into him, enjoying him and our walk by the cliffs. "Not everyone has to be a reader. But you do have all of those books in the bedroom."

"I read thrillers and a little fantasy here and there. I also consume a lot of online articles," he says, thinking it over. "Podcasts. That sort of thing."

"I'll listen to podcasts with you."

We stop in the middle of the path, and he gently grips the back of my neck in his palm, bringing his face closer to mine.

"Would you then, bumble?"

"Sure." *Christ, I love it that his accent is thicker when we're here in Ireland.*

"And why is that?"

"Because I love you, and spending time with you is my favorite thing."

His face softens, and he leans in to brush his lips over mine, making my stomach clench with desire.

"You're so bleedin' sweet," he whispers against my lips, the words almost getting lost in the wind.

"You're different here," I reply, watching him closely.

"How so?"

"You're always wonderful, but I notice you're not as tense here. You're calmer. A little quicker to smile."

He stands up straight and glances over my head at the property, the house farther away now, and then out at the water. After taking a breath, he turns his gaze back to me and cups my face.

"This is home. It's familiar and where I can be myself. That's why I wanted to bring you here, to spend a good amount of time with you."

"When was the last time you were here?"

"At least three months ago. Maybe more."

What?

"Connor, if this is where you're the most at home, why don't you live here more often?"

"Because you're not here, angel." He rests his lips on my forehead and takes in a breath. "I want to be wherever you are, and Montana is home for you. Montana is where we bloom together, and I do love it there. I would say that aside from this place, it's where I'm most at home because *you're* my home."

This man and his amazing way with words.

"I want you to be happy."

Now, he wraps me in his arms, palms the back of my head, and holds me to him, embracing me so tenderly and lovingly, it brings tears to my eyes.

"I'm so fucking happy, *a ghrá*." He kisses the top of my head, and then he leads me back toward the house.

"Well, for the record, I like it here a lot."

"I want to show you the world."

"Let me be clear." I pull him to a stop so I have his undivided attention. "I've been out here for about an hour, and I can tell you with absolute certainty that it's incredible. I don't need the world. If this is waiting for us, I'll come here with you *anytime*. Once a month? Let's do it. I—"

I don't get another word out before he's on me, kissing me as if I'm the air he breathes, holding on to me as if the mere thought of letting go will tear his heart from his chest.

"Hold this," he says, pushing his mug in my free hand. Then I'm in his arms, giggling as he carries me to the house. "I'd fuck you right out here, but I have security cameras, and Miller and his team keep an eye out."

"I'd rather not put on a show for Miller and Simon," I agree, pressing my face to his warm neck. "And I can walk the rest of the way."

"Almost there," he replies, not even breathing hard.

How does he do this? Carry me as if I'm nothing more than a sack of potatoes?

He pushes into the house through the glass doors. The next thing I know, I'm sitting on the kitchen counter, and Connor is stripping me out of my clothes, kissing every piece of my skin as he uncovers it. "I woke up wanting you, and you weren't there."

"Sorry." My hands fist in his shirt, yanking it over his head. "Won't happen again."

He laughs as I lift my hips off the countertop so he can pull my leggings and panties off, and then he squats, spreads my legs, and buries his face in my pussy, lapping at my core.

"Oh God." I lean back on my elbows, unable to stay upright, and reach down with one hand to clutch his hair in my fist. "You're so fucking good at that."

I close my eyes and let my head fall back.

"Eyes on me, or I stop."

My gaze flutters open and back to his, and then he licks me, from opening to clit, and every muscle in my body tightens.

"Connor."

"You're so bloody soaked, angel."

"Billionaire."

"Aye, *a ghrá*. What is it that you need?"

"You."

"More specific." I love it when his voice gets bossy and hard like this.

"*Connor.*" He pushes his tongue inside me, and I swear to all that's holy, I'm going to explode.

"Tell me."

"Please let me come. I need to come."

He rubs his thumb over that bundle of nerves and fucks my opening with his tongue. I fall apart, my hips pushing, circling, as I ride wave after wave, then Connor's kissing the inside of my thighs and up my hip to my stomach. As his teeth close around my nipple, I feel him nudge his pants down before the crown of his cock is pressed to my opening, and he slides his mouth to mine with a groan.

"You're so ready for me."

"Yes," I whisper against his lips.

"Is that what you need, *mo rúnsearc*? Do you need my cock inside you?"

"*Please.*" My nails dig into his shoulders, and with a satisfied grin on that impossibly handsome face, he slams into me and doesn't stop to wait for me to adjust to his size.

He pounds in and out, hands gripping my hips so hard, I'm bound to have bruises from his fingertips later, and I *can't wait.*

His face is mere inches from mine, and he's murmuring words in Gaelic that I don't understand, but they're so beautiful, they embed themselves right into my heart.

"Mine," he finally growls in English, biting me just under my ear. "You're mine, Billie. Every gorgeous piece of you. Inside and out."

"Yours," I confirm, hitching my legs higher on his hips. "Always yours."

He pushes twice more, then grinds against me, filling me so completely and hitting my clit *just so* until we're both rushing into oblivion together. He fucks me through his climax. Breathing hard, he braces himself on the counter on either side of my hips and nibbles the crook of my neck, sending more shivers through me, making me tighten around him again.

"Christ, I love you." He shakes his head and kisses my forehead. "Every glorious inch of you."

"I love you too, billionaire." I grin at him, then cringe when he pulls out of me, and we make a mess of the kitchen floor. "I'll clean that up."

"I have housekeepers," he reminds me.

"Oh, hell no. I'm not leaving that for a housekeeper." I push on his chest and reach for the paper towels, but he scoops me up, tucked under his arm, and carries me out of the room. "Connor!"

"I'll take care of it before they get here," he says. "But right now, I want you back in our bed."

"That's a lovely handbag, Billie," Maeve, Connor's mom, says to me as we sit in the parlor before dinner is served.

Their home is *bigger* than Connor's, and I didn't think that was possible.

I was dead wrong.

The Gallagher family is beyond what I can comprehend as wealthy. Their hotel and resort brand is on par with Hilton, The Ritz, and other luxury hotels, and I get that.

But sometimes, I'm reminded just how filthy rich they are.

I'm in a green Chanel dress with black Chanel heels and a bag from the same designer. All of it thrifted, which makes me immensely happy.

"Oh, thank you," I reply, glancing down at the bag in my lap. "I was excited to find it."

"I looked for months," she says, surprising me.

"You did?"

"Yes, I called every Chanel sales associate I know in Europe and the US, and no one could get their hands on one for me."

I blink at her, surprised, and aware that Connor and his father are listening to our conversation.

"I have to ask, where did you find it?" Maeve asks.

"At a consignment shop in New York," I reply with a wide smile. "Just this past week, when Connor and I were there. I was *shocked* when I saw it on the shelf, and I couldn't leave it behind because I knew it was hard to get."

Maeve blinks in surprise. "A consignment shop? Interesting."

"To be honest, my whole outfit is thrifted."

Her jaw drops. "But you're covered in Chanel, head to toe, darlin'. In fact, every time I've seen you this past year, you've been in designer labels. I admire your fashion choices."

"Yes, ma'am, thank you. All thrifted."

Her gaze moves to Connor's, and then back to me.

"Billie, I'm quite sure my son would be happy to buy you any labels you want, new from the shops."

"Oh, I know he would." I nod, not shy in the least. "Connor's incredibly generous, but I have to tell you, going on the hunt for designer labels through consignment and at a thrift store I found in a neighboring town is one of my favorite hobbies."

Maeve's green eyes don't look convinced, so I chuckle and lean over to take her hand.

"Honest, you'd be shocked at what I find. Most of the garments still have tags on them and have never been worn. I *love* the game of it, the thrill of the hunt, I guess you could say. And I'm obsessed with fashion. This is how I feed that obsession, which I'm happy to do on my own. Connor is already generous enough with his time, his affection, and so many other things. I don't need him to splurge on shopping."

"So tell me," she says, leaning in closer. "What else have you found? I want to hear about it all. And next time you're in New York, I'll meet you there and join you, if you don't mind."

I rub my hands together, thrilled to share my secrets with Connor's mom. I love that she'd like to go with me.

"Oh, I'd love that. Okay, I found so many amazing things. Do you remember ..."

Maeve and I spend the next thirty minutes talking about bags and shoes and clothes. When it's time for dinner, it's not Connor wrapping his arm around my shoulders to guide me to the dining room, but Patrick.

351

"You're a fine thing," he says with a soft smile. Connor resembles his father. "And a beautiful one. How have you been, Billie?"

"I'm doing well, thank you. And you?"

He looks down at me, almost as tall as his son, and appears surprised that I'd ask him how he is.

Does no one ask powerful people how they're doing? It boggles my mind.

"I'm grand, thank ye," he replies, showing me to my seat at the table.

"Are you enjoying retirement?" I ask him as I set my napkin in my lap.

"Goodness, no," Maeve says, shaking her head with a laugh. "He's bored out of his bleedin' mind."

Connor's eyes sharpen on his father. "Why didn't you say something?"

Patrick shakes his head. "I'll find things to fill my time. Golf isn't it for me."

"Da, you can come back—"

"No, lad." Patrick shakes his head again. "That's for you now. The truth is, I don't want to go back to the office. We enjoy being in Galway, and now that both you and Skyla are in Montana, we'll come out there more often."

"Perhaps, if someone would give us wee babies to hold and smother with love, we wouldn't be so bored." Maeve stares at her son, and I hide my smile behind my glass of wine.

"You're not as subtle as you once were," Connor says to his mother.

"I'm running out of time to be subtle," she insists. "I want babies to hold and love before I leave this earth, Connor Declan Gallagher."

I can't hold back the bubble of laughter that escapes, and Maeve turns her attention to me.

"Do you want children, Billie?"

Connor mutters, "Christ," under his breath, earning a glare from his mother.

"Sure, one day. For now, I spoil my niece, Birdie. Did you hear that Dani and Bridger are going to have another baby?"

"No, we hadn't heard," Patrick says, eyeing his wife with tender love in his green eyes. "That's lovely then."

"I'm sure your parents are filled with joy," Maeve says, her eyes welling with tears.

"You know what I think is really great?" I ask her, and she turns her attention to me, sniffling against her napkin. "That you don't have to be related to someone by blood to show them affection and love. I know, without a doubt in my mind, that my brother's new baby will need all the attention they can get. So please feel welcome to come to Bitterroot Valley anytime to get all the baby snuggles you need. Dani doesn't have parents of her own, but that baby will have a lot of people around to shower him or her with affection. And Birdie is the sweetest little thing, as you know. If I remember correctly, she loved hearing the Irish stories you told her, Patrick, when we were in London."

"We'll have to go soon. And then spend the holidays

there as well," Maeve says to Patrick, who nods while watching me.

Connor takes my hand in his and kisses my knuckles as dinner is served.

Chapter Twenty-Five

CONNOR

"Christ, you're a vision." Taking Billie's hand in mine, I lift it to my lips and pepper the back of her hand with kisses. She's in another off-the-shoulder black dress, but this one is shorter, hitting just above her knees and hugging her delicious curves.

"You simply take my breath away."

"Thank you. You always look divine in a suit. Is that Armani?"

With a grin, I gesture for her to get into the car, then follow her inside and pull her next to me. "Of course, it is."

She smirks and leans into me as we drive away from the house. "Where are we going? Do I get to know yet?"

It's been four days since we had dinner with my parents, and she made them fall almost as in love with her as I am. She made them feel like they were part of her family, and that's something about her that's so fucking special.

We've spent our time mostly at home, but I have taken her out to some of my favorite restaurants and gone on drives to show her the scenery. I've shown her my home, and she's soaked it all in, not just for my sake but because she's truly enjoying herself.

I've always loved travel, but exploring with my angel is a whole new experience that I'm quickly becoming addicted to.

However, tonight is special.

"We're going to an art gallery exhibit," I inform her.

"What kind of art?" She's already excited, those whiskey eyes alight with the idea of a new adventure, and my heart catches.

"Have I told you today how fucking beautiful you are, bumble?"

She presses her hand to my cheek and rubs her thumb over my lower lip. "What kind of art, billionaire?"

"Glass. Have you heard of Kane O'Callaghan?"

"Connor. Of *course*, I've heard of Kane O'Callaghan. Holy shit, there's a gallery here with his work in it?"

"Aye, he owns the gallery. And he has a new exhibit opening tonight, and we're his guests."

Her jaw drops. "I'm sorry, what?"

If I'm not mistaken, her hand starts to tremble in mine. "Hey, it's okay, angel. He's a good mate of mine from when we were lads, and he knew I'd be in town. You don't want to go?"

"Holy fucking shit," she whispers. "I *love* his work. I was in Seattle a few years ago and spent three days admiring the glass in the museum dedicated to him there.

It has to be *hard* work. It's so beautiful. It inspired so much emotion, and it was like it gripped me by the throat and didn't want to let go. I didn't want to leave."

A tear slips out of her eye, and I catch it with my fingertip. My girl feels things so fecking deeply.

"*A ghrá*, I don't want you to cry."

"I'm overwhelmed, and that doesn't happen often." She inhales, clears her throat, and dabs at her eyes, careful not to smudge her makeup. "I'm fine. Wow, this is fun. You know some cool people, billionaire."

I see how she's put on the facade of strength, not wanting to show too much vulnerability right before we get to the gallery, and I'll give it to her.

No one wants to have tears when they meet someone they admire.

But later, I'm going to hold her close and get her to talk to me.

Miller pulls up in front of the gallery, where some members of the press wait to take photos.

Kane is a big fecking deal, and this is an invitation-only event.

"Jesus," Billie mutters, those nerves back in place.

"You're gorgeous and have nothing to worry about," I remind her.

"You do realize that after this, we're going to be *very* public, Connor." She blinks at me, that vulnerability shining through. "Are you okay with that?"

"You're mine," I reply and cover her lips with mine. "The sooner the world knows it, the better. Come on, angel, I want to introduce you to my friends."

She smiles as Miller opens my door, and I climb out, then extend my hand to my girl.

As we walk toward the doors, Simon and Miller flank us, but someone calls out, "Mr. Gallagher! Can we get some shots of the two of you?"

"You okay with that?" I murmur to Billie.

"Of course," she says, and we stop on the red carpet. Miller and Simon step back two paces, and I wrap my arm around Billie's back and pose for the cameras.

After thirty seconds, I wave, then lead her the rest of the way inside.

"Well, that was interesting," she murmurs. "I might want copies of those pictures."

"I'm sure they'll show up on social media within the hour, and you can grab them," Simon says.

No doubt Billie will hear from *her girls* about that. Apparently, they've thoroughly enjoyed all the pictures she's been sending of us in Ireland. It's such a beautiful, rugged country, and having Billie in this part of the world has been incredible.

I snatch two flutes of champagne off a tray and offer one to Billie, and we wander around the room, admiring the magnificent works of art on display.

"He has such an eye for color and movement," Billie says as we stand before an impressive piece that looks like flames rising into the sky. "It's amazing to me how a stationary piece can look so much like it's moving. Like it's on fire and its own living being."

"Well, if that's not one hell of a compliment, I don't know what is."

We turn, and my old friend sweeps me up in a quick hug. He's grinning from ear to ear.

"It's good to see you," I tell him, but he's already turned his attention to my girl.

"Aye, it is, but I want to meet this lovely woman with an eye for genius."

Anastasia, Kane's wife, smirks beside him.

"This is Billie," I tell him. "Billie, this is Kane and his wife, Anastasia."

"Please, call me Bee," she says as she shakes their hands. "It's a pleasure to meet you. I'm a big fan."

"And now, I'm a fan of yours," Kane replies after shaking her hand. "Connor tells me you're from Montana?"

Billie's eyebrow climbs in surprise. "That's right. Do you two live here in Galway?"

"Only part of the year," Anastasia replies. I like Kane's wife very much. She's a beautiful blonde with the bluest eyes and a curvy figure, and she keeps Kane in line the way no one else has ever been able to. "The rest of the time, we're on a little island just across the Sound from Seattle. That's where I'm from."

"That makes sense," Billie says. "The museum there is amazing."

"Right?" Anastasia grins, takes Billie's hand, and pulls her away. "Kane's working on a new exhibit for the museum now. You really have to come see it. Now, come with me to the bar. I want to introduce you to Kane's siblings and their families."

They walk away, and I turn to my friend with a grin. "I like your wife."

"Aye, and so do I, mate. She's the best part of me."

"How are the kids?"

"Hopefully asleep." He laughs and claps me on the shoulder. "Come on, there's some whiskey around here somewhere."

"Don't you have to see to your other guests?"

"I've said hello, and that's all they need from me."

"And there you are, the grumpy bastard I've always known. I was worried there for a minute."

He smirks, and we each take two fingers of whiskey from the bartender.

"Your package was delivered this morning," he tells me. "Safe and sound."

"Excellent, thank you. She'll love it."

"It was supposed to be a part of that new exhibit my wife mentioned."

"I'm quite sure the two million I paid you will make up for that."

Kane laughs, then swallows his whiskey. "It took the edge off. And how are you and your pretty lass doing?"

"She's the best part of me," I reply, echoing his own words.

"I'm sorry to interrupt," Billie says as she sidles up beside me, slipping her hand into mine and linking our fingers. "I'd like to ask a question about a piece if you're open to discussing it. Some artists don't like to talk about their art."

"For you, fair Bee, I will talk about it. Which one do you fancy, then?"

"The one you've titled *Luminary*." She leads us both to the piece set on a pedestal that has to be about a square meter in size to accommodate the massive chunk of glass. It's wavy, resembles a shell with a pearl inside, and is colored the same as a pearl.

The discreet price plaque says it's fifty thousand euros.

And now, it's my bumble bee's.

"You have good taste," Kane says with a nod as the two settle in to talk about his process, and I step back, giving her time with a man she admires.

"She's wonderful," Anastasia says beside me as we both look on.

"She's everything," I reply.

"When you get married, I'd love to do the cake."

"I thought you retired from the cake business."

She shrugs. "I did, but I still work magic for the people I love. I'll come out of retirement for you."

"You'd deliver to Montana?"

"I'll deliver it wherever it needs to be, friend. You think you'd do it in Montana?" she counters.

"That's her home. Our home, now," I reply. "Her family and friends are there. I can't imagine her wanting it anywhere else."

"You know what I find intriguing? You're already talking about a wedding as if it's a foregone conclusion, but there's no ring on that girl's finger."

"Yet." I wink at my friend and watch as Billie makes Kane laugh. "Holy shit, was that a *laugh* out of him?"

"It happens once in a while," Anastasia replies. "Always shocks the hell out of his family, too. But the tortured artist has mellowed."

"Thanks to you and the wee ones."

She smiles brightly at that. "I like to think so. Bring Bee to Seattle sometime so we can spend more time together."

"We'd like that."

And then it hits me how distinctly different Anastasia's response to Billie is from Fiona's. Granted, Anastasia and I don't have a romantic history, but Billie's words flash through my mind, nonetheless.

"Sure, my good friends might ask questions and even warn him that hurting me means they hurt him in turn. But they wouldn't deliberately try to destroy something important to me."

Anastasia isn't in any way threatened by Billie. In fact, she embraced her simply because she's my friend. Because that's what a good friend does.

Well, that and because Billie Blackwell is irresistible. She and Kane see how important Billie is to me, and that's enough.

Fuck.

"But she and Kane might not make it out of the firing barn," I add.

"Kane doesn't let anyone in that barn."

We watch the two for a moment, how they have their heads together, deep in conversation.

"I bet my angel could talk him into it."

Anastasia laughs. "You could be right."

"I just got a text from Cassie." Billie frowns over at me from her seat on the jet as we're headed toward home. "She's asking me about our meal requests for next week."

"Good." I take my glasses off and rub my eyes. I've been staring at my bleeding computer for too long. "Choose whatever you like, bumble."

"Why is she asking *me*?"

"Because that's what will make you comfortable." I'll never forget that morning when Cassie and Billie met, and Billie was jealous as she walked into the bedroom carrying that tray. I hated the look on her face. "I won't have you uncomfortable in your own home, angel. From now on, you'll be Cassie's primary contact."

She blinks at me and then shivers. "I'm always so cold on planes."

"I got you something." I stand to walk to the back of the plane. Retrieving her gift, I take it to her. I open the soft wool blanket and drape it over her. "This is for when we fly. I know you get cold."

"Connor?"

"Yes, *mo chroi.*"

"You bought me a *Hermes* blanket. Just for when we fly?"

"Aye, I did."

She snorts and snuggles under it. "Thank you. Okay, I'll add it to my calendar to chat with Cassie each week."

"Thank you." I move from my seat to the one next to hers, and she shares her blanket with me.

"Were you cold, too?"

"No. I missed you, angel."

She flutters her eyelashes at me. "You're just trying to get into my pants."

I huff out a laugh and lean over to kiss her head.

"I had the best week with you," she says softly, leaning against me as I pull her to me. "Every minute of it was fun. Kane and Anastasia are *so nice*. I loved having dinner with your parents. And the view of the ocean from your house is just amazing. I even loved it when we fought."

"We didn't fight."

"In New York, we did, but then we had the makeup sex, and that was pretty fabulous. Also, I still can't believe you bought that glass piece from Kane. I wasn't trying to—"

"I know. But it was obvious that it was meant to be yours. Where will you put it?"

"In our bedroom." *In our bedroom.* "It'll go well in there. I'll see if someone will build a pretty stand for it. Chase Wild is an excellent woodworker. I bet I could talk him into it."

"Chase is a man of many talents," I reply.

"He's a good guy. The whole family is great." She snuggles up closer, and I tighten my arm around her. "When you hold me like this, it makes me sleepy. Not tired, but relaxed. And just like when I stood by the cliffs, it drowns out all the noise, and my mind quiets. It's like a drug that I can't get enough of. You're good for my nervous system."

"Good, because I have no intention of ever letting you go, *mo rúnsearc*. I want to be your peaceful place."

"You are. Since the night I met you." She looks up at me and brushes her fingers through my hair. "I wasn't lying or exaggerating the other day when I told you that I'd like to go to the Galway house often. It's serene. So freaking gorgeous. And it's where you're the most relaxed. Now that I've found my peaceful place, I need you to have yours, too."

"I do, baby. It's when I'm with you."

"You have relaxed considerably since I first met you." She kisses my shoulder. "But I saw the way your whole body relaxed when we were there, and I want you to have it as often as possible."

"We'll see what we can do."

Her phone buzzes next to her, and she grabs it. "Beck just canceled family dinner tomorrow."

"Oh?" My lips twitch, and I kiss her head.

Of course, he canceled.

I asked him to.

"Well, that sucks."

She sounds so sad, but little does she know that I'll more than make up for it.

"It'll be okay, *mo chroí*."

"But it's my birthday tomorrow, and I was excited to see them."

I tip her chin up and kiss her lips softly before deepening the embrace, and when she comes up for air, her eyes are shining.

"Don't worry. It'll all be okay. Trust me."

She presses her lips together and nods. "Okay. How long until we land?"

"About an hour. Take a quick nap."

"Do you want to go back to the bed and lie down?" she asks but snuggles closer, burrowing in.

"No. We're fine right here." I kiss her head again. I can't keep my hands or my lips off this woman. My cock would like in on that action too, but Miller and Simon are nearby. "Sleep for a while."

Chapter Twenty-Six

CONNOR

illie's right. I do love being in Galway, but I missed being with her, in our bed, in Montana. Maybe I'm becoming a sentimental arse, but we have memories in this bed. A history here.

This house, here in this town, is our home.

It's my angel's birthday, and she's sleeping soundly next to me. Last night, she insisted on unpacking her things herself and putting everything away just so—she's particular about her clothes—and it was darling to watch her coo and fuss over her pretty new finds from New York. Then we ordered in dinner from Old Town Pizza and curled up to watch a movie before we slept.

Jet lag is a bloody bitch.

But now, it's her special day, and I'm going to make it unforgettable.

Her skin is warm and smooth as I urge her onto her back and kiss her neck. She whimpers as she stretches her arms over her head, and I pull a nipple into my mouth as my hand roams down her soft stomach, over her thigh, and back up again.

"Good morning," she murmurs, her raspy voice full of sleep as her fingers weave into my hair.

"Aye, it is," I agree, kissing down her rib cage, her legs scissoring, my cock stirring when she gasps. "The best day of the goddamn year because you were born on it."

I nudge my shoulders between her thighs, spreading her open, and skim my fingers through her already soaked lips.

"So wet for me, *a ghrá*." I have to taste her, to consume her. I drag my tongue through her slit, up to her hard bundle of nerves. As I push two fingers inside her heat, she lifts her hips and moans.

"God, Connor."

"Aye, baby." Curling my fingers up, making a *come-here* motion, I rub over that rough spot that makes her lose her bloody mind. "Come on my mouth. You're such a good fecking girl."

Her walls clench around me, and she lets go, flooding my hand with her release. I growl as I sop her up, loving every sound, every shiver coming from her spectacular body.

Pulling back, I grip her thighs and flip her over, pull her hips back, and bite her arse before landing a loud *crack* with my palm.

"Fuck yes," she moans, making me grin.

My girl likes it a little rough.

Fisting my dick, I drag the crown up and down, from her clit to her tight ring of muscle, and back again.

"Is this what you want, angel?"

"Yes. Please."

She's pushing back, seeking my cock. "Tell me."

"Fuck me, billionaire."

I slam into her, bracing myself on either side of her, and nibble my way over her shoulder as I fuck her. I push my hand into her hair and fist it at her nape, holding her where I want her.

"Who do you belong to?"

"You." God, I fucking love her raspy voice. "Only you. Always."

"That's right, *mo rúnsearc*. Only me. I'm the only man who will ever be lucky enough to touch you like this. To see how perfect you are when you come apart."

"Oh my God."

I grip her hips and pound her into the mattress, then pull out and flip her back over because I need to see her eyes.

She wraps her legs around me as I sink into her tight heat again and cup her face, brushing my thumb over the apple of her cheek.

"Only you," she says, lifting those hips to meet me.

"You're everything," I whisper against her lips.

Tears fill her eyes as she frames my face and kisses me. I'm so damn helpless against this woman. She brings me to my knees.

With only a few more thrusts, she quivers, her walls tighten, and she cries out as she succumbs to her climax, pulling me over with her.

And when I've managed to catch my breath, I pull

away and clean us up, then cross the room. I open the secret coffee area I arranged to have installed while we were away and make her a cup.

"You already had it done?" she asks, sitting up and wrapping the sheet around her.

"You wanted it." I shrug as I cross to her and pass her the steaming mug, then drag my finger down her flushed cheek. "So you needed to have it."

"You spoil me, you know." Her eyes smile at me as she takes a sip.

"Complaining, bumble?"

"Never." She chuckles and pushes her hand through her hair, then stands, naked as the day she was born twenty-eight years ago, that coffee in hand as she walks to the bathroom. "I need ten."

"Take all the time you need."

After pulling on a pair of gray sweatpants, I walk downstairs to first check in on the project I had done while we were gone, and when I'm happy with what I see, I make my way to the kitchen. Cassie snuck in this morning and left waffles, crispy bacon, and fluffy eggs on a tray in the warming oven, so I take it upstairs to my girl.

"Wow, how long was I in the bathroom?" Billie asks when she sees me walk through the door. She's already pulled on leggings and my old sweatshirt that she stole out of my closet in Ireland, which I don't mind in the least.

She's sexy as hell in it.

"One of the few times I'll reach out to Cassie," I inform her as I set the tray on the bed. "She snuck in early this morning and left it for us. We can eat this here or take it downstairs."

"Here," she decides, crawling to sit on the bed. I sit opposite her, and we dig in. "I'm freaking hungry."

"Well, eat up, bumble, because today is just getting started. I have something to show you after this."

She stops chewing and frowns at me. "Connor, you've already given me so much. You don't have—"

I reach over and press my lips to hers, licking the tiny drop of syrup from them. "Stop, *mo chroi*. Let me make today special."

Her expression softens, and she rests her free hand on my leg, giving it a squeeze that I feel up to my groin. "You make every day special, billionaire."

Jesus Christ, what she does to me.

When our meal is finished, I take her hand and lead her out of the bedroom. Once we're at the bottom of the stairs, we head down the hall, past my office, and I hear her gasp.

"This place is way too big if I missed the fact that you added on while we were gone." She laughs.

I stop her before we reach the new area and frame her face. "Close your eyes."

She grins at me so wide and happy that I have to kiss her before she does as she's told.

"Keep them closed."

"Okay." She's still smiling as I lead her to the entry of the room. French doors open silently as I guide her forward, and once we're inside, I step around to stand at her side so I can see her expression.

"Open your eyes, *mo chroi*."

Those beautiful eyes widen, her jaw drops, and her hands fly up to cover her mouth as she takes it all in.

"Robin's egg blue," she whispers, her gaze skimming the shelves that line all the walls. A large window looks out to the mountains, but aside from that, the rest of the room is for bookshelves.

"Look up," I whisper.

She gasps, and tears fill her eyes.

The ceiling is wallpapered with blues and yellows, hints of pink. And the light fixture is crystal.

"Holy shit," she whispers. "It's too beautiful."

"Never." I kiss her cheek and then her neck.

"The chairs are amazing." They've been placed in the center of the room, with their own ottomans and tables for snacks and drinks. "I'm glad there's two of them. You can sit with me."

"That was the plan," I reply, happy that she's okay with me being in here with her. "The shelves are empty because I knew you'd want to arrange them your own way, but I did have your library from your old place carefully boxed up and brought here. They're in a guest room, ready when you are."

Her eyes are bouncing everywhere, still trying to take it all in. They land on the one section of shelves that isn't empty, and she hurries over.

"Connor."

"Yes, my angel?"

Her hand lifts as if she wants to touch, but then she pulls back again.

"Baby, tell me you didn't ... I can't ... *Connor.*"

"Hey." I wrap my arms around her from behind and bury my lips in her hair. She clings to me, her eyes still pinned to the books before us. "Take a breath."

She does, but it's shaky.

"These look like really old books."

"They're all first editions," I reply as my eyes skim the titles.

"And"—she swallows hard—"*Wuthering Heights* has Ellis Bell as the author. Oh my God."

"You can touch them."

"I don't have gloves."

I grin. "You know, I read somewhere that the gloves do more damage than your hands. Touch them."

Carefully, she reaches for *Wuthering Heights*, and a tear slips down her cheek as she opens the cover.

"No way."

"What is it?"

She shakes her head and turns to me, those eyes shining up at me, and it's enough to crack my heart open.

"It's signed by Ellis Bell. How in the hell did you make this happen in a matter of *days*?"

"Money talks, baby." I tip her chin up and kiss her lips softly. "Now, I know you're a wee bit overwhelmed, but there's one more thing in this room you haven't noticed."

She closes her eyes and leans into me. "I can't do anymore. This is too much. I don't deserve—"

"Finish that sentence, and I'll turn you over my knee, Billie."

She blinks up at me in surprise, but her lips part, and her pupils dilate.

"Thank you," she whispers.

"You're welcome, but we're just getting started. Come here."

"Wait." She carefully places the book back on the shelf, then slips her hand in mine. "Okay."

I had blue fabric draped over the piece that Kane sent over, and when we approach it, I pull the fabric off and toss it aside, and my girl gasps again.

"Stop it."

I laugh at that and tug her to me. "The blues and greens in this piece remind me of the mountains here, and when Kane sent me a photo of it, I knew you had to have it for this room."

"Connor." She's crying now, wiping at tears.

"He had it hand couriered over from Seattle, so it would be here when we got home."

She turns and launches herself against me, wrapping her arms around me tightly, and presses her face to my chest.

"Tell me these are good tears, *mo rúnsearc*."

"So good." She sniffs and wipes her face. "So glad I didn't put my makeup on yet."

With a chuckle, I kiss her forehead. "I do need you to be ready to leave the house within the hour."

She blinks up at me, frowning. "What? Why? I plan to spend all day in here, organizing my books and pretending I'm Belle from *Beauty and the Beast*."

"You're so fucking adorable." I shake my head and

kiss her once more. "That will have to wait. The surprises are just beginning for the day."

"Connor." She takes my hand before I can pull away. "I'm so grateful, so *stupidly* grateful, but you know I'm not here for this. I don't need you to spend all this money on me. I'm not a gol—"

I narrow my eyes, and she smartly folds her lips together.

"We'll never *ever* say that word. Do you understand me?"

Her shoulders droop, and she nods.

"You're mine, Billie. And in turn, I'm *yours*. Everything I am, everything I have, is also yours. I'm a wealthy man, and I make no apologies for that because I've worked my arse off for it. As have you. I will shower you with whatever your heart desires because making sure that you're happy and cared for is my number one priority."

"This is more than happy and cared for." The side of her mouth tips up in a rueful grin.

"It's a privilege to give you everything I can. I will give you the world, angel." I kiss her forehead, breathing her in. "Just as it's a privilege to sit and talk with you. To make love to you. The simple, the mundane, and the extraordinary. We can have it all."

"Thank you for sharing it with me. I'll never take it for granted."

"You have forty-five minutes to get your sexy arse ready to leave the house."

"I'll be ready." She wipes her eyes and turns to look at

her new library once more. "Holy shit, billionaire, this is *incredible.* Way to show off your billionaire status."

I bark out a laugh, shake my head, and leave her to ogle.

"Forty minutes, angel."

Chapter Twenty-Seven

BILLIE

Holy fucking shit.

He built me a library. A legit, enormous, two-story motherfucking library with a ladder and the softest chairs I've ever seen, and *oh my God*.

I'm so overwhelmed. This house already felt like home, even though I've technically barely lived here, but he's *made* it mine.

He built me a whole addition to this already gigantic house.

"Thirty minutes, bumble!" he calls out, which gets me moving.

"Coming!"

I run upstairs, directly to the bathroom, where I take a quick shower, shave my legs, and then brush out my hair and twist it up into a messy bun.

I don't know where we're going today, but it's still summer and warm in Montana, so I pull out my favorite summer maxi dress and sandals. After putting on makeup and grabbing my handbag, I rush downstairs with a minute to spare.

"I can be speedy," I inform him as I boost myself up on my toes to kiss him, then he's leading me outside.

But we don't climb into the SUV in the driveway.

No, he guides me around the house, and I stop in my tracks.

"No way."

"It's perfectly safe, *a ghrá*."

I shake my head, staring at the helicopter where Miller and Simon are waiting.

"I'll get sick."

"You're sitting up front, so you won't get sick," he says, soothingly rubbing his hand up and down my back. "You've got this. Trust me."

Tentatively, I stumble forward, and Connor helps me climb into my seat. He buckles me in, then hands me a pair of headphones with a microphone to wear.

Simon and Connor climb into the back, and Miller takes the pilot seat.

"You can *fly this*?" I ask Miller.

"I've done it once or twice." He winks at me, puts his own cans on, and starts the engine. The blades above us start to whirl, and my stomach is in knots. "Relax, miss. I was a helicopter pilot in the Air Force."

My gaze whips to his. "You were?"

He nods solemnly. "You're perfectly safe. The weather is calm today, so there shouldn't be many bumps. I'll get you where we're going in about an hour."

I blow out a breath and glance back at Connor, who reaches forward and squeezes my shoulder.

"Okay." I turn back around, and Miller lifts us off the ground, making me squeal. "Holy shit."

"Breathe, bumble," Connor says in my cans, and Simon and Miller chuckle.

I have to admit that seeing the mountains this close from above is absolutely spectacular. I forget all about being afraid or having motion sickness and am enamored with the herd of elk I can see through the trees.

"Two o'clock," Miller says, gesturing to our right, and I gape at the grizzly bear, meandering through a field with two little cubs in tow, romping around and playing.

"It's so damn beautiful up here," I murmur, taking in the blue water of rivers and lakes as we fly over the mountains. So green and full of life. But it's always the mountains that take my breath away.

An hour later, Miller sets us down on another helipad, and a black SUV waits for us.

"How did you get ... you know what? Never mind."

Connor chuckles and presses his hand to my lower back as he guides me to the waiting vehicle.

He changed into dark jeans and a blue T-shirt, showing off his magnificent muscles, broad back, and flat abs. I can't resist reaching out to drag my hand down his arm.

"Later," he murmurs against my ear just before I climb into the car and slide over, making room for him. With Miller and Simon up front, we take off.

"Where are we?"

No one answers me. Connor simply smiles over at me and kisses the back of my hand.

Soon after, I recognize exactly where we are, and my heart fills.

"Are you trying to make me cry all freaking day?" I demand as I feel the tears want to come. Miller parks in front of *Thrifty Threads*, and I burst out of the vehicle and run inside. Martha offers me a big grin and a tight hug.

"Hey, friend," she says with a laugh. "Happy birthday."

"Thank you. Oh, my gosh, Connor surprised me."

"I know." She backs away and winks over my shoulder, and I follow her gaze. Connor's standing about ten feet away, hands in his pockets, his happy gaze on me.

This man sees me like no one else ever has.

And I'm so fucking addicted to him.

I hold my hand out for his, and he presses his palm to mine, stepping forward to join me.

"Okay, I have instructions," Martha says, clearing her throat. "Anything you want, it's yours. I've held some pieces aside for you because you're going to *lose your shit* when you see what I've recently got in."

I'm jumping up and down by the time she reaches the end of her speech, then proceed to spend two hours hunting for designer gold.

Which I find in spades.

And the whole time, Connor hangs out, giving his opinion, smiling, and chatting with us. Not once does he take his phone out to see to work or to scroll.

I have all his attention, and it's the best feeling ever.

"This Louis Vuitton cross-body is *so cute*," Martha says, showing it to me. I tilt my head to the side, thinking it over.

"The strap is too short for me." I shake my head. "On a skinny girl, totally cute, but it would sit too high on me. However, that little top handle Gucci bag is adorable. Is that vintage?"

"You have such a good eye," Martha confirms. "This just came in."

"I like the red." I pick it up and pet the soft leather. "Someone loved this bag. I'll take it."

"Sold," Martha says with a grin. "Anything else?"

I eye the small pile of clothes and two bags that I found and shake my head. "This is great, thank you."

She folds and then bags everything up and passes it to Connor, but when he pulls out his credit card, she shakes her head.

"No, this is on me. Happy birthday, beautiful friend."

I blink at Martha in surprise. "Uh, I think you're supposed to charge people for your stuff when you own a business. You're doing it wrong."

Martha laughs but holds firm. "You always bring me books, and you are one of the sweetest people I know. This trip is on *me*. Next time, you can clean me out, and I won't even give you a discount."

I wrap my arms around her and hug her again. "Thank you."

"I hope you have the best day ever."

"I already have."

"Good." She steps back and smiles at Connor.

"Thanks," he says, his voice soft.

"My pleasure. Truly. Now, you two kids, go have fun."

I bark out a laugh. Martha is younger than me. "See you soon!"

Once outside, Connor passes my bag to Simon, who slips it into the SUV.

"We're walking over to the hotel," Connor informs the others.

Simon walks behind us while Miller drives the car to the hotel, and I breathe in the summer air around us.

"I can already feel fall trying to sneak in," I say as I grin up at my man. "It won't be too long now."

"What's your favorite season?" he asks me.

"Fall. I love a good pumpkin spice latte. And sweaters. And crisp leaves." I squeeze his hand as he leads me into the hotel he owns, where I saw him all those weeks ago, the last time I was in town.

And we're shown to a table in the restaurant.

"I know you own the place," I say when we're left with drinks and menus, "but have you tried the whipped feta cheese with honey and pistachios?"

"I can't say that I have."

I sigh and roll my eyes back in my head. "You have to. It's *so good.*"

As we munch on the best food *ever*, sip wine and chat about our businesses and families, it hits me just how well we fit together. How comfortable I am with him, how he puts me at ease, and makes me feel alive and sexy and smart, all at the same time.

Connor Gallagher is my person.

The love of my life.

"You're quiet, angel." With the meal finished, he reaches over to take my hand. "Is everything all right?"

I huff out a short laugh. "I'd say that's an understatement. I've been well and truly worshipped today."

He lifts an eyebrow. "It's not over yet."

"Connor, I can't do any more gifts. I'm telling you right now, I can't handle it."

"Trust me." He stands and helps me to my feet, and guides me through to the hotel lobby, where he's handed the key to a room. After a short elevator ride to the top floor, he unlocks a door, and we're in a beautiful suite with a view of the ski mountain.

"Wow, this is pretty."

"We're not staying the night," he says as he folds me into his arms. "But we're going to have a nap date."

I jerk back, staring up at him. "You remembered."

His thumb glides over my bottom lip. "I remember everything, *mo rúnsearc*. I'm going to get you naked, and we're going to climb into that bed and sleep, skin-on-skin, for a couple of hours."

"Holy shit, I love you."

His smile is a mile wide as he tucks my hair behind my ear and kisses me sweetly. "Other things might happen since nakedness will be involved."

I lift an eyebrow. "Really? What sort of things?"

I know exactly what he'll do. But flirting is fun.

Slowly, he leads me to the king-sized bed in the bedroom and squats before me, helping me out of my sandals. Then he grips the hem of my dress, and as he stands, he pulls it up my body and over my head. I'm left standing in a black thong and strapless bra.

"Christ," he whispers, taking me in. "There's nothing more beautiful than you, angel."

With a soft smile, I help him out of his clothes, and once we're both bare, we climb into the bed and he pulls me to him. We're lying on our sides, facing each other. He has one arm under my head and the other wrapped around my back, and I lift my leg to hitch it up over his hip, hugging him closer.

"Thank you for today," I whisper, loving the intimate quiet surrounding us. "For every single thing."

"You're welcome." His fingertips dance up and down my spine in long, lazy strokes, sending goose bumps over my skin. I'm so turned on, lying here like this, our mouths mere inches apart, being held by this strong, incredible man.

"Before we sleep ..." I reach between us and guide his hard cock to my opening, and he slowly, so slowly, pushes inside me. "*Yes.*"

"Is this what you need, *a ghrá*?"

"Always." He nibbles at the corner of my mouth, making me clench around him. "You always feel so damn good, billionaire."

"My angel," he whispers, moving so deliciously slow, I can't help but whimper. "My love."

"Connor."

"That's right, *mo chroi*." God, I love the Irish words. And his fingers move back and forth on my clit in the most delectable way, ensuring that I won't last long. "Come on my cock. Take what you need from me, birthday girl."

"Oh, Jesus." My leg tightens, pulling him so damn close, and I can't hold back the climax that works through me in delicious waves, tugging him with me.

"Love you, *mo chroi*," he says, peppering me with kisses. He holds me so tightly, his hands soothing me.

I love the way he touches me.

As if I'm a treasure. Something precious he can't live without.

"I love you so much it almost scares me," I admit softly, and he wraps his arms tightly around me.

"There's no need to be scared. I'm right here. And I'm never going anywhere without you."

He murmurs more words of love, of reassurance, until I fall blissfully asleep.

I highly recommend nap dates. Especially when they're accompanied by hot, intense sex.

And a gorgeous-as-hell Irishman.

"This was fun," I say into the mic as we near our home in Bitterroot Valley. "Thanks for today."

"You're more than welcome, bumble," Connor says in my ear, and he squeezes my shoulder.

The sun isn't quite ready to go down yet, and when we near the house, I see a bunch of cars parked out front.

"Who's here?"

Miller sets us down on the helipad, that I never noticed until today, and when we get closer to the house, I recognize the vehicles and wrap my arms around Connor's neck, launching myself at him, so he hugs me and twirls me in a circle.

"My family's here!"

"Among others," he agrees. "You needed them today. I just needed a little more time with you."

"I love you so much. God. Thank you."

He kisses me hard, and then I run into the house and find everyone—*everyone*—I love in the kitchen.

As usual.

"Happy birthday!"

I can't help it. I break down into tears. My brothers surround me, all four of them at once, giving me a group hug like they did when we were kids.

"Hey, no tears on your birthday," Brooks croons to me.

"You'll ruin your makeup," Blake agrees.

"We're so proud of you, baby girl," Beckett says, which only makes me cry more.

"Love you to the moon and back," Bridger adds.

"Hey, you guys have to share her." Skyla laughs, and when my guys pull away, I survey the room.

My parents are here, along with Connor and Skyla's parents, who are sitting together, smiling over at us.

Holden and Millie wave from the island where they're chatting with Mik and Benji. Bridger and Dani are snuggled up with Birdie, who's beaming at me.

Alex is sitting with them, and then Connor's arms are around me, hugging me from behind.

"Your parents are here," I murmur.

"They wouldn't miss this," he replies.

"Aunt Bee," Birdie says, rushing over to me as if she just can't stand it anymore, and I squat so I can hug her close. She presses her cheek against my own, and I breathe in her little girl scent. "Happy birthday."

"Thank you, my sweet baby." I kiss her cheek, then resume pressing it against mine. "I love you so much, baby girl. You know that, right?"

"Yes." She giggles and pulls back so she can see me. "Did you get a good present for your birthday?"

"The best," I assure her, tapping her nose with my finger. "But you know what?"

"What?"

"Seeing you here tonight is my favorite present. I missed you, peanut."

"I *am* a good present," she agrees, making us laugh.

"I want to see the library," Dani announces.

"Same," Skyla and Alex say at the same time, and Millie nods.

"Library tour." Mom claps her hands as she and Maeve join us girls.

"What, the boys don't want to see it?" I prop my hands on my hips, scowling at them all.

"We already saw it, squirt." Blake winks at me. "We helped."

Okay, that makes me melt. "You *helped*? You *all* helped?"

"I did not." Mik shakes his head. "Because Benji and I just arrived. So we need to see it with you."

"Oh God, you're going to make her leak again." Alex looks panicked and takes my hand. "Come on, let's go ogle your princess library."

"I want to be a princess," Birdie announces, skipping beside us.

"You already are, peanut." I smile down at her. "And don't ever let anyone tell you otherwise."

Of course, we all spend a crazy amount of time admiring my new space until finally, Brooks calls down the hallway.

"Okay, enough of that! Some of us want cake."

"Jackie made it," Skyla adds. "She wanted to come, but she went to the Iconic Women's Collective party tonight."

"Oh my God." I turn to Millie, eyes wide. "You should be there!"

"I'll stop in later," she assures me. "I'm right where I want to be."

I pull her into a tight hug. "I love you, Mills."

"Back at you, birthday girl," she says with a smile. "Now, let's eat cake and get a sugar high."

The massive cake is decorated with bumble bees,

which makes me smile.

"Cute," I say to Connor, who winks.

The birthday song always makes me feel uncomfortable, but after I blow out all of the candles—without starting a major fire—our moms cut the cake and serve it.

"I have one last gift," Connor says, and I set my plate aside.

I can't help my deep sigh. "Listen up, billionaire, you've done too much already."

"I love that she calls him that," Alex says to someone, making me smirk.

"I promise, it's the last one for the day." Connor passes me a box that has my heart stuttering and my head shaking side to side. "It's not that kind of box."

I shake my head, looking down at it. Scared to open it. Christ, what did he do now?

"Open it," my dad says.

"I'll probably cry again, and you know how I hate to mess up my makeup."

Connor slides his hand into mine, threads our fingers, and holds on tight.

"Look at me, angel."

"Gah, that's so sweet," Skyla murmurs, and my lips twitch as I turn my eyes to Connor's.

"I know, today's been a lot. Just humor me one more time."

I rub my lips together and flip up the lid of the box, and stare down at a key fob.

To a Porsche.

"Jesus, Connor." I swallow hard and feel my cheeks heat.

"What is it?" Millie demands. "The suspense is killing me."

"It's a freaking car."

"Not just any car," Brooks says, looking over my shoulder. "A Porsche. Nice, man. Macan or Cayanne?"

"Macan," Connor replies, and Brooks nods, clearly pleased with my new ride.

"I don't need a new vehicle."

Connor smirks. "Any time the words *my brother had to put new brakes on my car* fall from your perfect mouth, you need a new car, bumble."

"Swoonfest," Dani says, making me giggle.

"Please let this be the last thing for today."

"I promise," he says against my ear. "Want to have a look at it?"

"Are you kidding? I'm gonna give rides to everyone here."

"Shotgun!" Blake announces, and we all walk outside. I don't have to search for it. The sexy SUV is pearly white and adorned with a huge red ribbon on top.

"Holy shit."

Connor chuckles, slipping his hand in mine once more. "It should handle great in the snow."

Chapter Twenty-Eight

CONNOR

I t's been two weeks since Billie's birthday, and one week since I've seen her.

I'm going out of my bleedin' fecking mind.

"We'll be landing in Dublin in fifteen minutes," the pilot says over the speaker, and I turn to Miller.

"We should be headed home."

Miller works for me, but he's also my friend. One of the few people in this world who I trust implicitly.

"And why aren't we?" he asks with a raised brow.

"Because my bloody board wants a goddamn meeting." I scrub my hand down my face. I just spent a week in New York without my angel, and the penthouse felt ... *wrong*.

Everything feels so wrong without her.

I was supposed to go home two days ago, yet there have been issues and delays that keep me from going to Montana.

And it's pissing me the fuck off.

The plane touches down, and once in the waiting SUV, we head straight for the offices.

As I walk through the building to my office, everyone gives me a wide berth. I'm pissed as fuck, moody, and I don't know why I've been summoned here when I could have likely handled whatever they want to talk about from the comfort of my home.

With Billie in my lap.

As soon as I walk into the office, my phone rings, and I scowl when I see Simon's name on video call.

"Yes."

"I wanted to touch base, boss," he says with a sigh that has my eyebrows climbing.

"What's going on?"

"Miss Blackwell is safe." He rubs his hand over his eyes. "But she's been … obstinate."

"Obstinate?"

"Stubborn," he adds.

"Just tell me what in the hell is going on."

"She leaves without telling me," he says, and I feel every muscle in my body tighten in agitation. "Nothing crazy, but she'll go to the grocery store, or run over to one of her brothers' houses, or pick Birdie up from school without letting me know she's leaving the house."

"We have cameras," I remind him.

"Yes, sir, we do. Doesn't stop her from evading me. I don't think she's doing it on purpose. She's simply independent and thinks having a detail with her every time she leaves the house is excessive."

I rub my hand over my mouth. *She's going to be the bloody death of me.*

"I'll talk to her."

"The sooner, the better. I like this job."

I hang up and find Ronan standing in my doorway. "Bad time?"

"Come on in." I gesture to a chair. "Have a seat and tell me why I'm here."

"The board wants a meeting in person." He shrugs a shoulder when I glare at him. "That look doesn't work with me."

"I was here less than a month ago."

"I think they want to talk about Sweden."

"I swear, that property is going to send me out of my fecking mind."

He grunts in agreement. "How are things with your lass, then?"

"Good. She's brilliant. I want to go home to her. How are things with Fiona? Ronan—"

He puts a hand up, stopping me, and then sighs. "We had a long talk. She's not confused about us, and she's not pining after you. I think she really thought she was trying to protect you, or Billie, or hell, I don't know. I think her ego was bruised."

I scowl at my best friend. "What the hell?"

"You didn't love her. She didn't think you were capable of it. Now you love someone else, and it threw her for a loop because she thought she knew you better than that."

"I'm going to be brutally honest here, and I hope it

doesn't make you punch me in the face because she's your wife."

"Go ahead."

"Fiona only knows what I've allowed her to know. She's my best friend's wife, and that's all. I wouldn't expect you to know all of the ins and outs about Billie, even twenty years from now." I stare at him, and Ronan nods in agreement.

"That's pretty much what I told her. She needs to let her shite go. She will probably apologize to you, but I don't think she meant to try to scare Billie off." He shrugs and then grins at me. "Not that it would have worked anyway. That lass is in love with you, mate."

"I know." And the reminder of it never fails to knock me off balance. "And it's returned to her in kind. When are we meeting with the others?"

Checking his watch, Ronan says, "Thirty minutes."

"I'll see you in there, then."

He nods and leaves my office, and I make a quick call to my angel.

"Hey," she says as she accepts the video call. "You're a sight for sore eyes. I see you made it to Dublin."

"Aye," I reply, soaking her in. "Angel, I need you to do me a favor."

"Okay."

"I need you to stick with Simon. Let him drive you wherever you need to go."

"It's so annoying," she mutters and closes her eyes, and I can see her fatigue. Christ, she's not sleeping.

Because I'm not there.

The guilt is swift and all-consuming as I lean back in my chair, wishing I could pull her close and hold her in my arms.

"When was the last time you got a good night's sleep, bumble?"

She shakes her head. "I'm fine."

"Answer the question."

She nibbles on her bottom lip. "How long have you been gone?"

"Baby, come to Ireland. I'll send the jet for you right now, and you can be here by morning. Come to me."

"I wish I could." She sounds defeated, and it makes me ache for her. "I can't leave again so soon. I have too much work to do. But you'll be home soon, right?"

"I'm doing my best. Trust me, I don't like being away from you, either. It should hopefully just be a few more days, and then I'll be home for a while."

"Good." She smiles sweetly. "I have Birdie's dance recital tonight. Skyla's disappointed that you won't be here for it."

It seems I'm just letting all my girls down this week.

"I'm sorry I won't be there, but I'll call her after we hang up. Take Simon with you, Billie."

"Okay, billionaire, I'll take my babysitter."

"Not a babysitter. Your detail because I want you safe. I love you."

"I *am* safe. I'm home. Nothing's going to happen to me here, baby. There's always someone around."

I take a deep breath. "Try to get some sleep tonight."

"I'll do my best." She grins at me. "Don't worry about me."

"That's impossible."

"Go finish ruling the world so you can come home."

"Okay. Be good, keep Simon with you, and stay out of trouble."

"Who, me?" She bats her eyelashes playfully. "I'd *never* get into trouble."

"Right. Tell me you love me."

"More than all the stars in the sky, billionaire."

She hangs up, and I close my eyes. Christ, I miss her.

I check the time. Seeing that I still have a few minutes to spare, I call Skyla.

"And hello to you," she says with a smile. "A *video* call. Fancy."

"I wanted to tell you to break a leg tonight at the recital."

"I see you're not coming. Again."

I blow out a breath and shake my head at her. "I'm in Dublin, Skyla Maeve. It's not like I'm just across town and am blowing you off."

She narrows her eyes, but I see the humor in them. "Billie misses you."

"I miss her too."

"Don't worry, she's staying busy with work and all of us. She's coming tonight, along with Ma and Da."

Our parents decided to stay in Montana for a while, and I know that Skyla has enjoyed spending time with them. "I know, I just got off the phone with Billie a few minutes ago. Anyway, I have to go. I love you."

My sister grins at me. "I know. I love you too. *Slán abhaile*."

Safe home.

That's definitely where I want to be heading.

My entire family is in Montana.

I stand and button my suit jacket closed, something I've done a million times before. But today? Today, it feels as though my suit just doesn't ... fit.

I hadn't realized until Billie kept commenting on my body how seldom I didn't wear a suit. *Until her.* Until I had a reason *not* to don my armor every day. Until I had a reason to think outside of boardrooms, contractor meetings, and other business-focused affairs. Until I had someone who utterly and completely fit me.

And I her.

My other half.

My beautiful angel who rescued my soul from loneliness.

I need to wrap this up, so I leave my office, heading toward the boardroom. I need to get out of this suit and go home.

Chapter Twenty-Nine

BILLIE

Simon walks into my bookshop, and I scowl at him.

"Did you seriously *tattle* on me?"

It doesn't surprise me when he doesn't smile.

"I like my job, Billie. I need you to help me keep it." He assumes his position beside the front door, hands clasped in front of him, staring straight ahead.

"He looks like he could be the hero in one of the mafia books we read. All broad-shouldered and the obvious tattoos under that suit," Emily says from beside me, not bothering to keep her voice down. "You know he's muscled and can handle a gun. It's kind of hot."

Simon doesn't even blink.

I swear, the man is made of stone.

"He's not fiction. He's a real-ass man, Em." I roll my eyes and turn away from Simon. "Stop ogling my bodyguard."

"Hey, not all of us have sexy billionaire boyfriends," she reminds me with a smirk.

"Can we *work* now?" I ask dryly as I grab a bottle of my favorite water—which Connor always keeps stocked here—out of the small fridge behind the counter and unscrew the top. "I got an email from Catherine Cowles. She's going to do a signing for us next month."

Emily's jaw drops in surprise, and then she hops up and down. "Holy shitballs! She's my favorite, Bee. I'm going to make an absolute ass out of myself when I meet her. She's going to think I'm a moron."

"No, she won't." I laugh and take a sip of water. "She seems really kind. Plus, you'll pull yourself together before then. I need to order some books, have graphics made for social media, and a whole bunch of other things to get ready."

"We can do this," Emily says, giving me a mock salute. "No worries, babe, we're on the case."

I smirk as she hurries off to help a customer. Grabbing my laptop, I sit in one of the comfy chairs to place my orders and get some other work done for the day.

Just after I email the amazing woman I use for graphics, the door opens and in walks Juliet.

"Hey!" I jump up and wrap her in a hug.

"Hey, bug," she says with a smile. "How is every little thing?"

"Pretty damn good." I laugh. "And you? How's the new restaurant coming along?"

"Aside from plumbing issues in the building, a

freezer on back order, and a whole shipment of plates arriving broken, things are good."

"Oh no. I hope that doesn't delay your opening."

She shakes her head and pushes her pretty hair over her shoulder. "I'm determined to make it work. But I'm also trying to make myself relax in the evenings, and maybe some new reading material will help."

"You left here with a dozen books not that long ago."

She laughs and wraps her arm around my shoulders. "Honey, I've already read them."

"Well, I have you covered. What are you in the mood for?"

"Sports romance," she decides. "And maybe some billionaire romance, too."

"Lauren Blakely and Helena Hunting both have some new hockey releases out that are fabulous," I inform her, leading her to the sports romance section. "And billionaires? You can't go wrong with Sadie Kincaid."

"This is exactly what I need." She grins and gets lost in reading the back cover blurbs, tucking the ones she wants in her arms.

"Have you talked to Brooks yet?" I ask, and her face falls. "Jules, you live in the same town. The same *tiny* town. You're going to run into him sooner or later."

"I know." She sighs. "I'm just not ready for the rejection. I figured I'd get the restaurant up and going first, and then go grovel for forgiveness."

It's none of my business.

"Billie, I could use your help," Emily says behind the counter, catching my attention.

"Go. I'm good here," Juliet assures me with a grin. "I'm just going to shop for a while."

The afternoon moves by swiftly, and before I know it, it's time for me to close the store and head over to Skyla's dance studio for Birdie's dance recital.

"Let's grab a quick dinner," I say to Simon, who simply nods. "Hungry for anything special?"

"Nope."

"Are you originally from New York?"

"Nope."

"Are you at all interested in Emily?"

He pauses. "No."

I raise an eyebrow as he opens the back door of the SUV for me. "Maybe a little?"

"Where to?"

I sigh and bite my lip. "Let's just grab a pizza. I'll call ahead. Do you like pepperoni?"

"Fine." He nods and closes the door, and I place our order.

"You're a man of few words, Simon."

"It's not my job to chat," he replies, but his voice isn't hard or angry. "I'm here to protect you."

"What, exactly, does Connor think might harm me in Bitterroot Valley, Montana?"

"Doesn't matter. He's hired me to watch you, so that's what I'm doing."

"Miller said that he's former military. Are you as well?"

"No."

"For fuck's sake," I mutter, sitting back with an exasperated sigh. I catch Simon's lips twitching in the mirror. "I saw that."

"I don't know what you're talking about."

After we both scarfed down a couple of slices of pizza, Simon drove us over to the dance studio and has been by my side for the entire performance.

You'd think he was my date.

It's annoying.

"When is Connor coming home?" Dani asks.

"I don't know. Hopefully soon."

Birdie struts on stage and gives the performance of a lifetime, making us all cheer for her.

Even Simon claps.

Maybe he's not a robot after all.

After the recital is over and I've hugged my girl, Bridger turns to me.

"Want to go get ice cream with us?" he asks.

"Please?" Birdie adds. "It's my big night."

I grin and run my hand down her pretty braid. "Of course, I want to celebrate with you. Let's do it."

Filling my evening with my family helped to get my mind off missing the hell out of my billionaire.

But now I'm home, and I miss him so much that it hurts.

This house is massive. It's a mountain mansion, and I love everything about it. But without Connor here, I feel so ... *lonely.*

I take a long, hot shower and wash my hair, then spend an hour drying it and styling it so it'll be easy for work tomorrow. I go through my entire skincare routine, and while my face mask does its job, I walk into the closet and sort through some clothes I'll take to Martha the next time I go to Big Sky.

Before leaving the closet, I stop by Connor's suits and carefully smell them so I don't leave mask residue on them.

"I miss you, billionaire," I whisper before I pad into the bathroom to wash my face.

At around midnight, with no sign of sleep in sight, I walk down to the library and sigh happily when I turn on the light and the room practically glows.

I've spent most of my sleepless hours organizing this room while Connor's been gone. I unpacked all my books and lined them up, alphabetized by author.

Then I decided to reorganize them by genre, which I like better.

I have plenty of space to add more books, which I can't wait to do.

Tonight, there's no organizing to be done. I finished it all yesterday. The library is my happy place, and I don't think Connor could have found a better gift to give me.

He sees me.

And I love him for it.

Maybe I should adopt a cat. They're relatively self-sufficient and would be company for me when Connor is away on business. I could picture a little black cat curled up in my lap, here in the library, while I read.

It's definitely something to think about.

After grabbing a favorite title to reread tonight, I relax in one of the plush chairs and settle in to read the night away.

By three in the morning, I'm no closer to sleep, but my brain is too tired to make sense of the words on the page, so I stand and stretch.

Now what am I supposed to do?

It's a beautiful late summer night out, and remembering that I've hardly been able to drive my new car, I decide this is a great night to go for a drive.

I'm dressed in a loose T-shirt and shorts, so I shove my feet in some flip-flops, grab my handbag with the key fob inside, and deactivate the house alarm as I walk out to the six-car garage, open my bay's door, and fire the Porsche to life.

I *love* this car. I love the rumble of the engine, the soft leather seats, and I really love how fast this thing can go.

Moments later, I'm cruising down the driveway, through the gate, and onto the highway, headed out of town.

I'm careful not to go *too* fast because of all the wildlife that could pop out at any moment, but I do put the sunroof back and blare the music. As Taylor Swift sings about being the antihero, I belt it out with her and feel energized.

Getting out of the house, in the fresh night air, is exactly what I needed.

Driving my new car without Simon hovering? Even better.

I love driving around Bitterroot Lake. It takes about an hour because it's a *big* lake, but it's such a beautiful drive, even at night. I'm only twenty minutes away from the house when a vehicle drives up behind me, their lights flashing, and I hurry to pull over and let them by because they're clearly having an emergency.

Except they don't drive by.

They pull up behind me, and just as I'm about to speed away because *fuck that shit*, I look in the mirror and see ... *Simon?*

I jump out of my car and push him in the chest.

"You *scared* me!"

"*I* scared *you*?" He scowls down at me. "For fuck's sake, what are you doing? It's the middle of the goddamn night."

"I'm taking a *drive* in my new car. Not that I have to explain anything to you."

"No, but *I* have to explain to Connor why the woman he's paying me to protect is not with me in the middle of the fucking night."

This is the most emotion I've ever seen come from this man.

"I just went for a drive."

"And now you're going home," he says, schooling his face back into stone.

"No, I'm driving around this lake."

"Billie." He sighs, and I can see he's tired. He's in jeans and a T-shirt, something I've never seen Simon wear before. Emily's right. He *is* good-looking. Holy hell, the tattoos on both arms are ... wow. He's also a pain in my ass.

"Wait." I hold up a hand. "How did you know where I was?"

"There's a tracking system on your car."

My jaw drops. "What did you just say?"

"There's a tracking system on your car."

"You're a smart-ass."

"You asked."

"Why is my car being tracked?"

Simon sighs again. I'm clearly trying his patience. "In case anything happened to you, we could find you. There's one on every vehicle, not just yours."

I shake my head at him, so frustrated I could pull my hair out.

"I'm going home," I mutter, my nighttime drive ruined.

"I'll be right behind you."

"Of course, you will be. And if I get away, you'll be able to *track* me."

"Yes, ma'am," he says, without an ounce of remorse.

Dick.

I can't wait to get home so I can call my billionaire and give him a piece of my mind.

Chapter Thirty

CONNOR

I'm in the middle of a meeting regarding the property in the Maldives when my phone starts to buzz with an incoming video call from Billie.

"Excuse me," I say, standing to leave the room.

"Connor—" Fiona starts, but I shake my head, shutting down whatever she was going to say.

"I'll be right back."

Once I'm in my office with the door closed, I take the call. "Hello, angel."

"Don't you *angel* me," she says, her beautiful eyes hot. "Why is there a tracking device on my car?"

"Because there's one on all of the vehicles," I reply, sitting on the edge of my desk. "What's happened?"

"I went for a drive, in my car, *by myself*, and Simon freaking found me, pulled me over, and ripped me a new one."

"Good."

Her jaw drops. "Excuse me?"

"I asked you not to go anywhere without Simon. Wait, it's four in the morning there. Why are you taking a drive in the middle of the night?"

"Because I'm a grown-ass woman who can decide for herself what time of day she wants to go for a mother-fucking drive!"

I've never seen her this angry.

"If you weren't going to let me drive this car, why did you buy it for me?"

I pull my glasses off and rub my eyes. "Of course, you can drive it. It's yours. Just please take Simon with you."

"This is fucking insane," she mutters.

"Bumble, tell me why you're taking drives in the middle of the night."

"Because I can't fucking sleep," she retorts, her face flushed and eyes bright with frustration. "I can't settle. I miss you."

Her eyes fill with tears, and it's almost my undoing.

"Angel, I'm coming home tomorrow."

I had planned to stay the week, but fuck that. My girl bleedin' needs me.

"It's not your fault," she says, furiously wiping away the tears on her cheeks. "It's just stupid insomnia, and it's ridiculous that I need my person with me to sleep. That's an addiction or something. Maybe I need an intervention."

My lips twitch as I watch her. "I miss you too, *mo chroí*. So much it hurts. And I'm not sleeping well, either."

"We have a serious problem."

"Aye. We're in love, and being apart is brutal." That makes her lower lip quiver again, and I swear under my breath. "Hang in there for just one more day. Can you do that for me?"

"I'm sorry." She blows out a breath and wipes more tears away. "This is so silly. If I could just sleep, I'd be fine."

"I know." God, I wish I could touch her. She needs to be held and kissed. I'm not there to give it to her, and it's driving me out of my bleedin' mind.

"Simon might quit," she says. "I was kind of mean to him. But Emily thinks he's hot, so maybe we should try to keep him."

"Emily's attracted to Simon?"

"Yeah. And I asked him if he liked her, and he paused before he said no, which means yes."

I blink at her. "I'm not sure how I feel about that."

"It's romantic," she insists. "But I really pissed him off tonight. Or this morning. Whatever it is."

"Don't worry about Simon, except *please*, don't go anywhere without him until I get home. Now, I want you to go upstairs, get into our bed, and relax. Breathe. Take my clothes with you so you can smell me."

She sniffs. "Okay. I'm sorry I'm such a brat."

"No, you aren't." I laugh when she rolls her lips together and grins. "Get some rest, angel. I'll see you soon."

"Good night. Love you."

"I love you as well."

She hangs up, and I drag my hand down my face before shooting Simon a quick text.

> Just spoke with Billie. Thank you for getting her home safely. She will not ditch you again.

When I return to the conference room, I'm met with some scowls and silence.

"Is there a problem?"

Before anyone can reply, the door bursts open, and Miller strides in, his face a mask of rage.

"You need to see this," he says, shoving his laptop in front of me. When I scan his email, my blood runs cold.

"Where did this come from?"

"We're tracking it now," he says as my eyes scan.

They are photos, dozens of them, of my angel. Some from New York when we were there, others from Bitterroot Valley shortly after we got home.

But my heart stops when I get to one of her at Birdie's recital *last night*.

There's another of her working in her bookshop, smiling at a customer, also time-stamped yesterday.

"Jesus," I mutter, and then I get to the message.

Terminate the building of the resort in Sweden. It would be a shame for this beautiful woman to get hurt.

My eyes jump up to every person on my board, and I growl.

"We're pulling out of Sweden."

Fiona gasps, and there are rumblings around the table.

"This isn't up for discussion."

"Connor, as your attorney, I'm telling you, this wouldn't be wise."

"I have to agree with Fiona," Ronan says. "We'll lose half a billion euros at this point."

"I'm not asking! These motherfecking arseholes are threatening my future wife. Not just me. *My future wife!* I'm going home."

"Sir, we have so many important matters to go through with you, especially now that you're hardly here in the office."

I glare at Sean. "There's a stalker following Billie, taking photos of her, watching her so they can threaten us. So they can threaten *her*. I'm not there, not even on the same goddamn continent, but that arsehole *is*. If you think I'm staying here for one more minute, you're insane. Pull out of the Sweden project *now*. I don't care how much money we lose. We can afford it."

"We don't typically give in to threats like this," Fiona says softly and holds her hand up before I can bite her head off. "But I agree in this case. It's been a difficult project from the onset, and if it's going to lead to threats and danger, it's not worth it. I'll figure it out. Go home to your girl."

I blink at her, surprised, but she offers me a small smile.

"Go," Ronan agrees. "We'll handle it. If need be, I'll go to Sweden myself."

"We'll go as a board," Sean says, and the others nod in agreement.

"Thank you," I murmur and then turn to Miller. "Call and get the plane ready. We're leaving from here."

"Yes, sir." Miller nods, leading me out of the room.

"Is this the first time they've threatened her?" I ask as we stride to the elevator.

"Yes," he says firmly. "There have been several threats against you, but this is the first targeting her."

"Get Simon on the line and tell him to stick to her like goddamn glue."

"On it."

"Then find out who this photographer is, call Bitter-root Valley PD, and have them dealt with. I also want this goddamn extremist group dealt with. Call in our contacts with the FBI and CIA and have it ripped apart."

"Already started on that," he replies. "I don't *just* guard your ass, you know."

I nod, and when the elevator doors slide open, we rush to the SUV.

I need to get home.

Chapter Thirty-One

BILLIE

"I love this book club," Skyla says with a contented smile after the rest of the girls leave and just the two of us are left in the store. "Everyone always reads the books, and the conversation is so much fun."

"I agree." I smile at her as I gather the last few items for the trash, and Skyla helps me put the chairs away. "You don't have to stay, you know. I'm fine here."

"I've missed you," she replies, watching me with shrewd green eyes, so much like her brother's. "I know you're a busy woman with work and my brother, but I thought it would be nice to hang out for a minute to chat privately."

I can't help myself. I pull Skyla in for a tight hug. Her arms wrap around me, and she squeezes me just as tight, and it occurs to me how much I really needed a hug.

"Are you okay?" she whispers as she rubs her hand up and down my back.

"I miss him," I reply and pull back, eyeing Simon,

who's still standing by the front door, but he's looking at his phone. "My life has changed a lot."

She nods, obviously understanding. "He's a little overbearing sometimes, and he's feral when it comes to protection. Is it worth it?"

I frown at her. "Of course, it's worth it. I can't picture my life without him. But he's so ... *worried* about the safety thing, no matter how many times I explain to him that nothing's going to happen to me here."

"I thought I was safe here, too." And everything that happened just a couple of months ago with Skyla's stalker, her being in danger, her beautiful dog almost dying, comes flooding back to me. "My brother loves you, and there's nothing he won't do to keep you safe."

"I love him, too."

She smiles and cups my cheek. "Aye, I know you do. Isn't it wonderful that I fell in love with your brother, and you fell for mine, and we'll be best friends forever?"

"As long as your brother doesn't dump me, it's wonderful."

She barks out a laugh and shakes her head. "Not happening. Ever."

I laugh with her and pull away. "I'm just going to go turn out the lights and get ready to go. Would you like a ride home?"

"I drove myself in," she says. "But I'll wait and walk out with you."

With a nod, I walk to the backroom so I can flip the light switches. I hear Skyla speaking and then a lower voice, and I assume she's talking to Simon.

Once I've gathered my handbag from my office, I walk back through the store, and my eyes widen when I realize Skyla's speaking to Connor.

But before I can run and jump in his arms, I realize Connor doesn't look happy.

"You'll do as I fecking say," he says to his sister, who's frowning at him. "I've already called Beckett, so he's aware."

"We'll be fine," Skyla assures him.

"Hey." I offer my man a tentative smile, and then I'm yanked into his arms. He holds me so tight, it's hard to pull in a breath. "I missed you, too."

Suddenly, Simon shouts, "Get down!" He pushes through the glass door, his weapon drawn, and he's sprinting across the street with Miller right behind him.

Connor tackles me to the floor, and Skyla's down, too, and my heart thumps in my ears. There's no noise coming from outside, and I lift my head to look, but Connor growls.

"Stay down, angel," he says as Skyla scoots over to us, and I pull her close.

"What in the hell?" I ask.

"You'll stay here, both of you," Connor says as he goes to stand, but I yank on his hand, pulling him back to me.

"You're not going out there."

"I'm going to check it out," he says, kissing my forehead. "I'll be fine."

Absolutely fucking *not*.

"Let Miller and Simon handle it."

But my stubborn-as-hell man ignores my plea and stands just as the door opens again, and Simon rushes in, no weapon in sight.

"All clear, the suspect is apprehended."

What the hell is going on?

"Who?" I demand. "What was he doing?"

Simon doesn't even look my way. He's talking directly to Connor as Skyla and I climb to our feet.

"The suspect is apprehended, sir, but we haven't done a full canvas of the area to know if there are any more out there," Simon adds.

"Who?" I demand. "What was he doing?"

Simon doesn't even look my way. He's talking directly to Connor as Skyla and I climb to our feet.

"The police are with him, boss," Simon says.

"Miller called them in?"

"Yes, and they were literally a street away. They pulled up as we caught the guy."

What guy?

"Good." Connor tugs me against him. "Christ," he mutters against my hair. "Need to get you to our home, bumble. And I need you to listen to my instructions and follow them."

"*Who* and *why*?" I demand again, but no one's answering me.

Instead, Connor backs away and starts barking orders.

"Simon, follow Skyla home, and don't leave her until she's through the gate at their ranch. Miller, we're heading straight to the house. I want alarms set around the perimeter of the property and all cameras on."

"Sir," they both say, their faces grim.

"What's going on?" I ask as Connor opens the back door of the SUV and gestures for me to get inside.

But I don't get inside. Instead, my gaze is pinned to the short, skinny man with wire-rimmed glasses being led to the back seat of the police car where Chase Wild is reading him his rights.

"Who is that man?" I ask.

"Angel, I need you to get in the car now. Please." He gestures for me to get into the car, then slides in after me. I've barely got my seat belt on when Miller takes off toward home.

Connor holds my hand, but he's distant. His face is hard as granite as he stares out the window, grinding his teeth together.

"Who was he?"

Nothing. He takes a breath and grinds his back teeth together.

Okay, I'll try this another way.

"How was the flight?" I ask, trying to draw him into conversation.

"Long," he replies and pulls his glasses off to rub his eyes with his free hand.

I decide to keep my mouth shut until we're alone in the house, and I can ask what in the hell is going on.

I don't like that it feels like he's shut me out again. It feels like it did months ago, when we were fighting the attraction between us, and he was always so broody and growly.

Something's wrong, and he's not going to tell me what it is.

"Boss, the house and perimeter are secure. Jones and Weston have eyes on our approach."

I don't even know who Jones and Weston are.

Connor nods but otherwise stays silent.

Finally, Miller pulls up at our front door. I push out of the vehicle and walk inside after punching in the code to disarm the house alarm.

Connor walks in behind me, rubs his hand down my back, and marches to his office.

And I'm right behind him.

"I'll be upstairs in a few," he says, obviously dismissing me. "Go get comfortable, and I'll come hold you."

"Not until you tell me what's going on."

He takes off his suit coat, watching me with cool green eyes as he drapes it over the back of his chair. I prop my hands on my hips as he unfastens the buttons on his cuffs and rolls them up his forearms.

"I'd like you to let me do some work, and then I'll come upstairs," he tries again, obviously doing his best to rein in his frustration.

"And I'd like *you* to talk to me." I soften my tone slightly because I can see the torment in his eyes, and it makes my chest ache.

He's barely touched me.

He's so fucking distant, I hate it.

He's shut me out, and he looks exhausted. His hair is in disarray from his hands diving through it in agitation.

"I *need* you to talk to me," I try again.

"And I need you to do as you're bloody told," he retorts, fisting his hands at his sides.

I feel my eyebrows wing up at that. "I'm not a dog trained to obey you."

"*Fuck*," he growls and begins to pace the office.

"Something is obviously *very* wrong, and we're in a relationship, Connor. This is a partnership, not a dictatorship. I can help, you know. I tell you everything, so it's a slap in the face that you'd keep something from me. Something obviously bad enough that it has you pulling away from me and not even touching me. It's not fair. Who was that man? And why did Simon run after him with his gun drawn?"

He stomps to me, he grips either side of my jawline and throat, and he kisses me hungrily, drinks from me as if he's dying of thirst.

"Goddammit, you're not a fecking dog," he growls, still holding me, staring into my eyes. "You're my future wife. You're everything. My life doesn't work without you, and I won't apologize or ask your permission to use everything in my power to protect you like you're the most important person in the world because you *are*."

"I'm *fine*," I assure him, but he shakes his head. "Tell me who that man was, Connor."

"I don't know for sure who he is. I received threats." He swallows hard as if the words taste like ash on his tongue. "Christ, I received threats against you. They're here in Montana and had photos of you. Recent photos of you from the recital and around town, and I suspect that was the arsehole taking the goddamn pictures. I don't know if he was going to try to do worse. I don't know if he's alone or if he has a team with him. *I don't fucking know, angel.*"

My stomach drops. God, no wonder he's been so worried about my safety.

"Why?" I ask him. "Why against me?"

"Because the threats against *me* didn't get them anywhere," he replies, and the fatigue in his face deepens.

"Wait." I pull back so I can scowl up at him. "They've been threatening *you*?"

"Aye." He lets out a gusty breath. "It happens all the time."

"But you didn't tell me."

"They're mostly idle threats to try to scare me to do their bidding," he replies, but I'm shaking my head. "But when they dared bring you into it, they unleashed the fire of a thousand suns because I'll burn it all to the ground to make sure you're safe."

"Connor." My hands circle his wrists. "When did this happen?"

"Which ones?"

I blink at him. "All of them."

"It started in New York. But they didn't send me the photos of you until just before I boarded the plane to come home."

"You should have called me." I step out of his embrace and pull my hands down my face. "As soon as it happened, you should have called me and told me, so I could understand *why* you were so adamant about me being with Simon."

"I don't—"

"We're *partners*," I remind him, turning back to him. "You've said several times that you love my backbone. Well, here it is, billionaire. If you think that I'll sit back and let you dictate how things go without question, then I'm not the girl for you. You need to go find her. I deserve your respect as well as your love and protection."

His eyes narrow, still so hot, and then he slowly walks to me until he's just an inch away, but he doesn't touch me.

And it's torture.

Chapter Thirty-Two

CONNOR

She's so fucking beautiful, standing here in my office with her chin up, her whiskey eyes shooting sparks at me.

So bloody strong.

And mine.

"You think I need someone else, *a ghrá*?" My voice is low and hard as my stomach tightens at the mere thought of being without her.

"No, I'd kill any other woman who dared put her hands on you, but—"

That's all I need. I cup the back of her neck and yank her against me. Covering her mouth, I slide my tongue against hers and finally breathe her in.

With a whimper, Billie's hands grip my sides, and she pushes her stomach against my cock, leaning into me.

"Mine," I growl against her lips as I lift her, and she wraps her legs around my waist as I walk us up the stairs to our bedroom. Her arms loop around my neck, and she kisses me for all she's worth, and finally, I'm home.

Setting her down long enough to strip us out of our clothes, I guide her back to the bed and crawl over her, caging her in with my pelvis between her legs. I brush her soft hair away from her face and rub my nose over hers.

"I know you're strong." I love the way her hands skim up and down my back. "I know you can handle anything that comes our way, but a part of me will always want to shield you from shite like this because you're my heart, and I don't want you to worry."

Her expression softens, and she cups my face and lifts up to dust her lips over mine.

"And I don't want you to carry anything alone." Christ, she steals the breath from my lungs. "If they threaten one of us, they threaten both of us."

I slip inside her, making us both groan, and when I start to move, I cup her neck and jaw, and her walls tighten around me.

"If I tell you to be careful, I need you to do it," I growl against her lips.

"As long as you tell me why." She bites my lower lip and sucks it into her mouth.

"I need to know that you're safe."

"I know." She lifts her hips and her legs higher, opening herself so I slip in deeper. "It's your love language."

"*Mo chroí*," I growl against her ear, moving faster. "I've missed you."

423

She smiles and tightens around me. "Me too. So much. Oh God."

"You're so good for me." I lean up so I can watch where we meet, where her wetness coats my cock as I move in and out. "Look at how well you take me. I'll never get enough of you."

She whimpers again, and I can feel her body tensing, ready to fall into oblivion.

"That's right, come on my cock. Finish for me."

She cries out as her body convulses around me, tugging me over with her as I shoot inside her, over and over again as I fuck her through my climax, rocking into her until finally, I fall onto her and crush her to the mattress.

"Canp momb," she says against my shoulder, making me grin.

"What was that?" I ask as I pull up and pepper her cheek with kisses.

"Can't move," she repeats. "But that's better."

After one more soft kiss, I clean us both up and snuggle her to me, her front to my side, her arm wrapped around my middle, and her head on my chest.

She hitches her leg over my thigh, as if she can't get close enough.

"Oh God. Here it is. My peaceful place." She tips her chin up so she can look at me, and I see tears fill her pretty eyes. "No pressure or anything, but if you leave for that long again, I'll have to key your car."

"Which one?" I ask, tipping up an eyebrow.

"All of them." She chuckles, then her face sobers

again. "You look so tired, baby. Ireland wasn't good to you this time?"

"No." I kiss her forehead. "You weren't with me."

"Let's go to Galway soon." Surprised, I blink down at her. "I'll slip away for a long weekend or something. You need it."

"Christ, I love you." I tighten my hold on her, hugging her to me. "I think we both need it."

"Yeah, we do." She nuzzles against my chest, and I feel her muscles loosen. "I think I might actually fall asleep."

Brushing my lips back and forth over the crown of her head, I smile. "Go to sleep, *mo rúnsearc*. I've got you."

"I've got this," I say to Bridger, who nods and reaches for another box.

We're in town, and I'm helping the Blackwell men move their parents into the new house they bought. All four of them are here, along with their dad, Brandon, and Holden Lexington.

The women are at my house, having a lass's baking day. It's been a week since I got home. Billie wants to go to Galway later this week, but I need to talk to these guys first.

After the last box is unloaded from the truck, we gather in the small kitchen, and I clear my throat.

"I need to talk to all of you." They quiet down and turn their attention to me. I'm not usually one who gets nervous.

But today, my hands are sweaty.

"Are you okay?" Brooks asks, his brow creasing.

"Aye, I'm good." I tuck my hands in the pockets of my jeans. "I'd like to talk about Billie."

"It's happening," Blake says with a smug grin.

"I can head out—" Holden begins, but I shake my head.

"I'd like it if you'd stay. This worked out well, actually." I push my glasses up my nose and then look each of them in the eyes. "You all love her. You're her family. So it's right that I speak to all of you together when I tell you that I'm going to ask her to marry me next week. We're taking a trip to Galway."

Brandon blows out a breath, and the others share glances, shuffle their feet, and then look at their da.

"Why do you love my daughter?" he asks, crossing his arms over his chest.

"Did you know that her favorite thing in the world is to be hugged?" Brandon's eyes narrow. "She simply wants to be touched. She's picky about the bottled water she drinks. She'd rather spend hours hunting through secondhand clothing stores to find what she wants than spend the money on something new."

I chuckle and shake my head, then look down at the floor.

"She misses all of you terribly but would never make you feel bad because she hasn't seen you in a while. And Christ, does she have a backbone on her. She sticks up for herself and those she loves without batting an eye, and her tongue can be lethal. She's so bleedin' clever and quick-witted. Don't even get me started on her work ethic. Something I think she learned from all of you."

I look up to find all six of them grinning at me.

"I love the fire in her. Her stubborn side and her softness. I'll continue to love her, to protect her, until the last breath leaves my body, and I need her to be my wife. The sooner, the better."

Brandon nods, then pulls me in for a manly hug, patting me on the back.

"Welcome to the family."

Everyone shakes my hand, Beckett being the last. His eyes are sober as they hold mine.

"She's the best of us," he says. "She's the best there is, and she deserves everything in this world."

"Aye, she does. And I'm going to give it to her."

How could it be that simple? I answer one question, and they accept me without any other discussion? Without asking me if my family will insist on a prenup—which I'll fight—or if we'll move out of Montana—we won't—or any other questions at all?

The expressions on their faces are full of acceptance. Happiness, even. Welcoming me into their family so easily humbles me to the core.

It's not just my girl who's special. I'm grateful that

Skyla and I found their entire family. It's a privilege to be among them.

With that finished, we caravan over to Billie's and my home and join the girls in the kitchen, stealing cookies.

"These are still warm," Bridger says as he bites into one of the treats.

"I did it," Birdie says with a wide smile. "And Mom says when the baby comes, I can teach him how to bake, too."

Everyone goes dead quiet and turns to Bridger and Dani, who are both grinning at each other.

"Are you telling me you're having a boy?" Billie asks, her hands clasped over her chest.

"We were going to wait for dinner to announce it," Dani says as she leans into Bridger's side. "But yes, we just found out yesterday. Baby Boy Blackwell is on the way."

I look on as my girl starts to cry and pulls both her brother and best friend in for hugs. Everything I said earlier is true, but this is what I love most about my angel.

She loves so big, so completely, that it spills out of her eyes, as if her body just can't hold on to it all.

Her gaze finds mine, and she smiles widely as I cross to her and tip her chin up before brushing my mouth over hers.

"I love you, *mo rúnsearc.*"

She tips her forehead against mine. "I love you too, billionaire."

Chapter Thirty-Three
BILLIE

"**A**re you telling me you've found them?"

I lean on the doorway of Connor's office in the Galway house and cross my arms over my chest as I listen in. There's no need to eavesdrop.

Since returning to Montana several weeks ago, Connor has made it perfectly clear that he won't hold anything back from me.

It's only made me fall more in love with him.

He flips the phone to speaker and sets it on his desk, gesturing for me to join him. Rather than sit in the chair opposite of him, I round the desk and settle in his lap. Connor kisses my cheek and hugs me against him.

"We found most of the members of the extremist group," a voice says on the other end of the line. "They weren't even *in* Sweden."

"Where were they?" Connor asks.

"Alaska." The man snorts. "Apparently, they like to

cause trouble in the name of saving the trees, or the fish, or whatever the fuck, but they do it from their hideout in the wilderness of Alaska. Or they did. They've been wanted for a long time, and we have them in custody. We're still tracking a few members, but it won't take long."

"Good." I feel Connor relax behind me. "And the arsehole who was in Montana stalking my girl?"

"In jail," he confirms. "The police force there apprehended him quickly, as you know, and he'll go away for a while for stalking. He was also wanted on other warrants, so he won't be a problem for anyone but the federal government for a long while."

"Excellent," Connor says. "As always, I appreciate your help. I've wired your money."

"It's a pleasure."

The man hangs up, and I twist to look Connor in the face.

"Did you just bribe an official?" I ask him.

"I have no idea what you're talking about or who that man was." His face is calm, but his Irish eyes are full of mischief.

"Uh-huh. I don't believe you."

He leans in and plants his magical lips against my neck. "Let's go for a walk, *mo chroí*."

"That sounds nice." I hop off his lap, and he follows me through the house to the front door. After snatching up his hoodie, which is now *my* hoodie, I pull it over my head, and we make our way outside to the path that leads us to the cliffs.

We do this every day. We've been here for two days already, and we always make time to come out here to stare at the raging sea, breathe in the salty air, and just be here together.

It's my favorite time of the day.

With my hand firmly in Connor's, we walk down the path, and I point out the birds that never fail to make me grin.

My man stops and tugs me into his arms to hug me close. I love how physically affectionate my billionaire is. Maybe it's becoming one of his love languages, too.

"I love you, *mo rúnsearc*."

Grinning up at him, I reply, "I love you too."

Connor licks his lips, his gaze floating over my face. Stepping back, he suddenly kneels before me, and my heart stops beating as tears threaten.

"I can't go another minute without telling you how much I love you, Billie. There aren't words to explain the love that fills me up whenever I look at you. You take my breath away. I'm proud to be by your side. You're such an incredible woman, so smart, full of so much fire. You inspire me."

A tear escapes and drifts down my cheek, and he reaches up to catch it with his thumb.

"No world exists where I can live without you. You are my life force, the only thing that makes sense. And you showed me what real love is, and that I'm capable of it."

"You love me so well," I tell him with a trembling voice.

"Marry me, *a ghrá*. Build a family with me. Let me show you, every day, how much I love you."

He reaches into his pants pocket and pulls out a ring that takes *my* breath away.

"Holy shit."

His lips twitch. "I need an answer, bumble."

Taking his face in my hands, I lean in to press my lips to his. "Of course, billionaire. Nothing would make me happier than being your wife."

His smile is so bright, it lights me up inside as he pushes the ring, with the biggest oval diamond I've ever seen in my life, onto my finger. Then he stands, and I'm in his arms, and he's kissing me until my toes curl.

"I'm going to keep you on your toes," I inform him as we continue walking down the path. "There won't ever be a dull moment."

"I'm counting on it."

"How quickly can we have a baby?"

He stops and stares down at me and then tugs me to him once more, but this time, his hands slide down to my ass, and he presses his growing cock into me. "You want me to put a baby inside you, *a ghrá*?"

"Lots of babies," I confirm.

"I'll never deny you anything. But let's get married first. I'm thinking next month should be enough time to plan."

I laugh and cup his face. "That's no time at all. I don't think we can make that work."

"Money talks, bumble. We'll get married, and you can plan on being pregnant by Christmas."

I frown up at him. "That's fast."

"You want it." He shrugs and kisses my forehead. "So you'll have it. Anything you want."

"Tell me you love me."

His gaze softens. "More than all the stars in the sky."

Epilogue

BLAKE BLACKWELL

Denver International Airport is always busy. I have plenty of time on this layover, which I scheduled on purpose in case there was any weather to worry about. Of course, Denver's having a heat wave this year, so we won't have any issues taking off.

Which is good because I'm due back at the hospital tomorrow.

I make my way to the gate and see that they're boarding, so I get in line and find my seat in first class. I always sit in the aisle.

Just as I've fastened my seatbelt and settled in the seat, a woman who immediately has my attention boards the plane.

Hello, gray-eyed beauty.

She's tall and lean, with thick dark hair that's currently up in a messy bun.

She's wearing glasses, and those gray eyes narrow as she looks down the aisle toward the back of the plane.

As she waits for the person ahead of her to shuffle forward, her gaze lowers to mine. She doesn't smile. She blinks. And then, to my utter delight, she lifts one perfect eyebrow.

And I couldn't stop my grin if I wanted to.

She smirks and walks past me, and the moment is over.

The flight attendants go through their routine of making sure everyone is buckled up, and then, to my surprise, we're taking off on time.

"Hello everyone, this is your captain from the flight deck. We've reached our cruising altitude of thirty-four thousand feet. Should be a smooth ride up to Bitterroot Valley, but they are having some weather tonight that could make things dicey for us. If we have to divert, we'll keep you posted. In the meantime, sit back and relax and enjoy the one hour, fifty minute flight."

Christ, I hope we don't have to divert.

Why do I always agree to attend these conferences when the weather is the most unpredictable? Last year, I was stuck in Denver overnight because of a storm for this same conference.

I'll look for something different next year.

I'm reading an article about celiac disease when a flight attendant comes over the loudspeaker.

"Is there a doctor on board?"

Christ.

"If there is, please press your call button."

Resigned, I press the button above my head, and the attendant hurries up to me.

"Can you come with me, doctor?"

"Sure."

I walk behind her and am surprised to find the gray-eyed woman sitting in the middle seat next to a man in the aisle, in the exit row, with her fingers on his neck, taking his pulse. The man appears to be in his mid-sixties. He's pale and clammy, and I don't like his breathing.

"I'm Dr. Blackwell," I say as I crouch beside them.

"I'm Harper," Gray Eyes replies and licks her lips. "I'm a nurse. I don't like his color or his breathing."

"Agreed." She's fucking smart. "Sir? What's your name?"

"Ronald." He's panting as if he can't catch his breath.

"Do you have pain in your left arm, Ronald?" I grabbed my backpack on the way back here. So I pull out my stethoscope and put it in my ears, then listen to Ronald's heart.

"No," he says.

"Does your chest hurt or feel heavy?"

"No."

I need an EKG machine. I do have my smartwatch.

"Ronald, I'm going to put my watch on your wrist. It'll take a measurement of your heart for me. It's not perfect, and I'd rather we had you in my ER, but it'll do for now. Is that okay?"

Ronald nods, and Harper gives me a half smile.

"I was about to do the same thing."

She helps me get the watch on him, and I run the ECG function. It doesn't show a heart issue, but it's not a fail-safe.

I flag down the attendant.

"Do you mind if we put this gentleman behind me" —I gesture to the guy sitting across the aisle from Ronald —"in my seat, and I'll take his so I can monitor this until we land?"

"Of course." She escorts the other man to my first class seat, and I turn back to Ronald.

"I'm going to have the pilot call ahead to have an ambulance on standby to meet us when we land. Okay?"

"Yeah. I don't feel great."

"How *do* you feel?" I ask him.

"It's hard to breathe. I'm sweaty. A little dizzy."

"Are you prone to panic attacks?" Harper asks him. She's holding his hand, doing her best to keep him calm.

"Never have been before."

"This is your captain again. Unfortunately, we won't be able to land in Bitterroot Valley tonight. There's just too much fog and snow, so they've rerouted us to Missoula. We've begun our descent and should be on the ground in about twenty-five minutes."

"Shit," Harper mutters.

"Doctor," the flight attendant says, "there will be an ambulance waiting for us when we get there."

"Good."

Ronald's breathing has calmed down considerably, but he's still sweaty, and his heartbeat is fast.

He's nervous, and I can't blame him. I would be, too.

"Are you married, Ronald?" Harper asks. She's trying to distract him.

Smart girl.

"Forty-two years," he says. "Six kids."

"*Six,*" Harper says with a chuckle. "That's a lot of kids. Boys? Girls?"

"All girls. All gorgeous."

"I bet they are." Harper's humor-filled gaze finds mine, and she winks. "How old are they?"

"Oldest is forty. Youngest is twenty-nine."

"Any grandbabies?"

"Three." He nods. "Would be four, but one didn't make it."

"I'm sorry to hear that," Harper says quietly.

"He had a heart defect when he was born. Spent a month in the NICU. Never got to come home."

Harper nods sympathetically. "I work in the NICU. You're my first adult patient in a long time."

That gets a smile out of Ronald.

And me.

Christ, she's fucking beautiful.

"I don't envy your job," Ronald says to Harper.

"Some days suck," she admits. "Like on days when the babies like yours don't make it. Can I tell you a secret?"

He nods, and she glances my way and raises an eyebrow.

"Your secret's safe with us," I reply, speaking for the first time in a while.

"Every time a baby passes when I'm on shift, I spend my lunch break in my car, crying. You'd think after five years of doing this job, it would get easier. But it doesn't. But then there are the days when the babies go home, and that's the *best*. It's all about checks and balances, I guess."

The plane lands, and everyone is asked to stay seated while we get Ronald off the plane and onto a stretcher. When he's loaded into the ambulance, Harper glances my way, then grabs her bag and starts walking away.

"Hey," I say, and she stops.

"Yeah?"

"Where are you going?"

She looks around and then back at me. "I'm going to figure out how to get home from here."

I shake my head and hold my hand out for hers. "Come on. You're with me."

After just one second of hesitation, she slides her palm against mine, and I lead her away.

Are you ready for Blake and Harper's book, When You Blush? You can preorder it here:

https://www.kristenprobyauthor.com/when-you-blush

. . .

Turn the page for a PREVIEW of When You Blush!

If you'd like to read **Kane O'Callaghan's** story (Connor's childhood friend, the glass artist, from Galway), you can find it here:

https://www.kristenprobyauthor.com/dream-with-me

When You Blush Preview

Chapter One

Blake

"It's wild to me that Bitterroot Valley is so socked in with fog and snow that we can't land there, but it's not bad at all here in Missoula."

The gorgeous woman next to me, with her hand still clutched in mine, stares out the windows of the airport to watch the snow drift down softly as we wait for our luggage.

She's not my girlfriend.

She's definitely not my wife.

This intriguing woman is a complete stranger to me, but I absolutely do *not* want to let go of her hand.

I met her less than two hours ago on a flight from Denver to Montana, thanks to a medical emergency mid-flight with another passenger.

I was asked to help because I'm a doctor, and she was sitting next to the patient. All I know about her is that her name is Harper, she's a NICU nurse by trade, and she's so fucking beautiful, I can't take my eyes off her, with all that dark hair and gray eyes.

Oh, and when she tried to walk out of my life at the end of that tarmac, I told her she'd be with me and offered her my hand.

It wasn't a question or a request.

And she didn't argue. If Harper were *my* sister, I'd punch myself in the face. But she's not. She's a beautiful woman that I'm not ready to say goodbye to yet.

We're stuck in Missoula for the night, thanks to the early winter storm happening at home in Bitterroot Valley.

And I plan to make the most of it.

"Are you okay?" she asks, peering up at me with those gray eyes.

I'm fucking fantastic. Never better.

"I'm fine. And you? Will your family be upset if you don't make it home in time for Thanksgiving?"

Yes, this is my way of asking about her family. *Mine* will not be thrilled that I won't make it home in time for dinner.

"They'll be okay." She shrugs a shoulder, then points when she sees her black-and-red suitcase with a bright yellow ribbon on the handle come around on the carousel. "That's me."

I muscle it off the belt for her and set it on its wheels.

Then I spot my own luggage, and before long, we're walking away from baggage claim.

"I could just rent a car," she says thoughtfully as we walk, each one of us rolling our bags, still holding hands. "It's only a couple hour drive from here."

"In a storm," I remind her, shaking my head. "Let's find a hotel for the night."

She lifts an eyebrow, and her lips tip up with humor. Gray eyes flash. "Wow. Does that line work on all the nurses you pick up on rerouted flights, or am I just the lucky one?"

I grin at her. Christ, she's pretty. Even dressed so casually in leggings and a hoodie, with her hair up in a messy bun and in her glasses.

No makeup.

Absolutely fucking perfect.

And I can tell that she's attracted to me, too. This isn't one-sided. She's still letting me hold her hand, for fuck's sake.

"Two rooms," I reply, shaking my head. "I'm not trying to be a creep or anything."

"Good to know. I'll order an Uber."

"Already done," I reply, and chuckle when she narrows her eyes at me. "And you're welcome to join me."

Now she bites her lip. "Okay, I'm going to be brutally honest."

"Please do."

"You don't seem like a serial killer."

"Glad to hear it."

"But, Dr. Blackwell, I don't even know your first name."

I smile at her, nodding. "Blake. Thirty-four. Family practice and ER doc from Bitterroot Valley. The middle child out of five, I *will* likely catch some shit for not making it to dinner tomorrow, especially from my niece, Birdie, who is six and the apple of my eye. I'm not married or otherwise attached."

She's blinking at me, listening with wide eyes, and nods slowly.

"Your turn," I tell her.

"Uh, let's see. Harper I'm-Not-Telling-You-My-Last-Name. Thirty. NICU nurse, as you know. No siblings. Hell, no parents."

I tighten my hand around hers, but she doesn't seem to notice.

"My best friend and *her* family will miss me tomorrow, but like I said, they'll be chill about it. I like your niece's name."

I grin at that.

"We're all B names. My parents thought it was fun."

"Totally fun," she agrees with a nod. "You know, you could have made all of that up and could still be a serial killer."

I sigh and purse my lips. "You're right. I could have. Well, I guess you'll have to trust me."

"Or I could say goodbye and go fend for myself like the grown adult I am."

I lean into her, not touching her, and press my lips to the soft skin just below her ear.

Fuck me, she smells good.

"You don't want to do that, do you, Harper?" I pull back and hook a loose piece of her hair behind her ear. She licks her lips. *Yeah, she's fucking attracted to me.* "I promise, I'm not a danger to you."

She huffs out a laugh. "Why not live on the wild side, right?"

My Uber pulls up to the curb, and I load our suitcases into the trunk. The ride to the hotel is quiet as we take in the snow around us, getting heavier by the minute, and then we're pulling up to the hotel.

Harper walks next to me as we approach the front desk.

"How can I help you?" the receptionist asks.

"We need two rooms, please," I tell her, and she starts typing away on her keyboard.

"Do you have a reservation?"

"No," I reply.

She hums, wrinkling her nose. "Well, with it being the day before Thanksgiving and so many flights canceled, we only have one room left. However, it *is* a suite."

I glance at Harper, who shrugs.

"We'll take it," I reply with a nod and pass her my credit card, just as Harper offers her credit card as well. "Don't worry, I've got this."

"No way—"

"You can buy dinner," I tell her, and she frowns at me as I get the room squared away with the nice receptionist.

On the way up to the room in the elevator, I glance down at the woman beside me. She's worrying her bottom lip between her teeth.

"I'll take the couch," I inform her. "Just laying that all out there now, so there's no awkwardness later."

"You're super tall," she reminds me, and then her eyes skim over my chest and shoulders. "And … *broad*. I should probably take the couch."

"Let's see the room and then make decisions," I suggest as the elevator comes to a stop, and we walk out onto our floor.

Our suite is at the end of the hallway, and I open the door and Harper slides past me, pulling her suitcase behind her.

"Well then." She whistles and looks around the spacious space. "Big room."

A couch and chair are situated in front of a television, and the dining room table along one wall sits six.

Through a doorway is the bedroom with a king bed, and the bathroom is big enough for a soaking tub *and* a standing shower that would easily accommodate both of us.

I'm not going to lie. I'd love to fuck her in that shower.

"I'll fit on that couch," I inform her, although I sincerely hope that by the time it's time for bed, I'll be in the king with her.

Harper is gorgeous, smart, and completely fuckable.

And I've recently had a dry streak when it comes to sex.

I don't do relationships. Ever. My schedule is too messy, and I'm married to the hospital. No woman should feel like she's secondary to anything, especially a job, and that is unapologetically my priority in life.

But casual sex is something I have down to a science.

"Are you hungry?" she asks me, and I lift an eyebrow.

Harper rolls her eyes, making me laugh.

"For *dinner*, Romeo. I didn't grab anything before the flight. There's a restaurant downstairs."

"Then we'd best go get some dinner," I reply with a nod.

"Hold that thought," she says, raising a finger and pulling her phone out of her pocket. "I have to let Ava know that I won't be in tonight."

I nod and give her privacy. I use the bathroom and freshen up from the flight, and when I walk back into the living room, she's just finishing her call.

"I know, it sucks, but I can't control the weather, you know. Yeah, I'm safe." She turns and looks at me and bites that plump lip again. "I promise I'll keep you posted. I don't have a return ticket, remember? You'll get plenty of time with me. Jesus, Ava, you're fucking needy."

That makes me chuckle, and Harper smiles back at me.

Fuck, that smile.

"Yeah, yeah, love and blah, blah." I lift an eyebrow, and she rolls her eyes. "Yes. Yes. No. Okay, *mom*, eat some turkey for me. I'll be there as soon as I can, clingy girl. Okay, bye."

She lets out a gusty exhale, closes her eyes, and shakes her head.

"That girl needs a boyfriend. Hold on, I'm going to wash my hands."

She strides into the bathroom, and I shove my hands in my pockets.

Jesus. I like her.

Newsletter Sign Up

I hope you enjoyed reading this story as much as I enjoyed writing it! For upcoming book news, be sure to join my newsletter! I promise I will only send you news-filled mail, and none of the spam. You can sign up here:

https://mailchi.mp/kristenproby.com/newsletter-sign-up

Also by Kristen Proby:

Other Books by Kristen Proby

The Wilds of Montana Series
Wild for You - Remington & Erin
Chasing Wild - Chase & Summer
Wildest Dreams - Ryan & Polly
On the Wild Side - Brady & Abbi
She's a Wild One - Holden & Millie

The Blackwells of Montana
When We Burn - Bridger & Dani
When We Break - Beckett & Skyla
Where We Bloom - Connor & Billie

Get more information on the series here: https://www.kristenprobyauthor.com/the-wilds-of-montana

Single in Seattle Series
The Secret - Vaughn & Olivia
The Scandal - Gray & Stella
The Score - Ike & Sophie
The Setup - Keaton & Sidney
The Stand-In - Drew & London

Check out the full series here: https://www.kristenprobyauthor.com/single-in-seattle

Huckleberry Bay Series

Lighthouse Way

The Big Sky Universe

Love Under the Big Sky
Loving Cara
Seducing Lauren
Falling for Jillian
Saving Grace

The Big Sky
Charming Hannah
Kissing Jenna
Waiting for Willa
Soaring With Fallon

Big Sky Royal
Enchanting Sebastian
Enticing Liam
Taunting Callum

Heroes of Big Sky
Honor
Courage
Shelter

Check out the full Big Sky universe here: https://
www.kristenprobyauthor.com/under-the-big-sky

Bayou Magic

Shadows
Spells
Serendipity

Check out the full series here: https://www.kristenprobyauthor.com/bayou-magic

The Curse of the Blood Moon Series

Hallows End
Cauldrons Call
Salems Song

The Romancing Manhattan Series

All the Way
All it Takes
After All

Check out the full series here: https://www.kristenprobyauthor.com/romancing-manhattan

The Boudreaux Series

Easy Love
Easy Charm
Easy Melody
Easy Kisses
Easy Magic
Easy Fortune
Easy Nights

Check out the full series here: https://www.kristenprobyauthor.com/boudreaux

The Fusion Series

Listen to Me
Close to You
Blush for Me
The Beauty of Us
Savor You

Check out the full series here: https://www.
kristenprobyauthor.com/fusion

From 1001 Dark Nights

Easy With You
Easy For Keeps
No Reservations
Tempting Brooke
Wonder With Me
Shine With Me
Change With Me
The Scramble
Cherry Lane

Kristen Proby's Crossover Collection

Soaring with Fallon, A Big Sky Novel

Wicked Force: A Wicked Horse Vegas/Big Sky Novella
By Sawyer Bennett

All Stars Fall: A Seaside Pictures/Big Sky Novella
By Rachel Van Dyken

Hold On: A Play On/Big Sky Novella
By Samantha Young

Worth Fighting For: A Warrior Fight Club/Big Sky
Novella
By Laura Kaye

Crazy Imperfect Love: A Dirty Dicks/Big Sky Novella
By K.L. Grayson

Nothing Without You: A Forever Yours/Big Sky Novella
By Monica Murphy

Check out the entire Crossover Collection here:
https://www.kristenprobyauthor.com/kristen-proby-
crossover-collection

About the Author

Kristen Proby is a *New York Times*, *USA Today*, and *Wall Street Journal* bestselling author of over seventy published titles. She debuted in 2012, captivating fans with spicy contemporary romance about families and friends with plenty of swoony love. She also writes paranormal romance and suggests you keep the lights on while reading them.

When not under deadline, Kristen enjoys spending time with her husband and their fur babies, riding her bike, relaxing with embroidery, trying her hand at painting, and, of course, enjoying her beautiful home in the mountains of Montana.

Made in the USA
Middletown, DE
12 July 2025